AND SOMETIMES WHY

REBECCA JOHNSON has been a contributing editor to *Vogue* for the past twelve years. Her extensive career in journalism also includes writing "Talk of the Town" columns for a year at *The New Yorker* and working as a contributing editor at *Talk* magazine. She lives in Brooklyn and Pound Ridge, New York, with her husband, two children, and three stepchildren.

Praise for *And Sometimes Why*

"[A] heartbreaking debut . . . Johnson's portrayal of a family's grieving is exquisitely crafted."
—*Publishers Weekly*

"*And Sometimes Why* manages to be funny and painful, ironic and heartfelt all at once. In this portrait of a fractured family, Rebecca Johnson—long known as a gifted journalist—shows herself to be an equally gifted novelist. Using her prodigious skills as a social observer, she has created compelling characters and a powerfully moving story."
—Dani Shapiro, author of *Black & White*

"*And Sometimes Why* is a remarkable novel by a remarkable writer. Rebecca Johnson, in addition to having deep reserves of impressive writerly chops, possesses an equally deep wisdom and understanding of what makes us human, the bonds and bounds of love, and the very best and worst in us all."
—David Rakoff, *New York Times* bestselling author of *Don't Get Too Comfortable* and *Fraud*

"It is not often that a book makes me laugh and weep at the same time, but this one did. This is a novel filled with humor and wit and an ample dose of heart. I found myself charmed by its spell and surprised by its twists. Johnson is a masterful storyteller as she moves in and out of her characters and their lives. This is a story of love and loss and all that happens in between. At its core it is a book about family and redemption, and a beautiful one it is."
—Mary Morris, author of *The River Queen*

and

sometimes

why

REBECCA JOHNSON

A PLUME BOOK

PLUME
Published by the Penguin Group
Penguin Group (USA) Inc., 375 Hudson Street, New York, New York 10014, U.S.A. • Penguin Group
(Canada), 90 Eglinton Avenue East, Suite 700, Toronto, Ontario, Canada M4P 2Y3 (a division of Pearson
Penguin Canada Inc.) • Penguin Books Ltd., 80 Strand, London WC2R 0RL, England • Penguin Ireland,
25 St. Stephen's Green, Dublin 2, Ireland (a division of Penguin Books Ltd.) • Penguin Group (Australia),
250 Camberwell Road, Camberwell, Victoria 3124, Australia (a division of Pearson Australia Group
Pty. Ltd.) • Penguin Books India Pvt. Ltd., 11 Community Centre, Panchsheel Park, New Delhi–110 017,
India • Penguin Group (NZ), 67 Apollo Drive, Rosedale, North Shore 0632, New Zealand (a division of
Pearson New Zealand Ltd.) • Penguin Books (South Africa) (Pty.) Ltd., 24 Sturdee Avenue, Rosebank,
Johannesburg 2196, South Africa

Penguin Books Ltd., Registered Offices: 80 Strand, London WC2R 0RL, England

Published by Plume, a member of Penguin Group (USA) Inc. Previously published in a Putnam edition.

First Plume Printing, July 2009
10 9 8 7 6 5 4 3 2 1

 REGISTERED TRADEMARK—MARCA REGISTRADA

The Library of Congress has catalogued the Putnam edition as follows:

Johnson, Rebecca, date.
And sometimes why / Rebecca Johnson.
p.   cm.
ISBN 978-0-399-15452-2 (hc.)
ISBN 978-0-452-29007-5 (pbk.)
 1. Traffic accident victims—Family relationships—Fiction.   2. Teenagers—Fiction.   I. Title.
PS3610.O3727A84   2008   2007032608
813'.6—dc22

Printed in the United States of America
Original hardcover design by Nicole LaRoche

PUBLISHER'S NOTE
This is a work of fiction. Names, characters, places, and incidents are either the product of the author's
imagination or are used fictitiously, and any resemblance to actual persons, living or dead, business estab-
lishments, events, or locales is entirely coincidental.

BOOKS ARE AVAILABLE AT QUANTITY DISCOUNTS WHEN USED TO PROMOTE PRODUCTS OR SERVICES. FOR INFORMA-
TION PLEASE WRITE TO PREMIUM MARKETING DIVISION, PENGUIN GROUP (USA) INC., 375 HUDSON STREET, NEW
YORK, NEW YORK 10014.

To the Smiths—Andrew, Luke, Simon, Toby.
And my first, best, teacher, MFJ.

and

sometimes

why

*b*reakfast together was mandatory in the McMartin family. Not the eating of it, though Sophia McMartin, mother of Miranda, eighteen, and Helen, sixteen, was glad for the opportunity to urge food on her daughters, now that they had grown into young women willing to eat rice cakes all day to keep their weight down. There were, however, mornings when the tedious machinations of the family wearied Sophia, who only wanted to read her newspaper in peace.

"It's my turn."

"You had it last night."

"You didn't need it last night."

"Not relevant. Time used is time used."

The argument between the McMartin sisters centered on a third-hand silver-gray Honda Accord with 87,000 miles on it, a peeling "Visualize Whirled Peas" bumper sticker that now read "Visual Whirl P ," and a tendency to smell of cardamom on the rare humid Los Angeles day. Darius and Sophia McMartin had bought the car, believing (naively, it turned out) that their daughters could peaceably share, alternating days when each would get to use it. Neither had been given cars by their own parents and had long debated the ethics of such a gift. Were they spoiling their children needlessly, giving them too much while expecting too little? Would their daughters ever learn the value of a dollar if they were not forced to work for what they got? In the end, selfishness won. Los Angeles was a city built for cars, and they were sick of driving their children around. For the first year, while Helen had only a learner's permit, things had gone smoothly. But ever since Helen got her driver's license three weeks earlier, there had been nothing but trouble.

"Let's see if we can work this out." Darius McMartin put his paper down and regarded his two fuming daughters with bemused affection. Beloved English professor to thousands of freshmen and a lucky few seniors in his highly selective seminar on late Shakespeare, Darius loved the domestic cacophony of family life. He came from a family of nine. For him, the verbal hurly-burly, the jockeying for position, the thrust and parry as one child sought dominance over the other, was like the sound of twittering birds or a babbling brook. There but not there. Reassuring, soothing, a sign that life was as it should be and, therefore, easily ignored. Unless something caught his attention.

"What do you need the car for?" he asked Miranda, who was paying suspiciously close attention to the blueberries in her muesli.

"I want to go to freshman orientation," she said without looking up. This was a lie. Miranda wanted to go shopping. In two days, she would be starting college at the university where her father taught. She would have preferred an East Coast school, a place where the windows were made of leaded glass and the students could take an afternoon train into New York City, meet under the big clock at Grand Central Station, wear camel hair coats and drink martinis (she'd heard that nobody in New York carded), but the tuition was free for a full professor's daughter, and she saved even more by living at home. Everyone agreed it made financial sense to stay. Besides, she understood that her New York fantasies, cribbed as they were from old F. Scott Fitzgerald novels, probably had nothing to do with reality. Nevertheless, around the corner or across the country, college was a chance for reinvention. Having spent her high school years dressed as drably as possible in black Levi's and white T-shirts, assiduously avoiding any gesture that could be seen as ostentatious or attention seeking in any way, Miranda decided to branch out sartorially. New clothes, new life.

New Miranda. But the last people she wanted to admit this to were her family.

"Really?" Her father's face lit up. "I thought you said, 'Freshman orientation is for losers.'"

"I did." Miranda nodded. "But then I realized it was wrong to be such a snob."

"'Pride went before, ambition follows him.'"

Miranda smiled at her father. It was a game they had played since childhood. He'd quote a play and she would have to guess which one. Helen, who found Shakespeare impenetrable and had the built-in disadvantage of being sixteen months younger, refused to play. Early on, Darius had chosen the easiest, most identifiable quotes. "A rose by any other name," "To be or not to be," "Hark! What light from yonder window, etc." but lately, they had gotten much harder.

"A Henry?" Miranda guessed. Blindly.

"Which one?"

"The Fifth?" She had no idea.

Darius sighed. "The Second."

Sophia scowled at her husband. Artistic daughter of a Greek restaurant owner in Pittsburgh, secret smoker of cigarettes, and head of membership at a prestigious local art museum, Sophia was resigned to a husband who used his photographic memory to seduce people. It was when he used it on their children that she seethed. More than anyone, she understood its allure. In college, she had begged him to recite long passages from the pastoral comedies as she lay on his naked chest, tracing invisible patterns on his skin as love fireworks exploded in her brain for her husband-to-be, son of an Irish stone mason, lover of poetry, possessor of a head of hair as black and lustrous as an oil slick, and the first man to see her completely naked. Not only could he recite the entire Shakespeare canon from memory, but after only a fleeting glance at the back of a cereal box, he could also tell you the number of riboflavins and percentage of protein based on a 2,000-calorie diet within a portion, as well as the last known location for Katy, a missing moon-faced twelve-year-old from Evansville, Indiana. As a young man, his memory had earned him a reputation for brilliance, so when Darius McMartin fell in love with skinny, moody Sophia Theofanides, who sat four rows behind him in astronomy for poets, she could hardly believe her luck. But in the intervening twenty-two years, Sophia had come to view her husband's talent as something else. A cheap party trick. Mere mimicry. A thing that could win a Buick on a game show, but nothing more. Too late, she realized she had married a regurgitator, not a creator.

"Must we?" she asked her husband.

"Yeah," Helen seconded the thought. "It's a lot of pretentiousness before nine in the morning."

"'What early tongue so sweet saluteth me?'"

"*Dad*."

"Okay, honey, tell us why you need the car."

Helen opened her mouth and closed it.

"Is it a boy?" Darius asked.

"Is it ever anything else?" Miranda asked.

"Why don't you shut it?" Helen answered.

"Why don't you?" Miranda said.

"Forget it," Helen said. "I'll take the bus. My needs are always secondary in this family."

Whenever the girls fought, a cold front rolled through Sophia's heart. As children, the two had gotten along eerily well. Dolls, books, toys—everything was cheerfully interchangeable, as if Miranda and Helen had created a utopian society free of jealousy or envy. When other parents complained about the violent bickering between their children, Sophia wondered if hers were even normal. At night, after putting them to sleep in separate cribs, she'd go back to check on them an hour later and find Miranda, the older and more mobile, curled up in her sister's bed, their two small bellies rising and falling in sync. Sophia could watch them for hours. "It's so animal," she'd whisper to Darius as she crawled back into their bed. On the playgrounds where Sophia would bring the girls to while away the endless afternoon of motherhood, the girls were like a gated community with secret codes and passwords only they knew. If another child happened to wander into their orbit, they would turn watchful and quiet, wary of the intruder. Even Sophia sometimes felt locked out of their secrets. But when the wider world intervened, in the form of kindergarten, everything changed. At first, Miranda would sob and weep every morning when she left her mother and sister, but after a few weeks, she began to look forward to school. When she came home, she became bossy and impatient with her younger sister. "That's not how we do it in school," she'd announce imperiously whenever Helen suggested they play in their old way. The parenting books Sophia dutifully bought at the university co-op claimed the dynamic was natural. But when Helen got to school and started making friends on her own, she never seemed to forgive her sister that early betrayal.

In high school, the disparity in their social standing hardened. Technically, it would be wrong to say Miranda was unpopular. Nobody made the loser *L* behind her back or mooed like a cow when she passed. It was more that she was massively, mortifyingly ignored. She probably would have been welcome at the big keg parties thrown by the more popular kids when their parents were away, but nobody thought to invite her. Instead, she got by with one or two close friends: brainy, hardworking girls who nurtured their eccentricities to justify their isolation and waited for an age—twenty-eight, thirty-four, forty-nine—that suited them better. Helen, on the other hand, seemed born to be a teenager. The endless permutations of the social hierarchy; the obsession with clothes, cars, and boys absorbed all her attention. Especially boys. Helen's father was right. She did want the car on account of a boy, but not for the reason everyone assumed.

"Are you sure?" Sophia asked Helen. She didn't like the stricken look on her daughter's face. Because Darius loved his daughters so completely, it never occurred to him that attention paid to one daughter might leave the other feeling slighted. It was up to Sophia to notice the hoarded hurts, the widening of the eyes as a blow, even an unintentional one, was absorbed.

As the sister of a favored older brother, she was alive to the damage of love unequally parceled, and though she hated to admit it, when it came to the children, Helen was hers to protect, Miranda was his. Even in looks, Helen took after Sophia. They were both small, birdlike women with wide mouths, thick lips, and wrists so small that bracelets were always sliding off. They dressed alike, too, in sheer prints bought on sale from expensive boutiques on the west side of town. Miranda, on the other hand, was big boned and sturdy. "A peasant," she would say of herself, "made to carry a plow." People assumed sunny, bubbly Helen would be fine in the world, while moody, introspective Miranda would not. Sophia wasn't so sure.

"Never mind," Helen answered her mother's concern with a wan smile. "Maybe Siri can give me a ride."

2

*ile four of his daily six and no pain in the left knee. Harry
Harlow felt good. The sun shone, as it did every morning, high
in the hills of Los Angeles, with a specific brightness that always sent a
thrill through him. He'd spent mornings in the valley. Plenty. He knew the
light was different down there. Flatter. Deader. Up here, the air sparkled.
Especially this early, when the pachysandra was still a dew-wet green and
the freshly fallen jacaranda blossoms had yet to be crushed by the cars
descending through the sidewalkless streets toward the flat land. Harry
tried to hold on to the feeling, the way a shrink had once advised him to—
"Own it, Harry. Live in it, it's yours"—but every time he tried, he felt it
slip away. The problem was, Harry didn't really feel good. He felt lucky.
He moved the word around in his head, like a mint in his mouth, the electric thrum of it followed by the familiar wash of dread. He wished he could
feel that he deserved the things he had—the beautiful wife, the easy job,
the ready money—instead, they seemed like a Fruit of the Month delivered
to the wrong house but opened, nevertheless, and eaten. If luck could be so
randomly bestowed, couldn't it just as randomly be snatched away? When
he got to that point in thinking, Harry's pace slackened, as if he needed
complete stillness to process the thought. But just then, Harry spotted the
L.A. Times delivery truck he often passed at this hour in the morning.

Harry watched the driver slow, reach into the cab of his truck, and
heave the ad-bloated newspaper through the window so that it landed with

a thud on the driveway of one of the multimillion-dollar houses that rose improbably out of the hills. He looked for a cul de sac to duck down, but it was too late, the driver had spotted him. Harry pressed on, his pace steady, like a sailor steering into a swell. When they crossed paths, the driver—gut, mustache, Hawaiian shirt, straight out of central casting for the role of "loser," Harry thought unkindly—leaned out of the truck and said the same thing he always said when he saw Harry.

"Hey! Harry!" the loser yelled, "I'd rather be in bed."

Harry, close enough to register the color of his teeth—*abalone*—forced a smile. "Me, too!" he yelled. The driver beamed. Thrilled.

Oh, Jesus, Harry thought, congratulating himself for making the loser's day, how pathetic was that? Nevertheless, Harry's pace quickened, his spirits lightened by the exchange. He might know deep in his bones that everything that had come his way was the result of dumb luck, the random alignment of chromosomes that gave him that straight nose, thick hair, and right-angle jaw—looks that had been unremarkable until he hit seventeen, when suddenly girls fell silent around him. "Jesus, Harry," his mother had said to him, as surprised as he was, "you're a looker." He might fear losing everything, but whatever happened to Harry from this day forward, there was no getting around the fact that, for the time being, he was not driving a newspaper delivery truck. He was not a waiter. He was not mowing anyone's lawn. He was not auditioning for jobs he never got. He was not cutting hair or counting a client's sit-ups. He was Harry Harlow, the forty-five-year-old host of *Would You Rather?*, the most popular game show in America. He had been on the cover of magazines, both the self-important newsweeklies and the glossies. He made $5 million a year. Not including his bonus. He drove a BMW X5. He had a beautiful wife thirteen years younger than he. That morning, he had been awakened by the whir of the fax machine delivering the best overnight Nielsen numbers yet. Life was good. For now and the foreseeable future, Harry was lucky, and if he did not feel good about it, if he could not "own" the feeling, whatever that meant, it was nobody's fault but his own.

His pace back up, Harry rounded the corner of his driveway, legs pumping, heart beating. Lucky, lucky, lucky, he sang silently to himself. When he saw his agent's forest green Jaguar parked in the circular driveway behind his house, the dread sliced through again, as sharp as a paper cut. Aaron Kramer had been Harry's agent for four years, ever since he had picked Harry's headshot out of the hundreds of B-list (okay, C-list) actors the agency represented. He remembered the call well.

"You're an agent?" Harry had asked, lifting a cushion on the couch. He was pretty certain he had seen a quarter there earlier in the week.

Aaron proposed a drink. Harry countered with lunch. He could use a meal, and agents always paid. They settled on coffee. When Harry arrived at the Starbucks on La Brea Avenue, he ordered three mozzarella paninis, a cheese pastry, and a fruit cup, and asked the girl behind the counter to run a tab. It was against store policy, but the girl had been so undone by Harry's looks, she put the bill aside, just as he had asked. Her heart beating fast. When Aaron paid the bill, he raised an eyebrow theatrically at the total. Harry never forgave him for that.

Aaron Kramer was Jewish and from the East Coast. He had gone to Princeton but his roots were on Ocean Avenue in Brooklyn, where his grandfather had bought blocks of apartment buildings during the 1970s, when, as he liked to say, "the city was in the toilet." Today, the Kramers were the sixth richest family in the borough, a fact Aaron researched for his senior thesis at Poly Prep, an exclusive high school in the Bay Ridge section of Brooklyn. Most of Aaron's college friends had gone to Wall Street, but he was "creative," so he went to Hollywood. He had thick, black eyebrows that tapered together in the middle of his forehead and a body as soft as a woman's. His lower lip was round, red, and wet. A child's mouth. But his eyes were ancient.

"Your problem," Aaron had said, sipping a caffè latte as Harry wolfed down his second panini, "is you're too handsome." Harry smiled, thinking that was the cue for him to flirt. Not that he'd ever go to bed with a man, but he wasn't above putting on a white cotton sweater and standing by a pool with a drink in his hand if that was what it took to get a job. Aaron didn't smile back.

"You couldn't be in movies," Aaron continued, "because no star wants someone as good-looking as you on screen with them." Harry stopped chewing. It was true. He'd never been able to put his finger on it before, but the guy was right. Harry *was* too handsome. He could feel it every time he went out into the world. At the gym, in the grocery store, even at church those three months he had decided to give religion a try, people stopped and stared at him as if he were an alien. He'd learned to live with it, to act as if he didn't notice. But he hated it. Hated the way people seemed to expect something of him, though what that might be, Harry didn't have a clue. "WHAT??!" he always wanted to yell at them. Something in him stopped still at the irony. He was failing as an actor because he was too handsome, but he'd only become an actor because everybody had said to him, "You're so handsome, you ought to be an actor."

"So make me a star," Harry mugged, resisting the impulse to lick his fingers now that the paninis were done. Aaron didn't bother to answer.

"That would have left soap operas," Aaron went on, more to himself. Harry grunted. He'd been on a soap for two years. The hours were long, the work was dull, and the pay was mingy. Harry mocked the work along with the other actors, but truthfully, he loved the steadiness of the job, the camaraderie on the set, and the steady supply of good-looking women cycling in and out of the bit parts. You could make real money on the side by appearing at mall openings, but Harry's character on *The Fire Within* raped his stepdaughter in a drunken stupor, stole money from his father, and burned down the family house to cover his crime. Nobody wanted to hire *that* guy to sign autographs in a department store in Encino. When he complained to the writers, twin sisters from Baltimore who always wore black stretch pants covered in cat hair, they ignored him. "We just write the crap," they said. "Bill thinks it up."

"Bill" was Bill Ball, creator and part owner of *The Fire Within*. One of the wealthiest men in Hollywood, Bill was eighty-one and lived alone in an all-white house high in Beverly Hills with a roof that could open and close, just like a convertible. Ever since 1967, when he and his wife had entered a "Create Your Own Soap Opera" contest sponsored by the Ajax soap company, Bill had overseen every bend in the road, twist of fate, and turn of fortune for the eighteen characters who made up the longest-running soap opera in the business (though there were some in the industry who liked to say *The Fire Within* could use a new spark). Bill supposedly watched all the rehearsals on a live feed, but the actors only saw him once a year, when the entire staff of the show was invited to Bill's house for the annual Christmas party. Harry might still be working on *The Fire Within* if he hadn't gone to the party. He had been standing outside on a balcony, admiring the view, pretending the house was his own, when he turned to find the owner himself.

"Hell of a view," Bill said, leaning over the balustrade so his shiny black leather jacket scrunched up over his shoulders, making him look like a hunchback.

Harry nodded, his pulse racing. Rule number one on the set of *The Fire Within* had been drilled into his head from the day he signed his contract: Under no circumstances should any actor *ever* discuss his character with Mr. Ball. If you ran into him in the elevator, if you were seated next to him at the Emmys, if you were pissing next to him at Chasens, it didn't matter. *You never discuss your character with Mr. Ball.* But the way things had happened—it being Christmas, the old guy making conversation about nothing, as if trying to find a way to what mattered most—it had to be some sort of a sign.

"You know, sir, I've been thinking about Danny," Harry began, his heart throbbing like a sewing machine.

The old man had given Harry a look of such startled ferocity, Harry stumbled, momentarily losing his train of thought.

"Yes?" he asked.

"It's just"—Harry swallowed and went on—"he's *such* a son of a bitch, I just couldn't help wonder, are people really like that?"

The old man looked as if he were really thinking hard about the question, really giving it some serious thought. "You know, I'll have to think about that," he said. Then he touched Harry on his shoulder, looked him in the eye, and said, "Thanks for the feedback, son, I really appreciate it." Harry had felt great. It wasn't often that he defied conventional wisdom and took a leap, but look what happened when he did! He squared his shoulders and looked out at the lights of Los Angeles twinkling below like circuits on a motherboard. The old guy had actually thanked him. From now on, he wasn't going to be Mr. Rule Follower. Mr. Wimp. Mr. Go with the Crowd. He was going to stand up for what he believed in.

The next week, his stepdaughter killed him.

The woman he'd been sleeping with on the set, a brunette with a turned-up nose, fake breasts, and the disconcerting habit of wearing twenty tiny little-girl barrettes in her hair at once, came to visit while he was packing up his dressing room. "If enough fans complain about your death," she said, "maybe you can come back as the twin brother nobody knew about?" She had a particularly annoying habit of making every sentence sound like a question: "We're rehearsing at three?" "I'll miss you when you're gone?" "If you get famous, don't forget me?"

"I raped my stepdaughter," Harry said. "Who's going to want me back?"

The brunette frowned and interlocked her fingers together in a gesture that reminded Harry of the child's game—*This is the church, this is the steeple, now open the doors and see all the people*. "I could get my mom and her friends to write in?"

Since then, work had been spotty. He'd had a few small roles on television shows and a few call-backs for commercials, but if nothing changed, Harry would be in trouble. So when Aaron laid out the idea for the new game show he was casting, Harry listened closely.

"You know what the number-one rule in business is, Harry?" Aaron asked in the Starbucks that afternoon.

Harry's eyes wandered toward the glass display case behind the counter. Would a fourth panini be too piggish?

"Change," Aaron said, dead serious. "You stop changing, you die. Game shows were the most profitable sector of television in the seventies. People got stinko rich with that shit." Stinko? Harry wondered silently at the word. Was it something the hip people were saying now? Had he missed it? "You know those houses in the hills? The ones with seven-car garages, beautiful women coming and going in their little white tennis dresses? You think those guys made their money on 'quality' movies? No. They made it on *television*"—Aaron said the word as if Harry were hard of hearing—"that's where the real money is, and nobody made more money than people who owned a piece of a game show. But after they got rich, they got stupid. The same hosts, the same goofy gags, the same dumb questions—'Who wrote *Carmen*? What three presidents are on Mount Rushmore?'"

"Four," Harry interrupted.

"Excuse me?"

"There are four presidents on Mount Rushmore, not three."

"Yeah, but who gives a shit? The point is, the genre died because it went soft. People were too nice. Life is hard. It's full of suffering and humiliation and taking crap. If life is hard, why should the game be easy? If people want a trip to Tahiti for free, they should have to suffer. Game shows died because they didn't acknowledge that. They didn't grow."

Harry stared at Aaron. "You're going to hurt people on TV?"

"Not physically. Mentally. Remember that game you played when you were a kid? Would you rather eat your grandmother's toenails or slide down a giant razor into a vat of rubbing alcohol? We want to use things that tap into people's deepest fears and revulsions: public nudity, rats, worms."

"Rats?" Harry hated rats. "What about them?"

"To be determined. You could eat one, kill one with your bare hands. There are a lot of ways to go."

"You can do that on television?"

"The world is changing."

"Why me?" Harry asked Aaron the night after they'd filmed the pilot and were having a celebratory drink at the Polo Lounge.

"You have a mean streak," Aaron answered.

Harry stared at him. It was true, he did have a mean streak. He tried to be placid and nice on the surface. He wanted people to like him. But inside, Harry seethed. The woman in the Ford Bronco who cut him off on La Cienega that morning? *Fucking cunt!* All the idiots who hadn't given him the roles he auditioned for? *Get cancer, dickheads!* The phone company that cut off his bill because he was two months behind? *Eat shit and die, assholes!* Even he was appalled by the boiling cauldron of resentment brewing right under the surface of his personality, which was why he worked extra hard to hide it. So how had Aaron seen it?

"Don't worry." Aaron had laughed when he saw the expression on Harry's face. "It's going to make us rich."

Harry bent at the waist, letting his weight stretch the muscles in the back of his thighs. Through the back door, he could hear Aaron and Catherine laughing. He thought about going in the front door and bypassing Aaron altogether, but he knew his wife would come looking for him. "Harry," she'd say, forehead creased with concern, "how can you be so rude?" Easily.

He had married Catherine two years earlier, on the beach in Malibu after knowing her for six months. She was thirteen years younger than he, from a wealthy wine-growing family in northern California, and pretty in a blond, ethereal way, though Harry couldn't help notice how quickly her coloring went from delicate to washed out whenever she had a cold. She rode horses and painted big, pale abstract canvases. "What is it?" he'd ask, staring at one of them. "It's a feeling," she'd answer patiently, unflummoxed by his skepticism. That was the thing about people who grow up with money, Harry would think sourly to himself, they never wonder whether they're wrong or untalented. Maybe it wasn't a feeling, maybe it was just a blob of paint on a canvas, a thing without meaning, the manifestation of a woman determined to be creative at whatever cost, but Catherine never asked the hard questions of herself. She'd never needed to. Everything had been given to her so easily she never worried over the practical matters of life. If Catherine turned the lights off when she left the room, it was not to keep the electricity bill down, it was to save the world.

At first, Harry was charmed by her assumption of plenty. He had grown so disillusioned with the desperation of his female counterparts in Hollywood—the almost-made-it actresses whose eyes grew fearful as they approached thirty—like horses in a smoky stable. More than once, Harry had gone to get his hair cut at an expensive, marble-floored salon in West Hollywood, only to recognize one of the stylists from his early days of acting. "I couldn't take it anymore," the former actress would say, gently pushing Harry's head forward, scissors poised at the nape of his neck. "All that *rejection.*" Snip. Snip.

He pushed the door open. Wife and agent looked startled and then— was it Harry's imagination?—guilty. Aaron recomposed the smile on his face from genuine to fake in less than a second.

"Harry, my man." He stuck out his hand in that jokey way meant to evoke a ghetto where Aaron would never be caught dead. "Nice number last night."

Harry kissed Catherine on the cheek. An animal marking his territory. Catherine made a face at the dampness of his sweat. Aaron noticed it. Harry noticed Aaron noticing it, and his heart hardened fractionally toward his wife on account of it.

"What's this?" Harry asked, looking into an oil-stained bag on the counter.

"Aaron brought them," Catherine said, smiling at her husband's agent.

"Everyone should have an agent who brings them croissants for breakfast," Harry answered. That fattening shit might be fine for them, but he'd never put it in his own mouth.

"I'm here to watch the new promo." Aaron checked his watch. "Which should be on right about now."

Harry used the remote control to turn on the television. Almost immediately, the screen was filled with an image of him standing next to a dorky teenager in a University of Ohio sweatshirt. Harry remembered being grossed out by the way the kid breathed through his open mouth, no filter between his insides and the world.

"Tonight, on *Would You Rather?*" the announcer said, "host Harry Harlow asks, 'Would you rather conduct a survey wearing nothing but a bathing suit?'" The camera cut to footage of an old man in a tiny black Speedo, black socks, and shoes approaching two teenage girls on a crowded sidewalk in the mall. His body was long and pale, his breasts hung low, and the skeleton underneath the skin was visible, making him look like the figure of death from a medieval linotype. The girls recoiled in horror. The audience roared with laughter.

"Or," the announcer continued, "endure the dreaded Torturtron?"

The screen changed to a roller coaster–like contraption speeding toward the camera. The terrified face of a middle-aged woman, mouth open in a silent scream, flashed on the screen. The audience roared with approval as the announcer teased, "Tune in to America's number-one-rated game show, when host Harry Harlow asks . . ." Harry's face filled the screen as the audio switched to Harry's own, unmistakeable baritone. "Which *would you rather?*"

Standing on one leg, his hamstring stretched behind him like a wading bird at rest, Harry frowned and clicked the television off.

"It looked good," Catherine said, smiling at her husband. That was another thing about her. The glass wasn't half full for Catherine. It was full. Always. Even when it was empty. Harry had hoped to become a sunnier, happier person with Catherine, but it had not worked like that. Happiness, it turned out, was not contagious. Instead, Harry had grown to see her optimism as a personality flaw, one that leached the intelligence out of her. If everything was good, he once tried to explain to her, nothing was good.

"Everything can be good," she had answered, round-eyed, serious, filled with a pitying love for her husband. He was appalled by a sudden desire to hit her.

"I look like I have a double chin," Harry sulked.

"You don't have a double chin," Catherine said.

"I know that," Harry answered, "so why do they shoot me so I look like I do?"

"He's probably president of the 'Get Harry' cabal," Aaron said, putting on his jacket, "the one that's always trying to ruin your career."

"I'm not vain," Harry answered, "I'm protecting my assets. *Our* assets."

Aaron checked his watch. "I'm off," he announced, kissed Catherine good-bye on one cheek, and waved broadly in his client's direction. "So long, asset."

Harry leaned his head back to do the facial exercises his mother used to minimize her double chin. "Ayyyy, eeeeee, ayeee, ohhhhh, youuuuu," he enunciated, exaggerating the sound of each vowel so it stretched his mouth comically wide.

"And sometimes Y," Aaron added, shutting the door behind him.

"Everybody always forgets Y," Catherine agreed.

3

*m*iranda wished she could lie better. She had the feeling that her life would be wider and richer if she could make up things without her throat constricting or the capillaries on her cheek dilating with red heat. Even as a child, she'd been as easy to read as a large-print newspaper.

"Did you eat your vegetables?"

"Mmmhmm."

"Then why are your pockets full of broccoli?"

"How do you know?"

"I can see your face."

Having secured the car, Miranda found herself driving toward the university through the back streets of the west side, going to freshman orientation, just as she told her father she would. If she went shopping, as she had planned, she knew she'd never be able to lie convincingly when, at the end of the day, her father would ask, "How was orientation?" his face all lit up with paternal hopefulness. Unlike her mother, who seemed to accept the constant low-level disappointment inherent in parenting, her father would be wounded. She wasn't entirely sorry to be going. The orientation packet, with its promise of "human pyramid building" and a "literary scavenger hunt" was exactly the kind of thing she would have made fun of in high school, but all that cynicism, she had to admit, had left her with a pretty empty life. Instead of admitting the truth—she was shy and fearful of being wounded—Miranda chose the more comfortable but lonelier role of snob. Participation in group activities was the sign of an unoriginal mind, she told her parents when they asked why she didn't try out for soccer. Sophia, who shared more than a few of the same character traits, knew Miranda was missing out, but she also understood that children needed to make their own mistakes. As long as her grades and scores were fine, Sophia let her be. By the time Miranda understood that the kids who did play basketball or soccer, argue on the debate team, edit the yearbook, or star in the school play all seemed to be having a better time than she was, it was too late to change.

Standing in the freshman quadrangle, reading the name tags of her fellow scavengers, Miranda felt her resolve to be less judgmental weaken. What could she ever have in common with three Asian engineering students from Queens, New York; a goth lesbian from Manhattan Beach, California; a blond cheerleader from Dallas who drew a smiley face next to her name; and a lumberjack named Jason from a town called Prince Rupert, B.C.?

Miranda arched an eyebrow at Jason's name tag. "B.C.? Before Christ?"

"British Columbia." He looked at her chest. "Los Angeles? The acorn did not fall far from the tree."

"You have no idea," she answered.

An androgynous young man wearing a turquoise polo shirt (collar up) and khaki pants handed Jason their first clue. "Good luck," he said. Something about his walk made Miranda think of a gymnast approaching the uneven bars.

"Notice how the white man instinctively gives the clue to the only white man in the group," the goth lesbian observed.

"Wow." The Dallas blonde gazed at the lesbian, without elaborating.

"I think he handed it to me because I was closest to him," Jason said.

"The ruling class has always found justifications for its oppression of minorities."

"Right." Jason nodded amiably and read the clue aloud. "'But at my back, I always Hear, Time's winged chariot hurrying near.'" He looked up from the paper. "*Hear* and *Time* are capitalized."

One of the engineering students shook his head. "What's a winged chariot? A plane? A bird?"

"No," his friend answered. "Superman!" The engineers laughed.

Miranda said nothing. She thought the game moronic but was curious to see how the hayseed from Canada would solve the puzzle.

"Why are *Hear* and *Time* capitalized? That's the question," he mused.

The blonde moved closer to Jason. "Mmmm," she said, as if smelling something good.

The blonde's attention to Jason made Miranda look more closely at the broad outline of his shoulders, the set of his chin, and the short, military thatch of his haircut. If you ignored the plaid shirt and stiff new jeans, she could see his appeal. Something about him seemed more solid than the other students, like a person who had shouldered responsibility—a soldier, perhaps, on the eve of World War I. Her thoughts were interrupted by the campus bells chiming three o'clock. With each bong, Miranda stared more intently at her teammates, hoping they would intuit her intent, but nobody paid any attention to her. Finally, she couldn't take it anymore.

"Hello?!" Miranda blurted out, pointing to the bell tower. "Does anybody else 'hear time'?" It took everyone a second to process her strangely strident presence, but it was Jason's face that first lit up.

"Brilliant!" He grabbed Miranda, kissed her on the lips, and took off running for the bell tower. As understanding dawned on their faces, the others followed, including the goth who seemed suddenly girlish under her white foundation and burgundy lipstick. Only Miranda remained rooted to the spot, jolted by that sexless press of lip to lip and the sight of her teammates happily galloping away. How could virtual strangers bond so quickly? Like iron shavings to a goddamned magnet.

Jason was halfway to the bell tower, enjoying the spontaneous kiss with the girl from California, when he turned around to look at her again. More than a hundred yards away, Miranda stood in the exact spot where he had left her, a look of such sorrow on her face, he almost didn't recognize her. As the engineers and the goth ran past him, Jason walked back to Miranda.

"What's wrong?" he asked.

Miranda looked into his face. She saw bright blue eyes spaced a tad too wide, making him look vaguely lizardlike, a tiny constellation of zits at the right of his mouth, a high forehead creased with concern for a girl (woman, she corrected herself) he hardly knew, and thought to herself, *Well, why not?*

"It's from a poem," she said.

"I know," he answered, "Andrew Marvell."

Miranda blushed. She had underestimated him. How embarrassing.

"Come on," he said, taking her hand. She let herself be pulled, limply, reluctantly at first, until his will seemed to flow like transferred heat through the skin of his palm into hers. Suddenly, she too was running toward the bell tower. Laughing, skipping, like a kid trying to catch up. It wasn't that hard to get along. If someone was pulling you. If that someone had nice blue eyes and a perfect V-shaped torso. If that someone knew who Andrew Marvell was. If that someone did not resent you thinking he did not know who Andrew Marvell was. If that someone seemed like a grown-up. A man. A person who understood the laws of actions and reactions. Consequences.

After the hunt, Jason asked her if she wanted to see his dorm room. A few feet away, the Dallas blonde was pretending to make a call on her cell phone.

"Is that, like, some kind of code?" Miranda asked.

"A code for what?"

"You tell me."

"Are you always so suspicious?"

"Yes," she answered.

His room was a twelve-by-six rectangle of cinder-block walls painted peppermint green. The floors were linoleum, the lighting fluorescent. He had put nothing on the walls or over the windows. His bed, a single mattress without box springs, was neatly made with flannel sheets and a wool blanket.

"Have a seat," he said.

She looked around the room. The only place to sit was on the bed or a wooden desk chair on wheels. She sat on the bed, her hands folded primly in her lap.

"I think this may be the ugliest room I have ever been in," she said, unclasping her hands.

He sat next to her. "Are you always so honest?"

She tried to give the question real consideration, but her attention kept wandering to his hand on the bed. Did he mean for it to be so close to her thigh? Why did she suddenly feel so nervous and breathless? She stood and picked up the closest thing she could find, a bleached white skull of an animal she did not recognize.

"Dog?" she asked, holding it up to the light.

"Bear. Old Cyrus." He leaned back casually, like a sunbather. "He foraged in our backyard for years."

She placed it back on top of the bookcase and sat on the hard chair. "Old Cyrus. Osiris."

"The Egyptian god of the dead."

She blushed. Once again, she had underestimated him.

"You think I'm stupid because I'm from Canada."

"No." She shook her head, and sat back down on the bed, deliberately putting a few inches between their thighs. Why was he looking at her mouth like that? Did she have something on her teeth? Was her breath bad? How could you want somebody to do something and not want him to do it so intensely, and all in the same moment? "I don't think you're stupid because you're from Canada. I think you're stupid because you're eighteen, and most eighteen-year-old guys care about one thing."

"Baseball?" He moved closer so his thighs were touching hers.

"Football."

He pressed his lips against hers, the heat and smell of him covered her like a thick blanket. His saliva tasted like caramel.

"Ah," she said, mostly out of surprise.

He went still. "You want me to stop?"

"Uh," she exhaled. "Yes. No. Yes some more."

He laughed and maneuvered her back onto the bed, his hand poised thrillingly above her breast.

Miranda succumbed. Mostly. But not entirely. She loved lying next to him, intertwining legs, hands, lips, feet, and fingers. He smelled of soap and deodorant and something uniquely Jason, a kind of woodsy, feral smell, which she privately labeled the smell of Canada. This, she could see, would also be something easy to do, if somebody was pulling her along. But when he tried to unzip her pants, she tensed and moved his hand away.

"Not yet."

"When?" he asked.

"Don't you think you should at least ask me out on a date?"

"You want to go out on a date?"

"When?"

"Tonight?"

"Too soon."

"Tomorrow night?"

"Too far away."

Jason smiled. "I'll pick you up at seven."

4

to the public, Harry Harlow *was Would You Rather?* They assumed he picked the guests, wrote the questions, and devised the traumas for the daily half-hour show, which, at the end of the day, was nothing more than a child's game with better technology. Harry had initially hoped to have more input in shaping the show. Had even looked forward to the idea of regular work, a daily commute, lunch at the company cafeteria. He'd never gotten over the feeling that acting for a living was too easy. When he passed men doing real work, road crews tearing up the tarmac, repairmen untangling the mystery of water or electricity, things people needed to survive, he always felt a stirring of shame for the physical ease of his life. Even the sweat in acting—water spritzed from a plastic bottle between takes—was ersatz. It was one of the reasons he never shirked his daily exercise regime. At least there, in the middle of the eighth mile or the eightieth sit-up, he felt pushed.

The first few weeks of production, he'd gotten up at six a.m. and joined the morning traffic jam. At work, everyone began the day complaining about the commute. Not him. Traveling in the same direction as everyone else made him feel solid, like a citizen of the world. And he loved his office—the faux walnut expanse of his desk, the red light on the phone that blinked when he had a message, the bleakness of a brick wall through the window. As a child, he had imagined working in just such an office, conducting important business over the phone with a secretary waiting on his needs, though what business he was doing in the fantasy, he could not have said.

It didn't take him long to realize there was nothing for him to do. A young woman with a bullhorn and a smoker's hack was responsible for culling the audience, some snarky Ivy League types fact-checked the questions, an ex-agent worked the phones, bartering prizes in exchange for plugs on the show, and the executive producer oversaw everything else. The first time Harry walked by the glass-walled conference room where the staff was meeting, he had assumed they'd simply forgotten to invite him.

"Hey," he said pulling up a chair, "I didn't know we were meeting." A look he chose to ignore passed around the room like a secret code.

When the meetings continued and Harry still was not invited, he stayed in his office, a queasy rivulet of shame dripping through him. He had, he realized, become the "talent," the word on the set that inevitably came with quotation marks around it. He remembered it from jobs where he was the nobody, the extra getting $100 a day, meals included. In those days, it was easy to hang with all the other nobodies—the assistant grips or gaffers; wannabe union guys with their talk of pussy, beer, and blow. Harry remembered how they all felt about the star in the trailer—if he was friendly, he was a suck-up; if he was unfriendly, he was an asshole. There was no winning. Harry had seen it happen a hundred times. He just never imagined it would happen to him. He began staying home in the morning.

"It's better this way," Gus Morbane, executive producer of *Would You Rather?* and one of the truly conscience-free men Harry had ever met, assured him. "This way, we get you fresh."

Nevertheless, there were moments when Harry alone saw things that needed doing. The double chin was one of them. It might not seem impor-tant to Aaron, but Aaron was indifferent to matters of the flesh—how else to explain the extra thirty pounds of it he carried around? Unlike the smirky young people who worked on the show, Harry understood how people in middle America watched TV, because he was one them. He might not know where the Pyrenees were compared to the Azores or how many electrons orbited the outer ring of a hydrogen atom, but he knew who played Elizabeth Montgomery's mother in *Bewitched* (Agnes Moorehead) or the bumpkin oil heir on *The Beverly Hillbillies* (Max Baer Jr.). He understood the man on the couch who turned on the television as soon as he got home, a beer in one hand, the remote control in the other. He knew he would turn to his wife at the sight of that scallop of flesh under Harry's chin and snort like a pig. He knew she'd laugh guiltily, momentarily feeling a little better about her own fat stippled thighs and Buddha belly. But soon they'd turn on him. They didn't watch television to see their weaknesses made heroic. If Harry Harlow, who had nothing to do with his life but make himself look as good as he could, had a double chin, how was he better than all the fatties out there watching him? Harry went upstairs to his bedroom, showered and pulled on a pair of jeans, loafers, and a loose-weave Armani shirt the color of oatmeal. Outside his bedroom window, he could see his wife speaking to José, the gardener. Catherine was very proud of her Spanish, a rickety blend of tourist jargon and café patois she'd picked up studying art and getting banged by a guitar player in Cuernavaca during her junior year of college, but Harry saw the panic of incomprehension in José's eyes whenever she spoke to him.

When Harry got to the studio, the guard at the entrance booth, a genial middle-aged black man with a shiny bald head, waved Harry in, a big smile on his face.

"Afternoon, Mr. Harlow."

Harry smiled and pressed his fingers together in a beauty-queen wave.

"You know, Harry"—the guard leaned down so Harry could see the brachiochephalic red veins in his eyes—"I'd rather be golfing."

Inwardly, Harry rolled his eyes. Twice in one day? But he just smiled and said what he always said. "Me, too!" The guy laughed and waved him in.

Harry opened the door to the studio and literally bumped into Marian Blaumgrund, aka "the rat lady." It was not an uncommon experience to bump into her. Most days she seemed to be studying the floor for an answer to a deep and troubling question. But Harry thought she seemed even more preoccupied than usual.

"Are you okay, Marian?" he asked.

"Oh, Harry, no. I'm not. Thank you for asking. It's this new shipment of rats—"

Harry began to back away from her. He had a soft spot for Marian, if only because she was as marginalized as he was, but the woman had a tin ear for the ebb and flow of social conversation. Long past the moment things ought to start wrapping up, Marian would keep talking and talking. Harry often had the feeling she had recently been in solitary confinement and was relearning the art of conversation. "If there's a problem, Marian, I am sure you will work it out. There's nobody in the business better than you."

"Thank you, Harry. Lord knows I have put in my time." Twenty years to be exact, but Harry was already gone. Marian sighed. A few weeks earlier, Gus Morbane had told her to make the rats "nicer" after one of the contestants had complained to the *National Enquirer* about a bite on his left thigh. Marian wasn't worried about infection, she herself had inoculated every single rat in her care for rabies, TB, hepatitis, hantavirus, and a handful of other diseases. But rat bites didn't make for good public relations. She had tried every trick she could think of to calm the rats—she gave them lots of room and toys during the day, she fed them high-quality dog food with gravy. But rats were rats. They did not like stress. Dump them into a glass cage the size of a bathtub and turn hot, bright lights on them, coupled with loud music, and they were going to be stressed. And stressed rats are violent rats. In the twenty years she spent running the rat and mice lab at UCLA, she had seen stressed rats do astonishing things, including chewing off their own tails.

"I could drug them," she had said to Gus.

"Rats on valium?" He frowned.

"I could try a calmer breed . . ." she mused aloud to herself.

"Good idea." Gus seized on the suggestion.

"It could be expensive," she warned.

"Spend what you need."

The Chestnut rats had arrived special delivery on a British Airways flight a few days earlier. Even Marian, who had seen plenty of rats in her time, was impressed. Their haunches were sleek and muscular. Their coats were shiny without being oily. Their teeth were pearly, pointed, and even. Actors' teeth. They had almond-shaped brown eyes, pink tongues, and long whiskers that seemed to twitch with joy when Marian leaned down to look at them. Most adorably, they loved to do tricks. Marian could watch for hours as they did somersaults, walked on their back legs, rolled over and played dead. One could even do a back flip by scurrying up the cage, dropping his front paws so that his body dangled from the ceiling, then releasing his back claws so that the bottom part of his body jackknifed forward. Marian was enchanted. In the 1970s, Morrissy Chestnut had achieved worldwide fame for his skill in training English sheepdogs; in the early 1990s, when his arthritis got so bad he couldn't spend time in the field anymore, he had turned to rats. Clearly, the man had not lost his touch.

But there was one problem. The Chestnut rats didn't like American rats. Hated them, in fact. The minute Marian put one in the rat cage with ordinary American brown rats, the English rats turned mongoose. Their backs arched, their hair stood straight up, they bared their teeth and emitted a low, hissing sound. When another rat approached, they would fly into a rage, scratching and biting like a rabid animal until Marian put on her thickest work gloves and scooped the rat out of the cage. It would take a few minutes of petting and cooing before the rat's breathing returned to normal.

She had e-mailed the great Morrissy Chestnut asking for advice on the problem but the results were discouraging.

Dear Madam,

   Had I known the commercial use for which you intended the animals, I would not have sold them to you. Rats are intelligent, sentient animals.

Exploiting the irrational human hatred of a species is sadistic. Be a good soul and set them free.

> Yours sincerely,
> Morrissy Chestnut

P.S. The Baltimore Zoo has expressed interest in the bloodline. Perhaps you could send the litter on?

The e-mail sent Marian into a black funk for days. How dare he take such a tone with her? Hadn't she fought diligently for rats' rights for years? Wasn't she the person who wrote a letter to the *Los Angeles Times* just a month before, pointing out that rats were not, as is commonly assumed, responsible for spreading the bubonic plague—it was the fleas on rats that jumped from host to host. (The city council was debating rat-extermination techniques in the municipal sewer.) True, *Would You Rather?* was a television show and not a "pure" event like the yearly Manchester Rat Show, but it was certainly better than watching rats grow walnut-sized tumors on their head or endure toxic chemicals dripped into their eyes, or any number of other tortures she had been forced to witness at the UCLA lab. The fact that she had admired Morrissy Chestnut for years had made the blow all the more bitter. She could not help notice that there was no offer to refund the show's money in exchange for a return of the rats. Not only had she spent a healthy chunk of cash buying the Chestnut rats, she was no closer to solving the original problem. For the time being, she decided to ignore the problem by using the old brown rats. Perhaps Gus Morbane would forget he had asked her to solve the problem? Or maybe nobody would land on Rats!

Harry found the director, Maury Shore, standing in the middle of the set, frowning at "Sam" (short for Samsara), the wheel the contestants spun to decide their task. Initially, they had used an LED display to flash the choices—Rats! Truth Time! Roaches! Random!—but in focus groups, people said they preferred the low-tech spinning of a wheel. Getting the resistance right was, however, surprisingly hard—too much made it too hard, too little made it spin too long.

"Slower," Maury yelled into a mouthpiece attached to a headphone.

Harry could see it wasn't a good time to talk to the director, but it was never a good time with Maury, a tall but stooped man with a pot belly that sat weirdly high on his chest, as if somebody had strapped it on from behind. He had come to Hollywood a young man determined to make the plotless existential road movies briefly popular in the 1970s. After a movie starring a mechanical shark broke every box office record on the books, those movies seemed to disappear overnight. While waiting for them to return, Maury had taken a job in television. By not giving a shit about the medium, he managed to thrive. On the rare occasion when his self-loathing got too bad, a few snorts of cocaine could quickly silence the demon roar.

"Do you have a second?" Harry asked.

"Not really, no," Maury answered, turning his back so that Harry was facing the director's long gray ponytail. It looked as lifeless as winter wheat. Harry felt the man's snub like a blow to his gut. He knew he ought to let it go. Be a bigger man and all that crap, but if push came to shove, wasn't Maury more expendable than he? Who could even name a famous television director? More important, Harry could beat the shit out of him in a fight. That ought to count for something when two men came into conflict.

"I asked you once not to shoot me from below," Harry said. "It's Photography 101."

Maury turned slowly and looked up and down Harry's body. "You think it makes you look fat?" His voice was silky, intimate, mockingly sympathetic.

Harry could feel the malevolent eyes of the crew on the back of his neck. He and Maury locked eyes. Harry was surprised by the surge of emotion in him. He imagined hitting Maury in the face, breaking his nose, watching the blood spurt as he begged for mercy. It wouldn't be hard. Knowing that, Harry willed himself to calm down. He took a deep breath, like a hot-air balloon descending to earth.

"Yeah," Harry let the air out of his lungs, "I do."

Maury looked surprised. He'd made Harry look vain, like a woman, for caring about his weight, but once Harry agreed, there was no place left for him to go. He shrugged.

"They're Anton's angles," Maury gestured toward a prematurely balding young cameraman with light blue eyes and the large, angled nose of a cartoon witch. Harry vaguely recognized Anton McDonald from the set. Now that he looked more closely, he could see that he was different from the other cameramen. Younger. And he dressed differently, in black Levi's and black shoes with thick rubber soles. More like a Bohemian than a teamster. He was standing next to a camera, staring at the floor.

"You've been doing the handheld?" Harry asked.

Anton McDonald nodded. He had finished film school only six months earlier. His senior project—*The Truth About Bathtubs*—followed a police detective convinced the majority of the 891 yearly "accidental" drownings in bathtubs were actually homicides. Its deadpan irony and careful attention to the chiaroscuro of classic noir had won it every student award in the school. After graduating, everybody assumed Anton would take the usual route of script reader for the studios while he lined up financing for his first feature. But he was a purist. If he read too many bad scripts, he feared he might unconsciously absorb their lessons, like a virus. He believed great movies were built visually, frame by frame, and the only way to understand the eye of the camera was to work in the trenches as a cameraman. Unfortunately, the only two photography jobs available on the postgraduate job bulletin board were for porn in the Valley or a game show at the network. Being squeamish about sex, he had taken the latter. The pay on *Would You Rather?* was good but the work was frustrating. Whenever Anton tried to find an interesting angle or an expression on an audience member's face other than manic ecstasy, he'd hear Maury's voice in his ear: "Cut the artistic crap, Antonioni." The most he could get away with was shooting Harry unflatteringly from below, and that was only because Maury Shore disliked Harry Harlow.

"Don't shoot me from below, okay?" Harry said.

"Okay, but—"

"But what?"

Anton swallowed. The words had simply leaped out of their own accord, imprisoned all these weeks by the lonely invisibility of his job. A part of him was enjoying the attention.

"If everything is shot on the same level, it gets kind of boring to look at."

"If it's so boring to look at, why are we the number-one show in America right now?"

Anton blinked. It was a question he, too, had pondered. "I have no idea," he answered. He'd been aiming for a jokey, insider tone but as soon as the words were out of his mouth, he could see he had miscalculated.

Harry's face turned bright red. It was one thing for the director to treat him like shit, but a cameraman?

"Do you like your job?" Harry asked.

Anton did a quick mental calculation of his assets—$1,803 dollars in the bank, rent of $425 due next week, student loan payment of $83, utilities, food, car insurance, groceries, movie tickets, food, laundry, only fifty pages of his script written. Yeah, he liked the job. "I guess," he answered.

"You don't sound too sure."

In his mind, Anton was saying, "Yes! Yes! I love my job. Don't fire me." But somewhere between the saying and the thinking, the words had gotten tangled up, like a duck in an old fishing line. "Uh," he said.

"You're fired." Harry turned and walked away.

Anton's mouth dropped in surprise. If he were to write the scene in a movie, the violins would swell. His co-workers would stop what they were doing. Someone, probably a black man with large muscles and flaring nostrils, would start to applaud. The others, moved by Anton's courage, would follow, until a chorus of applause would lift Anton up and carry him away on a wave of love and adoration. But life was not a movie. Anton looked around the room. People looked away. They didn't think he was brave, they thought he was stupid. The show was hugely successful, what kind of an idiot antagonizes the talent like that? Only someone who didn't need a job, and if he didn't need a job, that made him different from them. And if he was different from them, he was better off. And if he was that much better off than they were, well, screw him.

"Don't worry," Maury said, "you haven't worked until you've been fired." Anton thought it was the other way around: You couldn't be fired until you'd worked. But in the last five minutes Anton had learned a valuable life lesson—this time, he managed to keep his mouth shut.

Harry sat in front of the mirror in his dressing room, waiting for Jeannine, the makeup woman, to arrive. He felt like shit. He looked like shit. Question: If a man feels like shit and a man looks like shit, does that mean a man *is* shit? He leaned forward and smiled at his reflection in the mirror. "Hello," he said, "my name is Shit. It's very nice to meet you." A network of lines appeared on his forehead and cheeks, all connected to one another like the map of a poorly planned city. Calcutta, maybe. He stopped smiling. The wrinkles went away. Salt Lake City. He smiled again. Calcutta. Shit. He really was getting old. Or maybe it was just the lighting? He'd complained about the cheap fluorescent tubes overhead a million times, but Jeannine always brushed him off. "If you look good in this light, you'll look good anywhere."

The thing is, he hated firing that kid. Growing up, he'd watched his mother get fired over and over by jerks who said she couldn't type or came in too late or left too early or talked too much or drank too much. She was always too something. Now he was one of them. A firer. One who fires.

The door opened.

"Hiya," Jeannine said. Harry half smiled, forming Tokyo, a busy city, but navigable. He leaned his head back, closed his eyes, and moaned her name. "Jeannnninnne." She stood behind him and put her hands on his head. "Transferring energy," she once told him. Jeannine had shiny eggplant-colored hair, pale skin, a nose a little upturned, and a mouth a little downturned, giving her beauty a melancholy uncertainty, as if it couldn't decide whether she was happy or sad, pretty or plain. She claimed to be a lesbian but Harry suspected she made that up so that nobody— including him—would hit on her. Makeup girls were reputed to be the easiest lay on a set.

"What's wrong?" Jeannine asked. Motherly.

Harry opened his eyes. He was eye level with her breasts.

"Have I ever told you how great your tits are?" Harry asked.

"Every day, perv," Jeannine answered.

"I fired someone today," Harry answered.

"*Ew*." She frowned, taking a jar of caramel-colored foundation out of the fishing tackle box she used to carry makeup. "Bad karma." She unscrewed the lid, dipped her fingers inside, and rubbed the cream vigorously between her palms. Warming it, she once explained to Harry, made it go on more smoothly. She applied daubs to his left cheek, his right cheek, his chin, and his forehead, then massaged his forehead with the palm of her hand, working the pigment into the skin. Harry closed his eyes, enjoying the familiar feel of her hands on his skin and the warm buttered-toast smell of her. Yoga-doing, wheatgrass-drinking, patchouli-wearing, cat-owning, psychic-seeking Jeannine might have lived in Berkeley or Greenwich Village a generation earlier, but these were apolitical times. Poverty had lost its allure. After a brief affair with an aromatherapist, Jeannine had drifted into the health and beauty industry, where the quest for perfect skin had gotten mixed up with the Keatsian quest for truth. "'Truth is beauty, beauty is truth,'" she liked to tell her clients, forty minutes into a makeup session.

From a financial perspective, Jeannine's timing could not have been better. She earned more than the governor of California, and could have made considerably more if she had taken up a major beauty company's offer to start her own line. Hairdressers, makeup artists, personal trainers, yogis, masseurs, an entire industry based on the delivery of personal hygiene had, in the last decade, supplanted drug dealers and prostitutes in Hollywood as the receivers of celebrity intimacies. Outsiders had a hard time understanding, but nobody was lonelier than a star. Genuine cover-of-*Newsweek* stardom required ruthless jettisoning on the way up—family, friends, lovers, anyone who might hold you back or mess you up with their complicating needs. There could be only one person. One career. Yours. If you got successful enough, a life would be handed to you. Parties every night, openings, closings, events, happenings, free clothes, free food, free flights, and lots of people always around whose sole purpose was to keep you happy. The problem was, you had to pay those people. The publicist, the manager, the agent—it was just a job for them. At the end of the day, they went home to their lives of carpools, rosemary bushes by the back door, and pool-maintenance problems only to make fun of you on Satur-day night, when their real friends came over and asked, "What is she *really* like?"

Jeannine was different. One, she had no life to compete with the client. No child, no husband, no house, no pool. Two, Jeannine had perfected an attitude of complete and total acceptance. In her mind, she was a helio-trope gently arcing toward the sun of fame, absorbing everything that was good and bad. The toxins and the nectar; the nettles and the petals; the vicious, petty complaints; the paranoia, followed by the paroxysms of hys-terical affection. She *understood*. Any idiot could make under-eye bags dis-appear, but how many people could make a client feel loved? It made her the most sought-after makeup artist in Hollywood. Her best customers would write her salary into the production budget of their latest project, ensuring that she flew first-class, stayed in the hotel room next door, and got a per diem as high as the star's. Other makeup artists were so envi-ous, rumors swirled about how far she would go to please her clients. In truth, Jeannine did not really care about the money. What she liked was being needed. She doted on the stars and their fleeting beauty. In her mind, vanity was good. It was the desire to stay one's best, to live up to the gift God had given. Not the God of the Old or New Testament, of course, but the universal God—Allah, Yahweh, and Buddha all wrapped up into one. If it hadn't been for the constant travel, she'd still be doing it, but even the best hotel rooms—*especially* the best ones, with the inevitable Regency reproduction armchairs covered in silk damask, the botanical print on the wall, the television and minibar hidden in a mahogany armoire—began to depress her. She might not have children, but she had cats, and she missed them. The cellophane-wrapped trays of room-service food made her want to weep. The unfamiliarity of the views from her window weighed on her. Sometimes she forgot what city she was in. Eventually, her good cheer dried up. The celebrities began to seem like overgrown children clawing at her for attention, like kittens fighting for the mother's teat, always suck-ing, sucking, sucking. She felt dried out and used up. Like an old lemon. She began to get as whiney and mopey as her clients. "You've changed," the stars began to note with disappointment. She tried acupuncture and aromatherapy, even a chiropractor. Nothing worked. So when a regular gig on *Would You Rather?* arose, she signed on. Her cats had never been happier.

"He disrespected the show," Harry tried to explain why he had fired Anton. "I had to let him go."

It seemed important that Jeannine understand.

She sharpened an eyebrow pencil and began filling in Harry's eyebrows to make them darker. More authoritative.

"But you always say, 'The show is shit,'" Jeannine said.

"I know the show is shit. You know the show is shit. But we can't go around saying that, can we?"

Jeannine didn't say anything. Harry sighed.

"He made me look fat."

Jeannine frowned, suddenly engaged. This was something she could understand. "Have you been doing those exercises?" she asked.

Harry leaned his head back. "A, E, I, O, U."

"And don't forget Y." Jeannine took his chin and gently raised it to blend the makeup into his neck.

In the control room, Maury Shore watched the set without saying a word. Who the hell was Harry Harlow to fire one of his cameramen? The kid had talent, any fool could see that. All around him, the crew talked in low, subdued voices, avoiding contact with him. They were familiar with his moods, and this was a bad one. Maury had already had four cups of coffee, trying to erase the metallic taste of anger left from the encounter, but nothing was working. He knew the most efficient way to get rid of the feeling was a line of coke. He also knew what his doctor, his ex-wife, and his sponsor at Narcotics Anonymous would have to say about that. Still, it took all his energy to keep his mind from falling into the canyon of memory carved by the craving. He could so easily imagine the straw angled up his nose, the quick, sharp inhalation through one nostril. The immediate chemical taste at the back of his mouth and then the sweet, pleasant flood of relief. It was like a film loop playing over and over in his head, torturing him, needling him. There was something wrong with a universe where bad things felt so good.

As the audience filed into the studio, Anton prowled the floor with his handheld camera, trying to appear normal. Ever since Harry fired him, he'd felt a strange weight on his chest, as if someone were exerting pressure on a vital organ. What was it about him that attracted trouble? He was a mild man. Small. Delicate, even. A bit of a wimp, actually. Not at all the type to start a fight. Violence disgusted him. But all his life, it seemed as if other men took one look at him and developed an instant need to crush him. He thought bitterly of his childhood terrors—the time they stripped him of his pants outside middle school, forcing him to walk home in his underwear. The time they tied a firecracker to his dog's tail. But then, just as the Mobius strip of self-flagellation was gaining more and more speed,

Anton derailed it. Fuck it. What did he care? He was an outsider and that was how it should be. Outsiders see things. They are the artists because they aren't afraid of the truth. They don't care about being liked or respected. Not like that cokehead director or the paranoid host. Let them drown in their own sea of mediocrity. If the price of seeing was not belonging, so be it. Anton would pay that price. The more they kicked him, the better it was for his art.

Having arrived at a justification for the shittiness of other men, Anton felt suddenly energized, as if he'd finished a long, healthful run. In the dead time before the show began, the other cameramen liked to pass the time zooming in on women's tits and asses. Anton used the time to scout expressive, unusual faces that might give him a good reaction shot during the show. Knowing it was the last time he would shoot the show, he suddenly found every face that day profound and meaningful. A young woman's excitement, an old man's melancholy, the way a couple held tight to each other, he saw his camera as a paintbrush, capturing each moment like a latter-day Daumier. A large woman in aisle ten stood up and began carefully moving down the stairs toward the bathroom. As she passed him, Anton followed the planes of her ass, shifting like dunes of sand in the Gobi Desert. That ought to keep them amused in the control room.

Backstage, Hank, the production assistant, gave "Dr. Davis," the resident shrink, a thumbs-up. Boyd Davis—calling him "Doctor" was Aaron's idea, he was only a Ph.D.—put down his copy of *The New Republic* and climbed into his booth. Like a goddamn toll taker on the New Jersey Turnpike, he liked to say to his wife. It was Boyd's job to place the polygraph sensors on the clammy skin of the contestants. He hated the acrid smell of adrenaline rising off them like some kind of sickness and the bright lights that made him blink like a convict, no matter how many times Maury had told him to knock it off. But it was the questions that galled him the most: *Have you ever cheated on your spouse? Have you ever lied on your taxes? Are you a virgin? Have you ever forced a woman to have sex against her will? Have you ever had a three-way? Have you ever shoplifted? Have you masturbated in the last week? In the last twenty-four hours? Do you ever eat your boogers? Do you like the smell of your own farts? Do you love your husband? Are you proud of your children? Do you like your mother-in-law? Do you think you're pretty?* Questions designed to grab hold of secrets and pull them into the halogen light of instant celebrity, where they lay on the floor, writhing in their death throes for everyone's amusement. Every show, Boyd silently prayed that a contestant would land on rats instead of him.

Hank continued to the rat room, where he saw two tanks of rats—the ugly brown ones and the cute black-and-white ones. But no sign of Marian Blaumgrund.

"Which rats are we using?" Hank spoke into his headset. "The brown or the black-and-white?"

"Fuck if I care," Maury answered. "You decide."

Hank leaned down to look more closely at the black-and-white rats. A large female with a black spot over her eyes raised herself up and twitched her nose at him.

"Hey there, Spanky," he said.

Having done his hair and makeup, Jeannine was giving Harry a back rub when a production assistant knocked once and stuck his head in the room.

"Showtime."

Jeannine began to pack up her makeup box.

"Last night, I dreamed my face was on a stamp," Harry said, his eyes still closed.

"How much were you?" Jeannine asked.

Harry opened his eyes and stood up. "I forgot to look."

As he stepped onto the stage, the roar of the audience, like rain on a metal roof, drenched him once again in the dread of the morning. Lucky, lucky, lucky, he repeated to himself. The stage manager lowered his hands like a conductor, the audience took their seats, and Harry faced the eye of the camera. "I think we need some contestants," Harry said, unfolding the piece of paper Hank slipped him on his way to the stage. Anton focused on the epileptic twitch of Harry's leg as he spoke. In the control room, Maury saw the shot but said nothing. In a few hours, the kid would no longer be his problem. A spotlight roamed the audience like police helicopters searching the undergrowth. People moved closer to the edge of their seats, ready to spring forward at the mention of their name.

"Mr. Henry Lee!"

Second row from the front, an elderly Asian man stood quickly and blinked into the lights, both hands moving back and forth in a circular motion as if he were cleaning a window. In the control booth, Maury Shore watched with disgust. "He doesn't have any teeth," he said, which was not technically true. Mr. Henry Lee had teeth. He just didn't have *front* teeth. Mr. Lee's wife grabbed his hand and covered it with kisses but he snatched it away. He was on to something new, something better. You could see the force of this idea pulling him forward as he made his way down the aisle, stepping on everybody's toes. As he passed, they all touched him, wishing him luck, yes, but also secretly wishing some of his luck would rub off. What were the chances of two contestants coming from the same row?

Harry looked at the paper again. "Paula Bane," he read the name out loud.

A small blond woman in a tight striped T-shirt jumped out of her seat and hopped down the aisle as if the ground were burning her feet.

"Finally," Harry read again from the paper, "Shawnia Moore."

Shawnia was the owner of the ass Anton McDonald had followed with his camera, and though she might well be as big as a house, she did not move like a fat woman. Bounding down the stairs; breasts so alive they seemed motorized; arms, stomach, legs aquiver; the audience gasped first and then laughed aloud at the pure pleasure of her. Shawnia shook her hips in appreciation.

"Shawnia," Harry said, smiling at her, "calm down."

"No, unh-unh, no"—she shook her head, so much, her thick gold earrings swung back and forth, thwacking her on the cheeks—"I am up and I am staying up!" She lifted her arms, turned to the audience, and began to clap.

Harry laughed. "All right, then, let's make some money." He reached into his breast pocket, pulled out a card, and turned to face the contestants. "Which of the following mountain ranges is *not* in the United States of America" he read out loud. "The Ozarks, the Sandia, the Brooks, or the Atlas?" Mr. Lee's console lit up first.

"Mr. Lee," Harry asked, "what is your answer?"

Mr. Lee looked confused. "Uh . . . could you repeat the question?"

"No, Mr. Lee, I'm sorry, that would be against the rules," Harry answered sternly. Mr. Lee's face was wet with sweat. People sometimes asked Harry if he felt sorry for the contestants who didn't know the answer. He said yes, but he didn't. Not really. Contestants who hit the button as soon as they could—whether they knew the answer or not— were cheaters, people who believed in blustering forward, confident the rules would be bent for them. Finally, Mr. Lee barked, "The third!" Harry frowned. "I'm sorry, Mr. Lee, but the Brooks Range is in the state of Alaska." The crowd exhaled "Oohhhh."

Anton had kept his camera on Mrs. Lee for a reaction shot. She did not disappoint. Her mouth an O of agony, she pressed her palms against her cheeks, and howled like a wounded dog. Seeing her face on the bank of monitors in the control room, Maury took the shot. He would miss the kid, nobody had the instinct for bathos as he did.

Harry turned to Shawnia. "It looks like you rang second. Care to give us an answer?"

Shawnia leaned into the microphone. "The Atlas?"

"We have a winner." Harry held out his hand.

Two buildings away, Marian Blaumgrund sipped her Earl Grey tea in the company cafeteria, oblivious to the death of the quartz battery on her wristwatch two hours earlier. When she checked half an hour before, she had been pleasantly surprised to see how much time was left before taping. Perhaps, she thought, time elongation was one of the perks of menopause and decided to treat herself to a piece of network-subsidized carrot cake, what *L.A. Magazine* called "the best reason to be an extra." While standing in line to pay for it, she glanced up at the clock on the wall and gasped, so flustered she dropped the carrot cake to the floor, shattering the china plate. In all the time she had worked on the show, she had never missed a taping. How would the rats function without her?

Harry and Shawnia stood in front of "Sam." Contestants were allowed two spins, then decided which of the two options they'd "rather" do. The set was high-tech modern pierced by shafts of halogen light, but "Sam" was wooden and painted red, like something from an old carnival. Shawnia raised her arms, grabbed the wooden handle, and pulled as hard as she could. The wheel stopped on a large brown rat.

"Oh, shit, I hate rats." Shawnia put a hand over her mouth. "Can I say that on TV?"

"No, you can't. The rodent lobby is going to be all over us. Try again."

Shawnia stuck out her tongue, giggled, grabbed the handle, and pulled.

As the wicket drew close to Rats! again, the audience let out a long "Oooohhh."

"No, no, no." Shawnia buried her face in her hands when it landed on Rats! a second time.

Harry put a hand on her elbow and walked her toward the rats. "It's destiny, Shawnia. Don't fight it." Shawnia peered into the tank. The Chestnut rats were blinking at the halogen lights shining in their eyes and pawing unhappily at the air. "Are those rats or hamsters?" she asked.

Harry laughed. "You know the rules," he answered. "One minute gets you a leather recliner. Two minutes, Hawaii. Three minutes, a car."

"I'm going for the car. I ain't afraid of no hamsters," Shawnia answered. She climbed up the ladder next to the tank and gingerly put one leg in, as if she were going swimming in cold water. The audience clapped in encouragement. The rats went still, warily watching as she placed another foot in the tank. Hands on the rim of the tank, she slowly lowered herself in, as if entering a tub of hot water. The rats began to hiss.

Harry looked offstage for Marian Blaumgrund. Why were the rats acting so strangely?

"They supposed to do that?" Shawnia asked.

Anton focused his camera on the rat Hank had called Spanky. Lips pulled back to reveal long, sharp teeth, she was leading the now-steady creep toward Shawnia's feet.

As Harry lowered the lid, Spanky leaped into the air and landed on Shawnia's head. "*Aaaeeeeiii*," she screamed. Harry was so surprised, he lost his balance and fell backward off the ladder. The audience gasped in horror as all two dozen rats converged on her flailing limbs. Harry scrambled back up the ladder, grabbed the lid, and lifted it off the tank. Blood was running down Shawnia's forehead. "Motherfucker!" she screamed, knocking Harry over as she scrambled out of the tank.

In the control room, Maury's mouth dropped open in shock as he watched the debacle unfold in front of him. "Be-yoo-ti-ful," he said. If he broke down and scored a little bit of blow tonight, there was no one in the world who could blame him. Not after the day he'd had.

5

*h*elen McMartin's parents were right. In a manner. She did want the car for a boy, but not for the reasons they suspected. She wanted to break up with Bobby Goralnick but felt it would be wrong to do it over the phone. Until a few weeks earlier, Bobby had been the bass player for a band called Highs, Mostly in the '80s—a joke referring to the marijuana the band regularly smoked and their repertoire of hard rock songs popular in the 1980s. She'd met Bobby at the Salty Cat, a bar in Venice that featured live music on the weekends and karaoke the rest of the time. She and her friend Siri had snuck in using fake IDs they'd ordered over the Internet. She was pretty sure the guy at the door knew they were underage, but they both looked so hot in their handkerchief halter tops and low-slung jeans, he let them in anyway. They ordered drafts of the cheapest beer and drank them slowly. A couple of guys tried to sit with them, but Helen lied and said they were waiting for their boyfriends.

Until just a few months earlier, Helen did have a boyfriend. The son of a well-known rock-and-roll biographer, Roy Beaudell lived three doors down from her in a mock Tudor house with a swimming pool in the shape of a guitar. At fifteen, Helen was so infatuated with Roy, she would scrawl his name followed by a string of hearts moving upward like bubbles from a fish's mouth in all her books. Just last week, her sister had picked up a once-beloved copy of *Zen and the Art of Motorcycle Maintenance* only to find the title page defaced by:

I Love Roy
I lOve Roy.
I loVe Roy.
I lovE Roy!!!

It was hard for Helen to believe it, but there was a time when she had actually gone to Venice beach to tattoo his name on her belly. Thank God for parental consent laws. Her family never understood what she saw in him, but she loved his swimming pool eyes, the way his skin seemed to hold the warmth of the sun even indoors, and the slim, loosely slung muscles of his body. Who knows? If they had never had sex, Helen might still be in love with him, but one November night when the Santa Ana winds had been blowing harder than usual, she finally said yes to Roy's constantly murmured "Please, baby, please, baby, please."

"Really?" Roy asked, pulling back. He was so taken aback by her sudden change of heart, he briefly lost his erection.

Unfortunately, the sex wasn't that good. In fact, it was kind of awful. Everybody said the first few times were always lousy, so Helen had reduced her expectations, but with Roy, sex started out bad and remained that way. When they kissed, everything was fine. She liked his warm breath on her neck, and the growly moans from the back of his throat made her feel powerful—who'd have thought she could transform passive, dreamy Roy into someone so animal? But once their clothes came off, his focus became single-minded, like a dog burying a bone. Lying underneath his huffing body, she felt that she could have been anybody. Or anything. Even his eyes were squeezed shut against her. Afterward, when he said thank you and collapsed sweatily on top of her, she felt even worse. Thank you? She tried to shift her body so that she could breathe more comfortably. Thank you? She had not done him a favor. Giving someone a ride was a favor. Lending him twenty bucks. Letting him use your cell phone. Wasn't sex supposed to be something they both liked?

Her love began to fade. People talked about what a romantic couple they were. Her girlfriends called her Mr. and Mrs. Roy. She smiled and played along, but inside she was wondering how she was going to get out of it. Then, at the beginning of the summer, Roy's father was busted for growing hydroponic marijuana in his basement under a set of old klieg lights he'd bought in an online auction. While reading the meter in the basement, a worker for the electric company spotted the plants and reported him to the police. Under the government's zero-tolerance policy, the Tudor house was seized as the asset of a felon. The arrest sent a shiver through their gently left-leaning community, where it was not uncommon for parents to be smoking marijuana in the master bathroom, windows open, exhaust fan roaring, at the exact same moment teenage children were doing the same in the basement, two stories below. Roy's father got three years in a federal prison and Roy was sent to live in New Jersey with his mother, an ex-model who had made her own fortune selling dietary herbal supplements. Everybody assumed Helen's heart was broken, but the truth was, she was relieved. On the eve of his departure, Helen told him he was free to date other girls.

"I don't want anyone but you," Roy protested.

"You're too young to tie yourself down," she told him. "You should experiment."

"You think?" he asked.

"I think," she said, and nodded. "But that doesn't mean we can't write."

"You're the best," Roy said, his eyes tearing up.

For her next boyfriend, Helen had resolved to find somebody older, a man of experience. Not a Polanski or anybody like that, more like someone's older brother. So when Bobby Goralnick approached her table at the Salty Cat, she could hardly believe her luck. "Y'all want to meet the band?"

"Yeah!" Helen answered before Siri could say anything. All night, she'd been watching him at the guitar. He wore a leather vest, faded blue jeans, and a bandanna around his head. The muscles on his arms were long and stringy, like a ballet dancer's. If she got to pick, he'd be the one. Backstage, the musicians greeted the girls by making the sound of chewing gum.

"Jaysus," Bobby laughed at the way they blanched in embarrassment, "how old are you two?"

"Old enough," Helen said, pretending a confidence she didn't have.

Bobby handed her a beer. A Heineken. "Oh, I think you are, darlin'." His long, floppy bangs stopped just above his eyes and his smile seemed to engage every plane on his face. He was from a place called Slidell, Louisiana, and could say things like "darlin'" without sounding queer. Somebody lit a joint. When it got to Helen, she passed.

"You don' smoke?" Bobby asked, inhaling so the end of it lit up and a piece of ash fell on the thigh of his jeans. She reached out her hand to brush it off. Bobby jumped with alarm.

"You had an ash," she said.

"I've got a fire now," he said. The men laughed. Helen wondered if she was in over her head.

Later that night, Helen and Bobby kissed for a long time in the alley behind the bar. She liked almost everything about it, from the way he pushed her against the soft leather cushion of his motorcycle to the confident way his tongue moved around her mouth, exploring the nooks and crannies of her teeth as if they were his own. She could see how different it was to kiss a man with experience—like the way he breathed calmly through his nose, so he didn't have to keep coming up for air, and the fact that there was no extra saliva to worry about the way there sometimes had been with Roy. He wanted her to go back to his house that very night but she said no. It was already long past the time she should have been home.

Two nights later, she snuck out the back door while her parents slept. Bobby picked her up on his motorcycle in front of Roy's old house. She tried not to dwell on the significance of that. In a gesture of loyalty, she and her friend Anya had stolen the For Sale sign out of the front yard the night before. She noticed a new one had already replaced it. This time, she and Bobby went to his place, the small back house of a ranch-style home three blocks from the beach. In his tiny bedroom, with its acoustic tile ceiling, stained carpet, and smell of unwashed clothing, she took a deep breath and lay back, letting him do whatever he wanted. The next morning, as the sun was rising, he dropped her a block from her house. She walked the rest of the way home barefoot, dangling her sandals from two fingers and paying close attention to everything about the morning—the *pht, pht* of the automatic sprinklers, the water on the sidewalk, her wet footprints on the concrete, the tangerine light of dawn—she wanted to remember it all.

For the next few weeks, she hoarded the pleasure of her secret, making excuses to her friends and lying to her parents about where she went at night. She'd only told Miranda about Bobby after running into her early one morning in the bathroom. "Nice pajamas," Miranda had said. Two nights later, Miranda came to see a show. Afterward, Helen asked her what she thought.

"Sexy," she'd said, and nodded, then narrowed her eyes. "But skeevy, too. You know?"

"Mmmm." Helen nodded, hiding her hurt.

After that, she would sit alone at a front table, nodding her head to the beat which, truth be told, was sometimes hard to find—even she could tell Bobby wasn't much of a bass player. Occasionally, there would be some trouble with club owners wanting to see some ID or guys hitting on her but she learned to say, "I'm with the band," without rolling her eyes.

Everything changed when Forrester, the lead singer, announced he was joining the navy. The remaining band members placed an ad in *Variety* looking for a replacement, but it seemed like every person they auditioned was worse than the next. When they did find someone who seemed promising, the candidate would inevitably turn them down. "That hurt," Bobby said to Helen of the rejection, pounding the spot on his chest where his heart lay beating.

To supplement his income, Bobby had always taken the occasional house-painting job. With the band gone, now it was all he did. Helen would look at his brown hair speckled with white latex paint at night and think, That's how he'll look when he has gray hair, a thought inevitably followed by, I hope I am not around to see it. Evenings they used to spend in clubs were now passed at his home, sitting around his dingy apartment watching television and drinking beer. She became restless. Helen had always felt that her parents shut themselves up in too many dark rooms on sunny days, a book propped in front of them. But the lack of any reading material in Bobby's apartment—not even a newspaper—began to grate on her. Even sex became less exciting and more of a chore. This is my boyfriend, she would sometimes think while they were doing it; he used to be in a band but now he paints houses. She knew the contours of the water stain on his ceiling like the back of her hand. "It looks like the boot of Italy," she said to him one night.

"Italy has a boot?" He took a swig of beer.

She might have been able to wait out the bad spell if it weren't for the drinking. When he was in the band, the constant beer in his hand was like a barely noticed but ever-present accessory. Since the breakup, the beer had become the main focus. What was the Latin phrase her father always used? *Sine qua non.* Without which nothing.

"Let's go for a walk on the beach."

"Let me just grab a fresh one."

"Let's go see a movie."

"After this beer."

She began to keep track of how much he actually drank—one for breakfast, two at lunch, four in the afternoon, and another six-pack before the night was over. Helen was used to the genteel drinking of her parents—wine with dinner and never during the day unless there was a special event, such as a wedding or bar mitzvah. Bobby drank on a different scale. The only time she ever saw his naturally sunny disposition darken was the night she told him she was worried about his drinking.

"If I wanted to date my mom, I'd still be in Louisiana."

A week before, he'd gotten so drunk he peed in the bed. She wasn't there to witness it, thank God, but he actually told her about it, thereby confirming what she was beginning to suspect—her boyfriend was both a drunk and a loser. Who would be dumb enough to admit something like that? Senior year of high school was starting in a few days. She could feel the promise of her life ahead of her like an engine in idle, and Bobby Goralnick was not part of it.

The last few days, she had been practicing with Siri how to leave him.

"I'm sorry, Bobby, it's just not working out."

"What are you talking about? I *looove* you." Siri answered in a bad imitation of a Southern accent.

"Siri, be serious."

"I am being serious. You're the one who is squelching my creativity as an actress."

"Please?"

Siri sighed. "Fine. 'How can you leave me now when I'm down?'"

"We're just too different. We have nothing in common."

"You liked me when I was in a band. Now that I'm a nobody, you think you're better than me."

"God," Helen answered, "you think he thinks that?"

"It's true, isn't it?"

"It's not his fault he had to drop out of high school."

"Just call him."

Helen refused. Breaking up over the phone was cowardly. She already felt guilty enough. She'd once read in a magazine that public venues were the best place to break up, because people were less likely to make a scene. She suggested lunch at an outdoor café in Venice Beach, her treat.

"How?" he asked suspiciously. Helen never had money.

"I babysat last night for the couple across the street."

Not getting the car threw a major wrench into her plans. She went upstairs to her bedroom and called Siri on her cell phone.

"Hey."

"Hey."

"What are you doing?"

"Nothing."

"You want to go to the beach?"

"I can't," Helen sighed. "I'm breaking up with Bobby today."

"Finally."

"But Miranda won't give me the car."

"No."

"*Please*, Siri."

"Do it over the phone."

In the end, she took a bus and arrived fifteen minutes late. "I'm sorry," she said. Apologizing already.

Bobby didn't seem to mind. He was sitting at an outdoor table, wearing Ray Ban aviator glasses in the bright sun and drinking a beer. From his good mood, she doubted it was his first of the day. "You know, sweetheart, this was a good idea." He leaned forward and squeezed her thigh in a proprietary way. "We ought to get out more often, see what the world has to offer."

Helen tried to smile and act normal, but the idea of normal with Bobby had already receded in her mind. Was she normally this nervous around him? The waitress, a bony brunette wearing cut-off jeans and peacock-feather earrings, brought a menu. Helen could tell by the unsmiling way the woman placed the menu in front of her that Bobby had been flirting with her before she arrived. She wished she could tell her to stick around, he'd be available soon.

"I'll have the Cobb salad and a Diet Coke," she said.

"That's good," the woman said, glancing at Bobby. "I was afraid you were gonna order a beer, and we don't serve minors."

"Well, then, you needn't have feared," Helen answered. Needn't? She cringed inwardly at the way she seemed to become her parents when she was offended.

The waitress rolled her eyes.

"Meow," Bobby laughed, watching her leave.

"Bobby," Helen sighed.

"Oh, I know, honey. You don't have to say it." He raised the sunglasses and winked at her.

"What do you mean?" she asked.

He finished his beer and pointed to the empty bottle as the waitress passed. "I might be dumb, but I'm not stupid. When your girl says, 'Let's have lunch in public,' I know what's coming. I don't blame you. I know being with me has not been a picnic these last few weeks. If I could break up with my sorry ass, I would, too."

Helen was so taken aback by his sudden stroke of perceptiveness that she wondered for a second if she was making the right decision. Then she remembered the faint smell of urine that lingered in his bedroom.

A Mexican busboy brought her salad. "'Njoy," he said.

Helen stared at the waxy patina of the Swiss cheese. The article had not mentioned whether it was better to break up before eating or after.

"You don't mind?" she asked.

"Naw," he answered, "you're just a kid, you got your whole life in front of you."

"Well." Helen pulled the salad toward her and began to eat. "Thank you. I mean, for being so understanding." Suddenly, she was ravenous.

"I do have one favor," he said.

"Anything." She was feeling magnanimous.

"How about one more for old times' sake?"

Helen stopped chewing. She could picture a "Sex with an Ex?" headline in the same magazine that advised breaking up in public, but since Roy was making no moves to come home, she hadn't actually read the article. In fact, the last e-mail she received from her ex had cryptically alluded to "the cool people" he had met in New Jersey, which she understood to be code for "I have a new girlfriend." Bobby's glasses were back down over his eyes and she was having some trouble reading his request. Was it a ploy to get her back or a wanton appeal for a futureless fuck?

"I'm not going to change my mind," she said.

"I'm not expecting you to. I have some news myself. Tomorrow I'm gonna sign up with the navy. Forrester gets a three-thousand-dollar signing bonus for every buddy he recruits. He's promised to split it with me. I only need to stay six months. I figure it's a good way to dry out, shape up, and get paid for it." He patted his belly as if it were fat.

Helen's head was reeling. It was all happening so fast—the breakup, the news that Bobby was joining the military, the acknowledgment that he had a drinking problem. She didn't know what to say, so she said what women have always said on the eve of their men shipping out. "I guess once more wouldn't hurt."

Bobby smiled and pushed the bill toward her. His four beers cost more than her lunch. In front of the restaurant, Bobby kissed her on the lips. "I miss you already," he said, handing her the spare helmet he always carried on the back of his motorcycle. The yeasty smell of beer on his breath made her feel queasy. She wondered if he had been drinking before they met, but didn't say anything. In a few hours, Bobby Goralnick's problems would no longer be hers. She tightened the helmet strap, swung a leg over the seat of the motorcycle, and put her arms around his waist. He leaned forward, forcing her body into the curve of his spine and down into his ass. She cursed her body for the tremor that ran through her. They had broken up, shouldn't that break the magnetic pull of his body?

"Hold tight," he said over his shoulder. Helen loosened her embrace. She hated it when people told her what to do.

"You'll take me home afterward?" She couldn't hear his answer over the roar of the engine.

6

What a nightmare of a day. Marian Blaumgrund had once told Harry that rats can be the most inexplicably vicious animals on the planet—a rat would bite the head off every chicken in a hen house simply because it could—but to attack a human like that? Harry put his turn signal on, checked the rearview mirror, and tried to change lanes, but a Mexican fuckhead in a beat-up pickup sped up and passed him on the outside lane. Harry gave him the bird. Was it his imagination or was traffic heavier than usual? One thing was certain, appeasing Shawnia Whateverhername was going to take more than a car. While Jeannine was cleaning the blood off the woman's face, she was already asking, "Is there a lawyer in the house?"

Harry dialed Aaron on his car phone. His assistant, Emmy, answered. (Aaron liked to joke it was the closest he'd ever get to an Emmy award.)

"Oh, my God, Harry, we heard already. It's so awful." Each word had a slight echoey delay, as if she needed half a second to think of what to say.

"Yeah, well, some days you eat the bear—"

"Can you hold? I've got another line."

In his left ear, Harry heard the roar of a motorcycle. He glanced at the rearview mirror and saw a flash of a man and a woman. He couldn't say more about the man, whether he was old or young, fat or thin, even whether he was white or black. He saw even less of the woman, only the top of her knees pressed against the man's thighs and two hands clasped around his

waist. Her face was covered by a white helmet. The man was wearing a black one. Then again, those might have been details he learned later, standing by the highway, watching.

What he did remember with startling clarity was the thud of the motor-cycle against the side of his car. It was a solid *thwack,* as if the man had intentionally hurled the machine against the car. Harry felt his heart leap in fear. Someone leaned on a horn. He put his foot on the break and checked the rearview mirror. The bike was down and the man and woman were on the ground, their bodies crumpled in strangely artificial poses, as if they were faking injury. Jesus Fucking Christ. Were they dead?

Emmy returned to the speakerphone. "Sorry about that."

"Emmy, call the police."

"Oh, Harry, I don't think that's necessary."

Harry hung up on Emmy and called 911.

Long after he had been questioned and the couple had been taken away in ambulances—their bodies cosseted by webbed belts across the chest, waist, and hips—Harry continued to sit in the backseat of a black-and-white police car. The adrenaline flooding his body after the accident had made him feel obscenely alive, like a superhero who could scramble up the side of a building. But now, more than an hour after the accident, he felt jittery, with a strange, ticklish sensation in the back of his throat, as if a feather had lodged in his thorax. The first police on the scene had sheep-ishly asked him to take a Breathalyzer test, which he had done, but since then, nobody had suggested it was his fault. Nevertheless, Harry felt a sick-ness inside that seemed to grow with each passing moment, as if accumu-lated remorse for everything bad he had done in his life were coming to rest at that moment of impact.

A few yards from the patrol car, half a dozen cops were standing around talking, filling out paperwork. Every now and then, one of them would walk to the car, lean down, and say, "You doing okay, Mr. Harlow?"

"Yeah, yeah." Harry would wave. "How much longer do you think you will need me?"

"It won't be long now, sir."

Harry turned to look at his car. Someone was taking a picture of it. There was no dent, no blood, no sign that screamed Death Car, but Harry knew he wouldn't be able to drive that car again. Thank God it was a lease. Tomorrow morning, first thing, he was going to take it to the dealer. Unless, of course, both the kids on the bike were okay. He leaned his head out the window. "Excuse me?" he said to a policeman in tall leather boots who was watching a tow truck remove the mangled motorcycle.

"Yes, sir, Mr. Harlow?" The cop touched his hat as if Harry were a four-star general. Were they being so solicitous because he was a celebrity or a shocked citizen?

"Is there any news on the couple that was hurt? Are they going to be okay?"

"Sir, they're at the hospital right now. We won't know for a while."

Harry wanted to point out that that was the same answer from a half hour before, and if the cop would bother to make an inquiry with his phone or walkie-talkie or whatever it was the cops used to communicate with one another, he might be able to turn up some real information. But instead he mumbled a muddy "Thanks."

Traffic, which had been completely blocked during the "investigation" began to flow in the far lanes. People slowed for a look and Harry sank lower in the seat. A policeman's face appeared in the window. "Sir?" he said, "would you like an escort home?"

"What for?" Harry asked.

"Just a courtesy," the man replied.

Harry shook his head. He already felt uncomfortably conspicuous as it was.

Back in his car, he noticed the hand that held his keys was shaking. Had he made a mistake in turning down the escort? Like a stroke victim forced to relearn the basics of life, he found himself second-guessing all the previously instinctual parts of driving. Was there a car in his blind spot? Was he merging too slowly? Too quickly? Usually, he was a fast, confident driver; now he stayed in the slow lane, carefully keeping the needle on fifty-five. His mind veered to the accident. Was it really not his fault? Maybe if he hadn't been so distracted by the incident with the cameraman and the disaster with the rat? In the quiet of his car, Harry felt like crying. He tried to calm himself down by visualizing himself on a beach, the way Catherine had taught him to do. But his beach was always thick with rednecks playing loud radios, medical waste washing ashore, and the rotting carcass of a massive whale. "Oh, Harry, that's so unnecessary." Catherine had lost her patience when he described the scene. The thought of going home to his wife at that moment was even less appealing than usual.

The phone rang. Harry hesitated. He'd been speaking on the car phone when the accident happened. Was there a connection? Had he unknowingly veered into the couple while talking to Emmy? No, he reminded himself, all the eyewitnesses agreed—it was the motorcycle that hit him. He reached a trembly finger toward the answer button and, heart thumping, pushed.

"Hello?"

"Harry?" It was Fields, the show's publicist, a sweet-faced young man from the South who was said to be the gay lover of a married head of a studio. Harry had no idea if the rumor was true, but he had noticed that people treated Fields with a deference rare for a publicist. "How *are* you? *Where* are you?" *How air yew? Whair air yew?*

"I'm okay," Harry answered, "I'm on my way home."

"Thank God you took a Breathalyzer."

"Any news on the couple?"

"Harry, it's not your fault. You know that."

Harry's bottom lip jutted forward. His eyes began to water. "Both?"

"The girl is alive, I think. I only know what the reporters tell me. Isn't it crazy? I've got to watch TV to know what's going on. Harry, there are going to be reporters at your house, don't say anything." *Ainything*.

"How do they know where I live?"

"They know everything." He sounded overwhelmed.

"I guess you're earning your salary this week, Fields."

"I guess so." *I gayess so.*

"Should we, like, send flowers or something?" Fields's response sounded something like "Krakatoa." Then the line went dead.

7

*S*ophia was seven minutes late for her lunch with Betsy Saunders, the thirteenth-richest woman in Los Angeles, as tabulated by the glossy giveaway, *Sunset Boulevard*. Most people wouldn't notice seven minutes. Betsy would. She noticed everything. If Sophia was wearing a new shirt or a different shade of lipstick. If she was tired or sad or happy, Betsy noticed. She was like a spider, tracking everything that came near her web. It made it exhausting to be around her but not entirely unpleasant. There was, Sophia had to admit, something invigorating about being noticed so carefully. Especially now that she was of the age when men, who had once looked at her without fail, barely registered her presence. More important, it was Sophia's job to like Betsy. Not only had she given millions to the museum, unlike most rich people, she actually enjoyed calling up her friends and berating them for not giving more. The words "It's not like you can take it with you" came out of her mouth so often, Sophia's assistant once had them printed on a coffee cup for her birthday present.

They were eating at L'Orangerie, a faux Georgian mansion flanked by fiberglass gargoyles and citronella torches lining the Belgian-block drive-way. The walls inside were a brownish orange and everything on the menu had something orange in it—duck à l'orange, fish poached in citrus, rack of lamb served with a cranberry-orange relish. Even the waiters wore orange vests, which, in Sophia's opinion, made them look like construction workers. When she was feeling low, she saw hate in their Aztec eyes; other times, the place was a comfort, a throwback to the days when neither money nor calories were an issue. Though, as Sophia had learned from working with the very rich, money was always an issue. She knew for a fact, for example, that Betsy liked to eat at L'Orangerie only because she owned the parking lot attached to it. And while she'd grown accustomed to the yellowed armpits of Betsy's silk shirts and the missing buttons on her Chanel suits, the first time she met her, she'd been shocked by the moth holes on the sleeve of her Bill Blass suit.

Sophia had requested the lunch to discuss an Agnes Martin that Betsy had promised the museum two years earlier, a bland sunscape from Martin's early days in Santa Fe. A week earlier, the director of the museum, a slim-hipped German with unblinking blue eyes, had called Sophia into his office to say he'd heard that Betsy had promised the same painting to the Guggenheim.

"That can't be," Sophia said.

The director raised a pale eyebrow.

"She does this stuff when she feels neglected," Sophia explained.

"Well, let's un-neglect her." He waved his hand as if to move a cobweb.

"An invitation from the director would mean more."

"I've got a very busy schedule." He neatened a pile of papers on his already spotless desk.

Betsy offered a white cheek rendered lineless by a surgeon's scalpel. When Sophia bent to kiss it, she felt as if she'd been brushed by a moth's wing. The fact that Betsy considered Sophia a friend made her unfireable at the museum but required a devotion that Sophia sometimes resented. Once a month, Betsy summoned her to dinner at her Bel Air mansion, a traditional Colonial filled with provocative contemporary art, which always struck Sophia as odd, like an octogenarian wearing a miniskirt. The guest list was random to the point of hostility. Betsy liked to sit at the head of the table and watch people struggle to make conversation. "It's the Darwinian struggle to survive," Betsy once explained to Sophia, "right there at my dinner table." When the guests did happen to get along well, Sophia couldn't shake the feeling that Betsy was angry.

"Well, well," she'd say, glaring at them, "look at you." Once, years before, a couple who had met at one of her parties actually got married. Betsy was still furious about it.

Sophia had gotten used to the old woman's misanthropy, the casual references to "faggot" curators, "pathetic" painters, and "idiot" collectors, but Darius, with his natural manners and tendency to think the best of everyone, was so taken aback by her vitriol he refused to go back.

"*So,*" Betsy put her hand on Sophia's. "Tell me everything."

Sophia sighed. What was there to tell? Her life had not changed much since their last lunch. She had the same job, lived in the same house with the same husband. She could talk about books she had read or movies she had seen, but she knew that would bore Betsy. She could tell her about her midlife fantasies of selling the house, cashing in the pensions, and moving to Provence or Italy or that small town in the Mexican mountains where everybody goes to drink. Once, she had even listed the house on one of those home-swap Internet sites but was so disappointed by other people's houses, their ugly couches and smug descriptions of the neighborhood—*We live right next to the sweetest park and the best café!*—that she took the listing down after a week.

Truth was, the most interesting thing in Sophia's life were her children. Watching them figure out a place in the world was endlessly fascinating to her. She could happily spend all day with them without ever getting bored, and the conversation she most enjoyed with her husband was always, always about the girls. *Was Miranda happy? Would Helen ever get over that silly Roy Beaudell?* But Betsy would not be interested in that. Because she had never experienced it from her own mother, nor felt it toward her own, nothing bored her more than maternal love. What interested Betsy was gossip—the more malicious, the better. Nothing made her happier than hearing about another person's misfortune. Once, in a moment of weakness, Sophia had made the mistake of confessing to a flirtation with one of Darius's colleagues. Ever since that day, Betsy would ask, "How's your marriage?" with a knowing leer that made Sophia cringe.

Safest of all was gossip from the art world, and in anticipation of her lunch, Sophia had made a few embarrassing phone calls to scrounge some up, beginning with the impending divorce of a German architect notorious for his taste in very young Asian girls.

"*Ew,*" Betsy said, wrinkling her nose, "remember the one he brought to the Biennial? Her skirt barely covered her twat."

Sophia did not remember the barely covered twat of a young Asian girl. Only curators went to the Biennial. Sophia was in development. It was the kind of mistake Betsy made all the time, gaffes that seemed innocent on the surface but always made Sophia's mood darken. She could have been a curator if she had ever finished her dissertation, "Render the Child: Flesh of Jesus in Early Florentine Renaissance Painting," but how was she supposed to write at home with a small baby constantly needing attention? With her cold heart and millions of dollars, Betsy could have easily handed the baby off to a minion, but that had not been an option for Sophia. Or had it? Sometimes, she wondered if she had used the unplanned arrival of Miranda so early in the marriage as an excuse for her failure as an academic. Truth is, Miranda had been an easy baby, happy to lie calmly in her bassinet, playing with her own fingers while Sophia tortured herself at the computer. It wasn't laziness that kept her from succeeding, it was ambition. She wanted so badly for her thoughts to soar and her words to sing, it paralyzed her. She'd write and rewrite a single sentence over and over until it no longer made sense, like a skier lost in a whiteout, no sense of up or down, sky or snow. Finally, she'd put it aside and go to the park with Miranda. Tomorrow, she'd think, when her mind was fresh, surely she'd be able to resolve the problem.

But the next day, when she read the sentence, she'd be appalled. How could she ever have thought the words acceptable? And so it went. Days and days would pass but she'd find herself no closer to an end. She was the snake eating itself. Sisyphus rolling the rock up the hill again and again. Darius, already an assistant professor, was full of advice in those days. "Don't be so hard on yourself. It doesn't have to be perfect." But he was wrong. It did have to be perfect. The longer she took to write it, the more perfect it had to be. No wonder she had embraced childbearing with such ardor—it did not matter what kind of a mother she had been that day. Whether she had let the baby cry or left a wet diaper on too long, couldn't find the burp after a feeding or bought jars of commercial food instead of using the food mill to grind fresh carrots, the child grew. Regardless. Not only that, she loved Sophia in a way nobody ever had. Who else lit up like a Roman candle when she walked into the room? Who else could stare lovingly into Sophia's eyes for hours, endlessly entranced by the mute bond of mother and child? Who wouldn't be more interested in the flesh of her own child than the bloodless flesh of Christ in a painting from the fifteenth century?

Sophia was on the verge of bringing up the Agnes Martin, when her cell phone began to vibrate. Betsy made a face. Usually, Sophia would let it go directly into voice mail but she was sufficiently irritated with Betsy for the Biennial comment that she decided to answer just as dessert—orange pound cake soaking in a puddle of melted Belgian chocolate—arrived. It was Darius. Something had happened to Helen. An accident. On the highway. The doctors were with her. She was alive. But. *But?* Sophia wanted to scream.

"You'll want to get here as soon as possible," Darius answered.

Sophia stood.

"My God," Betsy said. "What's wrong?"

She opened her mouth to answer but nothing came out.

Sophia drove cautiously, like a drunk overcompensating for impairment. Both her parents were alive, her grandparents had lived to reasonable old ages, and she had no close friends who had died untimely or freakish deaths—yet all her life Sophia had been silently steeling herself for disaster. Whenever she watched Darius or the girls leave for trips, her mind would immediately wander into the ways they could die—what if their plane, taking off from LAX, hit a flock of seagulls? She had read that a single bird caught in the engine turbine could cause the plane to stall mid-takeoff. What if the pilot of the plane was suicidal and slammed it into the ocean, determined to take with him as many as possible? What if a hijacker opened an emergency exit midair? The plane might stay aloft but everybody within a five-foot radius would get sucked out of the door. What if the girls ate a hamburger infected with mad cow disease? What if they got bitten by a mosquito infected with West Nile virus? What if there was an earthquake and they were swimming in a pool and a live power line fell into the water? What if a deadly jelly fish stung them while they snorkeled in the Caribbean? What if a common cold turned into pneumonia, then septic shock? What if a crazy, unloved adolescent brought a shotgun to school one day? What if they interrupted the arc of a stray bullet in the drive-through at Poquito Más, their favorite Mexican takeout place? What if a chunk of concrete fell off the truck in front of them on the highway and smashed their windshield at eighty-five miles an hour? What if a rabid bat bit them on a camping trip? What if they stepped on a rattlesnake in the spring, when its venom was most potent? What about avian flu? Legionnaire's disease? Cancers of the cervix, the colon, the esophagus, the pancreas. Skin cancer, bone cancer, uterine cancer. There were a million unthought-of ways that the people she loved could die. By thinking them through ahead of time, Sophia liked to think she had somehow prepared herself for a disaster when or if it happened. Driving to the hospital, Darius's "but" ricocheting through her guts, she saw what a rank amateur she had been in the pessimism department. She hadn't had a clue what it would feel like when something bad happened to her child.

In the hospital parking lot, a man and a woman walking across the street in surgical blue scrubs sent a wave of panic crashing through her. She parked at a cockeyed angle in front of the emergency room, under a large No Parking sign.

In the lobby, a rustic wooden cross with fake wormholes loomed over the foyer. Catholics. Good. Not because she was a believer, but she'd been raised in the faith and knew her way around it. "I'm looking for my daughter," she said to the woman sitting behind the information desk. The woman looked startled. Sophia realized that she had just yelled at her.

"Name?" the woman asked wearily, as if people had been yelling at her all day.

"Helen," Sophia answered meekly, as if to make up for yelling. "McMartin."

Information appeared on the computer screen. "She's in the ICU. Three floors up."

Sophia followed her directions, rolling the letters—I . . . C . . . U— around in her head, trying to remember what they meant. They sounded collegial—something-something university? But she knew that wasn't right. As the doors of the elevator closed, it came to her. Intensive care unit. Where they send the sickest. But not the dead. In the waiting room, Sophia found her husband and daughter looking pale and confused, as if they were recovering from a flu. When she got closer, she could see that the pupils of their eyes had shrunk to pinpricks. She hugged her daughter first.

"What happened?" she asked, dismayed by the flicker of blame dancing deep inside. *If you had given her the car, none of this would have happened.*

"There was an accident. A motorcycle and a car, that's all we know."

Darius listened with a detached expression on his face, as if he were trying to identify a far-off piece of music.

"Helen was in the car," Sophia said.

Miranda shook her head. "No, she was on the motorcycle."

"Who has a motorcycle?"

"I think it was the guy she was seeing. They asked us if we knew his next of kin. He might be dead. I don't even know his last name. Just that he was older and in a band."

"Helen had a boyfriend?"

"She didn't want you guys to know about him. She thought you wouldn't approve."

Sophia sat down and put her hands over her eyes. She thought of all the times in her life she had misused the words she needed now. A boring cocktail party was *a nightmare*. A traffic jam was *a disaster*. Now she was left mute by the enormity of a true tragedy.

Helen's surgeon—Dr. Rajiv Marjani—entered the waiting room. He offered his hand first to Darius, then Sophia. He was familiar with the father's handshake. Brief. Firm. Dry. The grasp of a man trying hard to hold everything together. The mother took his hand between both of hers, looked straight into his eyes, and did not let go. He got the message. If something happened to his son, he'd probably do the same. The sister did not meet his eye at all, and he made a mental note to send a psychiatric social worker around for a consult. He didn't like the girl's color at all. Much too pale.

"I am very, very sorry for what has happened to your daughter and her friend," Dr. Marjani began, secretly cursing himself for not being able to remember the patient's name. Ever since the day he had gotten a shooting victim's name wrong to a set of grieving parents, he had learned never to say the name without being completely sure. "I am afraid the young man died en route to the hospital."

"The driver?" Sophia asked.

The doctor nodded.

"What about Helen?" Darius asked.

The doctor sighed. "May I give you a lesson in Brain Injury 101?" he asked. No one answered. As a family, the worst medical emergency they had experienced was what Sophia's doctor called a "suspicious" Pap smear, which turned out to be nothing. Darius had once gone to the emergency room convinced his appendix had ruptured but half a bottle of Mylanta later, he felt fine. Without waiting, Dr. Marjani removed a plastic model of a brain from his pocket. It was bright blue and the size of a large fist; he had bought it at the Museum of Natural History's gift shop during an outing with his son. It added little to his presentation, but he liked to direct the attention of the family away from his own gaze, onto a neutral object. Sometimes, the pleading in their eyes was too much to bear.

"The brain needs oxygen to survive," he began, "which it gets from red blood cells delivered through thousands of tiny blood vessels attached to its walls. When there is a traumatic blow to the head, such as your daughter suffered, the brain is rocked back and forth violently." The doctor shook the model as if he were mixing a bottle of juice. "The movement tears those blood vessels away from the brain, causing it to swell, just as a finger slammed in a car door will swell in reaction to injury."

He could see he had lost them. "Because the brain is encased by the hard shell of the skull, when it swells it has no place to go. The pressure caused by that swelling is what causes the oxygen to be cut off."

"Helen's brain is swelling?" Darius asked.

"Yes," the doctor answered.

"Can you do anything to control it?"

"We have already drilled a hole into the skull to relieve the intercranial pressure."

"You drilled a hole in Helen's head?" Sophia asked.

"Oh, yes. Without that, she would be dead."

"I need to sit," Sophia said.

"Of course," Dr. Marjani gestured to a seat, silently dismayed. Once they sat, you could count on an extra five minutes of talking, and already he had been called to consult on an accident at Presbyterian Memorial across town where a young man had botched trying to kill himself with a gun to the mouth. It was the type of injury Dr. Marjani specialized in, and the doctors there were hopeful they could still save the patient. He had promised to come if he could, but the truth was, his heart was never fully into saving suicides. There were too many other patients who had been blindsided by fate for him to spend his energy on someone who wanted to die. No, he would stay with this family and answer the best he could; if they still wanted him at Presbyterian, he'd consult by phone.

"How is the pressure now?" Darius asked.

"To be honest with you, it's high. Much higher than I would like."

"But she's breathing?"

"Oh, yes!" Dr. Marjani responded, trying to sound optimistic. "We intubate right away. Breathing is the most primary goal at all times."

"But she's not conscious?" Darius asked.

"No, she is not conscious. She won't be conscious for a long time." The doctor debated adding the truth, that she may well never regain consciousness, but decided to wait.

"What are the chances that she will recover?" Miranda asked. He was surprised that the hard question came from the girl. She was tougher than she looked.

"It is too early to say." Dr. Marjani squeezed the gelatinous brain and put it in his pocket. "We are, unfortunately, still very much in the dark ages when it comes to brain injuries. The biggest danger right now is a stroke. Ninety percent of coma patients die of a stroke."

"She's in a coma?" Sophia asked.

The doctor mentally kicked himself. The word was an old habit. "We don't really like to use that word anymore. It's very imprecise." That and too many TV shows had given people the wrong idea about them.

"Okay," Miranda said slowly, "if this were ten years ago, would she be in a coma?"

"Well, yes," he answered. "Ten years ago, she would be in a coma."

"Is she brain dead?" Miranda asked.

Again, the girl asking the hard questions! "I don't know what it means to be brain dead. No one really does," the doctor answered. "So, no, I could not say your sister is brain dead. Not yet. But she is sick. Very sick. The best we can do is hope." He wanted to say "hope and pray," but the hospital ethics committee had already issued several warnings to him about mentioning God to his patients or their families.

"About her friend . . ." the doctor said.

"We don't know him," Sophia interrupted. "He was just a . . . a passing thing."

"Ah." The doctor nodded. "The police may want to speak with you about him. It seems that alcohol was involved."

"Helen was drinking?" Darius asked.

"Her blood-alcohol level was zero, but the man was, ah, well over the legal limit."

Sophia felt like she was going to throw up. "Can we see her?" she asked.

"Of course," the doctor answered. "But one at a time. Please."

Darius and Sophia looked at each other. She could tell from her husband's eyes that he wanted to go first. "You go," Sophia said.

"Are you sure?" he asked, already standing.

Sophia nodded. She wasn't being generous. The truth was, she didn't want to go into that room. Seeing Helen unconscious, hooked up to machines, a hole in her head, would make the nightmare real. For just a few more minutes, she wanted to hold on to her old world. The world before the end.

When Sophia saw Helen lying in the hospital bed, her head encased in a metal cagelike contraption, she felt dizzy, as if the blood in her body were suddenly flowing in the wrong direction, the way the ocean is said to recede before a tsunami. Helen's face was pale and expressionless, as if she were waiting to be born and given a personality. Neat black stitches formed a paisley pattern on her scalp. Like a baseball. Sophia wanted to gather her body in her arms and hold her but there were half a dozen tubes attached to her mouth, nose, arm, and up the inside of her leg, taking fluids away or putting them back. Sophia couldn't be certain which. Instead, she lowered her own cheek to her daughter's hand and held it there. A nurse entered the room.

"Can she hear me?" Sophia sat up.

"We don't really know," the nurse answered with an empty smile, "but it can't hurt."

Sophia tried to think of something to say. When she was pregnant, it had been fashionable to play classical music next to the uterus and read aloud. She'd gone along with it, reading *The Lion, the Witch, and the Wardrobe* in a phony, theatrical voice, but she felt as silly then as she did now. It was the same problem she'd always had with prayer—how do you talk to someone who can't answer?

"Helen?" she said, finally. "It's your mother." She wished the nurse would leave so that she would feel less self-conscious.

"Honey"—she cleared her throat—"I know it doesn't seem like it right now, but you're going to be out of here soon." She stopped, hating how false she sounded. Sophia had no idea whether her daughter was going to get better. Already, her mind was swimming with a newly learned vocabulary of disaster: *hematoma, ischemia, axonal, neuronal.* When Dr. Marjani was talking, she had tried to let her mind open, to take in the bigger picture and interpret what the doctor was saying, not from his words, but his tone. She had been encouraged by the fleeting smile with which he had greeted them. If Dr. Marjani thought Helen was going to die, he wouldn't have smiled, would he? But then she realized her error. Of course he would. The worse the news, the more he would want to comfort them.

Sophia decided to be honest. She had always resented the lies parents were forced to tell their kids. From an early age, her kids knew Santa didn't come down a chimney, storks didn't bring babies, and fairies didn't take the bloody tooth under their pillows. Maybe after death, you did go to a place where everybody dressed in white, lived on a cloud, and drank the morning dew, but if life on earth was anything to go by, she doubted it. But when she tried to say something true, the only word that came to her lips was *Sorry*. Again and again, it pushed itself to the surface like a beach ball that wouldn't sink. *Sorry. Sorry. Sorry.* Once she had her children, the only thing that really mattered to her was protecting them from harm. So where had she been when Helen got on a motorcycle with a drunk? Having lunch with a sick twist of an old woman. *I am so motherfucking sorry.* Useless word. But it was all that seemed to fit.

"Helen," Sophia said finally, "I am so sorry. I wish we could trade places. When you have a child, you'll understand." There it was again. That false note of optimism. *When you have a child.* The nurse poked her head in and pointed to her watch.

Back in the waiting room, she sat next to Darius. He tried to smile but the expression on his face was ghastly. Sophia took his hand and they sat in silence, which is how the pretty woman with the clipboard found them.

"Hi," the woman said too brightly, "my name is Marta. I am in charge of public affairs for the hospital." She smoothed the back of an already tight skirt and took a seat across from them. "You can't see it from here, but our parking lot is filled with reporters who want to know how your daughter is doing." The way she said it, as if they should be flattered, caused Sophia to develop an instant and unrecoverable dislike for her.

"Why?" Darius asked.

"Ah"—the girl licked her lips nervously—"because the driver was a celebrity?"

Sophia was confused. Helen's boyfriend was a celebrity?

"From what I have heard," the girl continued in a rush, "it wasn't his fault. He was driving his car and the motorcycle hit him from behind. But he is involved, and that means the media are going to care." She shrugged her shoulders, as if to say, "What can you do?"

"Who was it?" Miranda asked.

"Harry Harlow."

"Harry *who*?" Sophia asked.

"The host of that stupid show," Miranda said with a shudder. "The one where you have to humiliate yourself in order to win a prize."

"I don't think we want to say anything," Sophia answered coldly.

"I completely understand," Marta answered. Her hands began to play nervously with the clipboard while she spoke. "It's just, in my experience, sometimes these things go away more quickly if you do issue a short statement." The girl shrugged her shoulders helplessly. Sophia recognized something of her younger self in the girl's assumption that things would go her way if she asked nicely and looked pretty. She also remembered bitter older women with hair-trigger bad moods.

"Have you written something?" she asked, trying to soften her voice.

The girl handed over the clipboard. It was a generic statement from the family, thanking all the people who had showed concern, summarizing the wait-and-see position of the doctors, and requesting privacy. Sophia handed it to her husband. He took the clipboard and fumbled for his reading glasses. Ten years he had been wearing them, yet he had never managed to devise a constant resting place. Sometimes they were on his head, sometimes in his left breast pocket; other times, his right. Normally, watching him dither like a forgetful old man irritated Sophia, but in that setting, the familiarity of the gesture comforted her.

"You've misused 'its.'" Darius said when he finished reading.

"I'm sorry?" Marta asked.

"It's a common mistake," Darius said. "My students do it all the time." He read the offending sentence aloud. "'The family requests privacy in it's time of grief.' There's no apostrophe in 'its.' It's like 'his' or 'hers.'"

"Oh." Marta reddened.

"Actually," Miranda said, looking at her father for backup, "I think *their* would be a better choice. 'The family requests privacy in *their* time of grief.'"

"She's right, I think." Darius smiled at her. "I don't know why I didn't see it."

Sophia could imagine how they must appear to the woman. Dry-eyed, rational, debating the niceties of grammatical correctness in a press release. How many times had she watched her husband pause mid-argument to compose the right sentence or correct her grammar? It made him feel in control, but she often thought the self-conscious act of composition kept him from feeling anything too keenly. Now, sitting under the fluorescent lighting in the peach-colored family waiting room, she was grateful for her family's control.

"Yes, that's right," Sophia said. "The family requests privacy in their time of grief."

"Of course." The girl lowered her head and made the change.

8

*d*riving home from the accident, Harry found himself gripped by a sudden, intense yearning for his mother. Monica Odell (Harry's real last name) had been a terrible parent by every conventional measure. Half the year they had no phone service. Electricity was iffy. Sometimes she forgot to pick him up at school and she was forever bringing home different men. Harry's earliest memory was being woken one night by her voice whispering, "*Ssshhh*, you'll wake the baby." At first, Harry thought she had brought a baby home with her. When he realized she was referring to him, all he could feel was indignation. He was not a baby! He was almost six years old! But for all her faults, she had done her son the great favor of liking him. He could feel it every time they spoke.

"Harry!" she'd sing, whenever he called, "tell me everything, tell me now and start at the beginning." He would, too. Work problems, money problems, girlfriends, sex. He held nothing back from Monica. Because she'd never treated him like a child, it wasn't hard for him to treat her like an older, benign friend. It seemed a common thing, a parent who liked you, but the older Harry got, the more he realized how rare it was. Catherine's parents might have given her everything she wanted, but Harry could never escape the feeling that they didn't much like the child they had created.

In return for her affection, Harry had forgiven Monica everything. When he was very young, he used to watch while she slept off her hangovers, just to make sure she wasn't dead.

"What are you doing?" she'd ask, when she woke to find him staring at her.

"Nothing," Harry would mutter, going back to the television, convinced he'd saved his mother's life.

It was Harry's biggest regret that his mother died at fifty-eight, five years before his success. When the county hospital diagnosed stage-four lung cancer, Monica seemed almost happy, as if she had been waiting for it.

"It's God's will," she told Harry over the phone. Harry got on a Greyhound bus to Searchlight, Nevada, that night. Three weeks later, she died in a county hospice, a morphine drip dangling over her head like an exclamation point in a cartoon conversation bubble. When he tried to pack up the trailer, Spartacus, her little black poodle, growled and snapped at Harry whenever he went near it, as if it blamed him for her death. Harry gave it to the animal shelter with the understanding that it would be "put to sleep" within forty-eight hours if nobody adopted it.

"What are the chances somebody will take her?" he asked the man who did the paperwork.

"Zero," the man answered, "nobody wants an old dog."

When Harry tried to sell her mobile home he discovered that Monica had been living for the last five years on a complex scheme of revolving credit-card debt. Each time she maxed out on one credit card, she'd apply for another, paying the minimum possible until the principal ballooned to two, three times the original balance. It was a precarious pyramid scheme on the verge of collapse. No wonder she'd sounded happy at the prospect of an early exit out of her troubles.

Rounding the corner of his block, Harry was surprised to see television vans lining the street in front of his house. "*Harry! Harry!*" Beauty-pageant blondes turned entertainment reporters crowded around his car, phallic microphones in hand. Behind them, their cameramen silently recorded everything. Harry shook his head as if he were sorry to let them down but even without Fields's advice, it would have been easy to say no.

Through a back window, Harry could see his wife in the kitchen, her hair tied up in a red bandanna and a line of worry bisecting the area between her eyebrows. He knew he ought to go inside and talk to her but instead he circled the house to the pool, where the gardener, José, was pruning the jacaranda blossoms. Earlier in the week, Harry had complained that too many were falling into the pool. Already, José had cut back half of the tree. Seeing the tree shorn, Harry realized he'd made a mistake. He missed the purple roof of flowers.

"José," Harry said, "you can stop cutting now."

José looked at the lopsided tree and frowned. "It's no even," he said.

"It's okay," Harry told him.

José shrugged unhappily and began gathering the cut limbs. Harry had noticed this before. José hated leaving anything half done.

In the pool house, a dank two-room structure that smelled vaguely of mildew, Harry began to undress. Halfway through taking off his pants, he heard his wife's voice.

"Harry? Is that you?"

He recognized certain aspects of her tone—wounded irritation mixed with something he'd never heard before. Was it fear? Reluctantly, Harry began to dress again. Catherine opened the door and threw herself against him. Harry felt an unfamiliar vibration in her body, as if she were freezing and burning up at the same time.

"Harry!" she wailed. "How awful." He thought he smelled bananas.

"Let's go inside," he said. It embarrassed him to talk to his wife in front of José. Unlike Catherine, who'd been raised by professionals, Harry had never gotten used to having employees around the house. He couldn't get over the idea that they were watching him, taking note of his weaknesses, laughing about him behind his back. He imagined how he and Catherine must look to them—pampered, childless adults who couldn't or wouldn't clean their own clothes.

The house smelled of banana bread. "It's what we do in our family when something goes wrong," Catherine explained.

"Good idea. Maybe the reporters will want some."

"Harry, don't be flip. Not now."

"If not now, when?"

"We need to come up with a plan."

"What kind of a plan?" he asked.

"Something to protect our interests in this matter."

From the little moonstones in her ear to her chamomile hair and gooseberry eyes, people met Catherine and thought *pushover*, but Harry had lived with her long enough to know better. She craved success and material comfort no less than any other woman he had known. Maybe more. The difference was subtlety. Catherine had it.

"I don't know what you mean by my 'interests,'" he answered. "It was an accident. Nobody thinks it was my fault."

"Exactly," Catherine answered, her breath coming a little quicker now, "and if something terrible should happen, you shouldn't have to suffer."

"What do you mean?" Harry asked.

"You know," she answered, "sometimes people get spooked when something bad happens. Like when there's been a murder in a house— nobody wants to live there—even if it's great in every other way."

"A man is dead and a girl is lying in the hospital fighting for her life." There were moments in Harry's life when the words that came out of his mouth sounded suspiciously similar to the lines he'd spoken when he worked on the soap opera.

"It's terrible, yes, but there's nothing we can do about it. There is, however, something we can do about our future."

"What's that smell?"

"Goddamn it." Catherine opened the oven door. The smell of burned sugar filled the room.

*b*y eleven that night, Sophia's exhaustion was like the physical ache of too vigorous exercise. Darius was leaning his head against the wall, his eyes closed, breath slow and steady. She had always been jealous of his ability to nap anywhere. Once, on a trip to Costa Rica, she had found him snoring on the lip of an extinct volcano, oblivious to the jagged black rock under his head. A nurse sat across from Sophia. Peggy was older than the day nurses, with thick ankles, a turquoise cardigan of cheap acrylic that did not become her, and a head of tight silver curls. Still, Sophia recognized the unmistakable gleam of intelligence in her eye and gently shook her husband awake.

"There's nothing for you to do here tonight," Peggy said after introducing herself. "You ought to go home."

"We can't leave her here," Sophia answered.

"Well, you can't take her with you," Peggy said, smiling.

"What if she wakes up?" Darius asked.

Peggy put her hand on top of his. It was mottled like a piece of expensive Italian paper. "I've worked on this floor for thirteen years," she said. "Patients in your daughter's state don't wake up overnight. It takes weeks, maybe even months. You need to conserve your strength for the days ahead. You can sleep on the floor. I've seen others do it, but I'm giving you the best advice I know." Sophia searched the nurse's face for some hidden meaning in her comments but couldn't find anything.

"She's right," Sophia said, "let's go home."

Darius opened his mouth to argue but then stopped himself. "You'll call if there's a change. Any change. Good or bad?"

"Of course," the nurse answered.

Outside, in the parking lot, the night had turned cold and clear. Sophia's car had long since been towed. To make room in the backseat of her father's Volvo, Miranda had to push aside an assortment of books, papers, a sweater, a squash racket, several empty takeout coffee containers, and a twenty-pound bag of topsoil Darius had bought at the organic market and never gotten around to unloading. The dirt made the car smell loamy, like a garden after a long rain or, Sophia couldn't help thinking, a grave.

When they pulled into the driveway of their house, Sophia was startled by its darkness. Some member of the family was normally home by now or had left a light on, but today the family had left in the fullness of the sun and returned in pitch black. It was like the first time she returned to a winter on the East Coast after living in California. My God, she'd thought, looking at the bare trees and brown grass, how could she not have noticed the death all around her? In the kitchen, a mug half filled with coffee sat in the sink. Sophia stared at it, stricken by the curdled star of milk in its center. Was it Helen's? She thought of the relatives of those who died in the World Trade Center, how they'd combed hair out of brushes or submitted old toothbrushes in Ziploc bags for DNA samples.

"Look at that." Darius's voice knocked the thought out of her head. The number *30* blinked on the answering machine. He pressed the play button.

"Do we have to do this now?" Sophia asked.

Miranda leaned against the kitchen counter, arms folded, head down.

"I'm not tired." Darius sat down with a pen and pad of paper.

Sophia poured herself a glass of scotch and sat across from him. Usually, she drank wine but she felt the need for something stronger, more corrosive. She could tell from the happy, careless tone of the first messages that they had called pre-accident. Darius meticulously wrote each one down. Sophia sighed.

"She's going to want them when she wakes up," Darius answered.

After the fourth message, the calls changed. First, there was the sound of whimpering followed by the quivery voice of a girl asking if somebody was there. Was Helen okay? Could anything be done? Would they call and let her know how Helen was doing?

Sophia picked up her scotch and left the room. Miranda was about to follow when Jason's confident baritone filled the room.

"Miranda?" He sounded older and embarrassingly robust on the machine. Darius glanced at Miranda, who stood, riveted, red-faced, still pointed toward the door. "It's Jason. You just left an hour ago, but . . ." Miranda winced, mortified by the carnal suggestiveness of his voice. He might just as well be saying, "Thanks for the shag," or "Nice tits," or something equally awful when overheard by her father. But he wasn't that kind of person. Would she ever learn to stop underestimating him? "What I mean is, I'm glad we met and I'm looking forward to tomorrow. Okay. Bye."

Darius forced a smile. "I didn't even ask about today. How was it?"

"Fine," Miranda mumbled. "Good night."

In the bedroom, Sophia lay down on the bed, fully clothed, balancing the scotch on the hollow between her breasts. Every few minutes, she would raise her head to take a sip. She hadn't eaten since lunch but instead of making her drunk, the scotch seemed to make her more sober, able to feel and see things more acutely. Even the everyday sounds of the house seemed louder than usual: the soft swish of the passing minutes on the clock, the far-off rumble of the boiler in the basement, the sound of water running— had Miranda flushed a toilet? And beyond that, the delicate roar of the vast city as people pursued their lives—eating, drinking, fucking, fighting, running over one another. She thought of the morning a few weeks earlier when she had been wakened by the sound of water rushing through the pipes. When she went to investigate, she found Helen's room empty. Sophia had gone back to bed, troubled by her discovery. It was possible that Helen had woken early and wanted a shower, but Sophia doubted it. More likely, she had snuck out for the night and come home early. Sophia wondered if she should confront her. Her own parents had been so smothering, she wanted to give her children space and air to grow, the way plants do better when they're not crowded in the garden bed. Over breakfast that morning, Sophia had looked Helen right in the eye and asked, "Tired?" But Helen only shrugged. "A little," she'd answered. If Sophia could, she'd do it differently. She'd keep them home, away from danger. Away from men on motorcycles.

When Darius finally came to their bedroom, the scotch was almost gone. He smiled vaguely in her direction but their eyes did not meet. Was he taking more time than usual in the bathroom or was the elongation of time the work of the liquor? Normally, she relished having the bed to herself, but on this night, she could not bear to be alone. She went into the bathroom. Her husband was staring at himself in the mirror.

"Are you okay?" she asked.

"No," he answered.

She put her arm around his shoulders and they walked to bed together, awkwardly, like two drunks supporting each other. She crouched in front of him to take his shoes off.

"Don't," he said.

She sat back on her heels, embarrassed. Had he thought she was making an overture to sex?

"We should talk to each other," Sophia said.

He didn't answer. She tried again.

"For me, the worst is not knowing. If she was dead, at least I would know how to feel. Right now, I feel torn between hoping and grieving."

"You can't give up hope," Darius answered, "it's only just happened." He sounded angry.

"I know. I just want to be prepared."

"Why?" The word came out harshly, as if he were accusing her of something terrible. For the first time that day, she felt her throat constrict with the threat of tears. How typical, she thought, castigating herself, crying at the minor wound instead of the big one.

"We're going to have to be kind to one another," she said. "We're all we've got."

Darius turned away from her. "I'm sorry," he said. "Go to sleep."

Sophia turned off the light, glad for the cover of darkness. A few minutes later, her husband's snoring filled the room while she lay next to him, rigid and sleepless, her mind veering toward the accident and the questions she had not asked aloud. Why had the young man hit the car? Was it an accident or had he done it on purpose? How drunk was he? Had it hurt? Had she understood what was happening? Did she have a last thought? A last word? Sophia got up and moved down the hallway, guided by touch, toward Helen's room.

It always surprised her how girlish her daughters kept their rooms. More than once, she'd offered to change the pink tulip wallpaper Helen had picked out when she was eight years old, but always her daughter said no, she liked the way it looked. As a teenager, Sophia had banished the stuffed animals of childhood as soon as she was old enough to wear a bra, but she had been in a hurry to grow up. For all their sophistication, her girls seemed happy to linger in the carefree oblivion of youth. Sophia chose to take it as a compliment. She and Darius had worked hard to protect them from so much of life's unpleasant realities. Even when they fought their worst fights as a couple, the ones over money or Sophia's disappointment in her career, they'd been careful to do it out of earshot, in the basement or the bedroom with the door closed. The girls had been lucky, she guessed, to be children during years of peace and prosperity. Sophia remembered long lines for gas and effigies of Americans burning in foreign cities when she was little. Watching the nightly news with her parents, she had felt hated by young men with black hair and eyes, who kept their women covered in black, like furniture in mourning. On 9/11, the family had watched in fascinated horror as events unfolded across the country, but after the initial dread passed, the girls seemed largely unaffected by it. Sophia had even worried her girls might be made boring by the ease of their lives. How quaint that worry seemed now.

She lay on Helen's bed and turned her nose into the pillow, looking for her daughter's scent. Mothers, she had once read, can locate their children in a nursery through smell alone. When the girls were babies, she would have recognized the okra smell of breast milk and baby soap, but when she tried to conjure Helen now, she drew a blank. All her pillow smelled of was the green-apple shampoo she had bought at the health food store. Turning on her side, Sophia slid a hand under the pillow and hit something hard. She pulled a book out from the pillow and immediately recognized the illustrated copy of the Kama Sutra she had given Darius as a birthday present ten years earlier. It had been a half-joking, half-serious present, given at a moment in their relationship when the demands of parenting had seemed to drain the sex out of their relationship. He'd been pleased when he opened the package but the book had been a disappointment. The positions had names reminiscent of kitschy cocktails—Tiger in the Grass or Lotus on the Branch—and required either enormous flexibility or a two-foot-long penis. They had tried to re-create a few of the positions after the girls had gone to sleep but they'd ended up in the position they both preferred. Him on top. Her on bottom. Boring but effective.

Sophia opened a page and studied the drawings. The brown fish eyes, long nose, and sensual lips of the man in the drawings looked like somebody she had met recently. But who? Suddenly it hit her. He looked like Dr. Marjani, Helen's doctor.

The next morning, Sophia lay awake on Helen's bed when the doorbell rang. She held her breath. Was that how hospitals broke the news of a death? In person? Like the military? Of course not, she told herself, willing her pulse to return to normal. It could be anybody coming to the door at seven a.m.

Darius opened the door. Helen's best friend, Siri Bonavant, and her father were standing on the front stoop. He flashed back to a moment ten years earlier when he had gone to the Bonavants' house after Sophia discovered an expensive jade-and-diamond bracelet in Helen's sock drawer. When confronted, Helen admitted that Siri had given it to her. The Bonavants were overjoyed to see the bracelet—a family heirloom on the mother's side—and the girls had not been allowed to see each other for three months. Both sets of parents secretly blamed the other girl's influence for their child's misbehavior and hoped the friendship would die, but adversity had only seemed to strengthen the girls' bond.

Despite their history, Darius could not remember the man's first name.

"George Bonavant," the man held out his hand. "Good to see you. We can't tell you how sorry we are about Helen."

Siri let out a muffled sob. George Bonavant put his hand on his daughter's shoulder. It was meant to be comforting but something about the angle of his hand suggested reproach.

"Thank you," Darius answered. "I'd invite you in but this isn't the best time."

"Hi, George." Darius turned to find Sophia standing behind him. Her hair looked like someone had taken an egg beater to it, and she was wearing yesterday's clothes. If he had seen her on the street, he'd have thought, *Crazy woman*. Was that what separated the sane from the insane, he wondered, a night's sleep in your clothes?

"Siri has something to tell you."

Darius remembered that George Bonavant was a lawyer for the airline industry. He knew this because Siri had given Helen a ticket to go to Hawaii with her family the year before. All the McMartins had to do was pay for half her room and meals. Sophia had initially been against the idea. "She should work for the privilege," she'd said. But in the end, she'd relented.

Everyone waited for Siri to start, but each time she opened her mouth, she started to sob. George Bonavant frowned and began to speak. "Siri was there the night Helen met the young man on the motorcycle," he said. "Apparently, the two have been seeing each other for a few weeks."

Darius and Sophia glanced at each other. This was the second time they had heard the news, thus rendering it officially the truth. Sophia tried not to dwell on Helen's duplicity. There would be plenty of time in the coming days to ponder every aspect of the lies Helen must have been telling them all these weeks. Nights she was supposedly studying with Siri or Magda. Afternoons she was allegedly at the mall. How had she managed to look them in the eye day after day? And, more important, why? Had they prevented any of her schoolgirl crushes in the past? Even that idiotic stoner, Roy Beaudell, with the bad writer for a father. No parent could have wished such a child for a first love but they had not forbidden it. Children need to make their own mistakes. They knew that.

"Apparently, the boy was—" George stopped, unable or unwilling to complete the thought.

"A loser. Totally beneath her," Siri said. The prospect of watching her father further botch the narrative of her friend's relationship stirred the girl sufficiently to words.

"Beneath her?" Sophia repeated. For one unpleasant moment she imagined her daughter beneath Bobby Goralnick in a carnal embrace. Of course that wasn't what Siri Bonavant meant. She meant that Helen's boyfriend was from a different class. It surprised Sophia to hear the words coming from Siri; she imagined those old class distinctions had died among the new generation.

"He played in a band but it broke up. Then he painted houses. I guess he was handsome but Helen knew you two wouldn't approve. Also, she said he drank too much. Yesterday was the day she planned to break up with him. She wanted to start her senior year fresh."

Sophia was learning everything she yearned to know about her child, but in the wrong way, as if she were reading her diary.

"Do we know where his family is?"

Siri shook her head. "Somewhere in the South. I don't think he was in touch with them. When Helen asked, he told her they were dead or they may as well be dead. Something like that."

Sophia recognized Bobby Goralnick from Siri's description. When she was Helen's age, her Bobby Goralnick had worked in the kitchen at her parents' restaurant. His name was Yanni, he was several years older than Sophia, smoked cigarettes he rolled himself, and was in the habit of grabbing Sophia's breasts when nobody was looking. She knew she ought to tell someone but instead she found excuses to go to the kitchen when business was slow. Yanni had a Polish wife with a china-doll face who picked him up and dropped him off for work in a gold Buick with Florida plates. If he'd had a motorcycle, she would have gotten on it and gone anywhere he wanted to take her.

"Thank you, Siri, for coming and talking to us." Darius was impatient to get to the hospital.

"She asked me for a ride. I told her no, she should break up with him over the phone. I didn't want her to see him again." Her voice broke. Sophia knew she was asking for absolution, a sign saying they did not blame her for what happened. She knew she ought to say something to comfort her but something held her back. What if Siri had given Helen a ride? Sophia allowed herself a small puff of pride over her daughter's principles—Helen was right, you can't break a heart over the phone. Even Yanni had given her a gold locket the day before he stopped showing up for work. "Garbage," Sophia's father had sniffed when he realized he was without a short-order cook for the lunch hour. She still had the locket.

"It's not your fault," Sophia said. But clearly it was! Why couldn't she have driven her? What was so important that it couldn't have waited?

Siri nodded, grateful. "How is she?"

"Not good," Sophia answered.

"We don't know that for sure," Darius said, glaring at Sophia. "Not yet."

10

h arry lacked the talent for sloth. Even as a child, he had dreaded the open-ended aimlessness of the weekend, time set aside for the ritual of church, family, meals on the good china. Things other people did. When he once mentioned it to his mother, she had immediately insisted they dress up the next Sunday morning and go to the fried chicken buffet on Route 80.

"Really?" Harry had asked.

"You bet," she'd answered.

On Sunday, he'd gotten dressed in his best clothes and waited until ten o'clock before trying to wake her.

"Oh, honey," she'd moaned. Harry was familiar with the yeasty smell of alcohol on her breath, like bananas gone black. "Can I take a rain check? I think I have food poisoning." Harry had not minded her canceling nearly as much as he minded the lie. Food poisoning? Had she forgotten how often *he* had called her employers pleading the same so-called illness when the hangovers were too debilitating?

Later, during the soap years, when the money had seemed endless and a loose, easy kind of friendship had sprung up between him and a few of the other actors on the show, Harry had tried to fill his weekends with golf. He liked the idea of an activity that took up the whole day. When, somewhere around the fifth hole, one of the other actors would inevitably turn to another, inhale deeply, and say, "This is the life!" Harry would join in, but deep inside he could never escape the make-work feeling of it, as if he were digging a hole, filling it back in, and digging again.

Work was the only thing that stilled the itch, but it had been two weeks since the accident, and the network was still insisting he take time off.

"Be realistic," Aaron had said. "You've had a trauma. Someone died. A girl is in a coma. They say she's probably not coming out of it."

"It's not my fault. The guy was a sleazeball drunk."

"Well, the girl was an innocent victim. Have you seen her parents? Nice people. At the hospital every day, no comment to the press. Real class. They're a wreck. If you go back to work like nothing happened, you will look like a heartless schmuck."

"I was hired because I'm a heartless schmuck."

"That's a game. This is life. I want you to go see Boyd."

"I don't need a shrink."

"I'll leak it that you're seeking professional help. This way, the show will get double publicity."

Hooking television-show contestants up to a polygraph was not the career Boyd Davis had envisioned for himself when he was a young man studying psychology at Princeton. He'd been mid-complaint about the crushing boredom of clinical work when Aaron, his old Princeton roommate, suggested the job. Boyd had taken a sip of the seventeen-dollar martini Aaron was paying for, and laughed.

"Why not?" Aaron pressed, suddenly taken with the idea. Two clients on the show would mean two commissions. "You'd give the show class."

As a child, Boyd had fallen in love with psychotherapy after his parents had taken him to see Dr. Mordechai Eisenmann, a psychoanalyst who lived and practiced out of a cheerful yellow Victorian in the center of Greenwich, Connecticut. Boyd, a pudgy, morose child, prone to pastries and historical novels, found the father he had always wanted in Dr. Eisenmann, a Holocaust survivor in his late sixties who was not intimidated by the silence of a ten-year-old boy. His first three visits, Boyd had not said a word. After five minutes of that, the doctor had shrugged his shoulders and begun paying bills, filling out forms, even talking on the phone, while the boy sat furiously staring at his hands.

When his fifty minutes were up, Dr. Eisenmann would announce that the session had been "highly revealing." Boyd glared at him. He knew when he was being laughed at. Finally, on the fourth visit, he couldn't take it anymore. "I really don't think you should be doing that!" he had sputtered when Dr. Eisenmann began typing a letter on an old manual typewriter that made a terrible clatter.

"So," the doctor said, looking pleased, "you're ready to talk." Boyd noticed he did not phrase the sentence as a question.

"What do you want to know?" the boy asked suspiciously.

"What do you want to tell me?" the doctor asked.

"Nothing. Everything about me and my life is utterly banal and boring."

The doctor laughed as if he found his young patient genuinely amusing. It was the opposite of how Boyd's parents treated him. His father, a thin-lipped Episcopalian who worked in trusts and estates and, as Boyd now realized, was probably a closeted homosexual, would grow visibly agitated at his fits, angrily denouncing his selfishness. His mother, a pretty, underfed blonde who wore pearls when she dropped off groceries to the needy every Friday afternoon, would try to cajole Boyd out of his moods with hugs and chocolate-chip scones, which is how Boyd developed the weight problem that got him mercilessly teased at school. What Dr. Eisenmann called "a vicious cycle."

"Vicious is right," Boyd responded.

After six months with Dr. Eisenmann, Boyd learned to say no to the scones.

"Are you sure?" his mother asked, nervously eyeing the pastries she had just baked.

Boyd could hear Dr. Eisenmann's voice in his head. *Do you think your mother will survive if you say no?* Boyd wasn't sure. Sometimes, baking seemed her only pleasure. If he didn't eat them, who would?

"Why don't we take a walk instead?" Boyd asked, just as Dr. Eisenmann had suggested.

"Oh." His mother's hand flew to her clavicle where it nervously played with her pearls. "Okay, I'll just get a cardigan."

In six months, the extra weight was gone. More important, he had discovered things about his mother he had never known. "You see how the Moores have planted their rhododendrons in full sun?" She'd shake her head sadly as they passed a mock Tudor ablaze with the showy purple flowers. "Rhododendrons are undercarriage shrubs that thrive in filtered light, under big trees. I've seen them grow to fifteen feet in Scotland, where they're native. The Mexican landscapers who do the planting around here don't understand. They're sun people—*la más sol, el mejor*—but plants are like people. Take them out of their natural setting, they can survive, but they won't flourish." Boyd learned to see his mother as somebody more than the disappointed woman sipping a six-o'clock martini as she steamed green beans.

After the weight loss, his pleased parents made noises about stopping therapy, but Boyd resisted. Dr. Eisenmann was not one of those silent shrinks who insist the patient figure things out on his own. "I am Toto," he told his young patients, "pulling back the curtain to reveal the wizard." Seeing him every week was like getting through adolescence with Cliff Notes to human behavior.

"If a girl is inexplicably cruel, that means she likes you."

"How do you know this stuff?" Boyd would ask, amazed, when his explanations proved correct.

The doctor shrugged. "We all like to think we're more complicated and original than we are. Read your Darwin. Variations from the mean are slight and gradual." It was Dr. Eisenmann who had first dropped hints to him about the nature of his parents' misery, allusions Boyd had chosen to ignore. It was one of the few things he and the doctor disagreed on— Boyd believed there were some things we were better off not understanding. Mordechai Eisenmann, whose parents died in Bergen-Belsen, believed denial was the root of all evil.

When Boyd got to college and declared his interest in the field of psychology, he could see it disappointed his parents, who made vaguely derogatory comments about men in "the helping professions." As a student, he'd found the subjects of Freud's case histories—Dora, the Wolf Man, the Rat Man—far more gripping than any made-up character in a novel or play. It was only when he began treating real-life patients that he realized how removed those theories were from reality. In his heart, he was his father's son, a Yankee stoic secretly disgusted by whining. The depressives were the worst. Whenever a new one came to see him, Boyd could feel his own spirits sink at the sight of their ashen faces and the dullness of their lives. He tried to view his contempt as useful countertransference, a living example of how the rest of the world viewed the sad sacks, but deep in his heart, he knew he had failed at empathy, the sine qua non of his profession. He was glad Dr. Eisenmann had not lived to see what a mess he had made of his career.

"Okay." Aaron had shrugged after Boyd turned him down. "But why don't you think about it for a week? Talk to your wife."

In the days that followed, Boyd found himself increasingly drawn to the idea. He knew Aaron was simply buying his Princeton degree. He also knew that, after graduation, there had been little to brag of in his career: one article published in eight years, countless hours of clinical work, constant fighting with insurance companies for reimbursement. Why shouldn't he trade that expensive degree for some decent money—what good was it doing him? A week to the day, he called Aaron.

"Fantastic," Aaron answered when he got around to returning the call. "You'll have to take a screen test, but it's nothing. Just a formality."

Everybody agreed that Boyd's preppy good looks—curly hair the color of rolled oats, tortoiseshell glasses, oxford blue shirt—looked good on camera, but they worried about his stiffness.

"Muffy, dahling, be a dear and bring me a fresh martini," one of the production associates said mockingly after watching his tape.

"I think it works," Aaron responded, "he's the real thing. You don't see that enough on television."

Boyd was surprised at the ways financial success improved his life. His wife wanted to make love more often, old friends began calling, even his mother seemed to thaw, dropping wistful hints in the middle of the winter about the weather in California. Was it nice? It's so cold in Connecticut these days.

He tried to justify the job. Didn't Freud do the same? Excavate the unspeakable, the desire to fuck our mothers, kill our fathers, smell our poop, and then analyze it? Only Boyd knew better. He saw how confession diminished people. Sometimes, he felt the impulse to comfort them, but what could he say? You were right to humiliate yourself for the promise of a Jet Ski or an all-expenses-paid trip to some shithole Caribbean island? The world is a better place now that we know you've worn your wife's panty hose under your jeans?

Worst of all was the way that fame gave total strangers the license to accost him in public. *Dr. Davis, can I talk to you for a minute? My husband is having an affair. My son is smoking pot. My daughter is a slut. I hate my job. I hate my life.* He shrank in their presence, appalled by the hot breath of their needs. Sometimes he pondered quitting, especially in the spring, when the Princeton alumni magazine arrived full of news about his former class-mates. *So-and-so is now lead counsel for the FCC. So-and-so has joined the board of the Council on Foreign Relations. So-and-so is now head of trading for global fixed income at Morgan Stanley. So-and-so is on the short list for doing something normal to make his mark on the world.* But now that he lived in a big house with a pool, a nanny to help with the kid, a twenty-foot Etchells he took out on weekends, he knew he couldn't go back to his old life. So when Aaron Kramer called and asked him to see Harry Harlow for a consultation, what was he going to say?

"God, Aaron, I don't know. I mean, I haven't seen any patients in a while."

"Has the field changed in the last three years?"

"Well, no, but Harry Harlow is a colleague. I think it would be pretty questionable for me to treat him. I mean, in terms of confidentiality."

"All I am saying is, see him a few times. Let's see how it goes."

"I don't even have an official office anymore."

"What about your study?"

"It's going to be awkward, but if it's important to you . . ."

"It is important to me."

Two days later, Harry found himself in front of Boyd's house fifteen min-utes earlier than scheduled. "Is it a problem?" he asked. "I didn't know how long it would take to get here."

"No, no." Boyd moved his body in front of the open laptop in the kitchen. He didn't want Harry to see he'd been playing an online game of Scrabble.

Harry looked around the room. The house was humming with the elec-tricity of machines washing things but no visible humans. Boyd had told his wife earlier in the day that she needed to be out when Harry arrived. "No problem," she answered. "I need to pick some things up at the mall." He started to open his mouth to complain. Her constant shopping was beginning to look like a classic case of compulsive behavior, but this time he let it go. He needed the house empty.

Harry looked around the room, the stainless-steel appliances, the honed granite countertops, the fruit bowl on the center island piled high with bananas. "Is this where you see people?" he asked.

"No, no. This way," Boyd ushered him into the study.

"You don't want me to lie on that, do you?" Harry pointed to a leather chaise.

Boyd did not. He always gave patients a choice but felt awkward when they opted to lie instead of sit. As he told the ones who chose a chair, Freud instituted the couch only because he himself did not like being looked at. When Harry chose the leather club chair, Boyd was relieved. In his limited experience, the couch gave people the license to ramble even more than usual.

"So," Harry said, "how does it work?"

"How does what work?"

"You know, the whole therapy thing."

"How would you like it to work?"

Harry smirked and shifted his weight as if he had sat on something sharp. "I would like you to tell Aaron I'm ready to work."

Boyd was surprised Harry thought he had that much power. The realization made him sit up a little straighter. His problem, as he was well aware, was that he suffered from a persistent case of deep, unshakable skepticism regarding the way he made a living. Every time a patient walked through his door, Boyd had needed to wrestle with his suspicion that the whole field of psychotherapy was a massive load of shit. Why had nobody ever been able to quantify the beneficial effects of talk therapy? All those PET scans and MRIs that were supposed to justify the field had ended up showing a big fat zero. And why were there so many different, contradictory approaches—Jungian, cognitive, Gestalt, Reichian, Rolfian, Sullivanian, rational, behavioral, blah, blah, blah. Any crackpot with a ficus tree and a knockoff van der Rohe Naugahyde chair could hang a shingle as a therapist. And if shrinks were so damn good at unraveling the twisted knot of the human condition, why were they such messes themselves? Most of the very men who purported to be experts at understanding the human psyche were themselves deeply dysfunctional narcissists. Assholes, in a word. Boyd squashed these thoughts as quickly as he could. He knew they would get him nowhere fast in the here-and-now of his life.

"Why do you think Aaron thinks you *aren't* ready for work?" Boyd asked.

"I have no idea."

"Do you want to go back to work?"

Harry shrugged. "Do you?"

Boyd didn't answer. Aaron had already warned him that Harry didn't know that the show was planning to resume taping next week with a handful of substitute hosts—an African American comic who said "nigger" so many times the show was unusable, a retired football player famous for a paternity suit, a fat lesbian comic, and an aging movie star who had run unsuccessfully for the Senate a year earlier.

"I can't sit here and say, 'I love my job,' but"—Harry shrugged—"it's what I do."

Boyd knew he was supposed to hold back, to let the patient suggest corridors of conversation, but he didn't have the patience for that. "What about the accident?" he prodded.

"What about it?" Harry asked, crossing his arms over his chest. Even he could hear the defensive tone creeping into his voice.

"How do you feel about it?"

"I feel great," Harry answered angrily. "How do you think I feel? Some asshole decides to kill himself and his girlfriend by throwing himself against my car at sixty miles an hour. How am I supposed to feel? But it wasn't my fault. Why does nobody seem to believe that?"

"Who doesn't believe you?" Boyd asked.

"I mean, I'd have to be a monster to feel nothing. I think about it all the time. I wanted to visit the girl or send flowers or something, but my wife was, like, 'Don't do that, you'll be admitting guilt. They could sue us.' I called the hospital to get information, but they won't say anything unless you're family." Harry sighed loudly and rubbed his forehead as if to erase the contents. "What I want to know is 'why?' Did he do it on purpose? Or did he lose control? And of all the idiots on the road at that moment, why did he have to choose my car? Was it me? Did I swerve into him? Maybe I did something without even realizing it. But everyone said he swerved into me. So I don't know. I don't think I'll ever know. I mean, how could I know?"

"Have you discussed this with anyone else?"

"Like who?"

"Your wife. A friend. A brother or sister."

"I'm an only child. My mother died a few years ago. I never knew my father." After Harry got famous, a man who claimed to be his father once tried to contact him through Aaron's office. He still had the man's name and address in Memphis, Tennessee, but he had never responded, and the man had never tried to contact him again.

"It's a lot to carry around—guilt, uncertainty." This was a trick he had picked up from Dr. Eisenmann—name the emotion and express sympathy.

"But that's just the point," Harry said. "I do feel guilty, but I don't think I should. It wasn't my fault."

Boyd tried to smile in an understanding way. "You have guilt for feeling guilt. Meta-guilt."

"I guess," Harry shrugged. "I didn't go to college."

Boyd cringed. Harry was reminding him of how he appeared to the rest of the world. Preppy, smarty-pants, perpetually boyish. "Unfortunately, we don't always get to choose what we feel. Our work here is to understand how those feelings . . ." Boyd paused. What? Destroy our livers? Shred our insides? Make us fuck everything up? ". . . impact our lives." He decided to stay with platitudes. Much safer. Especially in the beginning.

"Our work here?" Harry repeated. He had hoped one visit would be it, and now the guy was talking as if this was going to be a regular thing.

Out of the corner of his eye, Boyd was annoyed to see his wife's minivan pull into the driveway. She was at least half an hour early. He leaned forward in his seat and cleared his throat to signal that the meeting was over. "Maybe in our next session"—Boyd moved closer to the edge of his seat—"we could explore your relationship with your wife? Why it is you don't feel supported."

The door to his study flew open. "Daadddeee!" A girl in pigtails flung herself onto her father's legs.

"Not now, pumpkin, Daddy's working."

The girl turned and glared at Harry. "That's not work," she said.

Boyd tried to laugh. "From the mouths of babes. Same time next week?"

Harry hesitated. It hadn't been quite as bad as he had thought it would be. He did feel a kind of lightness around his shoulders, the way he once imagined he'd feel after acupuncture but never really did.

"Unless I see you before that. At work."

"Right." Boyd smiled. Harry squatted in front of the little girl. "You sure are pretty," he said. "What's your name?"

The girl pressed herself farther into her father's legs. "No." She shook her head. "I don't like it."

"Honey, that's not nice," Boyd said.

"It's okay," Harry stood up. "Kids and dogs never like me."

Boyd started to say forensic psychologists believed those were the classic signs of a sociopath, but then thought better of it.

11

S ophia was cleaning out the refrigerator when the doorbell rang. What
a silly tradition, she thought, opening yet another Tupperware container of lasagna brought by friends in the days following the accident. As if
eating were on the mind of people grieving a death. Near death, she corrected herself. She had dutifully shoved each container into the refrigerator.
Now, three weeks later, the food had turned green and black with mold.

Again, it rang. Darius and Miranda had gone to the organic farmers'
market. If she ignored it, who would know? The third ring, a short burst,
followed by a longer, more insistent lean, told her the intruder knew she
was home and wasn't going away. Reluctantly, she peeled off her plastic
gloves, went to the front hallway, and looked crossly through the windows
that flanked the door.

"Mrs. McMartin?" a man asked, holding up a badge. "Louis Carone.
LAPD."

She could see right away that he wasn't an ordinary policeman. Not that
she knew anything about police beyond the detectives in the movies. In real
life, the cops who had stopped her over the years for speeding had always
seemed like surprisingly nice men willing to let you off, provided your excuse included a child. The man at the door was more like one of Darius's
colleagues. Scholarly, gentlemanly, with murky gray eyes, sandy hair, a bit
of a belly, a shirt with a collar, and a jacket with leather patches on the
elbow. If she saw him on the street she might guess doctor. A pediatrician.

"Yes?" She opened the door, reluctant to let him in the house. Nothing in his eyes indicated good news.

"Could we speak?" He tilted his head as if he were looking for someone behind her.

"Um." Sophia tried to think of a good reason to say no.

Carone followed her into the kitchen, where she leaned against a counter, crossed her arms over her chest, and watched as he took in the stack of Tupperware on the counter, the sour smell of food gone off, the chaotic bulletin board three deep with coupons, xeroxed poems, pictures of the girls, unpaid bills, grocery lists, expired tickets to the philharmonic, a computer printout of important phone numbers, handwritten cell-phone numbers added to the bottom, a recipe for veal piccata she had wanted to try until Helen told her she was going to hell for even considering cooking with veal. Watching his unreadable face, she suddenly felt uncomfortably exposed, as if she'd forgotten her pants and only now realized it.

"Something to drink?" she asked.

"Water. Thanks."

Sophia turned to get a glass. She noticed a tiny piece of dried food stuck to the inside of the glass. For any other guest, she would have used a fingernail to scrape it off. For him, she left it on. As she filled the glass with tap water, she felt his eyes clinically appraising her. What was that thing doctors used to look in your ear? An otoscope. That was it. Louis Carone was otoscopic. He drank the water without noticing the fleck of food. Or he didn't care. Either way.

"I'm trying to guess why you're here," she said. "But nothing is coming to me."

He leaned down, opened a briefcase, and took out a sealed plastic bag. Sophia recognized Helen's wallet and keys.

"Ah," she said, sitting down. If God existed, which He so clearly did not—Helen's accident was proof of that—the pressure on her shoulders was like His hand guiding her into a seat. A cosmic maître d' concerned for her comfort.

Sophia touched the rippled green leather of the wallet through the plastic bag. She remembered the day Helen bought it at the mall. It was on sale, but even so, Sophia had hesitated. Wallets that belonged to her daughters had a way of getting lost. Now the leather seemed to be radiating some powerful grief-inducing force field. Sophia forced herself to look away from it, into the policeman's unblinking eyes.

"I'm sorry," she said. "Did you say something?"

"I was going to tell you about your daughter's friend. He had a complicated life."

"The boy?"

"Not exactly. He was thirty-seven years old."

Sophia felt her stomach lurch. All this time, she'd been picturing a reckless man-child made stupid by beer and youth, one of those drivers who sends your heart racing when he passes you going ninety miles an hour on the freeway. Did Helen know how old he was? Siri said he was in his mid-twenties, so that meant Helen probably believed it. Shit. Not only did he kill her, he lied to her. Sophia would have known better. The skin hangs differently on a thirty-seven-year-old than it does on a twenty-five-year-old. But Helen was so young, so inexperienced.

"They barely knew each other," she said, wanting to put as much distance as possible between her family and Bobby Goralnick. "Her friend told us she was breaking up with him the day of the accident."

The policeman took a small reporter's notebook out of his jacket pocket and made a note. She'd seen poet friends of Darius from the university do the same thing when a description or a phrase struck them in the middle of dinner or a party. She'd always thought the gesture excessively self-cherishing.

"Did the friend say anything else?" he asked.

"Like what?"

"About Bobby. His work, his past."

"Maybe if you told me what you were looking for."

Carone looked around the kitchen again, as if he were looking to change the subject to something more pleasant—the advantages of Corian over granite for countertops. "You have a nice house," he said. "You can tell the people who live here are cultured, you know? You don't see that a lot in my line of business."

Sophia knew she was supposed to feel complimented but instead she felt offended on behalf of the people he had just maligned. "I'm sure the people you deal with have a culture," she said primly.

"Oh," he said, nodding, "they do. It's just very loud. Everything here is so quiet. You can hear yourself think. You could probably hear the grass grow."

Sophia looked down at the floor. The policeman, she noticed, was showing no signs of wanting to leave. Something in the tilt of her head must have communicated her impatience because, suddenly, he changed the course of conversation. "The man Helen was with that day, you called him Bobby Goralnick. That wasn't his name. We think it was Virgil Tilden."

Sophia winced. Ever since the accident, she had worked hard to keep from thinking about Bobby Goralnick. As far as she was concerned, he was nothing. A nobody. A piece of dirt under the fingernail. Not worthy of a moment's consideration. Or so she told herself. Truthfully, if she thought of him at all, she feared her hatred would grow and grow like a toxic mold until it killed all the life around it. So she had worked to forget everything about him. And now here was this man in her kitchen forcing her to consider the facts of his life. As she feared, her mind went to the darkest places she could imagine: crystal meth labs in abandoned Iowa farmhouses, racist skinhead plots to kill liberal senators, child prostitution rings exchanging boys and girls at Disneyland. The kinds of stories the nightly newsmagazines could tease out to fill an hour of prime-time television. How had this happened to her daughter? All she could think was, Bobby Goralnick must have been a great lay. Helen wasn't dishonest by nature. Mostly, she was a good girl, eager to please, slow to anger, not terribly rebellious or, thank God, original. For her to have strayed so far, it had to have been the swamp pull of sex. Which meant her mother and all the disapproving priests; the old biddies she remembered from childhood; the spinster sex-ed teachers in high school, with their sensible shoes and tight buns; the moralistic painters from the fifteenth century she studied in graduate school; the right-wing loonies in the White House; the Bible-thumping, toupee-wearing preachers on the upper reaches of cable channels—they had all been right. Sex could kill you. Sophia had tried to revolt against this idea. She herself had sought out experiences, allowed Yanni Twardokea to put his hands on her breasts right there, next to the industrial-size vats of olives and the putrid-smelling barrel of feta cheese at her parents' restaurant. Left home as soon as she could. But when it came to defying her mother's beliefs, she never really left anything. She married the first man who fucked her because—much as it appalled her to admit it—something of her mother's fear of sex had seeped into the groundwater of her cerebral cortex. On the spectrum of rebellion, she'd scored a tepid 2 out of 10. Who knew how far she might have gone if she hadn't been hobbled by that unwelcome legacy of fearfulness? She had tried to free her daughters from the strictures of her youth. She taught them to protect themselves from diseases, unwanted pregnancy, and even offered to loan them her updated copy of the *Joy of Sex* (*Mom! Gross!*). But all along, it was her mother who was right. Sex kills.

"I can't help you." She finally forced herself to meet the policeman's false friendly gaze.

"If she kept a diary or had an e-mail account, we might be able to get some more information about Virgil's activities." He was all business now.

"You think she was involved in something illegal?"

Louis Carone craned his neck to the side and vigorously scratched a patch of hair next to his ear. Sophia had seen dogs do the exact same thing. "We're in fact-finding mode."

An orange flame of fury danced inside her. "Even if she kept a diary, which she did not, I would never give it to you."

"I could get a search warrant."

The flame danced higher, singeing her cornea, licking the hairline. "May I remind you that I am the grieving parent?"

"Okay." Carone fished around in the breast pocket of his jacket and brought out a business card. "If you change your mind."

"I won't," she said.

He looked disappointed. "You know, Mrs. McMartin, we could get rid of all the crime in this country if people who knew things would just step forward and say what they knew."

"Here's what I know—my daughter was not, is not, and never has been a criminal."

"For whatever reason, she may have been hanging out with one."

"She thought he played in a band."

"From what I understand, nobody who knew anything about music would have been fooled by that."

"If you have come here to accuse her of having a tin ear, guilty as charged. It runs in the family."

"Look, I really don't think she was involved in anything illegal." Carone suddenly seemed determined to make peace with Sophia. "We're just covering our bases." He stood and ran his hand over his stomach, as if checking to see whether the belly that spilled over the top of his belt had miraculously disappeared while he was sitting down. Sophia had seen Darius make the exact same gesture. "He definitely had his enemies. That's for sure."

Sophia wished for the discipline to resist the information he was dangling in front of her, but it was useless. "What do you mean?" she asked.

"We found sugar in Tilden's gas tank. It's a suburban myth, something teenagers do when they want to get back at somebody. Like setting a sack of dog excrement on fire, then ringing the doorbell. They think the sugar will get in the engine and ruin it, but it's not true. The sugar dissolves or the fuel filter catches it. In Bobby's case there was a substantial amount—so there's a small chance it contributed to a malfunction in the engine, but in my opinion, it was probably the six-pack he drank before getting on the bike that killed him."

"Do you know who put it there?"

"This type of crime, it's usually a kid. Or a woman. I gather he was something of a ladies' man." Betrayed women and angry children, the dyad of the unstable. Sophia thought of Yanni's wife and the heart-shaped misery of her once-beautiful face.

After Carone left, Sophia sat at the kitchen table, trying to make sense of what she had learned. It had been six months since her last secret, stolen cigarette behind the garage. Now the craving was back, stronger than ever. She squeezed her left hand with her right, willing it to pass. When it finally receded, she reached for the plastic bag that held Helen's wallet and keys. The plastic reminded her of the bags she used to keep food in the freezer. Written across the top was "Property of the LAPD." She unsnapped the wallet. On one side, the plastic cards lay neatly in their appointed slots. On the other was the billfold for money. She used her thumb to slide out the credit card they had given her for emergencies only. The first month she had it, there had been a big fight after she used it to buy three hundred dollars' worth of clothes at the mall.

"Mom," Helen had argued, "it *was* an emergency. Everything was *so* on sale."

Sophia was glad now she'd given in and let her keep the clothes. She ran a finger over the raised letters of the credit card, then studied the picture of Helen on her driver's license. She had complained bitterly about her half-closed eyes in the picture but Sophia had refused to pay the additional thirty dollars for a new picture.

Even as a little girl, Helen had a tendency toward vanity. "Mommy," she'd ask, "am I pretty?"

Sophia hadn't known how to answer. "Truthfully, you are devastatingly beautiful, but looks," she finally told her daughter one day, "are the least of it."

"It?" Helen had asked.

"It. You know, life."

"Looks are the least of life," Helen repeated, justifiably confused. Who was Sophia kidding? Even seven-year-old Helen McMartin, the recipient of a thousand "Aren't you cute?"s from hordes of well-meaning, temporarily insipid adults, had figured out that looks were not the least of it. Looks were everything.

Sophia studied Helen's picture more closely. Even with the eyes closed and the poor-quality reproduction, she was struck by how alive Helen looked. The eager smile, the way the skin hugged the bones of her face, the pinkish blue of her skin. Such a contrast to the empty expression of the girl lying a few miles away in the hospital. She turned the license over. On the organ donor box, Helen had ticked "I hereby make an anatomical gift to be effective upon my death, of any needed organ or part." She'd even had two of her friends—Siri and Anya—sign as witnesses. The date was two months earlier.

Before Helen's accident, Sophia had never experienced the kind of grief that suddenly rose up and engulfed, like a rogue wave in an otherwise calm ocean. She could feel the warning signs now—the way the walls of her throat thickened; the buzzing, nervous tickle in her stomach. She also knew she didn't have to succumb, she could swim away if she wanted. She shoved the driver's license back into the wallet and turned her attention to the key ring. The fake "What's lucky about losing your foot?" rabbit paw, a birthday gift from Siri, who was into the animal-rights movement, made Sophia smile. She slid the house and car keys off the ring. They could go in the communal kitchen key drawer for the inevitable moment when someone in the McMartin household would panic over a lost key. And when (if) Helen recovered, Sophia would know where to find them. Only one key remained on the ring. Silver and cheap, as if the door it opened was flimsy hollow core. Across the top was written a brand name. SCHLAGE. She thought of the Bohemian family in *Howards End*, a favorite book of hers in college. The Schlegels. An allusion, a professor had claimed, to the objective idealism of Hegel. Sophia, so keen to improve her mind, had dutifully gone to the library and checked out a book by the philosopher. She'd spent ten minutes on one paragraph and still had no idea what he was talking about.

Darius and Miranda came through the door, carrying white plastic bags filled with vegetables. "Hi," Darius said, smiling brightly, weirdly, as if trying to hide something.

"What's wrong?" Sophia asked.

Miranda busied herself unloading vegetables.

"We have a surprise for you," Darius said, the smile fading incrementally.

Outside, Sophia heard the hysterical yelps of a dog.

"No," she said.

"You haven't even met her. Him." Darius said.

"You can't be serious."

"This could be a good thing. It could be a distraction."

"*Could* be?"

"Just meet him."

Darius went outside.

"I told him," Miranda shook her head. "He insisted."

Darius returned, holding a leash. At the end of it, a greyhound pranced manically in place, whether from excitement or fear, Sophia couldn't tell and did not care. She had never been a dog person. Whenever she saw the woman who brought those doomed greyhounds to the organic market, she always felt sorry for her—who would ever want to adopt a retired race-track dog? Apparently, if you ever let one off the leash, it would run away at forty miles an hour and never come back.

"If we don't take him, he'll be killed tomorrow." Darius leaned down to pet the dog, whose eyes rolled back in ecstasy. Sophia thought he looked like a mosquito on crack. His fur, a yellowish white with patches of gray, looked like rancid milk.

"Is it even house-trained?" she asked.

Darius hesitated.

"You didn't ask?"

"How could he be house-trained? He's never lived in a house."

"What are we going to do? Throw some hay in the corner of the kitchen?"

"Greyhounds are extremely intelligent dogs."

"Does he have a name?"

"Monty. Apparently, he was a real champion. In his day."

Sophia knew she ought to fight harder. When the girls were little he used to periodically threaten her with a puppy, but she always managed to talk him out of it. The walks, the shit, the fleas, the kennel bills when they went on vacation, the trips to the vet. She could make dog owning sound like a nightmare when she put her mind to it. This time, however, she lacked the will. Anyway, maybe he was right. A dog would be a distraction. Already the despair caused by Louis Carone had loosened its grip on her intestines.

"What's that?" Miranda asked, looking at Helen's wallet.

Sophia told them everything about Louis Carone, except the part about the sugar in the motorcycle gas tank. She told herself it was because the detective had made it sound so inconsequential—why give her family one more thing to worry about?—but it also had to do with Sophia's own confusion about the news and its consequences. Could such a childishly malicious act really cause an accident? And what sort of mind would think of such a thing? A vicious simpleton. A vexed child or, as Carone hinted, a jealous woman. When Sophia was done with her story, the only sound in the room was Monty's heavy breathing.

"What kind of crimes did he do?" Miranda asked.

"I didn't ask."

"Why did he change his name?" Darius asked.

"I don't know."

"Sophia," Darius said.

"I'm sorry. I see I didn't ask any of the right questions. I was in shock. The sight of her wallet and keys, they just . . . Anyway, he left a card." She took the card out of the pocket in her cardigan sweater and put it on the table. Nobody touched it.

"Well," Darius said.

"I know," Sophia nodded, understanding what he meant.

"Do you know what this is?" She pushed the Schlage silver key to the center of the table.

Darius held the key up to the light.

"Could it be a school key?" Sophia asked Miranda. "To a locker or something?"

"They don't let you lock things up at school anymore. You've got to carry everything with you and get scoliosis by sixteen. A kid in Buena Vista is suing over it."

"It looks like a house key," Sophia observed.

"Maybe it's Roy's," Miranda said. "Helen used to feed their cats when they were away."

"Right," Sophia nodded, relieved to have the mystery solved. When she had a chance, she'd slip it under the door of the house.

12

*i*n the month since he'd been fired, Anton's days had followed a similar pattern. He'd wake early, steal his neighbor's newspaper, read it, carefully refold it so it fit in its bag and return it to the stoop before the neighbor, a bartender who kept late hours, woke up. After two cups of strong Central American coffee, the kind that came in a can and was often on sale at his local Ralph's supermarket, he would sit at his computer to work on his latest script, *King Lear* set in Silicon Valley. The king was the CEO of a Fortune 100 software company, his three daughters worked for the company. After a stroke that left his mind intact but his body twisted like a grapevine, the board of directors pressured him to step down. Instead, he turned the company over to the girls who eventually forced him out. When Anton began the project, he'd been filled with enthusiasm for its potential, but his agent's lack of enthusiasm had made the work hard going.

"Office politics starring old people?" she said over the phone. "What happened to your romantic comedy for teens?" In the background he could hear the click-click of a computer keyboard. The bitch was multitasking! He tried to work up some outrage but it lacked muscle. Whatever heat he'd had coming out of film school was cooling fast, being fired from the hottest game show in America didn't help, and, frankly, she had a point. Scene after scene, he found himself laboring to make typing exciting. In an effort to be original, he had deliberately set out to ignore the one piece of advice he'd heard over and over in school, "Film is visual." Office politics are not visual. The computer industry is not visual. Old men are not visual. Since the conversation with his agent, he'd been trying to enliven the story by injecting a romantic interest for the Lear figure—maybe one of those older actresses desperate for a role would even put up some money for the production? But his mood had stayed dark. He was lonely. Staying home all day was no fun. He had always done his writing in between something else—a job or school—and had never experienced the crushing boredom of his own personality for such an extended period of time. Day after day, it was the same thing. Words written. Words erased. Words rewritten. And in the end, something that wasn't total shit. Hopefully. He missed school. He missed knowing people and seeing them every day. Even a bad television show had provided some semblance of community. There was that cute cashier in the cafeteria who smiled at him when he bought his banana and coffee. True, she had politely declined an actual date with him but there had never been any hard feelings after that. If anything, she had seemed a little friendlier. Once, she didn't even charge him for the banana, though that could have been an oversight. Then there was that lady with the rats who liked to talk about how misunderstood vermin are. Actually, scratch that, she was a bit of a bore. But the security guard who always said, "Hey, man, how you doin'?" never failed to make him smile. They were small nothings, little points of recognition, but taken together, they added up to something more than sitting alone in your room parsing the degree of disinterest expressed by one's agent.

His gloom was made worse by the dwindling of his bank account. Already, he'd cut out the nonessentials—coffee to go (cheaper to brew his own), movies in the theater (cheaper to rent), and driving (cheaper to bike). He'd canceled his gym membership and downgraded his cable package to the bare minimum. There wasn't much more fat to be cut, but still the money disappeared, which was why he finally sucked up his pride and made an appointment to apply for unemployment benefits.

Even though he had left his house at seven a.m., there was a long line of people ahead of him when he arrived at the building where the interviews were held. A uniformed guard gave him a number—87—and told him to watch the board. He took a seat and stared at the board. His favorite deli had the same system. He'd take a number and wait his turn to place an order for a sandwich. For some indiscernible reason, the numbers here were not in sequence. The number 96 would light up, followed a second later by 14. Also, the time in between the numbers' lighting up was much longer than the time it took to make a chicken salad wrap. He could imagine the logic of the bureaucracy—what else did unemployed people have to do with their time? But it was like playing an excruciatingly slow game of bingo. He needed to go to the bathroom and would have liked a cup of coffee but was afraid of leaving. If they called his number while he was gone, how would he know? And what would happen when he came back, if his number had been called? Would he have to start over with a new number or would they take him right away? An hour and a half later, his number lit up. He jumped out of his seat. A woman with the turned-up nose and beady eyes of a horny toad lizard told him to see Mr. Dumond in room 312.

Anton wandered down the hallway. Like the numbers on the board, the offices also were out of sequence. Room 308 was followed by 319, then 312.

"Cyrus Dumond." A large black man with massive hands stood and extended one toward Anton. Feeling his own hand swallowed by that massive envelope of flesh made Anton feel uncomfortably vulnerable. If he wanted, Cyrus Dumond could smash Anton's fingers with one squeeze. His hand suddenly freed, Anton handed the man his application and sat down.

"Film director?" Cyrus read aloud. Anton recognized a faint Southern accent in the way the man pronounced "film," with a long *e*, instead of a short *i*. *Feelm director*.

"Well, you know, someday," Anton answered, chastened even more than usual by the gap between the scope of his ambition and the reality of his situation.

"Have you ever worked as a *feelm* director?"

"I don't expect to be one right away, but it's what I studied in school."

Actually, he had thought he would be one right away. It was only lately he had begun to have his doubts. Whenever he calculated the chances of him, or anyone he knew, actually becoming a feelm director, he was stunned by the overwhelming unlikeliness of it. Once, sitting in his agent's office, he had seen a piece of paper listing the names of the top movie directors working in America at that moment. He had always assumed that the A-list was a metaphor, but there it was, right in front of his eyes. The A-list. It included Oscar winners, action directors, comedy directors, and a few foreigners who had managed to cross over. What they all had in common was one thing. Success. But there were only forty of them. Thirty-nine, actually, since a promising young video-turned-feature director had suddenly dropped dead during a game of pickup basketball the week before. When Anton thought of all the would-be directors in his film school, then multiplied that by all the other film programs scattered around the country, then multiplied that by the years the programs had been in existence, and then factored in all the other screenwriters and actors and set designers and costume makers and valet parkers and God knows who else who nurtured the dream of becoming a director, what were the odds? Ten thousand to one? One hundred thousand to one? It was exactly the kind of reasoning his father, a professional chemist, had used to try and dissuade him from his chosen profession.

"What do you want me to be?" Anton had shouted back. "A loser living a lost dream in a loser city in a loser state?" The memory of that fight always made his cheeks burn. He'd always been proud of his dad's profession—at least his father knew how to do something useful. What was he but a person who took pictures?

"Anyway," Anton said to Cyrus, "a person can dream, can't he?"

"Oh, yes," Cyrus said with a laugh, "a person has got to dream. But a person has got to eat, too. And so has a person's wife and children."

"I don't have a wife," Anton answered.

"A single man."

Anton nodded his head.

"A lone wolf. An island."

"Not really," Anton answered, "just waiting for my ship to come in before I, you know, make a commitment." God, he hated that word, *commitment*. He was committed to his art, what was wrong with that?

"Well, don't wait too long," the man said, "you know what John Lennon said, 'Life is what happens to you when you're busy making other plans.'"

Anton must have looked surprised.

"I know you don't think I wanted to work in the unemployment office when I was a young man," Dumond asked, head lowered like an ironic bullfighter.

"No, no," Anton answered, looking at his massive hands and wondering what he had wanted to do.

Dumond cantilevered his considerable weight forward in his chair to reach the leather wallet in his back pants pocket. With a surprising delicacy, he thumbed through its contents, extracting a business card and handing it to Anton between two sausagelike fingers.

CYRUS DUMOND
Pianist Extraordinaire

Specializing in Weddings, Bar Mitzvahs, Funerals, Birthdays,
and All Occasions Requiring That Something Extra

"Cool," Anton said.

Cyrus nodded. "You know the Hyatt out by the airport?"

Anton didn't, but nodded anyway. Didn't every airport have a Hyatt?

"Friday nights, seven to nine. Fiesta night. For fourteen-ninety-five, all the fajitas you can eat, plus my music. Stay away from the pork, though you didn't hear it from me. If you ever do settle down, you should think about having live music during the ceremony. My rates are surprisingly reasonable. All things considered." Anton glanced again at his massive hands, wondering if that was what he was referring to.

"Now," Cyrus said, changing his tone into something more business-like, "you're entitled to six months of unemployment benefits not to exceed sixty percent of your past income. A check will come every two weeks to your home address. No P.O. boxes allowed. In order to continue receiving benefits, you must prove to this office that you have made three efforts per week to look for work."

"How do I do that?" he asked.

"You provide us with the names of three businesses or three business contacts with whom you have discussed employment in the previous week."

"Won't that be kind of embarrassing for me, you calling them to check up on me?"

Cyrus raised his eyebrows at Anton. "I did not say we call them to check up on you, but it could happen. If we find you are not 'actively look-ing for work,' we will be well within our rights to revoke your benefits."

"Has that happened?" Anton asked. Cyrus slid a piece of paper toward him. "Sign here to attest that I have fully explained all the laws regarding unemployment compensation under Article 456 of the California State Constitution."

Anton signed where Cyrus had made a big sloppy X.

"I'm not saying it has happened, and I am not saying it hasn't, but I don't think you want to be the one to find out?"

"No, sir," Anton answered. It wasn't like him to use the word "sir," but something about Cyrus inspired it in him.

"Good luck, son." Cyrus held out his hand to signal that the interview was over. Anton hesitated a moment before entrusting his own, suddenly puny fingers to the man's monster grip.

13

*

—Hi Helen. I am sure you can probably tell from my voice who I am. But just in case, this is Anya. I'm here with Siri.

—Hi, Helen.

—And Magda.

—Hey, Helen.

—And Louisa. They won't let us visit you yet, so we thought we'd make you these tapes so you would be able to keep up with what's going on. Not that there's anything exciting happening beyond you. I mean, I don't mean it's *exciting* what happened to you, I just mean, it's out of the ordinary.

—You wouldn't believe all the attention you've gotten. The first day it happened, like, ten television vans came to school. Mrs. Denberg made an announcement over the loudspeaker that we weren't supposed to talk to any of the reporters but some of the kids were, like, "That's a violation of my right to free speech" so they were, like, claiming to be your best friend.

—Jeff Cummings was on *Entertainment Tonight.*

—Isn't that pathetic? He barely knows you.

—And Hope was on the local news. What a phony.

—Meanwhile, we, your best friends, didn't say anything because we thought it was really gross the way those people were, like, cashing in on their fifteen minutes of fame.

—But don't worry, everybody said nice things about you.

—Even Jeff was, like, "Helen is the nicest person in the school. Blah, blah, blah."

—Like he knows.

—Tell her about the mural.

—No. Gross.

—She'd want to know.

—You tell her.

—Somebody had the idea that the whole school should sign one big get-well card that you could read when you woke up, so Miss Brainard from the art department, you know that teacher with red hair who never wears a bra? Well, she took this long roll of white paper and put it up on the first floor, outside the gym. And then she hung, like, Magic Markers from strings. The first day everybody was, like, "Get well soon." "We love you." Like when you were a kid and broke your arm and people signed your cast. But then some total loser decided it would be funny to write some gross stuff.

—It wasn't that bad, it was just, like, "Helen McMartin is hot."

—But not nearly so civilized.

—Yeah, I mean, it was really stupid. Because then somebody else drew pictures of, like, these big, like, well, you know, *dicks*. They looked like banana splits or something.

—The one I saw looked like a rocket. Only instead of sparks coming out of the end . . .

—I think that's more than she needs to know.

—It was so retarded.

—Miss Brainard was really upset. I think she tried to cut the bad parts out but then it had, like, all these big holes and it looked kind of suspicious. Like, what were they trying to censor? So the next day they took the banner down.

—And then some students were, like, you can't censor people. Art for art's sake and all sorts of stupid stuff.

—I think Miss Brainard is keeping it, so if you ever do want to see it, you can.

—Did you know somebody wrote, "Miss B's tits hang low"?

—Are you serious?

—Totally.

—What else can we tell you?

—I lost five pounds by cutting out all bread, rice, and pasta.

—Fascinating.

—Right. And everything *you* say is so riveting.

—The point is, everybody misses you, and we think about you every day and we can't wait for you to get better so we can crash the totally queer senior prom and get meaningless, low-paying jobs at the mall and flirt with surfer losers at the beach.

—Bye, Helen. We love you.

—Big smooch.

—I'm sorry this tape has been so trite. Next time, it will be much deeper. I promise.

—Does that mean you won't be coming?

—Very fucking funny.

—Why are you so defensive? It was just a joke.

—Can we erase that last part and start over?

—I don't . . .

Click.

14

ᔒ

Sophia was sitting next to Helen's bed, trying to care about the latest issue of *ArtForum*, when she realized that the patient in the room next door—an eighty-two-year-old woman in advanced stages of Alzheimer's—had just died. Nobody cried, raised their voice, or even walked faster than usual, but having spent every day of the previous month there, Sophia had begun to absorb certain truths about life in the intensive-care unit. Death was signaled by a great deal of unhooking— tubes, machines, sterilized bags. From where she sat, she could see the flotilla of stuff passing Helen's open door. Next came the housekeeping staff, young women in white outfits and latex gloves who wordlessly bundled the sheets off to central laundry and spritzed the room with a pleasantly lemon-scented antibiotic. It wasn't all that different from checking out of a hotel.

But the paperwork! Dying was even more complicated than taxes. The bureaucracy wanted to know everything: How much high school? How much college? How many marriages? At what age? Children? Grand-children? Stepchildren? Career? Years in career? Yearly income at death? Years in current address? Years in previous address? Service in the army? How long? How discharged? Year moved to state? And so on. As the days went by, Sophia had watched more than one family puzzle over the paper-work, shamed in the middle of their grief by how little they actually knew about their loved one.

More disturbing were the differences she began to notice in how the staff treated patients. The very old, suicides, drug overdoses, patients who had no visitors, no insurance, no flowers delivered to their room, no pictures of grinning grandchildren taped to the wall next to them—all of them seemed to die more quickly than patients like Helen. When Peggy, her favorite nurse, came to check on Helen, she worked up the courage to ask her about it.

"It's not like we put a pillow over their faces," Peggy answered defensively.

"I know, it's only something I've noticed."

"Well," Peggy answered dropping her voice, "at a certain point, when there's no family saying, 'Do everything,' you do stop going the extra mile."

Sophia said nothing, wondering what the extra mile looked like.

"Mostly," Peggy said, "pneumonia gets them. You see their lungs filling up, you ask yourself, should I call the doctor? Half the time, they don't even visit those patients on their rounds. They know who's who. I mean, if the patients don't have health insurance, who's going to pay those bills? You know what a day on the unit costs? Medicare stops paying after twenty days. Oh, don't look at me like that. Believe me, it's not the worst way to go. We always make it as painless as possible."

"What about Helen? Would you go the extra mile for her?"

Peggy looked her straight in the eye. "Don't you think we see you sitting out there every day?"

Sophia turned her head, trying to breathe her way through the cloud of grief she had wandered into. Peggy made a clicking noise in the back of her mouth that was supposed to express sympathy, but Sophia knew the women who worked on the ICU had long ago learned to unhook their emotions from the work they did. She didn't blame them. If they let themselves feel for every wasted body wheeled through those double doors, they'd never get anything done. Pain was debilitating. If you let it in, it could take over.

Peggy checked her watch. "Time's up," she said. For no reason Sophia could discern, hospital policy limited visits in the ICU to thirty-minute blocks, one person at a time. In an hour, Darius could come sit with her. Back in the waiting room, she found him with his arms around a small, dark-haired woman wearing a pink tank top and denim cut-off shorts with the words "Cutie Pie" written across the back in pink script. She was holding a balloon figure on a stick.

"This is Linda," he said, over the woman's messed-up hair. "Her boy was in an accident at Disneyland."

Sophia nodded. With each fresh sob, the balloon man did a gentle jig. Until he turned fifteen and discovered sex, Darius had entertained the idea of becoming a priest. Comforting strangers in pain seemed to take him back to that earlier, purer version of himself.

A man with a square head and pale lips burst into the room like a gunslinger in a western. The woman detached herself from Darius and threw herself into his arms.

"Let's get some coffee," Darius said to Sophia.

"Where's Miranda?"

"Wandering," he answered.

It had been like that since the day of the accident. Both Darius and Sophia could sit silently for hours, everything in them trained on the door through which Dr. Marjani or one of his minions would make their regular rounds. It was different for Miranda. Every few minutes, she would jump out of her seat and pace the floor. Occasionally, she'd windmill her arms or roll her neck like an athlete getting ready for a big race. After a few minutes of that, she'd announce that she was going for a walk. Once, after she was gone for three hours, Sophia went to look for her. She found her daughter curled up in a fetal position on the back pew of the nondenominational chapel provided for family members. A rosy pink light from the stained-glass window covered half her face. Her eyes were open. She looked beautiful. In normal times, Sophia would have asked, "Are you okay?" but these were not normal times and she already knew the answer. Instead, they sat together in silence for a good twenty minutes until suddenly Miranda sat up. "Daddy will be worried," she'd said.

In the cafeteria, Darius told Sophia how the mother had yelled at the boy for not buckling his seat belt. To spite her, he had stood up just as the ride entered a tunnel and hit his head on a fake boulder. The mother, who was sitting behind him, had been forced to watch the unconscious boy's body jerked the length of the ride. Sophia was so disturbed by the story that she didn't see Miranda rushing in.

"She opened her eyes!" Miranda, normally so fastidious about the attention of strangers, ignored the stares from other diners. "I was standing right there. I wasn't supposed to be there but I felt like seeing her, and all of a sudden she looked right at me and then she closed them."

"Did she say anything?" Darius stood up.

Miranda shook her head.

"Did she seem to recognize you?"

Miranda hesitated. She could see how much her father wanted her to say yes. "I don't know. Maybe."

Darius hugged her and sprinted out of the room, his wife and daughter following close behind. Ignoring the rules, the family crowded around Helen's bed.

Darius brought his face close to Helen's pale face. "Honey?" he said quietly. "Can you hear me?"

Nothing.

"Helen?" He tried again. "It's Daddy."

"Did you say something in particular?" Darius glanced at Miranda.

"No, I was just, I mean, I was . . . actually, I was praying."

Sophia and Darius exchanged a look of surprise. Religion was not a factor in their lives. When the girls had been little and the Methodist church around the corner had offered free child care during services, Sophia had occasionally taken them to church so that she could have an hour by herself in a setting that required nothing more than standing and singing an occasional hymn. She had only half listened to the sermons, which she found uniformly banal.

"I'm not turning into a God freak," Miranda said when she saw the look pass between her parents, "it's just something I do."

Dr. Marjani appeared in the doorway.

"She opened her eyes," Miranda said.

Dr. Marjani looked as if the news tired him. He nodded. "Did she seem to recognize you?" He took a slim flashlight out of his pocket, lifted an eyelid, and shined the light into Helen's eyes.

Miranda glanced at her mother. She was tempted to lie and say yes. They had all noticed that Dr. Marjani had stopped paying as close attention to Helen as he had the first few days. Miranda could feel his hopes for Helen waning. If he thought she was showing progress, maybe he would be more interested? But she'd already told her mother the truth.

"No," Miranda shook her head. "Not really."

Dr. Marjani frowned. "Patients in your sister's condition can seem to mimic the normal sleep/wakefulness cycle, but studies of MRIs on these patients have revealed no such consciousness."

Miranda wished she could dismiss his opinion. "You said, 'When she wakes up, it will be a breakthrough.'"

"I'm quite certain I said 'if' she wakes up. Unfortunately, opening and closing the eyes are not the same as waking up."

"So why did her eyes open?" Miranda pressed.

"A muscular reflex. Almost certainly not connected to volition."

"Almost certainly?"

Dr. Marjani sighed. Generally, he disliked bringing up the level of uncertainty inherent in his specialty. Every year, someone who had been written off as hopeless flummoxed the medical profession by suddenly waking up, befuddled but healthy. The media loved those stories. Marjani hated them. They gave people too much hope and undermined his authority. At the same time, he was a man of principle. He knew perfectly well that medicine was built on a constantly shifting sandbar. He was only forty-three years old, but already he had seen the experts completely reverse themselves on several procedures that had, until recently, been considered the gold standard of care. The McMartins were educated people. How could he stand before them and claim to know something without a doubt?

"As best we know," he amended his statement. "Now is probably a good time for a family conference to discuss Helen's future."

"We're not pulling the plug," Darius said.

Dr. Marjani flinched. After the accident, a colleague in the medical school had lent Darius a first-year medical textbook on injuries to the brain. Ever since then, he had worked hard to understand the nature of Helen's injury. At night, he'd make Sophia quiz him on the orbital lobe versus the parietal, the cerebellum versus the cerebral cortex. She used her Latin to puzzle out the root meanings of the words: *corpus callosum*, a "firm body"; *cerebellum*, a "little brain," but, unlike Darius, she could not seem to retain any of it in her mind. When the doctors gave them updates on Helen's condition, she focused only on the big picture—was she better or worse?—while Darius used his new knowledge to grill the doctors over specifics. How were her "o sats"? What was the diastolic pressure? But if he thought the doctors would appreciate his amateur's enthusiasm, he was wrong. Every time he asked a question using his new knowledge, Dr. Marjani seemed to bristle defensively.

"We never 'pull the plug,' as you put it," Dr. Marjani responded to Darius's comment, "without the full consent of the family." Sophia thought about Peggy's "extra mile" but said nothing. "Nevertheless," he continued, "the ICU is not the place for a long-term stay." He consulted his watch. "Could you meet me in three hours?" Of course they could—what else did they have to do?

Twice, they got lost trying to find the room where the meeting was scheduled. When they arrived, the only person there was the social worker whom Sophia disliked. Darius ostentatiously checked his watch.

"I got a page from Dr. M," she said. "He's on his way. How are you guys doing?"

No one answered. It was the kind of rudeness they would not have allowed themselves a few weeks earlier, but the accident had burned away all their false cheeriness. The woman's face reddened.

"We're okay," Sophia relented.

"I'm sorry," Dr. Marjani announced, bustling into the room a minute later. Sophia was surprised to see a spatter of what looked like fresh blood across the bottom of his white coat. Usually, he was meticulously clean. Without waiting for a response, he slid a DVD into a computer and turned down the lights. A series of images appeared on a large screen attached to the wall. Sophia knew they were CAT scans, but she could never reconcile the lime, red, and blue blobs on what looked like a horseshoe crab with what was, in fact, a picture of her daughter's brain. Darius had once tried to explain what the squiggles and lines meant, but it was like the stars in the night sky—others might see the hanging belt of a warrior, but Sophia never could. Instead, she looked to Darius's face while he studied the images, trying to decode his expression. He looked as confused as she felt.

"These are the latest scans?" he asked, pointing to two black-and-white images.

"I don't know how well you can read them," Dr. Marjani said, nodding. "But the main thing is to look here, along the falcine." He pointed to a hazy white cloud. "The brightness indicates fresh bleeding."

"How can that be?" Sophia asked, confused. "The accident was four weeks ago."

"Yes," the doctor agreed, "but as I have indicated previously, the initial trauma is sometimes only the beginning in a severe case. In the days and weeks that follow, a chain of biochemical events is set in motion that continues to inflict even more damage to the central nervous system. I'm afraid that that is what is happening in your daughter's case."

Sophia looked to Darius for confirmation, but he was staring at the doctor vacantly, as if his mind had wandered off someplace more pleasant. She noticed white patches appearing around his eyes. The blood draining away in a checkerboard pattern.

"I don't understand," Miranda spoke up, pushing her body forward so her torso was leaning against the table.

"Unfortunately, we don't, either. As far as we know, the body responds to injury by releasing an influx of neurotransmitters—chemical messengers that create activity between the neurons. In a minor injury, this begins the healing process, but when the trauma is severe, sometimes the activity doesn't stop. It's like the body's signaling switch is broken. As time goes on, that flood of neurotransmitters actually creates more damage."

"Excitotoxicity," Darius said slowly.

"Exactly," Dr. Marjani said, repeating the word with a slight correction in pronunciation.

Sophia felt like a child in the middle of a game of keep-away. Her husband knew things, and so did the doctor, but they were tossing them over her head, out of her reach.

"In a healthy person, cells die and they are replaced," Dr. Marjani continued. "When a person is gravely injured, the body continues to lose its ability to regulate itself. Blood pressure becomes unstable, the heartbeat becomes irregular. I don't know if you have noticed it, but Helen's EEGs are becoming increasingly labile." Sophia did know something was up. Only yesterday she had been sitting with her daughter when the green line on the heart monitor had suddenly spiked, as if something had spooked her.

"What was that?" Sophia had asked Peggy, who happened to be on duty.

"Nothing to worry about," Peggy had said, and smiled, "probably just a nightmare." Sophia had to stop herself from pointing out how often she had been told that people in her daughter's state don't dream.

"Is there any treatment?" Miranda asked.

The doctor looked down at the table. His head moved slightly back and forth. "I think we may have exhausted all of our options."

"There are experimental treatments," Darius said slowly, as if repeating words someone was whispering into his ear. "Cell regeneration using olfactory glia cells, neurotransmitter antagonists."

A vertical line of annoyance appeared between Dr. Marjani's eyes. "Those experiments have been performed only on animal models," he said. "Even if they were close to the human trial stage, which they are not, your daughter would not be a candidate. She can't fully breathe on her own. Surgery is not an option."

"If she's going to die anyway, why not take the chance?" Darius asked.

"As her doctor, I could not endorse it, and I don't think you'll find a legitimate doctor who would." Marjani looked to Sophia, then Miranda. "In my experience, the family that realistically prepares for the future is better prepared for the event when it happens. It is up to you, of course, but I have seen families ruin themselves emotionally and financially forestalling the inevitable. If she were my daughter, I would seriously consider making the rest of her life as comfortable as possible."

As if on cue, the social worker leaned forward and pushed a booklet toward Sophia. "I can help with that," she said in a whispery voice. Sophia glanced down at its cover—an oak tree with no leaves under the title "Crossing Over." Sophia had a sudden, frightening desire to plunge a knife into the woman's heart. She closed her eyes and willed the image to pass.

"You want to pull the plug," Darius said.

"No." Dr. Marjani shook his head. "I want your daughter to get up and walk out of this hospital, but I know the likelihood is remote."

"That means there is a possibility."

"Infinitesimal. But we will support the family's wishes. We do, however, need to move her out of the ICU, as recovery is no longer an expected outcome and those beds are needed by other patients."

and sometimes why 127

Sophia noticed that Miranda's body seemed to be sliding lower and lower in her chair. "Move her where?" she asked.

"There are support facilities."

"Can we bring her home?" Darius asked.

Marjani hesitated and glanced at the social worker. "Some families do decide to bring the patient home and try to care for them in that setting. I think, however, it is not a good idea. The strain of having a critical patient in your home is not something that can be underestimated." Sophia felt a distinct pressure somewhere in the region of her solar plexus. It was the feeling she sometimes got when she ate too much chocolate. Speedy, odd, sick. "We'll need to talk it over," she said. "As a family."

In the parking garage, Sophia tried to catch her husband's eye, to gauge where his feelings lay, but he seemed to be deliberately avoiding her eyes. Buckling her seat belt, Sophia recalled once reading that the best way to talk to teenage boys was in cars, where the distractions of the road kept them from getting too self-conscious.

"Darius?" she said as he put the key into the ignition.

"Yes?"

"Shouldn't we talk?" A van pulled up next to them. A young man leaped out of the driver's seat and hurried around to the other side, where a frail, elderly woman with fly-away white hair was struggling to get out of the car. The young man tried to reason with the woman, but she kept pushing him away. "*I can do it,*" she snapped.

"What is there to say?" Darius asked.

"The doctors just gave us a very grim prognosis. I think there is a lot to say."

"Sophia, every time a doctor gives you an opinion, you accept it as if it were written on a stone tablet."

"Obviously," Sophia answered as calmly as she could, "you understand Helen's condition better than I do, but I would be pretty surprised if you knew more than Dr. Marjani." Right after the accident they had looked into finding a new doctor, but everyone they interviewed said the same thing—in the field, Dr. Rajiv Marjani was one of the best. Sophia wanted to say more, to tell him how tired she was of hearing him begin every sentence, "According to my research . . ." but she knew the things said in the next few minutes could have repercussions for the rest of their lives. She wanted to make sure she got them right.

"I may not have their experience," Darius answered, "but I have something they don't have. *I* have hope."

She could tell from the way he emphasized *I* that he did not include her in that description. "If there was a chance Helen might recover using some experimental therapy, don't you think I would want that as much as you do?" Sophia knew her voice had begun to rise, to become shrill and accusing, but she felt powerless to stop it.

"I would have thought so, but lately I've begun to wonder."

"The difference between you and me is that I am realistic. I don't want to spend the rest of my life staring at my daughter's dead body, hoping for a miracle. It's bad enough to have your heart broken, but I am not going to be a fool about it."

"If you think hope makes you a fool, you're a sad woman."

"Fuck you. You're not the only person in pain here. When are you going to stop thinking only about yourself and *your* feelings?"

A low moan from the backseat made them both turn around. Miranda's forehead was pressed against the window. A curtain of black hair hid her face.

Sophia felt a stab of remorse for her childish outburst, followed by a more powerful wave of self-pity. She tried to protect herself from its hydraulic force by concentrating on her breath—in, out, in, out, she told herself—but it kept sucking her in, pushing her down so she couldn't breathe. She drew her knees to her forehead and tried to ride it out. The rest of the way home, nobody said a word.

When they got home, Miranda was the first out of the car. Sophia watched her daughter run up the flagstone path leading to the back door. Such a hurry to get away from us, she thought, sadly. The light in the kitchen went on, followed by a scream. Darius ran inside. Sophia followed more slowly. She could tell the scream was one of pique, not fear. The kitchen floor was strewn with the bloody cotton entrails of a used sanitary napkin that Monty had strewn across the floor.

"This is disgusting!" Miranda snapped.

"I'll clean it up." Darius took a broom from the utility closet.

"Forget it," Miranda said, grabbing the broom from his hand.

Sophia knew her daughter was embarrassed over the sanitary napkin. "Why don't you take Monty for a walk?" she said to Darius. The dog was staring meekly up at them, his body flattened against the ground in submission.

In her mind, Sophia had asked gently, as a peacemaker, but everything was so out of place in her head, she must have sounded accusing and angry. "Why don't you stop telling me what to do?" Darius replied, leaving the room. For once, the dog did not follow Darius.

"Great," Miranda said, banging the dustpan against the garbage can.

"Fine, I'll walk the damn dog." Sophia took Monty's leash off the hook Darius had inexpertly sunk into the drywall. Monty's tail whipped back and forth with such force, the whole rear end of his body shook. Sophia was beginning to see the appeal of a dog—who else, at this precise moment in time, took any pleasure in the fact of her existence, except for this needily neurotic dog looking at her so ecstatically? Outside, the light was changing so quickly from sepia orange to violet blue that she felt time and the planet itself racing forward at some incomprehensible Einsteinian speed. Normally, the feeling filled her with a vague melancholy, but that night she welcomed it. Only time could wash these wounds clean, and even then she wasn't so sure. As Monty pulled her down the sidewalk past the neighboring houses, she could see the ghostly blue glow of television sets turning on as people began their evenings. Through a double-height Palladian window, she glimpsed a woman's back as she leaned over to water a plant. Was that woman happy? Sophia wondered. Did she love her job? Her husband? Were her children healthy and strong, grateful to her for the years of work and worry? Was she afraid of death? Were her parents alive? Did they love her? Monty lifted a leg to pee on a lavender bush. Sophia looked around guiltily but nobody was around. The woman through the window straightened up and put a hand to her lower back.

Suddenly, Monty jerked the leash taut.

A few feet away, a squirrel peered down from the branch of a tree, its bushy tail flicking back and forth tauntingly, like a stripper with a boa.

"Monty," Sophia said, "no!"

The muscles under Monty's fur quivered with furious desire. Sophia thought about reaching down, unhooking the leash, and letting him go, but what would Darius say if she came home without the dog? Instead, she loosened the leash, letting the dog pull her with him on his mindless gallop. For the last several years, Sophia had faithfully attended exercise class three times a week at the YMCA around the corner from work. Since the accident, she hadn't been once. Despite the wrong shoes and a bra that offered no support, it felt good to run. After ten minutes and two left turns, she looked up and found herself in front of Roy Beaudell's old house. The whole time Helen had dated Roy, Sophia had been in the house only once, for a book party Roy's father's publisher had thrown him. The most vivid part of the evening had been the anguish she felt getting dressed. Everything she owned felt too old and conservative. Finally, she'd borrowed a mini-skirt from Helen. When she caught sight of herself in a full-length mirror at the party, she'd been horrified at the sight of a middle-aged woman trying to look like a young woman. Mutton dressed as lamb. "How could you let me wear this?" she'd whispered to Darius, who'd shrugged and (rightly) pointed out that nobody in the whole place was looking at them. Like that was supposed to make her feel better. "Anyway"—he'd kissed her ear—"I think you look terrific."

Across the For Sale sign in the front yard, a red-and-white Reduced! sticker had been pasted. She'd heard from a neighbor that Roy's father had purposely overpriced the house to annoy his creditors. Sophia felt her pocket for her keys and looked up and down the block. It would be good, she thought, to get rid of Helen's key. Plus, she'd stomped out of the house without stopping to go to the bathroom. Going down the driveway, she felt like a kid sneaking into the neighborhood haunted house. The key went easily into the lock on the back door but then refused to turn. She held it up to the light from a neighbor's lamppost. The metal was fine, neither bent nor rusted. She tried again, wiggling first one way, then the other. Nothing. She walked to the front door of the house but the key wouldn't even go in. Monty watched her with an expression of pleasant incomprehension. How nice to be so utterly stupid.

She walked home, fingering the keys like a rosary. Back home, she gave Monty a rawhide and called Siri's number from the list next to the phone.

"Hello?" Siri's frightened voice.

"I don't have news."

"Oh." She sounded both disappointed and relieved.

"I have a question. Did you ever give Helen a key to your house?"

"No," Siri answered. "Why?"

After they hung up, Sophia poured herself a glass of wine. She had just taken her first sip when the phone rang.

"I think I might know what the key is," Siri said in a strangled voice. "He gave her one, so she could let herself in if he was working late."

"Oh," Sophia answered. It had never occurred to her the key might have anything to do with Bobby, but it made sense. Her girl had been becoming a woman. A man had given her the key to his house.

15

*h*arry stopped leaving the house. He even gave up running for swimming. He told himself it was because of the reporters who'd camped
in front of his house, but the truth was, the reporters had left after the first
day. He stayed home because he couldn't think of anywhere to go. He
would have been happy to keep his appointments—the personal appearance at a fund-raiser for scleroderma, the paid endorsement of a casino
opening in Vegas—but Fields had strongly advised against it.

"But I *want* to go," Harry said, misunderstanding.

"*Hairy*," Fields answered, "don't get me wrong, but they don't want
you. You're bad news right now."

"But—" Harry answered.

"I know it wasn't your fault," Fields stopped him before Harry could say
it. "But sometimes people can get an aura. *Lack* when you've been to a club
where everybody is smokin'. You weren't, but you smell like you was. You
just got to let your clothes air out, *Hairy*. People will forg*ayt*, you'll see."

"That's just what I'm afraid of," Harry said. "People will forget."

Fields laughed professionally. "You're funny, *Hairy*. Nobody could
ever forget you."

For a minute he let himself believe that Fields was telling him the truth.
People would never forget him. He created that show. Practically.

Catherine entered the kitchen. It had been a month since the accident,
but still she looked surprised whenever she found him there.

"Do you think I'm memorable?" he asked.

Suspicion made her features hard and pointy. Like an okie. "In what way?" she asked, shaking a bolus of Red Zinger tea into a strainer.

"In the 'anals' of television history," Harry said.

"Funny," Catherine said flatly. She hated anything to do with the anus. The one time early in the relationship he'd suggested anal sex, she'd burst into tears. "If that's what you're into, I don't think I'm the woman for you."

Harry sighed and sipped his now-cold coffee. "Never mind." Of course the publicist was sucking up to him. That's what they were paid to do. "Hey," he asked, "how many yards are in a mile?"

She looked pained at the question. Catherine's parents had spent a great deal of money on her education—a "fortune" was the word her father liked to use—but the schools were the sort that ignored math in favor of art. For her college thesis, she slept in a tree for a week, then created a diorama made of toothpicks to represent the experience. "For, you know, the micro in the macro."

"It's something like seventeen hundred yards," Catherine answered, "or seven hundred. I'm not sure." That meant Harry was swimming either a mile a day or ten miles a day. He liked how the exercise had changed his body, building up his shoulders and narrowing his waist.

"Harry?" Catherine sat across from him, one hand cradling her steaming mug of tea. "We need to talk."

"You want a divorce?" he asked.

"Be serious."

"All right. Hold on." He slid off his stool and closed the door to the hallway where Rosalba, one of their housekeepers, was sweeping.

"Okay." Harry sat down. "You want to talk instead of just having sex." A joke. They hadn't had sex in seven weeks.

"Don't be flip. Not now."

"Sorry," he said, without conviction. If not now, then when?

"The point is, we need to come up with a plan. To protect our interests in this whole matter."

"I don't know what you mean by our 'interests,'" Harry said testily. "The accident wasn't my fault."

"Exactly. Which is why I think you should talk to my brother."

"Your brother is a real-estate lawyer," Harry said.

"He knows people."

This was the crux of the issue. Catherine knew people. Catherine's brother knew people. Harry didn't know people. He was only married to someone who knew people. He stood up.

"Where are you going?" she asked.

"To swim," he answered.

"Oookaaay."

When she was offended, Catherine had a habit of elongating her words. "What time do you want luuunch?"

"You know," he answered, "we don't have to eat every meal together."

"We're married."

"Married people usually eat one meal a day together. Not three."

"Which meeeaaaal would you like to eat with me?"

"Probably dinner," he answered, "it's traditional."

"Right," she said, smiling, "then we can talk about what we did during the day."

"Sarcasm?" he asked.

"You can't swim your problems away, Harry. This has to be dealt with."

From the pool, he could see Catherine's pale, worried face watching him through the kitchen window as she talked on the phone. The laps began to add up. Twenty, thirty, fifty. The fatigue spreading through his muscles was like an answer to an itch. Catherine was on the verge of a decision about him, he could feel it. He felt he should help her out somehow. Talk it through or do whatever it was that couples did in these situations. He knew what women thought of him. God knew he'd heard it enough through the years. *We're not partners. You never talk to me. You live in your head.* And then, finally, toward the end. *I'm lonely.* He tried to reassure his disappointed partners that they were missing out on nothing. The inside of his head was a remarkably uncluttered place. In the beginning, Catherine had seemed to appreciate his comfort with silence. The first time they drove up to Sacramento to see her parents they'd talked on the freeway as they left L.A., but by the time they reached Santa Barbara, there was nothing left to say. Instead of panicking, the way he'd seen some women do, by asking stupid questions nobody cared about. (*What were you like as a child? What did you want to be when you grew up? What's your favorite food?*) Catherine had simply shut up. They rode the next 300 miles in complete silence. Occasionally, he'd glance at her to see if she was suffering but she looked remarkably serene. Happy, even. It was on that trip that he first thought of marrying her. Now the silence had gone sour on them. During meals, she brought kitchen and bedding catalogs to the table. If he heard her coming down the stairs he wasn't above hiding around the corner to avoid her. Partly, he feared telling her what he himself was slowly realizing. He wasn't missing work. Not seeing Maury Shore or Gus Morbane every day turned out to be a great relief. Greater still was the relief he felt at not having to respond to the fans who were constantly besieging him with their annoying *Hey, Harry, I'd rather be whatevering.* Hey, loser, I don't care.

On his eighty-third lap, Harry noticed a pair of Adidas sneakers standing at the edge of the pool. He looked up. A short, muscle-bound man in a tight gray T-shirt, blond hair pulled back in a ponytail and green-gold eyes that glittered in the reflected light of the water, was watching him.

"It's good to see a person swimming," the man said. "Sometimes you begin to wonder if anybody actually uses the darn thing."

"You're the pool man?" Harry asked. He'd never been home during his monthly visit.

"The one and only. Joe Fisher." The man crouched and put a hand in Harry's face. Despite the muscles, his grip was soft, like a dead fish. He gestured to a large plastic jug near his feet. "I usually tell people it's not a good idea to swim for at least an hour after I put the chemicals in."

Harry hauled himself out of the pool. "Can I watch?"

"Be my guest, but be forewarned: Once you know what goes into it, you might not want to swim again." He cackled after he said it, and Harry wondered if he was stoned.

Fisher dipped a glass vial into the water, added a few chemicals and shook it.

"What are you testing for?" Harry asked.

"Bacteria. You'd be surprised how dirty humans are."

"Piss?"

"A common misconception. Urine is actually sterile. It's all the other things we're constantly shedding—hair, skin, oils. And then there's bacteria in the water itself." He put on a pair of plastic gloves, a mask, and opened a jug of chemicals. He said something to Harry that sounded like "Mumbai."

Harry moved. Fisher poured a yellowish liquid the consistency of vegetable oil into the pool. A chemical odor burned Harry's nostrils. Joe Fisher was right. Seeing what he was swimming in filled him with dismay.

"Do we have to use all those chemicals?" he asked.

Fisher shook his head. "I know. And then we all wonder why we're getting cancer at forty-five. I've been trying to convince my boss to sell the all-natural pool."

"How does that work?"

"You stock the pool with a couple of algae-eating fish—the Thai flying fox, a couple of candy-stripe plecos, a few rubber-nose peckies—add some oxygen-producing plants, keep the pump and filter on high, and you're re-creating the swimming hole as God intended it."

"You swim with the fish?"

"Just like the ocean. Without the waves, the salt, the sand, the high parking fees. Or girls in bikinis. But no plan is perfect."

"Why is your boss against it?"

"A man without vision." Fisher tightened the cap on the jug.

"But you know people who have done it?"

"In Europe, I understand it's very popular."

Harry watched as the yellow liquid dissolved. "Maybe we should try it here," he said.

"Yeah, right." Fisher answered like Harry was making a joke.

"No, I mean it. My pool could be, like, a test case. A beta model. People pay a lot of money to swim with dolphins, don't they?"

Joe's golden eyes widened. "Are you shitting me?"

Harry looked at Fisher more closely. A flicker of doubt leaped and danced inside him. Did he want to be in business with this odd little man who, he realized now that he'd had a moment to consider him more closely, strongly resembled a recent convict?

"Why not?" Harry answered Fisher's question.

"You're really serious?" In his growing excitement, Fisher began shifting his weight back and forth between his two feet, like a boxer getting ready for a fight.

"Yeah. I've been looking for—" Harry had started to say, "a new project," but stopped himself.

"Because not only would we be making the world a better place, but I think we could also get very rich." Harry opened his mouth to tell him he ought to be careful what he wished for, but then closed it. Let him figure it out for himself.

16

S ophia." Darius's voice sliced through the darkness. She felt his hand
on her shoulder. Her eyes flew open. She put her hand to her forehead. It was damp.

"You screamed," he said, yawning.

"I'm sorry," she answered. Since the accident her dreams had turned
suddenly violent. In college, she had taken a psychology course taught by
a Jungian, who encouraged his students to write down their dreams immediately upon waking. Every morning, Sophia would try her best, urged on
by the piece of paper she had taped to her alarm clock. DREAMS!!!! But try as
she might, she could never remember a single one. One day, she raised her
hand and asked the professor, an aged hippie who wore white Mexican
wedding shirts and Birkenstock sandals to class despite his gnarly old-man
toes, "What if you never dream?"

"Everybody dreams," he answered, moving his eyebrows up and down
in that ironically flirtatious way so confusing to young women yearning to
be taken seriously. "It's the human condition."

His answer had sent her into a funk. Am I not human? she wondered.
Am I lacking an imagination? A personal underworld? She began listening
closely to her classmates as they read their dreams aloud—*I was running and
I was naked and I was falling and I could fly and there was a test but I had not
studied, had not even enrolled in the class, then I woke up*—and used their
images to make up her own dreams, throwing in a few sexual images to keep

things interesting. A large cylindrical tower often loomed in the distance. She tried to climb it. It was slippery. Sometimes, water or a "viscous fluid" spurted out of the top. In the margins of her dream journal, the professor made neat little checks next to the dirty parts. She got an A in the course.

Now she was dreaming too much, waking up shaken and scared by vivid images of babies mired in bloody purple mud, infant bodies full of adult teeth. Sometimes they could fly, their arms distended like a pterodactyl's, flapping in the air, coming toward her, as if they wanted something essential from her, a lung or a liver. Always, she woke up before they reached her, but the adrenaline would still be coursing through her body, making her limbs tingle with a terrible electricity. When the terror receded, she felt bruised and exhausted, as if she had physically done battle in the night. Again and again, she had to remind herself of the first rule of dreams—the dreamer never dies.

Darius turned his body toward her and stroked her arm, following the curve of her hip down to the curve of her ass. "*Sshhhhhh*," he whispered. She accepted the caresses, willing her heart to slow down, her body to relax. After a while, his hand went from her stomach to the hollow in between her breasts and then to the nipples. The feel of his skin on her breast made her nauseous, the same way she had felt when she'd been pregnant with the girls and he'd wanted to make love.

"I'm sorry," she said, taking his hand and moving it away. He sighed loudly and turned his back.

She felt bad. Sex had always been the invisible glue between them. When the household chores, the relentlessness of meals, the dickering over driving, the parent-teacher conferences, the assemblies, the soccer games, the trips to the mall for cheap clothing the girls would outgrow in a few months, and always, always, the worries about money had become too tedious for words, sex had been a respite, a place where they could once again believe something in their life was transcendent. Normally, her desire was equal to his. Except for the times she was pregnant, she almost never turned down a sexual overture. Nor could she ever remember him saying no to her. When her friends complained about how much sex their husbands always seemed to want, it had been a secret source of pride for Sophia that she wanted it as much as he did. But now, when their marriage most needed its balm, sex had once again become linked in her mind to the bloody, unerotic mess of conception and birth. In the middle of the month, she'd get strange stabbing pains in her ovaries, as if her reproductive system had been pressed into active revolt, punishing her for her indifferent stewardship of its issue. When she mentioned it to her gynecologist, he had looked perplexed, then ordered a battery of expensive tests, all of which came back normal.

"Should we talk about this?" Sophia asked Darius's spine, visible beneath the black hair of his back and the pale Irish skin.

His answer was a faint hiss of air, like a tire going flat. He'd gone to sleep. Or was pretending.

When she woke up the next morning, Darius was gone. It used to make her feel strange waking up alone after going to sleep with him. If she could sleep through a 215-pound man heaving himself off a queen-size mattress, opening and closing a bathroom door, showering, shaving, and dressing, what else could she miss while slumbering? Now it didn't bother her. In fact, all of her old neurotic fears—empty parking garages at night, coffeemakers that spontaneously combusted, moles that outgrew their borders, flat tires, cockroaches in the cutlery drawer, colon cancer, gums that bled, audits by the IRS—had ceased to worry her. As far as the universe was concerned, she felt she'd used up her bad luck quota for decades to come. And even if one of those terrible things did happen, how small a burned-down house would seem compared to the tragedy of Helen's accident. As in painting, perspective was everything.

Downstairs, she found Darius reading the paper. Monty was asleep at his feet. He glanced ostentatiously at the clock on the wall—8:35—and went back to the sports pages. It was a sore subject between them. Every morning, he wanted to get to the hospital as early as possible. If he had his way, he would set up a bed in Helen's room and live there. Sophia didn't see the need. If there was any change in Helen's condition, the hospital had been instructed to call them, regardless of the time.

"Should we get Miranda up?" he asked. "It's getting late."

Sophia poured herself a cup of coffee, took a sip, and grimaced. It was even more burned than usual.

"Sorry," Darius said, watching her. "I've been up a while. I can make a fresh pot."

"No," she said, and waved at him, acknowledging his peace offering. "It suits my mood."

Sophia walked up the backstairs, toward Miranda's bedroom. Ever since the girls hit puberty, Darius had become shy about entering their bedrooms.

"They might be, you know."

"Oh, honey, even if they were, which they probably aren't because, trust me, it's different for girls, they'd be doing it under the covers."

But Darius, who had never gotten over the shame of being caught by his mother masturbating at thirteen, was adamant.

Sophia knocked once before entering the bedroom. Miranda was awake but still lying in bed.

"Rise and shine," Sophia said.

"Trying," Miranda answered.

Sophia went into her closet and picked out a long, flowy dress in dark blue.

"What about this?" she asked, holding the dress in front of her daughter.

Miranda fingered the material sadly. "I've never worn this."

"Maybe it's time to light the rose candle." A family joke. On her deathbed, Sophia's great aunt was supposedly asked if she wished she'd done anything differently in her life. Her answer—"I wish I had lit that damn rose candle"—had become part of family lore.

When Miranda pushed the covers off and swung her legs out of bed, Sophia noticed a small patch of cellulite on her upper thighs. It made her sad for a second. She had hoped the perfection of youth would last a little longer for her daughters.

"Mom?" Miranda stared at the floor.

"Mmmm."

"I don't want to go anymore."

Sophia had seen it coming. The first month after the accident, Miranda had risen promptly every morning, but for the last four weeks, she'd been getting up later and later. When she did finally get to the kitchen, she acted like a petulant fourteen-year-old. Not having her around might actually be a relief.

"I know." Sophia had thought about bringing it up with Darius, but she was having her own problems with her husband. Once, she believed their opposing temperament had kept things interesting long after most marriages had gone flat, but now, when it really mattered, his refusal to face up to the bleakness of Helen's prognosis was making her crazy. She sat next to Miranda on the bed, thighs and shoulders touching; they tilted their heads toward each other so the bone of their skulls met.

"If I could just give her some of my health . . ." Miranda said.

Sophia had had the same thought many times. It was in the paper all the time—mothers who gave kidneys or bone marrow to their sick children. She had no desire to die, but if there had been a way to give Helen her own brain, she would have. She'd lived long enough to get the gist of life. The museum would let her stay on, neither promoting nor demoting her, until a reasonable retirement age, when they'd give her a farewell cocktail party with their B-list caterer. She could practically taste the custard of the mini-quiches now. Darius might finish the book he had been working on for the last ten years—a biography of Shakespeare's abandoned wife—but probably not. That book had never been written because there was virtually no material. The house would get too big and too expensive to maintain. They'd move to an apartment. There would be meals and movies and books. On and on. Same old, same old. If it meant giving Helen a chance, she'd be willing to give all that up.

"Let's go talk to your father."

When Darius saw Miranda come down the stairs in pajamas, he looked to Sophia for an explanation. It had also been that way when they were babies. One of the girls would start to cry and Darius would look to Sophia, panicked. "Two short coughs and a cry means 'I'm bored,'" she would try to explain. "A constant wail means 'I'm hungry.' An arch of the back means 'I'm tired.'" But he was a young associate professor trying to get tenure. Understanding the inscrutable language of babies took time he didn't have.

"What's going on?" Darius asked.

"I'm not going to the hospital today," Miranda said quietly.

"I'm sorry?" Darius asked as if he hadn't heard correctly.

"It doesn't do any good. She doesn't know we're there. If it would help her for me to sit in that depressing waiting room, I'd be there. You know I would."

Darius opened his eyes wide, as if to take in more of the scene around him, then bent his head toward the table while massaging the creases on his forehead. Sophia was as familiar with the gesture as any zoologist who spent her days studying the habits of a single species. He was angry and hurt. The anger did not worry her. It was a quick blue fire that would dissipate quickly. The hurt was another matter. Already, she could feel that her husband's sense of the world had been dangerously destabilized by the accident. Even though he'd left the baby stage largely to her, he had never been one of those fathers more attuned to the world of work and men than the needs of his family. The bulk of the household chores still fell unevenly on Sophia's shoulders, but when it came to the ritualized intimacy of family, the ceremonies and events that marked the passage of time, it was Darius who did the work. He planned the family vacations, ordered the organic turkey for Thanksgiving four weeks in advance, bought the embossed leather photo albums and then filled them with pictures of each milestone in the girls' lives. As the sixth of nine children, he had grown up feeling lost in the crowd. Once, he confessed to her how crushed he had been when he came across a set of baby books for only the first four children in his family. "I couldn't believe it," he said, "for the rest of us . . . nothing." As the only girl child who had suffered under the too intense scrutiny of overprotective parents, Sophia tried to reassure him that he had missed nothing, but he couldn't hear it. All his life he'd mourned the lack.

"Can you talk to her?" Darius looked at her.

Sophia shrugged helplessly. What could she say? She was inclined to agree with her daughter. What was the point of all of them sitting in that room day after day? Sophia was in no hurry to go back to work. How could she pretend to care whether Betsy Saunders gave her Agnes Martin to the Guggenheim when Helen was so ill? It was different for Miranda. She had a life ahead of her.

"What should I tell her when she wakes up?" Darius asked. "Her sister sends her regrets, but she thinks it's too depressing to be here?"

"The thing is, Dad, I don't really know if she's going to wake up."

"Well," he said quietly, "I do."

"Then you know more than the doctors, because when I hear them talk, I hear them say, maybe next month, maybe next year, and maybe never. And the longer she goes without waking up, the less optimistic they sound."

"You know," he answered coldly, "maybe it's better you don't come. We really don't need all that negativity." He stood up, emptied his coffee cup into the sink, took the Volvo keys off the hooks next to the door, and said to Sophia, "I'll be waiting for you outside."

Sophia kissed her daughter on the top of her head. "Don't worry," she said, "he'll get over it." It was her role, the maternal anodyne, but inside, Sophia wasn't sure if any of them would ever really get over what had happened to them.

It could have been worse. In the worst-case scenarios Miranda had rehearsed, she imagined her father would burst into tears. If that had happened, there was no way she would be able to stand her ground. That he turned icy on her, telling her he was "disappointed," had been one of the best-case scenarios. It made him seem judgmental and sanctimonious. It was a child's birthright to disappoint her parents—hadn't he done it by marrying her mother ("A Greek?"), studying literature ("Stories?"), and moving ("California?")? She poured herself a cup of coffee and stared at the cordless phone on the table in front of her. She pushed it to the left, then the right. Picked it up, then put it down. It took exactly six minutes and fifty-eight seconds for her to work up the courage to call him.

He answered on the first ring. She liked that. People who let the phone ring two times even though they were sitting next to it were ridiculous.

"It's me," she said, heart thumping, "Miranda."

"*Hi.*" He sounded pleased to hear from her.

"I'm sorry I didn't return your calls, we had a family—"

"I know. I heard. I am really sorry. Are you free? Can I come see you?" She hesitated.

"Don't worry. Just as a friend."

She was glad he couldn't see her blush through the phone. "Okay," she said. She sat at the kitchen table and waited. Since the accident, he must have called twenty times. Each time she listened to a new message, her heart had twisted with desire, guilt, yearning, and about twenty other feelings that she could not name. In the end, they all left her in the same paralyzed place. How could she think of seeing him when Helen lay where she was? Sometimes, she'd call him when she knew he was in class or working his shift at the campus bookstore just to listen to his voice. "This is Jason. You know what to do." "Actually," she'd want to say, "that's the problem. I don't know what to do."

The doorbell rang. When she opened the front door, he was holding a bouquet of flowers wrapped in a cone of cellophane. A few pink carnations peaked over the top.

"Carnations!" she said.

"You don't like them?" He looked stricken.

"I love them." She hated them. But she loved that he had brought them.

He put his arms around her. "I don't like them, either, but it was all they had at the grocery store and I wanted to get here as quickly as possible."

She started to cry. How was it possible for someone she barely knew to understand her so well?

"It's okay," he said, patting her back.

"I'm not crying for her," she said into the faded blue flannel of his shirt. "I should have called you sooner." She pulled away from him.

"I didn't mind being the last thing on your mind."

Miranda sniffled. "I thought about you every day. That's why I couldn't call you. I felt so guilty." Being close to him was making her inexplicably drowsy, as if she had taken a sleeping pill. "I need to sit down," she said.

"Where?"

She looked around the house—the living room seemed too formal, the kitchen too public. "My room," she said, pointing up the stairs. He followed without looking around the house. She liked how he made her feel like a person with a future, not somebody attached to a past, a family, a house, a sick sister. During those endless hours at the hospital, when her mind would wander around the landscape of her life, projecting itself forward onto various life scenarios, she sometimes imagined she and Jason would marry, live on a farm somewhere, and raise happy, loudmouthed children who could recite "Jabberwocky" from memory. It made her sad that he and Helen had never met. Could anyone really know her without knowing Helen? But maybe it was better this way. With Jason, Helen would always be an abstraction. Growing up, she had gotten used to the idea that Helen would always be sunshine while she, Miranda, would be shadow. Light and dark. Easy and difficult. Smooth and prickly. While she had to assume that the man who liked Helen would never like her and vice versa, a part of her would always wonder. If you could choose between the two, why would you choose Miranda?

In her room, they lay on the bed together, facing each other. She put her leg over his hip. He put his hand on the small of her back and pressed her pelvis toward him. She had meant for them to lie together and talk but once she was close to him, she felt her body pulled into a current of desire. She put her hand to his head and drew his lips toward her mouth. His tongue found hers. Her hands moved into his hair, using it like a handle to pull him even closer. Their breath grew short. His eyelids grew droopy. In one swift movement, she maneuvered herself on top of him.

"I want to do it," she said into his ear. Before, her desire had seemed superficial, a thing to be resisted. Now it felt important, something that urgently needed doing. She couldn't even remember the nature of her objections.

"Are you sure?" he said.

"How can you ask?"

"I had to, it's in the student rulebook."

He put his hands around the elastic waist of the pants she was wearing and pulled her pants and underpants down. She gasped and worried about a million stupid things, the unsexy cotton underwear she was wearing, her unshaved legs, the soft mound of her belly, the way she smelled down there. He pulled his shirt over his head. His chest was broad and muscled, with a tuft of coarse brown hair in the middle. She stopped thinking about her own body and kissed one of his nipples. He groaned and unzipped his pants. She pulled slightly away.

"I'm a virgin," she said.

"I know," he answered.

"Is it obvious?"

"Yes. No. Don't worry. You are perfect in every way."

Miranda smiled. "Hyperbole will get you everywhere."

Afterward, she wasn't sure how she felt. Relieved to have it done, that was for sure. Slightly disappointed, but she had expected that—she didn't have a single friend who'd found the first time completely pleasurable. What disappointed her was how quickly it was over. It wasn't that he hadn't lasted long enough, he'd been courtly in that way, asking if she was ready. She'd acquiesced out of cluelessness: Ready for what? Now that it was over, she wanted to go back and examine everything, to understand what it had all meant, but already the memory was slipping away from her.

"It's always strange at first," he said into her hair.

"So they say."

"You're not regretting it, are you?"

"God, no," she reassured him. "I want to do it again and again."

He laughed and put a hand on her breast. "We will." He turned suddenly serious. "Are you really okay?"

"I don't know," she answered. "Life does go on. You think it's not going to. The first morning you wake up, you go to brush your teeth and you think, How can I brush my teeth while Helen's in the hospital fighting for her life? But if you don't brush your teeth and your breath stinks and the bacteria grow and your teeth rot out, how has that actually helped your sister? You've just fulfilled some kind of narcissistic need to dramatize your pain."

"I guess that's why the Jews don't cut their beards for thirty days when they're in mourning."

Miranda raised her head to look at him, surprised he would know that. "Do you know a lot of Jews?"

"My mother. Me. Matrilineally."

Miranda held her breath, waiting for more.

"She was a bush pilot and an ob-gyn in Anchorage. When women in remote villages needed an abortion, my mother would get in her plane and go to them. In Alaska in the winter, there are no roads."

"A hero." Miranda was impressed.

"Not everybody thought so. She was always getting death threats from the anti-abortion kooks. One morning I went outside to play and there was a fetus in a plastic salad container on our front porch. I thought it was a bird."

"How awful."

"They slashed the tires on my dad's truck, they spray-painted the side of our house with red paint. A kid at school asked me why my mom killed babies for a living. My dad begged her to stop, but she wouldn't."

Miranda could feel his breathing get shorter as he spoke. "Then one day, she went up in the plane and never came home. My dad believes it was sabotage. He maintained the plane, so he knew there was nothing wrong with it and she was a very careful pilot. If there was bad weather, she always stayed home."

"What did the police say?" Miranda could feel something wet between her legs. She wondered if it was blood but didn't want to look down in the middle of his story.

"The wreckage was on the side of a mountain too remote to access. My dad hired one of the best mountain guides in the state to retrieve her body. He tried three times but every time he went up, bad weather sent him back. Finally, we decided to leave her up there. They say the permafrost at that level will preserve things forever. We used to fly by the site every year on her birthday."

"How old were you?" she asked.

"Nine. After that, my dad quit his job—he was a lawyer representing indigent clients for Legal Aid—and we moved to the bush. It's weird because both my parents had been really liberal do-gooders, but after my mom died, my dad turned into an off-the-gridder. He went from 'It's my duty to help people' to 'People are responsible for themselves. If you're too stupid to take care of yourself, tough shit. You're on your own.' There's a lot of people in Alaska like that, so he wasn't alone, but none of his old friends could understand how he changed. Eventually, they stopped talking to him. Now he cuts down old-growth trees for a living and represents the occasional Inuit against drunk-driving charges, which is actually great, because they pay him in Chinook salmon, the best in the world."

"It must have been terrible, losing your mom."

"It was." He picked up a handful of her hair, held it to his nose, and inhaled deeply. "But it's like you said, you get over it. Unless you don't want to. The first time I went through a whole day without thinking about my mother, it was like learning to walk again after being paralyzed. I was so happy, I told my dad about it, thinking he'd be pleased, but he looked at me like I'd taken a dump on her grave. He didn't want to move on, and he hasn't."

Miranda reached a hand down between her legs. She tried to make the gesture look casual, as if she had an itch. When she looked down at the wetness on her fingers it was clear, like water, but sticky. She wondered if it was him or her but couldn't bring herself to ask.

"What made you decide to tell me this now?" she asked.

"I always tell girls the story right after I deflower them. It's a tradition in our family."

He moved a hand in between her legs. She tensed. Was it too wet down there? Was that normal?

"Seriously"—he moved his hand away—"I know what it's like to have something terrible happen to you out of the blue. I wanted you to know that." She closed her eyes to cool the sting of gathering tears, then put her hand between her leg.

"Is this me or you?" She held her hand in front of his face.

He took her hand and licked it. She shivered with repulsion and desire. Sex, she saw, was like a different country. A place where things that would usually gross you out—saliva, sperm, body odor—became parts of desire. She took her fingers out of his mouth and put them in her own.

"It's us," he answered.

17

*J*oe Fisher pulled up in his van just as Harry was finishing his morning swim. "Hey there, pard'ner," he said, "you ready to unload these babies?"

"I need to get dressed," Harry grumbled. Pard'ner? Babies?

Fisher frowned.

"What?" Harry asked.

"It's just these kids have been in these cans a while . . ."

Harry climbed into the van and peered in. The water swarmed with fish. "Oh, all right," he said.

"Excellent!" Fisher rubbed his hands together. It was, Harry reflected, as if the man had cobbled together a personality from an instruction manual. *Be agreeable. Be enthusiastic.*

Together, they dragged a can to the edge of the pool and lowered it into the water. "These are the pleckies," Joe said. A childlike expression of joy glazed his face as he watched the fish wriggle out to the aqua depths of the swimming pool. After so many hours swimming its length, Harry had come to feel he and the pool were one. Man. Water. Water. Man. But watching the platinum grace of the fish, he saw his delusions. He was a lumbering bear. Not even. The other night he'd watched a nature documentary and been surprised by the fluid beauty of a bear in the water.

Beside him, Joe was making noises like a new father. "Let's get the flying foxes in there before the pleckies feel like they own the place. When I got my first aquarium, I didn't know any better and mixed angelfish with monkey fish after the angels had lived in the aquarium for a few weeks. The next morning, I went to feed them and it was, like, fish massacre. Fish My Lai. Fish Shiloh. Fish Antietam. Fish—"

"Okay," Harry stopped him. *Be smart. Impress people with random historical allusions.*

"The next day, I went back to the fish store and I was, like, 'What the fuck? You said these fish get along,' and the guy was, like, 'Did you add them at the same time?' and I went, 'No,' and he was, like, 'Dude, fish are like gangs. You put the angels in first and they're, like, 'This is angel territory.' It's all trial and error. That's how I found out the pleckies and the flying foxes get along. I've got the two living in a tank right now and it's totally harmonious. Fish Switzerland."

In the water, the pleckies and the flying foxes circled each other, wiggling their tails and bumping noses, as if courting.

"I've written out some instructions for care." Joe reached into his back pocket. "You want to feed them twice a day, but only as much as they will eat within two to three minutes."

Harry was startled. Somehow, he'd imagined the fish would feed themselves. Just like in the ocean. "What if I miss a feeding?" he asked.

Joe blinked. "What do you mean?"

"I mean, what if I'm out for the night and forget?" That was never going to happen. He never left the house anymore. But he didn't want Joe Fisher to know that.

"I can't believe anyone could forget to feed their fish. I mean, you don't forget to feed your kids."

"I don't have kids."

"Fish are a responsibility."

"What happened to, 'Fish are low maintenance?'"

"They are! I have three golden labs. I have to run them for thirty minutes, twice a day, off leash. Their hair needs to be brushed daily. When I think they haven't got enough antioxidants in their diet, I make them vegetables in chicken broth. Fish are low maintenance, but they're not 'no maintenance.'"

Harry said nothing.

"I've disconnected the light and the pool heater," Fisher went on, less heartily.

"Why?" Harry asked, peeved.

"These fish live in waters warmed by the Gulf Stream, but until they're acclimated, cold is best. You know, a lot of my clients don't use their heaters this time of year."

Harry knew it cost a fortune to heat the pool. Catherine was always making snide comments about it. "It's like swimming in someone's old bath water," she complained. But Harry loved the warm water. Being rich hadn't been nearly as much fun as he thought it would be. Once you got used to the upgrade in your creature comforts—the softer sheets, the faster car, the fresher food, the flatter TV—everything felt pretty much the same. His mother, who never owned anything of value, had somehow been right on this point. "It's not what you have," she used to say, "it's what you're used to." But the one thing that exceeded his expectations was the pleasure he got from a warm pool, so if Joe Fisher thought he was going to give that up to keep some fish happy, he was wrong. As soon as he left, Harry turned the heat in the pool back up to 85 degrees.

Harry was mid-nap—a new post-job habit that suited him surprisingly well—when a set of high-pitched screams roused him from his sleep. At first he thought they were part of a bad dream, a psychic aftershock from the accident, but as the fog of sleep lifted, it seemed clear that the sounds were real, coming from the direction of the pool and made by children. He sat up, pulled on his pants, and went outside without bothering to put on a shirt. Over the past two months those doughy little dollops of flesh that used to hang over his belt had disappeared with the swimming, why not flaunt it?

Next to the pool, three young boys in bathing suits were flapping their hands in distress, like sea lions at feeding time. Harry thought they looked familiar, but all children had a way of looking alike to him.

"What the fuck, Harry?" his wife screamed.

"*Catherine!*" a lemon-faced woman in a gingham sundress remonstrated her.

"She said the F-word!" the boys hooted with joy.

Harry recognized the woman's long eyelashes and protuberant bottom lip. She was the wife of one of Catherine's brothers. The children must be hers.

Catherine breathed in deeply through her nose. "What. Are. These?" She pointed to the fish-filled pool.

Harry looked at the fish. They were spread out more evenly now between the shallow and deep end. That seemed like a good sign. "They're some pleckies mixed in with some Thai flying fish."

"Don't get cute with me, buster."

Buster? When Catherine was in the grip of an emotion that she could not control, she reverted to strangely anachronistic words like *buster*, *golly*, *gee*, or his favorite, *gosh*.

"What. Are. They. Doing. In. Our. Pool?"

"Eating algae."

The sister-in-law moved closer. Harry remembered her better now. Once, at a Christmas dinner, glass of merlot in hand, her foot had pressed against his under the table. He hadn't pressed back but neither had he moved it. As a rule, women made carnal by alcohol reminded him too much of his mother, but he hadn't wanted to offend and he had guessed, rightly, that she hadn't the guts to follow through.

"Tell me this is some kind of a joke," Catherine begged. Harry looked at the woman. In the sunlight and sober, she had a warm, maternal charm that was sending some kind of chemical messengers to his groin. Was there any way to get the woman alone? It had been ages since he and Catherine had touched. Probably not. Even if he could ditch the wife, there were children to be considered.

"It's the next big thing," Harry said. "Pools without chemicals. If the fish eat the algae, we won't need all that poison in the water anymore."

"Fascinating." The sister-in-law smiled at him.

"No, it's not fascinating, it's idiotic," Catherine answered. "Who wants to swim with fish?"

"What do you do in the ocean?" Harry asked. Before the accident, Harry was pretty certain Catherine would have shared his enthusiasm for the project. Wasn't she the one who was always writing checks to eco-terrorism groups or clucking her tongue disapprovingly whenever a Hummer passed them on the road?

"Harry," she said, "I want those fish out of the pool. Now."

The sister-in-law began to wrestle her boys into shirts. Disappointment made their limbs unwieldy. Plus, they sensed an adult fight brewing and didn't want to miss a word.

"It's okay," the sister-in-law said. "We'll come another time."

Harry watched the woman's thighs strain against the fabric of her dress as she squatted. There was an appealing, unexercised quality to her flesh that one didn't see often in Los Angeles. He imagined her body would be soft and comforting, a place of solace.

"Why don't they try swimming?" Harry asked.

The sister-in-law swiveled her hips toward him. Through the dark shadow of a V-shaped tunnel of leg, he could just make out a triangle of white cotton underwear. The boys looked from their mother to Harry. "Yeah!" They jumped up and down. "Let's swim with the fishies!"

The mother looked at Catherine uncertainly. "Is it okay?" she asked.

"I don't think it's very sanitary."

"The filter is on. What could happen?" Harry asked.

"How should I know?" Catherine responded. "I'm not a fish expert."

"We're going to swim with the fishies!" the boys chanted, bouncing up and down on their toes.

Harry began to remember her name. Rhonda? Rachel? He was certain it began with an R.

"If you want to risk it, Ruth, that's up to you."

That was it. Ruth. From Philadelphia. A Vassar graduate with a degree in landscape architecture. It was all coming back to him. She'd married Catherine's overbearing older brother, an allergist with bad breath, after he'd identified her toxic reaction to foam rubber. She'd been to eight specialists before she found him.

"I was so grateful," she'd explained to Harry, "I had to marry him." She'd looked Harry right in the eye when she'd said the word. Grateful. Not love. Or lust. Gratitude.

"I guess there are worse reasons to get married," Harry had answered.

"Mmmm," she'd answered, finishing off another glass of wine.

The boys flung their shirts off, ran to the edge of the pool, lifted their knees to their chins, and hurled themselves into the water, cannonball style. So much water splashed out, a few fish landed on the stone surrounding the pool. Harry used the side of his foot to gently nudge them back in the water.

Ruth smiled at Harry in that "Aren't my kids cute?" way. Harry's ardor flagged. Why do all parents assume their brats are charming? Harry never would have had the confidence to plunge himself so recklessly into a pool like those children. He'd been too busy worrying about his mother. Only children who never doubted the hands that fed them could enjoy themselves so wholeheartedly. Watching them, Harry felt the pain of his missed childhood throb like a scar on a damp day. His thoughts were interrupted by a loud "Ow!" coming from what looked like the youngest boy, a pale blond child with a wide gap between his front teeth. "Something bit me!" He pumped his legs in the water like a mixer on high.

The other boys stopped swimming and watched as their brother began to cry. *"Mommmeee!"* he shouted.

"Angus," Ruth said, "get out of there."

The boy launched into a furious dog paddle and pulled himself out of the pool. He was shaking and shivering. Ruth squatted and wrapped a towel around him. "What happened, goose?"

"Something bit me on my leg," he said in between hysterical gulping.

His brothers watched from the pool, torn between being afraid and wanting to stay in the water.

"Show me where," his mother asked.

The boy turned his leg out like a ballet dancer and looked down. The adults gathered round.

"I don't see anything," Harry said.

Sensing skepticism, the boy began to look. "There," he pointed to two tiny red marks just emerging on his calf.

"Oh, my God," Ruth said. "Boys! Out. Now."

"That's not possible," Harry said, "these fish don't bite."

"Ruth," Catherine said, "I am so sorry. Will you bring them again when we get this mess sorted out?"

"Of course!" She kissed Catherine on the cheek and put a hand on the back of each boy's head, without waiting for them to change out of their wet bathing suits. Harry watched her ass as she left.

"Well done, Harry," Catherine said sarcastically.

"Is there a reason you have turned into such a hellacious bitch?" Harry asked.

"Who's the bitch, Harry? You're the one who doesn't have the balls to confront the people who fired you."

"I'm not fired. I'm on a mental-health leave."

"Hello?" Catherine laughed. "Earth to Harry. Everyone and his brother has auditioned for your job since the accident. It's all over the Internet."

"There is a lot of misinformation on the Internet."

"Have you asked Aaron?"

Harry tried to think of some way to contradict her, but everything did seem to be pointing in the direction of her argument. Harry closed his eyes. In his earlier life, rejection at the job had been a constant refrain and he had learned not to take it personally. When he was let go from *The Fire Within*, the executive producer, a sallow, thin-faced man with an intermittent tic and a wardrobe of polka-dot bow ties, had stammered, "This is my least favorite part of my job." Harry stopped him right there.

"Jesus, Harry," the man said afterward. "I wish everyone was as easy to fire."

But this was different. Harry had truly believed that he and *Would You Rather?* were inextricably bound. One and the same. He hadn't asked Aaron because a part of him preferred the illusion that he was still employed, but maybe Catherine was right. Ignoring reality was making him Aaron's bitch.

"Okay," he said, opening his eyes. "I'll go talk to him."

In the elevator, Harry could feel the eyes of a well-dressed middle-aged woman on his face. He knew from the way she glanced at him, looked away, and then glanced back, that she was trying to place him. It was rare for someone to have trouble remembering his face. Even the people who never watched *Would You Rather?* had seen commercials for it during other prime-time television shows. Had he dropped from the radar that quickly? After the woman got off the elevator, Harry studied his reflection in the chrome of the elevator door. It was the hair. For years, he'd been having it lightened to a creamy butter yellow every two weeks. The day after the accident his colorist had come to the house for their usual appointment, but had been scared off by the reporters who swarmed her Audi, demanding information about Harry's "state of mind." When she called later to apologize, he told her to forget it. Until they started taping again, there was no need for the chemicals that made his eyes itch and head ache. Within a week, he'd been surprised by the quarter inch of brown hair that had grown out of his skull. Now, it was a full inch and a half with streaks of gray running through it like an agate geode. The remaining blond hair had acquired a greenish tone from all the chlorine in the pool. No wonder the woman hadn't been able to place him.

The receptionist at Aaron's office smiled coldly at Harry. He knew her type. The rest of America saw Hollywood as a babe magnet sucking the country's beauties west with the promise of stardom. There was truth in the cliché—park yourself on Sunset Boulevard on a Saturday night and you could easily believe the world was populated by preternaturally toned young blondes with pneumatic bosoms and eyes hardened by the reality of beauty for sale. But for every one of those girls, there were three like the appraising receptionist. Bright, ambitious, well educated, they came to Hollywood because the maleness of Wall Street turned them off, publishing paid nothing, Silicon Valley was too geeky, nonprofits were depressing, and universities weren't hiring. Entertainment was one of the few industries where women could rise to the top, and unlike the arrogant young men who began with them, they had no problem starting as assistants who picked up dry cleaning and answered phones. If the boss needed her birth-control prescription filled or her kid picked up from a playdate? Not a problem. On weekends, they read scripts, wrote "coverage" on them, and went out drinking with their peers. If they were any good, in two years they could count on a development job with an expense account and a job title sufficient to impress their parents back in New Jersey. As long as they hadn't passed on the next *Star Wars*, from there, it was on to a studio job, a house in the hills, and if they were lucky—the man shortage was a constant refrain—a husband, kids, and a full-time nanny.

In general, they did not date the "talent" but Harry had gone out with a few early in his career. Always, the dates went the same. She showed up looking good in a short black dress, no stockings, high heels, hair slicked back in a ponytail both girlish and mannish. Over dinner (broiled fish, no butter), she drank a lot of white wine, "split" a dessert, talked mostly business gossip, let Harry pay the check, invited him in for "a nightcap," had vigorous sex with him, and then asked if he wouldn't mind leaving, since she had an early meeting. At first, Harry thought the women liked him. Why else would they initiate sex like that? Without asking himself whether he actually liked them back, he'd call the next day. He didn't want to be like those shmucks who made his mother cry. If the women were high up enough to have assistants, someone would take a message that was never returned. Sometimes he saw their names on top of projects for which he was being considered. He never did get those jobs.

Some details had changed in the intervening years. The ponytails were gone, replaced by a long, shaggy haircut. Short skirts had been replaced by pants cut low on the hip and high heels with pointy toes, but the receptionist giving Harry a cold eye was definitely one of them. No question.

"Hallo, Mr. Harlow," she said, "what time is Mr. Kramer expecting you?"

"He's not, actually. I wanted to surprise him." Was that the newest thing, Harry wondered, a phony English accent?

"Lovely," she answered. "If you'll have a seat, I'll let him know you're here." She waited until he was seated, just out of earshot, to make the phone call. He picked up the latest copy of *Variety* on the coffee table and, out of habit, went straight to the back, where auditions were announced.

Hispanic male 24–26, attractive, for Tostitos commercial.

Hip kids, 8–10, for cereal commercial.

Tap dancers who can sing, under 30.

No ads for a forty-five-year-old game show host with gray-green hair, but one did catch his eye:

Tired of acting in dreck? Need to revitalize your career? Consider Shakespeare. The role of a lifetime. Renowned English director now casting *Hamlet*. GREAT SHOWCASE POTENTIAL. Males, 20–60. Female, 25. Any ethnicity.

Shakespeare. Harry had never bothered. On *The Fire Within*, he used to make fun of the pretentious East Coast actors who talked about the "bard" they'd done in New York. *Barf* was more like it. Now, however, something in him stirred at the idea. He was a big success, wasn't he? Why not stretch a little at the height of his powers? He coughed loudly as he ripped the ad from the page. The receptionist smiled vaguely in his direction, mimicking sympathy.

"Harry!" He looked up to find Aaron's assistant, Emmy, looming over him. He stood and let himself be enfolded in a cloud of green tea and baby powder.

When she pulled back, Harry saw she was wearing a telephone ear- and mouthpiece like a Secret Service agent or an old-fashioned telephone operator. "How are you?" she asked, pushing aside the mouthpiece.

"Fine," he said, with a shrug. "I'm not the one who was hurt."

Emmy nodded, never taking her brown eyes off him. "I know, but just being there, that can be hard, too."

Harry nodded. "Well, thanks, Emmy. I appreciate your taking . . . notice."

"Of course." She squeezed his arm. Emmy wasn't like the hard-eyed girl behind the desk. She was sweet, a little plump, and would make some- body a very good wife, but she wasn't the kind of girl Hollywood dickheads wanted to date. Aaron once told him she spent a lot of time in the bathroom crying.

"Is Aaron around?" Harry asked.

Emmy shook her head, as if saddened by something. "He's on the set with a client. He'll be so sorry he missed you."

"Oh." Harry nodded. "Tell him I dropped by, will you?"

"Of course!" Emmy nodded her head.

Together, they walked toward the exit. When Emmy used her em- ployee ID card to open the door leading to the inner offices, Harry put a hand on the door, holding it open for her. He saw fear in her eyes.

"Thank you, Harry."

"Not at all." He pointed down the hall in the opposite direction from her office. "I'm just going to use the little boys' room."

"Okay." She smiled, and glanced nervously toward Aaron's office.

In the bathroom, Harry pissed, washed his hands, splashed water on his face, and tried to pretend his heart was not racing.

When Emmy saw Harry walking toward her desk, her eyes widened in terror. "Harry," she whispered.

"Relax, Emmy, I'm not going to shoot you."

In his office, Aaron was calmly staring out the window, as if he'd been waiting for Harry.

"When were you going to tell me?" Harry asked, sitting across from him in a leather club chair from the 1920s that supposedly was owned by Fatty Arbuckle.

"It's on my list of things to do, right under getting a colonoscopy."

"Why?"

"You know what they say. There are four stages of life in this town: Harry who? Get me Harry. Get me a young Harry. And, Harry *who?*"

"I thought I was 'Get me Harry.'"

"You were. But then you had a high-profile accident when your contract was up for renewal. A show gets too associated with one host, that's not good for business. You might get greedy. You might die. Who knows? The network saw an opportunity."

"Son of a bitch."

"We had a good run. That's all you can ask for. Remember when I found you? You couldn't even buy lunch. Besides, you told Boyd you didn't even like the job."

"Isn't that, like, privileged information?"

"He works for the show."

"Can't we fight them?"

Aaron made a steeple with his fingers and pressed them against his forehead. "Sometimes, things are done that can be undone. But not in this case."

Harry looked out the window. On the street, the light had been flat and oppressive, the sky the color of wet cement, but in Aaron's office, the room glowed with the golden light of a wine commercial, an effect produced by a special uv filter made of finely spun fourteen-carat gold. "You don't want to know what it cost," Aaron had once told him, his voice swollen with pride.

"Are you going to continue to represent me?" Harry asked.

"How can you ask?"

Harry shrugged. How could he not? Aaron started to chew on a hanging cuticle.

"What do I do now?" Harry asked.

"Nothing. I'm trying to hammer out as big a severance package as I can." It wasn't what Harry meant.

"Maybe this is a good thing. I've been thinking I ought to stretch my wings. Maybe do a little Shakespeare."

Aaron smiled. "I am sure there are people who would pay to see that."

"The problem is, I'm not a very good actor."

"For a man without talent, you've done very well. That's something."

Harry had a sudden urge to smash his fist into Aaron's smug face.

By the time Harry got back to his car and paid the parking garage, rush-hour traffic had begun. He slowly eased his car out of the garage exit but sat frozen, waiting for someone in the line of cars crawling down the street to let him enter. Before the accident, he would have nosed his car into the mass, forcing someone to let him in. Behind him, an asshole in aviator glasses beeped. Harry went back to concentrating on the traffic. A gap appeared. Heart thumping, he turned on his signal and slowly merged.

When he got home, the house was dark. Catherine had left a note. "Out for the evening. Dinner in oven. Heat 450, 10 mins. C." He lifted the tin foil. Vegetarian pizza. When they were first married, Catherine insisted he go everywhere with her but now she went out without even asking if he wanted to go along. It occurred to him that maybe Catherine was getting ready to leave. He let the novelty of the idea settle into him, waiting for some kind of reaction. Wounded pride. Loneliness. But there was only relief. Not for the first time, he found himself wondering if he was even capable of love. Every time he thought he'd found it, the feeling would always fade. Sometimes sooner. Sometimes later. But, eventually, it always died. When it came to love, he had a black thumb.

He decided to go swimming. Emptying his pockets, he came across the page he'd ripped out of Aaron's *Variety*. *Tired of acting in dreck? Need to revitalize your career?* He walked over to the full-length mirror in their closet.

"To be or not to be?" he asked his reflection, one eyebrow arching. Even he could see it was all wrong. More like a parody of a snooty waiter.

He tried again. This time, he wiped all inflection out of his voice. "To be or not to be?" he asked in a monotone. But that was wrong, too. He seemed depressed. Like a hollow man.

He took off all his clothes, wrapped a towel around his waist, went outside, and lowered himself slowly into the warm water of the Jacuzzi next to the pool. Tiny bubbles clung to the hair on his thighs. His prick looked small and shriveled in the aqua blue water. He'd been reassured on several occasions that he didn't need to worry in the size department, but how could he trust what any woman said? They were all so damn eager to please. Until they weren't. And then they turned so mean. Or sad. Even his own mother. As often as he had offered to come visit her when she complained about her loneliness, he'd always been secretly relieved when she'd said no.

One thing was certain, he wasn't going to try out for that play or any other. As of that night, Harry decided to give up being an actor once and for all. He was sick of trying to do something he wasn't good at. He'd been around enough talent to understand that the people who could make you believe without feeling embarrassed for them, the ones who mysteriously blossomed in front of a crowd, were naturals. They weren't smarter or funnier or happier or better-looking than Harry. Usually, they were pretty miserable sons of bitches or just barely sane women, but they had something Harry did not. Talent.

Having made the decision, Harry felt suddenly unburdened. Lighter. Freer. Like he could run a mile in a minute. He climbed out of the Jacuzzi and went to the edge of the pool. In the dark, the fish seemed to be executing an elaborately choreographed ballet of intertwining chains of flesh, their silver skin twinkling like Mylar in the wind. Harry eased his body into the water. On his first lap, the fish gave him a wide berth. On the second lap, he felt something hard touch his left leg. What the fuck? He looked down into the water but could see nothing. Something nipped him on the back. Harry lunged for the stairs, gripped by a sudden atavistic fear of dark water. He turned on a light in the pool house and looked at his calf. There, above his ankle, were two tiny red marks. The kid was right. The fish were biting.

The next morning, Harry left an angry message on Joe Fisher's voice mail. "I guess you forgot to tell me the fish bite. Call me."

Half an hour later, he watched Joe Fisher's van pull into the driveway. He knew he ought to go outside and confront him. Instead, he went to the kitchen and took his time brewing a cup of cappuccino. Normally, he found the ritual of grinding coffee beans, monitoring the water level of the steam valve, waiting for everything to reach the boiling point tedious at best. Today, he took his time with each step, glad for an excuse to avoid confronting Fisher. He knew he ought to be angry. The problem was, he liked the fish. It made him happy to see them swimming in the pool, reclaiming the water as their own, redeeming the vainglorious scoop of concrete and water. But Harry also liked to swim. How, he wondered, did people in Europe manage it? He took a sip of the cappuccino, scalding his tongue on the too-hot liquid. He looked up when Catherine appeared in the doorway. Usually she wore sweatpants or stretchy leggings around the house but today she was wearing a fitted shirt and pants that looked uncharacteristically grown up, as if she were getting ready for a job interview.

"We need to talk," she said, lowering her herself onto one of the bar stools that lined their counter. The chairs were Shaker-style, webbed with bright yellow and red cotton. She bought them with the help of an interior designer whose bill for services was twice the cost of the actual chairs. Harry watched as she took a deep breath and looked down at the folded hands on her lap. When he'd worked on the soap opera, he'd seen a million bad actresses do the exact same thing right before delivering bad news. Take a breath. Look at hands. Confess infidelity. Take a breath. Look at hands. Announce you have cancer, had sex with your brother-in-law, spent the household expenses on cocaine. What, he wondered, accounted for the sameness? Had all women watched so many of the same movies that they unconsciously absorbed the behavior, or was it something deeper, more atavistic? Look at your hands in readiness for a fight, take a breath in preparation for flight?

"I want a divorce," she said.

Harry held his burned tongue against the roof of his mouth. He remembered a similar morning only a few years ago when Catherine had worn the same pinched expression, as if she were wearing shoes that didn't fit. "My family wants you to sign a pre-nup," she'd said, "but I trust you and I don't need that." In fact, he had often thought of that morning as he wrote checks for the clothing bills or the massage therapist or the hair cutter or the shrink or the new car, or all the other things he paid for in Catherine's life.

"Okay," he answered, "have your lawyer talk to mine."

Catherine's eyes widened in surprise. "That's it? You don't want to talk about it?"

"Not really. Do you?" Harry could see that his answer had thrown Catherine off her script.

"What about closure?" she asked.

"I think it's been closed for a while."

"I was hoping you'd move out of the house," she said in a small, wavery voice.

Harry laughed. "Why would I move out of my house?"

"*Our* house," she corrected him. "We live in a community-property state."

"I bought the house before we were married."

"The house has doubled in value. I picked it out. My father says I'm entitled to half the appreciation."

"Since when is your father a lawyer?"

"He knows about these things."

"Is this what you meant by 'closure'?"

"I don't want this to get ugly, Harry."

"Divorce is ugly," Harry answered, putting his cup on the counter. "I have to go. The pool man is waiting for me."

"Is he getting rid of the fish?"

Outside, the air was uncharacteristically crisp and clear. Somewhere, high above, Harry had the sensation of winds sweeping the sky clean.

He found Joe Fisher standing, naked, in the pool, his back to Harry as he slowly raised and lowered his arms. All around him the fish swirled, occasionally butting their heads against his flesh. Harry couldn't decide whether to be afraid—the man was clearly nuts—or angry, so he settled on a mixture. "Hello?" he asked.

Fisher turned slowly, like a man with whiplash. "Friend," he greeted Harry, slowly raising an arm.

"Can I ask?" Harry asked.

"Testing a theory. On a reef, a big fish pulls in and these guys rush over to eat him clean. It's called symbiosis. One species helping another."

"I know what symbiosis is," Harry answered, folding his arms over his chest. Why did people always assume he was more ignorant than he was, and how could Joe Fisher stand to let the fish get so close to his dick?

"What we need to do is get these fish used to humans. Once they understand that I don't have any barnacles or algae growing on my skin, they'll stop bugging me."

"How long do you think that will take?"

Fisher shrugged. "I've been here half an hour and they're still munching."

Harry tilted his head to the side. "Can I ask you a serious question?"

"Shoot." Fisher ducked. "Ha, ha. Just kidding."

"Are you, like, crazy?"

"People have said so."

"Have any of them been wearing white coats?"

Fisher pirouetted slowly, trailing a boa of fish. "One or two, but don't you have to be a little crazy to get out of bed in the morning? I mean, otherwise, the news is pretty bad."

Harry was inclined to agree, but he didn't want to be aligned with someone like Joe Fisher. He rolled up his pant legs, sat on the edge of the pool, and cautiously lowered a leg into the water. A few stragglers bumped and bit his leg, but he forced himself to keep it in the water. If you were prepared for it, the bite wasn't so bad.

"Anyway, how sane are you?" Fisher asked, prancing like a satyr, half man, half goat, one leg up, one leg down. Harry tried not to look at his prick flopping through the water. "You live in a big house you never leave. You don't seem to like your wife. You're famous, you're rich, you're good-looking, but . . ." He shrugged his shoulders.

"Maybe I'm not a people person," Harry said.

"Everybody is a people person."

"What makes you such an expert?"

"I'm a student of humanity."

"Are you married?"

Fisher shook his head.

"Girlfriend? Boyfriend?"

"Negativo. I realized a long time ago that most of life's problems could be traced back to sex. Getting it, losing it. Getting it again. Losing it again. If I stopped having sex, I'd no longer be sending all that useless energy into the world."

"Are you serious?"

"Never more."

"Do you jerk off?"

"I used to, but then I decided it was like saying you're a vegetarian who eats chicken." He took a breath and submerged himself underwater. A few bubbles escaped to the surface.

Harry watched his gold hair undulate gracefully under the water, like sedge grass in the sea. "Are you lonely?" Harry asked when he reemerged.

"Sometimes. But then I go to a meeting."

"What kind?"

"It doesn't matter. Alcohol. Sex. Drugs. Food. It's all the same. What matters is being in a room where people are not full of the usual shit. You'd be surprised how life-sapping the superficial can be." He tilted his head, one eye closed—piratelike—against the glare of the sun. "You should come with me sometime."

"I don't drink."

"Me neither."

"Isn't that, like, against the rules?" Harry remembered a controversy a few years earlier when people started using AA meetings to hook up.

"The rule is, there are no rules. That's the beauty." Fisher looked down into the water. "Look at that."

Harry craned his neck to see better. A few of the more stubborn fish were staring lidlessly at Fisher's leg, as if they were expecting it to suddenly grow a barnacle. "I don't see anything," he said.

"Exactly," Fisher agreed. "They stopped biting."

"Wow," Harry said.

"People think fish are stupid, but they can learn from their mistakes."

Somewhere, over the euonymus hedge, a house door slammed. Harry felt the muscles on his shoulders tense as his wife's feet crunched on the gravel of the driveway. Her face, furious, squinched, and red, rose above the hedge. "You haven't heard the last from me, Harry Harlow." For a brief second, he thought she was going to stick her tongue out at him. Instead, she turned, slammed a car door, and was gone.

"That's my wife." Harry looked at Joe Fisher. "She's leaving." He started to add a pronoun. *Me. She's leaving me*, but then Harry thought better of it. "When's the next meeting?"

18

ờ

S ophia was standing in front of a bulletin board outside the ICU, contemplating the implicit heartbreak of an ad for a size 20, never-worn wedding dress when the social worker whom she disliked approached.

"How are you?" the girl asked. Her braided hair lay inert and obscene across her shoulder, like a fat black sausage.

Sophia let herself sigh theatrically. She was so weary of the question. "Terrible," she answered. "But thanks for asking." She turned her attention back to the bulletin board but the girl refused to go away.

"Have you considered getting some support?"

For a second, Sophia had the confused idea that the girl was talking about support hose, those stockings that kept everything smooth but left her feeling as if her organs had been smushed. She shook her head, partly to dislodge the image that was tempting her to giggle.

"People say it helps," the girl said.

"I'll think about it," Sophia promised.

When she got home that night, the girl's voice was on the answering machine, leaving the address of the next meeting of PALOC (Parents Accepting the Loss of a Child). Against her better judgment, Sophia wrote down the details. The next day, she waited for an excuse not to go. When none appeared, she found herself driving to a Methodist church off Wilshire Boulevard in the middle of rush-hour traffic. *I don't have to do this*, she kept telling herself, even as she pulled into the mostly empty parking lot.

Six o'clock, she checked her watch, the hour of heading home from work and starting supper for the family. But not in this crowd.

The meeting room was depressive-functional—metal folding chairs, a chalkboard with no chalk, a Mr. Coffee, and a can marked CONTRIBUTIONS WELCOME with a smiley face next to it. Racially, it was a surprisingly diverse group—black, white, Asian, Hispanic—a regular UN of grief. But Sophia recognized certain shared traits—a sad, ducking way of entering the room, as if to avoid a cobweb. But also a flicker of defiance, that wondered, *Why me?* What had they done to bring on this fingerprint from hell? There wasn't even a word for what they were. Mothers without children. It left them feeling marked. Cursed. Into every life a little rain must fall? Fine. Let a job be lost. A tire blow. A ceiling fall. But not this. And if it must be, let it happen to someone else. Not me.

Only one woman, a youngish redhead with the soft body and engorged breasts of a recent mother, had her husband with her. It did not surprise Sophia that men avoided that room. When she told Darius she was thinking of going to the group, he had looked horrified.

"Why?" he asked.

"It can't hurt," she had answered, unsure if that was actually true.

Some of the women smiled in Sophia's direction. She wondered if they recognized her from television and that awful day when the cameras had caught the family ducking in and out of the hospital, but decided against it. They were smiles of complicity for the newcomer, meant to make her feel included, but all they did was make her feel raw on the inside, scraped free of the skin she had worked so hard to grow over her wound. Maybe it had been a mistake to come.

At fourteen minutes past six, a plump woman with frizzy white hair bustled into the room like someone who was chronically late. She smiled vaguely at the faces turning her way. Her name, she announced in between pants, was Helen. Sophia exhaled noisily at the coincidence. Helen was a nurse. She got the idea for PALOC four years earlier, when her only child, a five-year-old boy, had drowned at a birthday party in a swimming pool teeming with children. Helen was not at the party. She had volunteered for overtime that weekend. The pay—time and a half—was too good to turn down and she was saving up for a trip to Sea World, an obsession her son had developed after seeing the movie about the whale and the little boy that had been so popular that year.

"For years," Helen said, rocking back and forth from the heels of her feet to her toes, "I blamed everyone—the children in the pool, my husband for not wanting to go to the party, the other parents for watching only their children, the EMS workers for not getting there sooner, the hospital administrators for asking me to work overtime, the people who made the film about the whale, the whale. I even blamed Timmy for going swimming in the first place. He was only a 'guppy,' but he thought he was a great swimmer because that's how kids are, isn't it?" Helen surveyed the room, looking for agreement. Sophia was surprised at how inattentive most of the women appeared, but then she realized that they must have heard this story many times. Only the redhead was sitting on the edge of her seat, a look of ecstatic sympathy animating her features. Go on, her body language screamed, then what happened?

"I think that's what we love about our children," Helen continued, "they don't know they aren't good at things. In Timmy's mind, he was a shark, and that's why it's so easy for me to understand what happened next. He was in the shallow end, where he'd promised his mommy he'd stay, but over there"—she gestured toward an imaginary pool, somewhere in the back of the room—"in the deep end, he could see the older kids playing and he probably thought, That looks like fun . . . so he started heading toward them, using the doggie paddle, the only stroke he really knew." It alarmed Sophia to see Helen mimic a dog swimming, cupping her pudgy hands and moving them back and forth in a digging motion.

"What I can't understand," Helen said, the sweetness draining from her voice, "is what happened next. He drowned in only five feet of water. Five feet! Did Timmy panic when he realized how far he had wandered from the shallow end? Did he start to thrash around and call for help? What did the children around him think he was doing? I guess I've spent a thousand hours watching kids play in the pool and I've seen it again and again—there's always one who likes to pretend he's drowning. 'Help! Help!' he'll yell, breaking your heart with worry until you get there and he starts laughing and smiling, as pleased as punch that he fooled you. Maybe that's what the kids thought Timmy was doing. Maybe that was why nobody took him seriously. They probably didn't even know him because he didn't really have a lot of friends. He was a little shy and a little overweight. That was one of the reasons we were so pleased that he had taken an interest in swimming. We thought it might help with the weight. And when he got invited to the pool party, you should have seen how happy he was. . . ."

As she spoke, her face flushed a deep red, as if she had been exercising vigorously. She reached into her purse, took out a white Kleenex, and blew into it loudly. Sophia thought of her own Helen. Would it have been easier to lose her at five, instead of sixteen? Five was such a good age. The best, really. Old enough to be out of diapers and bed wetting but still filled with the awe of the world and still needing you to explain it. By sixteen, you have a glimmer of the way they will abandon you, seeking love in the arms of boys or respect from adults against whom you will be unfavorably compared. Even as you know it is right—children who stay forever coddled in the family home seem particularly pathetic—it breaks your heart a little. No, Sophia decided, she should count herself lucky compared to this wreck of a woman; not only did she still have Miranda, she had the luxury of seeing her Helen almost whole. Almost an adult.

She smelled him before she saw him—a mixture of alcohol, unwashed clothes, and the raw-onion smell of old body odor. She turned to look. A thin, pale man with several days' growth of a scratchy white beard was sitting at the end of Sophia's aisle. Her stomach flopped at the smell but after a few seconds, she let herself glance at him again. His once-white T-shirt was gray and misshapen, his tan corduroy pants were filthy, and he exuded a frightening fury. At first, she assumed he had mistaken the meeting for Alcoholics

Anonymous, but some of the women seemed to recognize him. If one could call the look of revulsion that passed over their faces recognition.

"Of course," Helen continued, "the person I blamed the most was me. I was Timmy's mommy. I should have been there, looking out for him, but I wasn't. And no matter how many 'grief counselors' have told me again and again that it wasn't my fault, it was. I know it. You know it. We all know it. If I had been there, there is no way Timmy would have drowned." Helen began to weep openly. A woman jumped out of her seat to put an arm around her. The man on Sophia's aisle crossed his arms and let out a sigh of contempt. Something in her was gratified by his attitude. She had a lump in her throat from Helen's story, but a part of her resented having her emotions stirred, the way she would hate herself for crying at a sad song or a sentimental movie. She might have left, had it not required squeezing past the crazy man.

Finally, Helen's tears subsided and she looked up, surprisingly calm and composed. "That's what we're about here at PALOC," she said, "having a place where you can break down and cry and nobody is going to judge you. Nobody is going to tell you 'Move on,' or 'Put the past behind you.' You don't have to put on a brave face or say you're sorry for crying your heart out. We know it's not easy. We know what it's like to have friends who don't want to see you anymore because you're too much of a downer, or lose your job or your spouse because you can't pick yourself up and move on. For some of us, it's not possible. Not now. Not ever. You might not always feel that way, but if that's how you feel right now, well, we are here to support you." Everyone in the room applauded, except Sophia and the man in her aisle.

"I see there are some new people in the room tonight," Helen said, looking directly at Sophia and then the redhead. "If you would like to get up and say something, we welcome you." Sophia shook her head slightly and looked at the floor, but the redhead stood and eagerly walked to the front of the room.

"Hello, my name is Kathy."

"Hi, Kathy," the crowd responded.

"I can't tell you how happy I am to be here," she began in a gush and then stopped herself, suddenly aware of how wrong her words sounded. "I don't mean happy . . . what I mean is, I'm happy to have found a place." She looked to her husband for help, a large lunk of a young man with huge hands and feet, whose short hair and fit body made Sophia think he was, or recently had been, in the military. He continued to stare at the ground. Kathy took a breath and started again. "All my life, all I wanted was a large family for me and Craig. Nine months ago, it seemed like God had answered my prayers, when I found out I was pregnant with Melissa." She touched her stomach when she said the girl's name, as if the fetus were still swimming around in her amniotic mush. "I did everything I could for Melissa. I painted her room pink and filled it with dolls, I ate a lot of vegetables and took all the right vitamins and I prayed all the time, thanking the Lord for sending us such a gift but for some reason, I was sick all the time throwing up with terrible headaches, and my body kept swelling up, getting bigger and bigger." She looked at her own hands in wonderment, as if they belonged to someone else. "I knew God intended women to have pain in childbirth as punishment for what happened in Genesis, but he didn't say anything about *before* birth. I had to quit my job as a dental hygienist because everything about the job made me throw up. People were nice at first, the dentist I worked for told me to take my time, go home if I needed to, but by the fourth month of my pregnancy, I could only work an hour a day. After that, I just stayed home, lying in bed, watching television and eating as much as I could to keep the nausea away.

"The only thing that made it worthwhile was feeling Melissa kick in my belly, knowing that she was there, waiting to get out and say hello to the world. One day, about a month before my due date, I noticed that Melissa hadn't kicked in a while. I thought, Oh, well, that's fine, she's just resting, getting ready for the big day, so I didn't really think anything about it. And that is one of things that bothers me to this day, because my doctor said to me after the whole thing happened, 'Why didn't you tell me she had stopped kicking?' But how was I supposed to know? Melissa was my first baby.

"So I went to the doctor for my regular appointment and I urinated in the cup just like they told me to and put out my arm for my blood pressure, and right away I knew something was wrong, because the nurse took my pressure three times. After two times, she even switched me to a different room to use a different machine, because she couldn't believe the number she was seeing was correct. And the look on her face, I'll never forget it. 'Stay here,' she said to me, like I was going to go anywhere. The next thing I know the doctor came in the room, looking all worried. He took the pressure again, just to make sure, and he can't believe it, either. Then he asks, 'How's the urine?' and the nurse, who's looking kind of panicky, says she'll check. And once I am alone with the doctor he starts asking me questions about pain in my stomach, headaches, nausea, swelling. I tell him I've had it all, but then I've been telling him that the whole time, and he always said, 'Don't worry.' Then the nurse comes running back and she doesn't even look at me, she just says straight to the doctor, 'Three plus.' Nobody tells me what that means, but the doctor says, 'Damnit,' which I didn't really appreciate because I am a Christian, but then he looked at me very serious and asked me to lie on my back, they're going to check the baby's heartbeat, so I pull up my blouse and lie down and wait. It was always my favorite part, listening to her heart race so fast, like a horse's hooves.

"I know the doctor is worried but I'm not. If something was wrong with Melissa, I'd know. I mean, I was her mother. So he started moving that thing that looks like an electric shaver over my belly. And he moves it here and there and I can hear something that sounds like a heartbeat pounding away, but he keeps looking. So finally I say, 'Isn't that it?' and he looks down at me like he's forgotten I'm even there, and he finally kind of smiles at me in a nice way and says real gentle, 'No, Kathy, that's your heartbeat.' And I am kind of surprised, because he's so far from my heart down there and we've never had that problem before, so I lay back down and wait for him to find Melissa. Finally, he hands the thing to the nurse, who's looking even sicker now, and leaves the room.

"Now I am beginning to get a bad feeling, and I ask the nurse what is going on, but she just tells me not to worry, it's bad for the baby for me to get upset, which seems funny because everything they've done has made me upset. Then the phone rings and the nurse picks it up, and it seems that the doctor has called an ambulance to take me to the hospital, where they are going to do a sonogram to get a good look at Melissa. I ask if I should call my husband, who has just gotten a job as an assistant manager at a Home Depot out by Toluca Lake, and the nurse says that would probably be a good idea. So I got up and they let me use the doctor's office so I could have some privacy. I make the phone call sitting at his desk where I can see all the pictures of his kids and a few of a black dog. The store pages my husband. It takes a long time, and when he finally got on the phone, I didn't want to worry him too much, so I told him I'm at the doctor's office and they want me to go to the hospital. I guess that was the wrong thing to say, because he assumes that I am going into labor and says, 'Honey, that's great! I'll be right there.' And I am trying to tell him I don't think it is so great, but then I decide, maybe he's right. Maybe this is it. So instead of getting sad about it, I decide to get happy. Maybe the good Lord has just decided that we have waited long enough and Melissa is ready to meet her mommy and daddy.

"At the hospital, I have to wait a long time for the man who does the sonogram to show up. Luckily, my husband, Craig, was there by then, and he was keeping me in good spirits saying, 'Any minute now,' and asking if I was in pain and if he should start timing the contractions. I didn't really have the heart to tell him I wasn't in pain so I'd say, I think that might have been one every few minutes. Then finally the guy who does the sonograms shows up and they wheel me into a room, and it's really dark inside, and I am a little surprised that he's an Oriental man and it's just him, there's no nurse or anything else, but I guess it's okay because my husband is there with me, and he holds my hand, and the man starts moving that thing over my stomach and punching things into a computer. Right away, I can see that Melissa looks different from the last time. She only moves when the man pokes her and her hands look kind of floppy. The man who's doing the measurements frowns and I try to catch his eye so he can tell me what's going on, but he just keeps staring at the screen. And I just figure that's how it is with Orientals, you never can tell what they're really thinking, but still I am beginning to feel really bad and then all of the sudden he gets up and says he'll be back.

"While I am lying there, I just get a really bad feeling and the only thing that makes me feel better in times like that is the Lord's Prayer, so I just start saying it out loud. 'Our Father, who art in heaven, hallowed be Thy name,' over and over. I think I had repeated it about twenty times when the door opened, and in comes this older nurse, a black woman, which kind of makes me smile, because the whole hospital is like one big melting pot. And she takes my hand and sits down next to me and asks how am I feeling and would I like a glass of water or a Coke? I say no. I haven't been drinking Coke ever since I got pregnant. I didn't think the caffeine would be good for the baby and she nods and says I'll be a very good mommy someday. And I kind of regret giving her that opening because then the next thing she says is that this child was not meant to be and I start arguing with her right there, saying Melissa was definitely meant to be. I know, because the Lord told me, and I can see she is glad that I am a believer because she's also wearing a little gold cross around her neck, and she starts saying that the Lord works in mysterious ways and maybe this baby was too good for this world and that is why the Lord sent her straight to heaven, and that's when it hits me full on in the face. They think Melissa is dead.

"I didn't even cry right away. I just swallowed real hard and got very serious and said, 'What do we do now?' because I knew they were wrong. I knew she was alive. So I figured we would just deliver her and then everyone will see that she is just fine. I could see the nurse was glad I wasn't going to fall apart on her right there, though she would have been a good person to fall apart in front of. She had nice hands. Warm and dry and callused, like she had spent her whole life working hard, probably raising plenty of her own babies. I can see why they'd go find her whenever they had bad news. So she tells me she is going to find me a room and get a doctor to talk to me about the next step. And then just to show her that I am not a person without a sense of humor, I tell her, I believe I will have that Coke now, and she smiles and says, 'Right away.'

"As soon as she leaves the room, I sit up and tell Craig not to listen to them. Melissa is fine. But I can tell from his face that he is torn apart. It's like a truck drove over him and all he can keep saying is, 'I don't believe it, I don't believe it.' And I tell him he should pray with me, and I got down on the floor right there and closed my eyes and prayed as hard as I could. A few minutes later, some men came with one of those beds on wheels. I told them I could walk just fine but they said something about insurance regulations, so they wheeled me down a bunch of hallways and I kept my eyes on the lights on the ceiling, thinking that all the people I was passing probably thought I really was sick. And then I was in a room with one of those beds you can adjust up or down and a television on the ceiling, and a doctor finally came to see me. A woman, which was interesting, because all my life I'd only had men doctors, and she started off saying how sorry she was about what had happened, but I waved my hand and told her I didn't want to talk about it, so she got down to business, telling me there were two ways we could do this, either by inducing delivery with drugs, or a C-section, which she said would be quicker and less trying on me, though the recovery would be longer and I would have a scar for the rest of my life, but it would only be small and I could still wear a bikini if I wanted to. Not that I would ever wear a bikini. I asked her which would be better for the baby and she looked kind of surprised. 'Kathy,' she said, 'that doesn't matter anymore.' And then I asked her what she would do, and she said that under the circumstances, she thought a C-section would be best. So I said okay, and I signed some papers, and she left to get cleaned up.

"Next thing I know, they wheeled me into a room with a lot of bright lights and strapped my arms down like I was Jesus on the cross, and a young man who looked Jewish told me he was going to give me a shot and then asked me to count backward from ten, and I think I got to four and I was out. When I came to, I was still on the operating table but I couldn't see anything because they'd set up a big blue tent over my body and all I could feel was a little bit of tugging, and that was when I started to say the Twenty-third Psalm, which I had been saving for just such an occasion: 'The Lord is my shepherd, I shall not want, He maketh me to lie down in green . . .' And then somehow I knew Melissa was no longer in me, because everybody looked at me and I could see a flash of something that was purple, like the color of a bruise, and I tried to move or make a noise, but I couldn't move anything, and then the next thing I knew I was out again. When I woke up after that I felt strangely pleasant, like I'd had a long, refreshing sleep. Craig told me that was the drugs, and it surprised me because I've never taken drugs and somehow I always thought they'd make you feel evil, but these didn't. They made me feel good. So of course the first thing I said was 'Where's Melissa?' But nobody knew, not the nurses or my husband. One nurse said she'd find out. After about ten minutes nothing happened, so I pressed that button next to my bed with the nurse hat on it. Someone came in my room and I said it again, 'Where's Melissa?' She said, 'Who's Melissa?' and I said, 'She's my baby,' and she said she'd try to find out and that was how it went for about two hours before the doctor came in. I told her I wanted to see Melissa and she said, 'Are you absolutely sure?' and I said, 'Yes, of course I am,' and she told me it might not be good for me, they were still monitoring my blood pressure and there was a risk of seizure and it wouldn't be good for me to experience too much stress, but I told her I didn't care. She could see I was adamant on the topic and wasn't going to be swayed so she left.

"About ten minutes later the black nurse who first told me about Melissa came in with a bundle of white blankets. She looked very sad, not like someone who is carrying a baby at all. 'Here is your precious angel,' she said, handing me the bundle. Inside was the funniest-looking creature I'd ever seen. It didn't even look human, more like something from *Star Wars*, with rubbery purple skin and a little bit of hair on her head. And she was so tiny, not like a baby at all, more like one of those troll dolls they used to sell when I was little. I was so sure that she wasn't Melissa, I gave her back right away and said there was a mistake. That was when the black lady and my husband looked at each other in that so-called meaningful way. I told everybody I was very tired and I wanted to sleep and they should leave.

"They both turned to go, but, then I started to panic. What if that really was Melissa? This would be my last and only opportunity to really look at her. So I said, 'Wait a minute. Just leave her for five minutes.' The nurse and my husband looked at each other like they didn't want to do it, but I told them I'd be fine and I guess they realized they didn't really have a choice, so the nurse brings back the bundle and leaves, but my husband stays and I tell him I just want a few minutes alone with her, so he leaves, too. And then it's just me and that little-old-man monkey. I could still feel a little warmth of life on her skin. So I unwrapped her and held her head next to my cheek, and her skin is surprisingly soft. Like a baby. And I looked at every single inch of her, from her perfect toes and feet to her tiny fingers, about the size of an inchworm, and that's when I know that it probably is Melissa and that's the only time I'm ever going to be able to hold my baby."

She had the room in the palm of her hand, that overripe redhead with her embarrassed husband and her bewildered sincerity. Even Sophia. Even the angry man on her right. Even with all her talk of Jesus and the Lord and the Bible, everybody wanted to hear what happened next. They wanted to know how she got up the next day and the next and the next. She knew it, too. It was obvious from the way she looked around the room and held her audience's gaze. She knew she had a story so terrible that nobody could turn away from her, a girl who'd never had the presence or the wit to hold the attention of a room full of people in her life. Even when she got married, she'd been aware of people in the back pew talking among themselves. She could not have anticipated how good it would feel to be the center of all that attention but for the first time since she held that dead child, she felt free, unburdened by the story that had been brewing inside, twisting around her entrails with its feverish desire to be told. Ever since Melissa died, she had wanted to yell at every face in the grocery store, at church, in the hospital, everywhere she went. Sophia understood. Everybody in the room did. They felt it, too. It was the outrage of the survivor. How dare the world continue so utterly indifferent to their grief?

"I knew then," the redhead concluded quietly, "nothing would ever be the same for me again." If only she had stopped then. If only she could have left them with that one small, bitter truth. But she could not. So she did what she had been taught to do all her life.

"But I can't be too sad." A false smile strained her face. "Because I know Melissa isn't dead. She's just gone to heaven. Because on that day, God must have needed another angel." And then she sat down, leaving behind an embarrassed silence as people contemplated the implausibility of the logic. Why would God do such a thing? Sophia suddenly became aware of the agitation of the man next to her. His hands gripped and ungripped the back of the seat in front of him as he battled some invisible gryphon.

"God didn't take Caleb!" he suddenly yelled.

"Now, Anthony," Helen stood as if to create a barrier between the troubled man and the young woman. Sophia could see flecks of white spittle coming out of his mouth.

"The devil took my boy," Anthony said.

The redhead opened her mouth as if to offer an argument, but nothing came out. Beside her, the husband was suddenly roused from his torpor, rising to his full height. "Just a minute," he said, "you can't talk to my wife like that." Anthony's palms opened and closed. Sophia thought of a sea horse furling and unfurling its tail. She suspected that Anthony would welcome violence.

"Why would God take a little boy?" he asked contemptuously, "because there is no *God*, there's only shitty luck, and everybody in here has it." Sophia was inclined to agree.

Helen spoke in a surprisingly gentle tone. "Anthony, why don't you give us an update on Caleb?"

Sophia, and every parent in Los Angeles, remembered the story. More or less. The boy was young, maybe eight or nine. An only child and some kind of a musical prodigy on the cello. Or maybe it was the violin. Usually, his parents walked him to the bus stop, but one day, after much begging, they let him walk alone. All day, his mother worried. At three o'clock, when he didn't get off the school bus, she called the school. Caleb never made it to class that morning. In the aftermath, everybody agreed it had been a terrible chain of events. The school should have called when he didn't show up, but it was a public school—one of the good ones, but over-crowded and overwhelmed with children who regularly did not show up to school. There was talk of a lawsuit. She could remember Caleb's face from the extensive coverage on the news—jughead ears, crooked smile, straight brown hair trimmed unfashionably in a bowl cut. Even years later, one occasionally came across a tattered old poster. Have You Seen Me? Caleb's face asked in each of them, listing an 800 number. The media onslaught had been relentless, driven by his frantic parents, who made nightly appearances on the news. The father was an engineer. The mother worked in health care, or maybe she was a social worker? It seemed impossible that the man on Sophia's right could be that man.

"Update?" Anthony said the word sarcastically. "There's no fucking update. Caleb left our house at seven forty-six a.m. on a Thursday morning and never returned. No one has seen or heard from him since. And now nobody gives a shit because he's yesterday's news." The redhead Kathy began to cry softly. Her husband took her arms and tried to lift her up. "Come on," he said, "let's go."

"Anthony," Helen said, "I've already told you, we can't have that kind of language in here."

The redhead was standing, tears streaming down her cheeks. Her husband was trying to get her to move, but her arms hung lifelessly at her side as she stared at Anthony.

"I remember Caleb," she said. "We prayed for him at church."

"Yeah? Well, it didn't work."

"I'm so sorry," she said.

Anthony looked away as the husband pulled her down the aisle, past Sophia and Anthony.

"God loves you," she said as she passed.

Anthony shook his head. "Bullshit." But his voice lacked its earlier fire.

Sophia could see the meeting was about to break up, so she rose, determined to leave before anybody could approach her. In the back row of the room, she passed two strange-looking men, both of whom stared at her as she passed. She thought they might be a gay couple, as one of them had the fading cartoonishly handsome looks of a comic-book character. Los Angeles was full of men who looked like him, but they tended to live on the other side of town and never bothered to look at people like her. However, this one was openly staring, as if he'd been expecting her a long time. She frowned slightly and looked away. As she passed, he rose from his seat, as if to follow. She quickened her pace. His leaving had to be a coincidence, she told herself.

"Excuse me," Harry said to Sophia's back as she put a hand on the door leading to the parking lot.

Sophia tried to pretend she hadn't heard, but then the man was next to her, addressing her face-to-face.

"Yes?" she answered with a frown.

He opened his mouth. "I wanted to say . . ." Harry began, and then stopped. He wasn't sure what he wanted to say.

Sophia made an effort to soften the expression on her face. Perhaps he and his gay lover had lost an adopted child, one they'd had to jump through numerous hoops to get in the first place. Maybe they had adopted an AIDS baby who had died of complications from the virus. Or a Romanian orphan who'd hit adolescence and killed himself with an overdose of pills. Who could tell what kind of trauma people carried tucked into their solar plexus, just out of sight, ready to leap out at the first sign of sympathy?

"I'm Harry Harlow."

Sophia brought her hand to her mouth. "Shit," she said, dropping it again. Harry Harlow was a name she had come to hate almost as much as Bobby Goralnick, a.k.a. Virgil Tilden. The police said it wasn't his fault and he had never been charged, but in the same irrational way she secretly blamed Siri for not driving Helen, she had come to hate Harry for being there. In that car. At that moment. His celebrity only made matters worse. What would it matter to him that a girl's life had been crushed like a cigarette butt? His life, in all its glittery fineness would go on unchanged, untouched by the tackiness of tragedy. Then again, why was he at the meeting? Was he stalking her? She forced herself to look him in the face. Close up, Harry looked older than he had on television (she had watched a rerun once for five minutes so she would know what he looked like). The skin around his eyes had gone soft. His flesh had that velvety droop that presaged old age, and his hair was a weird yellow, black, white, and gray, like a wild mushroom she'd once seen in a rain-soaked forest. Under his chin, a small swell of flesh that would only grow as the years passed seemed to quiver at that moment with some unexpressed emotion.

"I want you to know," he began to say, "how very, very—"

Sophia held up her hand. "I know," she said. She looked toward her car longingly. How much more of this would she have to endure before he would let her go? "You're very, very sorry. Everybody is very, very sorry. I know that." She rattled her keys and took a small step toward her car.

"If you think I'm crazy, I'll understand, but do you think I might come visit her sometime?"

Sophia gasped at the audacity of the idea. "No. My husband would . . ." She couldn't finish the sentence because she didn't actually know what Darius would do. Punch him? Hug him? Once upon a time, she could have predicted with reasonable accuracy how Darius would react to things. Not anymore. It was as if they lived in a new world. That she and Darius looked the same, sounded the same, dressed the same, seemed irrelevant. Inside, they were as altered as could be.

"Of course." Harry looked down. "It's only, I've been thinking of setting something up. Some kind of fund. Maybe a memorial. A foundation." He was winging it now, making things up, throwing words around. He'd never had those thoughts but now that he was saying them, he liked the sound of the words. The meeting seemed to have tightened his focus, given him insight into what ailed him. It was the girl, of course. He'd been too afraid to really think of her before, but seeing the mother somehow made it possible. The man driving the motorcycle was dead. There was nothing he could do for him, but the girl was alive. If he could help her, he might actually feel okay again. Better than okay. In some perverse way the accident had actually improved his life. His bad job and lousy wife were gone. The girl had done that but he had only brought her misery. Running into Sophia had to be part of a design, the universe reminding him that a bill had come due.

"It's not necessary," Sophia said, moving toward the parking lot, away from Harry's obsessed, feverish gaze. He raised a hand as if to stop her, but Sophia turned and ran to her car.

19

Miranda crossed the busy commercial street that bordered the campus on the west, mulling the tone of Jason's voice on the phone.

"Are you breaking up with me?" she'd asked when he suggested coffee, trying to make a joke out of it. The four weeks since they had slept together had been the happiest of her life. She was only slightly reassured by how quickly he'd answered. People blurt good news out on the phone; it was bad news that required a face-to-face meeting, the solace of flesh on flesh.

"If you were breaking up with me," she pressed, "would you tell me?"

He'd taken time to give the question genuine consideration. This, she'd thought in the synapse of the moment, was why she loved him. He took her seriously, even when she was being stupidly, girlishly insecure.

"Probably not," he'd finally answered.

"Well, you can't break up with me. My sister is in a coma."

Miranda scanned the Starbucks for a good table, miraculously finding what she was looking for right next to the window in the front. A good sign, she tried to tell herself as she placed her books on the round table. As she sat, she looked up to find a scowling young woman holding a container of coffee.

"I was about to sit there," the girl said.

"I'm sorry," Miranda answered, "I was obviously here first." *Bitch,* she silently added, using a napkin to push a constellation of crumbs on the floor.

The girl stuck out her bottom lip. "You don't even have your coffee yet," she observed.

"I'm waiting for my boyfriend. When he gets here, I'm going to order." Miranda resented having to impart so much personal information to a virtual stranger, but there was no way she was giving up the table.

The girl turned her head to look for another empty table, then sat down. "Fine," she said, "we'll just share it." She took out a book—*Ideology and Utopia*—and started reading.

Miranda glared at the girl. In principle, she frowned on people who fought with strangers, but the girl's assumption that she could do as she wished, combined with the arty knee-high stockings she wore, the little-girl tartan kilt cut high on her thigh, and the ubiquitous dangling iPod earphones around her neck, infuriated her. She curled a hand around the girl's coffee and stood up, holding the cup at shoulder height. The cardboard was warm to the touch. "You can't sit here." The shock on the girl's face made Miranda feel powerful and reckless, like a person who could change the world.

"*Excuse* me?"

"No, you're not excused. This is my table. I was here first. I can't share it with you because someone is about to show up and he will need that chair. I asked you nicely."

She watched the girl scan the room for someone who could help. A few of the students at nearby tables were watching them with interest, but when the girl tried to catch their eyes, they looked away. On the other side of the room, Miranda saw Jason enter the shop. She saw how she would look to him. A crazy woman holding a latte hostage. But backing down at that moment would be impossible. She had made a stand and had to see it through to its end. From the concerned expression on his face as he approached the table, Miranda guessed that Jason was probably not going to understand how important it was that she prevail.

"Miranda?" he asked, staring at the coffee, which she was holding awkwardly, like an unfamiliar weapon. The girl seemed to sense that Jason would not support Miranda. "Could you get a muzzle for your girlfriend?" she asked.

"I was minding my own business, waiting for you, and this woman walked up and put her coffee down. I told her I needed the seat, but she refused to leave."

"Obviously, this table is more important to her than it is to us," Jason said slowly, looking around the room for another table.

"Actually, this table is important to me," Miranda answered. "She can have her coffee back when she leaves."

A boy—barely twenty by the looks of him—appeared. A tag on his shirt read "Tom, Manager," but he looked as if he'd rather be anywhere else. "Can I help?" he asked.

"Thank God," the girl said. "Can you please tell this crazy woman to give me back my coffee?"

The boy's forehead was shiny with a thin layer of perspiration. Suddenly, Miranda's anger guttered like a spent candle, replaced by a queasy sense of embarrassment. When did she become the kind of person who could not let go of a slight? Was this, she wondered, what happened to people who had been hurt by the world? Did they became powder kegs, ready to blow at the slightest provocation?

"Fine." Miranda walked to an empty table a few feet away and put the coffee on it. When she returned, the manager was handing the girl a gift card. Jason was staring at one in his hand, a bemused smile on his face, as if he thought it was all a big joke. The value was ten dollars.

"Let's go," she said to Jason.

"Come again," the manager said, nervously pointing a card toward her. She shook her head.

"I don't know why you are giving her one. She's the one who created the scene," the girl said.

"Pathetic." Miranda rolled her eyes at the girl.

"Freak show." The girl sneered.

Outside, on the street, she felt absurd but right. "Sometimes you have to take a stand," she said, without looking at Jason's face. He took her elbow and guided her back toward campus and the always empty lawn facing the math building. A long time ago, her father had pointed out that the lawn in front of the English building was always packed, while this one was always empty. Miranda sat cross-legged and sullenly picked a blade of grass. If he was going to leave her, she had certainly made it easy for him.

"What's up?" she asked.

"Nothing. We can talk about it later." He ran a thoughtful finger up her bare calf, as if he were counting the follicles of black stubble beginning to sprout.

"Look, it was stupid of me to get upset. But we can't always control how we feel." She withdrew her leg, making a mental note to shave that night.

"Tell me about it." He took her hand and kissed the open palm. Miranda willed herself to relax. A person who was going to break up with you wouldn't kiss you like that.

"Tell me what you wanted to talk about. I'll be in a bad mood until you do."

Jason sighed and rolled over on his back. The bright sky made his eyes a deeper, almost violet blue. There were times when the sheer loveliness of him left her breathless.

"I have to go back to Alaska," he said.

"I know."

"No, I mean I have to go back next month, at the end of the semester."

"Oh." She hoped it sounded innocent, a small word registering surprising news and not what it was, a reaction to a knife in her gut. "Why?"

He sat up. "I told you my dad represents a lot of Native Americans who get stopped on drunk-driving charges?"

"Yes." Miranda nodded her head, trying not to ponder the ethical implications of that fact.

"They've done studies. The Indians lack a chemical for metabolizing alcohol. More than two beers, they're blotto. But up there, they have to drive fifty miles to get anywhere, so when the cops are bored, they round them up. They never pay him because it's paycheck to paycheck for most of them, if they even have a job, and my dad doesn't want to take money out of their families' mouths. So it's more like a hobby than a paying job. Anyway, there's this one guy, Willy Loman."

"Really?"

"No. His real name is Lomaw, or something like that, but a judge got it wrong once and the name stuck. Willy is Athabascan and one of the worst offenders. His driver's license has been suspended a dozen times, but my dad has been friends with him forever. Anyway, last month the government announced it was opening up the Tongass region to logging."

Jason looked at her to see if the name meant anything to her.

"It's old-growth spruce. Usually it's shit for anything but pulp, but this stuff is top grade."

"They cut down the old trees?"

"They leave every third tree standing. Letting air and light in allows the saplings to grow. Still, it's controversial. This is an area that has literally never been logged. To make the tree huggers happy, the government is only giving permits to Natives with valid logging permits. It's kind of a sham, because they need the money upfront to rent a helicopter."

"What for?"

"Heli-logging. There's no roads and the nearest river is ten miles away. It's the only way to get the wood out. It's dangerous, but my dad knows a guy who flew a medevac in Vietnam. He can get anything out of anywhere. Willie's got a permit for six months only. After that, the region could be closed for another fifty years. To pay my Dad back, he's giving his permit to my father. Or he's making him a silent partner. My dad will give Willy a percentage of the profit, but he needs me to come help. I know it might sound silly, but in the logging world, this is like winning the lottery. He could make enough money to retire."

"Oh." He *was* leaving her.

"I'll be back," Jason said.

"No. You won't."

"Yes. I will."

"Things will be different."

"Things are always different."

"Don't get philosophical. You're abandoning me."

Jason rolled over and pinned Miranda down with the full weight of his body. "Can't you wait for me?"

He must have weighed fifty pounds more than she, but somehow, it was easy to breathe with him on top, as if their breaths were inversely coordinated. She out. He in. A lock and a key. That wasn't something you walked away from.

"Take me with you," Miranda said.

He laughed.

"No." She pushed him off. "I mean it."

"Believe me. You don't. For the next four months, the sun will rise at ten in the morning and set at two. People go crazy this time of the year. They shoot each other or drink themselves to death."

"People shoot each other here because someone changed lanes without signaling. I'm getting in arguments in coffee shops over a window seat. It would be good for me to get out of here."

What she didn't tell him was that she was failing all her classes. The accident had happened so early in the semester, she'd missed half the lectures. It might have been okay if she were at all familiar with the topics, but over the summer, she had pored through the course catalog, self-consciously choosing a syllabus that was, as her father said, "all over the map."

"I thought it would be good to, you know, expose myself to a lot of different things," she'd answered.

"You can't go wrong with Professor Dalton," Darius had said approvingly of the art history teacher, "but I don't know anyone in economics or environmental science."

"I think that's the point," Sophia had observed over the rim of a wineglass. Once Miranda finally started attending classes, she wished she had heeded her father's advice. Listening to econ lectures about supply-demand curves or monopolies versus duopolies, it all seemed both incredibly obvious and extraordinarily difficult.

"There's nothing to do up there in the winter," Jason said.

"I could help you out. I could make your lunch, keep the house clean."

Jason laughed. Miranda was not noted for her neatness.

"You're saying no without even thinking about it."

"Miranda, we don't live in a nice house with curtains and Oriental carpets."

Miranda winced at the description of her family's bourgeois home. "I don't care," she insisted.

"You will when it's twenty degrees below zero and you have to use the outhouse because we don't have indoor plumbing."

Miranda blinked. What happened to piss at those temperatures—did it freeze midstream? Was that possible?

"Or when the only people you ever see are loggers who haven't had a shower in weeks. And the only green thing you eat comes from a can, and you're so sick of dried salmon, the thought of it makes you want to puke."

"Okay," Miranda said quietly.

"Or when you can't get a satellite signal for a week because it's been snowing for five days and no plane can get through."

"Jason."

"Or you're boiling coffee grounds for the third time."

Miranda stood, hoisted her book bag onto her shoulder and started walking. She regretted the petulance of the gesture but wanted to be alone, like a dog, with her pain.

He followed her. "Look, don't you think I'd love to have you there?" he asked.

"Apparently not."

"Listen to me." Something unfamiliar in his voice made her stop.

"It's my dad. I try and paint him as this 'colorful' character for people, but honestly, he's not colorful, he's fucking crazy."

"How crazy?"

"Crazy like he hasn't had a shower since I left."

"I don't believe you."

"Crazy like threatening to scalp the census taker. Crazy like his toenails look like something from the *Guinness Book of World Records*. Crazy like he and Willy Loman can drink Everclear for three days then threaten each other with chainsaws and nobody raises an eyebrow because it happens all the time."

"The logging thing was a lie?"

"No. It's all true. But, apparently, ever since I left he's gone downhill. If I can get the trees cut, I might be able to get him some real help."

"Honey." Miranda put her arms around him.

"I don't want anyone to feel sorry for me," Jason said stiffly.

"I don't feel sorry for you. I feel sorry for him."

"He just wants to be left alone. But if I don't do something, he'll die of something stupid like gangrene from an ingrown toenail, and I'll spend the rest of my life feeling guilty."

"I want to come. There's nothing for me here. I'm failing my classes, my sister is a cauliflower, and my parents don't know I exist. We can help each other. If I can't stand it, I can come home."

"I might be able to find a house. People move up there all the time thinking they want to live off the grid. After one winter, they're ready to go home."

"It sounds perfect."

20

S ophia and Darius seemed to be leading separate but parallel lives. They took their own cars to the hospital, sat apart in the waiting room, and timed their meals so that they would not be in the cafeteria together. At home, Darius had begun to sleep in the guest bedroom, a small afterthought of a room tucked under the attic staircase. As they had upgraded the furniture in the rest of the house, the bedroom had become the repository of all the un-wanted, mismatched objects accumulated along the way: the nightstand painted a muddy eggplant, the clunky Colonial headboard, the rag rug heavy with years of dust. Next to the bed, a gooseneck faux-Tiffany lamp left by a favorite aunt gave off an ochre light insufficient for reading. The small, diamond-shaped window under a dormer hadn't opened in years. A loud, square fan circulated the trapped, stale air. Sophia alternated between satisfaction that he was suffering in such an uncomfortable room and a physical ache over his absence. They'd never had an argument linger so long, and the strain was beginning to take its toll on her body—her neck and back hurt, as if she'd tried to lift something heavy. At the hospital, she could feel the nurses taking in their new, estranged seating arrangement. Mind your own business, she wanted to say to them. But did not. It had been four weeks since their fight. Three months since the accident. It was time to make up with her husband.

"I'm leaving now," she said to the top of her husband's head, bent over a heavy textbook he'd been lugging around the last few days: *Spinal Injuries: Causes and Cures.*

"Mmmm," he said, without looking up.

"I'm going shopping and then I am going to make dinner."

Darius looked up. His glasses had slid halfway down his nose. She had to restrain herself from reaching forward and giving them a push.

"Dinner," he repeated, his voice flat.

"Yes." Sophia nodded. She knew she ought to say more, to invite him or say something conciliatory, but she felt she'd gone far enough. Darius knew her well enough to understand that this was as close to a peace offering as she could manage.

"Okay," he said, ducking his head. "We'll see you then."

He always used the impersonal *we* instead of *I* when he wanted to let someone know he did not entirely approve, but Sophia knew what he meant. Invitation accepted. Détente. For now.

Shopping at the overpriced gourmet grocery store in their neighborhood, Sophia ignored the prices and bought what she wanted—ripe red tomatoes from Chile, massive shrimp from Indonesia. She could feel a festive stirring inside, as if she were planning one of the dinner parties she used to give when Darius was a young academic, striving to impress his elders. In line, she smiled sympathetically at a woman with two black eyes and a gauze headdress. Postoperative. People used to be embarrassed about plastic surgery, but now they went everywhere in the bandages. Sophia used to look down on those people, but now that her own face had begun to sink and sag in unfamiliar places, she found herself rethinking her position. Once she'd gone so far as booking an appointment for a "consultation" with a plastic surgeon but had canceled the day before. Where was she going to get $5,000 for an eye job when her kids were about to start college?

When Darius arrived home, Sophia was at the sink, deveining shrimp. On the counter lay the stalk of fennel he had bought at the organic market a few days earlier. Its edges had gone a little brown, but with some careful trimming it should be just fine. She had already opened a bottle of Pinot Grigio—because the sauce needed it, she told herself—but was struggling to keep from finishing a whole glass before the meal was prepared.

"Bouillabaisse," he observed. His favorite dish. Sophia nodded, waiting to see if he would acknowledge the peace offering. Monty came scampering down the back staircase, his long toenails clicking on the wood floor. Darius sat at the kitchen table and scratched the dog's ears. A good sign. The last few days, he'd come home, gone straight to the library, and ordered Indian takeout without asking if she wanted any. Sophia slid a paring knife across the back of a shrimp, extracting the glassine-like thread of its digestive tract. It was her least favorite part of the preparation, and when she was feeling lazy, she left it in, but tonight she was carefully removing every trace of black.

"Is someone special coming?" he asked.

"I asked Miranda, but she was seeing her boyfriend."

"Jack."

"Jason," Sophia corrected him. It was a mistake he never would have made a few months earlier, when the appearance of a young man in Miranda's life would have occasioned much speculation between the two of them. As it was, they'd only met him once, briefly, in the driveway, when he'd dropped off Miranda after a movie.

"He seems like a nice young man," she ventured. "I think he actually called me 'ma'am.'"

"Yes," Darius agreed, trying to remember something distinct about his daughter's first boyfriend. Having been a professor so long, he had developed a classification system for his students. Mostly, they weren't that different from when he and Sophia had been in college. There were the stoners and slackers who arrived at class messy haired and glassy eyed; the jocks with their coiled, confusing energy; the hipsters wearing black and affecting an ironic diffidence way beyond their years; recently, he'd noticed a whole new category he privately called the thugs. Kids, sometimes black, but usually white, who dressed like gangsters with do-rags on their heads, jeans that barely covered their asses, and oversized basketball jerseys. Jason was at the other end of the spectrum, in a category he dubbed "Mormon." Respectful white kids from the middle of the country who dressed conservatively, called men "sir," and inevitably wrote their papers on concepts like honor and duty in the Henry plays.

"He's not at all what I would have predicted," Darius said, squeezing his bottom lip between his thumb and forefinger.

Sophia used the tip of her knife to remove the black shrimp feces lodged under her fingernails. "Who were you expecting?" she asked, taking a sip of wine.

"I don't know. An East Coast kid. Someone with a goatee. The hipoisie."

Sophia moved on to the fennel, expertly slicing the end off the bulb. The cooks in her parents' restaurant had taught her the proper technique, using the fulcrum of her shoulder, instead of the wrist, the way most amateurs did it.

"I see the charm in him," she said. "He's got a low-key, Gary Cooper thing going. You were like that, at his age."

Darius grunted. Handsome men usually had something cruel in their face, a mouth that got meaner with time or a brow that expressed permanent impatience. With Darius, his face had gotten kinder, more generous. Out in the world, women responded accordingly. She could not leave him alone in the produce department without some divorcée asking the best way to cook manioc. "Uh," he'd answer nervously, looking for Sophia over the woman's shoulder, "I could ask my wife."

Sophia dumped the shrimp in the broth.

"Did you know," Darius asked, "there's a paralyzed man in Peru who is communicating with his doctors through a computer chip?"

"What's he saying?"

"He's just responding to simple yes-or-no questions, but it shows that he can think, even if he can't move."

"*Je pense, donc je suis,*" Sophia said.

"Exactly." Darius smiled. She immediately felt guilty. Just because she understood his viewpoint didn't mean she agreed with it.

"Has anyone asked, 'Do you want to stay alive in this state, yes or no?'"

"No," he answered coldly, glancing at his watch. "I think I'll grade a few papers before dinner."

As soon as he left, she drained the glass of wine and poured herself another. Over dinner, the silence hung awkwardly between them, sapping her appetite. Once upon a time, conversation had flowed gracefully between them. Like good dancers attuned to each partner's move, they had intuited each other's responses, ceding space and time accordingly. Now it was all herky-jerky fits and starts, as if the weight of their secrets were making them stumble.

After the dishes had been put away—a joint exercise in civility—she suggested tea in the room they ambitiously called the library. While Darius made it, Sophia tried to formulate a strategy of what to say and when, but it was like playing chess. Two moves in, and her mind shut down, overwhelmed by possibilities. Darius put the tray on the coffee table, something vaguely Art Deco made out of teak that they'd picked up twenty years earlier in a Goodwill in San Francisco, certain they'd replace it when they felt prosperous enough.

"I hear you've been talking to Kelly," he said, lowering himself onto a seat across from her. Kelly was the social worker who had suggested the PALOC meeting. Mostly Sophia tried to avoid her. It was Darius who seemed to have long, intense conversations with her in the hallway outside the family waiting area. "She says we need to decide where to send Helen by the end of this week." Darius carefully brought his teacup to his lips.

Sophia looked away. Something about his gesture made him look old and frail, as if she had glimpsed a future version of themselves. "They've been saying that for weeks," she shrugged, drinking her tea quickly, like whiskey, to offset her husband's daintiness.

Darius reached into his pocket. "I think they mean it this time." He handed Sophia a list.

She read the addresses—San Pedro, Simi Valley, Harbor City, nothing within a forty-five-minute drive. "These are terrible," she said.

"There are other options," he answered.

"No." Sophia shook her head.

"Don't you want to hear what I have to say?"

"I know what you're going to say."

"She's our daughter. She has a right to come home."

"We're not trained professionals, we're not capable of taking care of her."

"It's not hard to learn. People make the choice all the time. I've been to a group. You should hear what people say. It changes their lives."

Sophia imagined her daughter upstairs in her bedroom, hooked up to a ventilator, limbs twisted into a semi–rigor mortis, tubes coming in and out, suppurating bed sores, the constant wheeze of the machines filling the house twenty-four hours a day. What would happen if a lung collapsed or her heart stopped? In the hospital, Darius always left the room when the nurses changed Helen's catheter or wiped her behind after a bowel movement. Who would do all that? Sometimes Sophia liked to imagine Helen was conscious inside her head, silently watching everything that was going on around her. Other times, she looked at her and saw only inert proteins— blood, bones, hair, teeth. It was possible for her to hold both versions of Helen in her head. All Darius ever saw was a Helen who had gone into a temporary slumber. Despite what every doctor had told them. "Why does every doctor say she's gone?" she asked.

"Doctors say what they were taught to say in medical school. The field is changing every day. A hundred years ago they were burying people in comas because they thought they were dead."

"I think"—she faked a yawn—"I'll go to sleep."

"They've found coffins with scratch marks on the *inside*."

"Good night."

"I told you about the autopsy in Madrid? The one where the patient woke up? They drove that doctor out of town on a rail."

The next morning, Sophia stayed in bed until she heard Darius's car pull out of the driveway. She tried to think of a reason to get out of bed, but the best she could do was coffee. She went downstairs to make a large pot. Ever since she had started drinking more heavily, her mornings had begun to feel queasy and blurred. When she was younger, a medium-rare cheese-burger and a hot shower were enough to clear up hangovers, but now they seemed to linger longer, even gaining in strength as the day wore on. She tried to read the paper but her mind kept wandering to Darius. They would make it up somehow, wouldn't they? Everything that bends does not break, does it? And yet even as she repeated those teabag aphorisms, a part of her feared this was different. Something had changed. He seemed uncharacter-istically irrational to her, like one of those anti-abortion kooks and their mindless veneration for the primitive blastocyst. It wasn't as if she wanted to pull the plug and he didn't. She wanted to keep hope for Helen alive as much as he did, but not by turning their home into a hospital. It wasn't the work that frightened her. She'd sat by her bedside long enough to know that taking care of an inert body wasn't all that different from tending a newborn. You fed them, you cleaned them. If you loved them, you did it gently, with tenderness. If you didn't, you did it with indifference. What frightened her was the relentlessness of it. Home was a refuge, a place to escape sickness and death. If she gave that up, she didn't know if she could survive what had happened to them.

Yet the more she and Darius argued, the more convinced each had become of their own positions. Sophia remembered that this was what it was like to be a child. To have such strong feelings but no way of bending the world to your will—it was why two-year-olds threw tantrums.

"Stability," she said out loud, "is an illusion." It was an old joke between them. They'd been renovating their kitchen when the contractor, a philoso-phy grad student who never managed to finish his dissertation on Wittgen-stein, had pulled up the linoleum to discover joists that looked like brown cornmeal. "Termites," he said, as if he'd been suspecting them all along.

Sophia had kicked the rotten wood, instantly creating a five-inch gash. "Oh, my God," she'd said with a shiver, "this could have collapsed at any moment."

"Stability is an illusion," the contractor answered.

The phrase became a shibboleth to the universe of their marriage. Upon hearing that the couple across the street was breaking up, finding their favorite restaurant shuttered, or watching a colleague depart for a better job, Darius and Sophia would look at each other, shrug, and say it. "Stability is an illusion." But before, the joke had always been on others.

To get her mind off the subject, Sophia tried writing thank-you cards for the food and flowers that had arrived after the accident.

Dear Max and Judy,

And then she stopped. What was there to say?

Thank you for the veal meat loaf you brought by when our daughter's skull was smashed like a pumpkin after Halloween. The garlic was just the right touch to make us forget the motherfuck fuck fucking tragedy of our lives.

Eventually, she settled on:

Dear Max and Judy,

Thank you.

She stared at the two words on the card. They seemed cold and lonely, without any kind of buffer to warm them up. She took her pen and added a short vertical line over the period.

Thank you!

Breezy, given the circumstances, but it would have to do.

21

a nton was reading a short story by a Czech writer in a six-month-old copy of *The New Yorker* when the phone rang.

"Hello?" He did his best to sound like a citizen of the world, filled with optimism about the near future, but the chances were high that the person on the other end of the phone was from the Punjab and calling about a bill that had not been paid. He had learned to dread the polite persistence of their rhetoric. "We value you as a customer, when do you think you might be able to make the payment?"

"Mr. McDonald? Have you directed any *feelms* yet?" The voice laughed. Cyrus Dumond. Anton's heart began to race. Every week, he had been writing down names of former film school classmates as proof of his alleged job search. Most of them had jobs in the business, but none had the power to actually give him a job. Having worked his way through the class, he'd begun to recycle a few names. Was Dumond busting him?

"A job came in you might be qualified for. 'Experienced cameraman needed. Union not necessary. Day rates, two hundred fifty dollars.' That's more than I make."

"Really?" Anton asked.

"I'm not in the habit of making jokes about a man's livelihood."

"Do they need a reel?"

"A what?"

"Nothing."

"Given the fact that they want you to start work tomorrow, I gather the previous employee walked off the job in a somewhat precipitous manner." Dumond gave him an address off Ventura Boulevard in the Valley, told him to show up at eight a.m., and wished him good luck.

Anton stared at the address. Outside, the sun was the deep yellow of an egg yolk. Headache-making light. He rarely went to the Valley but he knew its reputation. Korean nail salons. Sushi restaurants. Moms in SUVs. Pornography. The grease pan collecting the film industry's leftovers. Did Cyrus Dumond know that? Anton's friend Scudder once worked as a grip on a two-day shoot filmed on a boat moored off the Catalina Islands. The first day, he said, he had a hard-on the whole time. The second day, he was disgusted by the sight of a human body. His girlfriend claimed Scudder was never the same in bed after the experience. Anton wasn't sure what she meant and never asked.

He needed the money. More important, he needed an adventure. In the three months since he had lost his job, he'd been having the literally sickening feeling that the world was moving forward while he was stuck in one place. Like the inner-ear confusion of sitting on a stopped bus watching another bus in motion. But Anton was afraid of sex. He'd done it once in high school and a few times with two girls from film school. Each encounter had been a fumbling, knee-bumping, nose-crushing exercise in awkwardness. Every time he got close to a girl, he could smell the onion odor of fear rising off him. His hands trembled like an old man's, and he could hardly breathe long enough to maintain a decent kiss. Everywhere he thought to put his hip, there was girl flesh getting crushed, her whimpering a soft "ow." Sorry, sorry, he'd mutter.

At first, he thought it was because he liked the girls too much. So when pale, square-faced Maddie Famm, who had a mouth like a grouper fish and protuberant eyes that took everything in without blinking, had asked him out, he'd said yes. Maddie wanted to be a screenwriter, but nobody could tell if her scripts were comedy, suspense, or horror.

"Let's just say, it's a metaphor," she'd say unhelpfully in the seminars in which students discussed their work.

"Well, Maddie, you're either a genius or an idiot," the teacher answered.

"Genius. Definitely."

Maddie was flat as a board. When she walked, it was as if her torso were connected to a different body. Hips swiveling to the left, waist arching to the right, like a robot. Also, her arms were disproportionately long, which made her look vaguely simian. Anton decided her unfortunate personality had been formed defensively, in response to the cruelty of other children. But when he mentioned as much to her, she laughed.

"No fucking way. I was totally popular."

Like him, Maddie would go see any movie. When they ran into each other at an Iranian film festival at the Los Angeles Academy of Art, it would have been more awkward to sit apart, so they sat together, allowing a provisional friendship to spring up between them. She was the only person he knew who could happily debate the merit of all ten films in Kieslowski's *Decalogue*. They even agreed on which was the best (the first) and the worst (the eighth). He probably never would have made a pass at her had she not said on their fifth outing. "So, are you, like, waiting for an engraved invitation or what?"

"What?"

"Are you going to ball me?"

"Ball?"

"Fuck. Shag. Hide the salami. Do the nasty. Whatever you want to call it."

Interestingly, things had gone better with Maddie than with any other girl. In bed, with her boyish breasts and wide hips, he felt like an Iowa farmer making love to his plain, hardworking wife. A woman chosen not for her feminine charms but her ability to pull a plow, pop out babies. If only she'd kept her mouth shut, things might have worked. But in bed, Maddie had a mouth like a longshoreman. "C'monbaby," she'd whisper in his ear during sex, "fuckmehardwithyourbighardcock." It made Anton blush and, worse, go temporarily soft. It surprised him that she never noticed.

"Is there something wrong?" she finally asked one afternoon. Her bare breast was pointing toward the ceiling, but if it hadn't been for the dark aureole surrounding the nipple, he wouldn't have known it was a breast.

"No," he answered. "Why?"

"Sometimes you look like you're in pain."

"I'm just not used to so much, you know, talking."

"All the books say communication is healthy."

"I'm not sure if 'Fuck my wet pussy' is communication." He'd meant it as a sort-of joke, but he recognized the offended look on her face from their writing seminar.

"Well, I'm a verbal person. That's what gets me off." She'd raised herself up on both elbows, filling the sacs of her breasts with flesh.

Anton hadn't known what to say, so he'd stayed quiet. In retrospect, he could see that had been a mistake.

"You know," she said, "maybe this isn't working out."

"Okay," Anton said, and nodded. Too late, he saw her cringe from the phantom blow of his rejection. And he had only been trying to be accommodating!

After that, his love life had been a desert. The idea of sex, so deliciously tantalizing when he had been around women on a regular basis, was beginning to look more and more like something he would never understand, an obscure sport to watch, briefly, during the Olympics like curling or rhythmic gymnastics. He knew that other men in his position turned to pornography as if it were no big deal, and he would smile knowingly when they mentioned it casually, laughingly: "Last night, while I was jacking off to this porno . . ." But inside a filament of shame quivered at the mention. The few times he let himself wander porn sites on the Internet, he'd been overcome with a nagging fear that his future capacity for love was being tainted by what he had seen.

He called the number Dumond had given him. A voice-mail system directed him to leave a message for Hippocampus Productions at the beep. He hung up instead. That night, he watched an old video of *Last Tango in*

Paris. People called this pornography, he told himself as Marlon Brando mounted the skinny French girl, but it had been miscategorized. All he saw in their coupling was animal sadness, the kind you can't be talked out of.

The next morning, Anton woke earlier than usual. Technically, he hadn't yet made up his mind to take the job, but as he showered and ate his breakfast he could feel his movements powered by a sense of purpose. Today, he was going somewhere. People were expecting him. That had to count for something.

The attendant at the parking lot was huge, three hundred pounds at least. A red bandanna was tied around his head and his ears were pierced in half a dozen places. A pirate parking cars.

"Can I help you?" The pirate leaned his head into Anton's car and craned his head toward the backseat.

"Hippocampus Productions?" Anton asked.

He asked Anton to open the trunk of his car. Anton turned off his engine and got out of the car. His trunk was a jumbled mess of things that seemed to belong to someone else—a Frisbee, a swollen paperback book, an old beach towel. The trunk of someone without a care in the world. The fat man leaned over, picked up a tire iron and weighed it in his hand, like it was a melon he was thinking of buying. "Amazing how much damage you can do with these things," he said.

"To a tire?" Anton asked.

"Heh, heh," the man chuckled, and threw it back. "Okay." He waved him in.

The Hippocampus office reminded him of his dentist's waiting room. Gray carpet, acoustical tiling on the ceiling, a banana tree in the corner. Not sleazy but not fancy. A utilitarian place for conducting business. He gave his name to a receptionist through a thick sheet of what looked like bulletproof glass (a touch lacking at his dentist's office) and took a seat. After staring at his feet a full minute, during which he ascertained that nobody in that room gave a shit about him, he allowed himself to look openly at the women surrounding him. He was used to the poignant hopefulness of casting calls but there was something different about the girls in the waiting room. They seemed harder, meaner, immune to disappointment and therefore, he had to admit, somehow sexier. You couldn't hurt these girls even if you tried. The girl sitting to his right, a freckled redhead wearing cutoff jeans and white go-go boots, leaned forward in her seat and held out her hand.

"Misty Moon," she said. Her legs were long and shapely but her body was lanky and lean, more like a fashion model's than a porn star's.

"Really?" he asked.

"No. But have you ever noticed that the girls who've made it big in this business are all named after natural phenomena? Savannah. Fern. Canyon. River."

Anton nodded. *Abyss, chasm, gap,* he thought, but did not say. His leg was bobbing up and down like the needle on a sewing machine.

"No offense"—she dropped her voice—"but you don't look like you're here for an audition."

"I'm a cameraman."

"Really?" She perked up. "Do you have any, like, tips for me? This is my third audition."

Anton could feel the other girls in the room staring at them.

"Don't look into the camera."

When the girl laughed—a rattley sound like a tin can being kicked down an empty alley—Anton realized that she was as nervous as he was. It gave him the courage to look at her more closely. Big pale blue eyes, the color of window cleaner; the well-defined clavicle of a ballerina; and an eager, uncertain smile that kept wavering on and off, like a broken filament in a lightbulb. She wasn't like the others. This girl could be hurt.

"To be honest, you don't really look . . ." Anton began, but didn't know how to finish.

"Tell me about it." The girl rolled her eyes, stretched her long legs straight out in front of her, and blew a stream of air upward so that her bangs fluttered in the jet of air. "I was reading the autobiography of the biggest star in adult cinema, and she got turned away five times until someone gave her a chance. These things work in cycles. Blond hair and big tits—that's only interesting for so long. Taste changes. And when it does, I'm going to be there."

She looked at Anton defiantly, ready for him to disagree.

"Have you always wanted . . ." He wasn't sure how to finish the sentence.

"To be an actress?" She finished the sentence. "Most definitely. Ever since I was Becky in *Tom Sawyer*. I got every good role in town. Annie, naturally, thanks to my hair, what's her name in *Our Town*, Mary in *Godspell*. Everyone said I was good so, naturally, I came here to find out. I told myself, 'Six months.' If I didn't make it in six months, I was going back to Amarillo." She checked her watch. "Tomorrow, it will be seven and a half months, but I'm not ready to go back. Six months wasn't long enough. I can see that now. Los Angeles is expensive. Did you know a girl can make twenty-five hundred dollars in one day doing this stuff?"

"Ten times what they're paying me."

"Yeah, but you don't have to worry that your English teacher from the seventh grade will happen on a picture of you on the Internet blowing three guys."

Anton smiled. Misty wasn't stupid.

"Anyway, nowadays it's easy to diversify. Did you know Savannah owns a winery? And Fern has a clothing line?"

He didn't know that but he also didn't know who Savannah or Fern was. "Couldn't you, like, waitress or something?" he asked.

"Yesterday I made forty-one dollars in tips on the lunch shift. Last night, I slept in the long-term parking lot at Burbank Airport. Don't look like that. I drive a Mercury Sable—that's a Ford in a tuxedo—the backseat is very comfortable. In the morning, I shower at the gym. Most gyms have a free two-week membership. I'm on my third. This one is my favorite, though, they have a salt scrub in the shower that makes your skin glow.

With the new digital cameras, that's especially important. They pick up *everything*. One pimple and—"

"If you need a place to stay . . ." Anton interrupted her, suddenly overwhelmed by a desire to help a stranger. If he'd had time to think it over, he never would have blurted it out. Already, the smirking faces of the women who had been listening to their conversation made his face burn with embarrassment, but for that one moment, he felt like one of those inexplicable heroes who jump into freezing water to save a drowning person.

She tilted her head, as if to let his invitation penetrate deeper in her skull. "Thanks," she said. "I was living with my boyfriend."

"I didn't mean romantically." And he didn't. She talked too much. Besides, her kind of fragile beauty made him feel uncomfortably beastly.

"I know. I can see you're a gentleman. Not like my ex. He was in a band. His house was a few blocks from the ocean. You couldn't see it but you could smell it and, at night, when there was no traffic, you could hear it. First time I went there, I thought it was heaven."

A fiftyish woman with thinning blond hair, pale pink lipstick, and the surprised expression of a newly hatched gosling opened a door and read names from a list. Misty went suddenly still, like a bird-watcher hearing a rare trill in the forest canopy. Anton looked down at the piece of paper in her hand. There was a list of questions with a *yes*, *no*, and *maybe* box next to each.

1. Will you do anal?
2. Will you do gang bangs?
3. Will you perform girl/girl scenes?
4. Will you do interracial?
5. Will you perform in bisexual/transsexual movies?

Misty had marked *maybe* next to all of them.

"Misty." Anton tried to get her attention.

"The problem was," Misty said, eyes still glued to the woman, "he did not believe in being faithful." She brought her gaze back to Anton.

"'Monogamy equals monotony.' That was his favorite saying. He met someone new. Someone young. Really young. Jail bait. So I had to let him go." Her hands were squeezing and unsqueezing the strap to her purse.

"Misty?" The blond woman scanned the room impatiently.

When she stood up, Anton saw she was even taller than he had first thought.

"Do you have a card?" She looked down at him.

Anton took out his wallet. Last Christmas, his mother had surprised him with a box of business cards containing his name, his address, phone number, and the word *filmmaker*. "Mom," he'd responded, flushed with embarrassment, "I'm just a cameraman."

"For *now*," she'd answered.

Misty read the card without blinking. "Cool," she said, and nodded, shouldering a white leather bag ringed with beaded fringe. As she walked away, the fringe of the bag danced like the tail of a horse.

Anton tried to sort through the cocktail of emotions churning through him. Relief—the last thing he needed was a homeless, would-be porn-star roommate—but also regret. As she walked away, Anton felt the earlier promise of the day's adventure fade like a passing song from a car radio.

"Anton McDonald." He looked up. The same birdlike blonde who had taken Misty behind the door was looking at him.

"We're waiting." She raised an eyebrow at him. Or, rather, she raised the area of skin where an eyebrow should be. On her, it looked as if the eyebrow had been erased, then penciled in half an inch higher.

"I'm sorry." He shook his head. "I can't do this."

She looked surprised, then pulled her lips back, baring her teeth like an aged cheetah. "Oh, for fuck's sake. Don't be such a pussy."

Anton's mouth dropped open in astonishment at the word he had just been called. *Pussy!* He tried to suppress the giggle tickling his solar plexus, but the more he tried, the more it seemed to insist on bursting free.

22

*d*arius insisted on parking.

"You don't have to," Miranda said from the backseat.

"I know that," Darius answered without taking his eyes from the snarl of traffic leading into Los Angeles International Airport.

"We want to," Sophia turned from the front seat and smiled. She regretted the phony cheerfulness of her voice but didn't want Miranda's last memory to be of her parents bickering. She was, as they said, "making an effort."

"I don't have to park and you don't have to go." Darius glanced at his daughter in the rearview mirror.

"I know." Miranda tried to modulate her voice so it sounded mature, wise, and suffused with a sad kind of love for her parents. The most important thing was that they not hear the tremor of excitement running through her at that moment. She was going to Alaska to meet her lover! She had dropped out of school! Okay, "taken a year off." She was having the adventure of a lifetime, getting away from these sad, sad people who happened to have given birth to her. But whatever. She would not be sucked into the vortex of their despair. She might be leaving Helen, but Helen, of all people, would not have wanted her to stay. Helen was the one who used to encourage her to live life, take risks, wear something other than black. Helen once told her she was an idiot not to lose her virginity sooner.

"Nobody's going to want you when you're old and crinkly," she had once told Miranda, who had, at the time, been offended but now saw her point. Especially given what had happened to Helen.

"The point is"—Sophia glanced irritably at Darius—"you can come back anytime. We'll pay for your ticket. No questions asked."

"If there's any change with Helen, you know I'll be back in a second," Miranda answered, looking out the window. Who was she kidding? The medical literature was practically unanimous—if there wasn't a change after four months, there probably never would be. "Why do you think the airport is called LAX?" she asked, trying to change the subject. "Where does the X come from?"

"It would take at least twenty-four hours to get back, which would probably be too late," Darius answered. "But that's your choice."

Miranda did not answer. There was no need to go through the fight again. It had been a painful last two weeks since she announced her decision, and more than once, she had found herself resorting to "I'm eighteen years old, I can do what I want." But in the end, they had come around, had even given her a credit card "for emergencies," and gone shopping with her at an outdoor clothing store, where she'd loaded up on bright yellow Gore-Tex clothes—"So you can be found easily in case of an avalanche," the salesman explained. "I'm not going skiing," she started to explain, but then stopped herself. Let him think what he wanted.

After cruising the entire first floor of the parking garage, Darius went up a level and took the first available spot. Level B, area 9.

"B–nine," Miranda observed from the backseat. "Benign."

Darius cracked a small, reluctant smile. It was a childhood game. Whoever devised the best mnemonic in the parking lot got the front seat. Miranda, being older and more verbal, usually won.

"Benin," Sophia played along. "Wherever that is."

"West Africa." Darius turned off the engine. His photographic memory made him hell on trivia games.

Miranda got out of the car and struggled with an overstuffed duffel bag. On the phone from Alaska, Jason had tried to lecture her on packing light, but his rapturous description of material deprivation had had the opposite effect. Stuffed inside her bag was a down pillow, three pounds of good coffee, two dozen CDs, three tubes of toothpaste, a plastic bottle of extra-virgin olive oil, six bars of dark Belgian chocolate, six months' supply of tampons, five tubes of ChapStick, four packages of dental floss, and twenty-four AA batteries. Among other things.

Darius left to rent a luggage cart.

"I'm jealous," Sophia said, when he was out of earshot.

Miranda did not answer. She hated the idea of her mother being jealous of her.

"I should have done more adventurous things when I was young."

"It's not too late."

Sophia shook her head. "It's different when you're older."

"You're not old."

"I always felt sorry for people who ate alone in restaurants. That was my mistake."

Miranda was about to ask her mother what she meant when Darius came careening around the corner, both feet on the cart. "I found it next to the elevator," he said happily. "Free!"

"You do like your bargains," his wife observed dryly.

"It's the little things in life." He grabbed the duffel bag, moaning theatrically at its weight. "You don't think they sell bricks in Alaska?"

"Ha, ha," Miranda answered.

Sophia let herself relax. This was the best the family had gotten along in weeks, maybe months.

Inside the terminal Miranda was surprised that the line for Alaska Airlines consisted mainly of old people in windbreakers and white sneakers, all carrying aqua blue nylon bags with the words "Buccaneer Cruises" written in the shape of logs.

"You have a seat assignment?" Darius asked.

"A window." Miranda nodded. "You really don't have to stay."

"As long as we're under an hour, the parking garage costs the same," Darius pointed out.

A beleaguered-looking woman wearing a Buccaneer Tours baseball cap arrived and asked all the "Buccaneers" to form a separate line to the left, leaving only Miranda on line.

"That was fast," Sophia said, after the bags were taken away and the overweight fine (fifty dollars) was reluctantly paid by Darius.

"I guess I should probably get going." Miranda looked at her watch.

"You've got an hour," Sophia protested.

"It could take a while to get through security," Miranda answered.

Sophia glanced at Darius in a sudden panic. What if something were to happen to Miranda? This could be the last time they ever saw her. They should wring every last moment they could out of her presence. "Let's buy some magazines. My treat."

"Mom, I've got enough to read."

"Coffee, then," she said too brightly, like a Buccaneer tour guide.

"Soph," Darius put a hand on her shoulder.

"Oh, shit. All right." Sophia shrugged. She knew when Darius thought she was being too emotional.

There were only a dozen people on line at the security checkpoint, but after a quick, hard hug from Darius and a more lingering one from Sophia, nobody suggested prolonging the good-bye. Miranda handed her driver's license to the security guard and kept her head down. If her parents were still watching, she didn't want to see. All those years growing up, Miranda had taken her parents' physical closeness for granted. When she was a child, their sexual energy had made her squirm with confused embarrassment, but it also reassured her. Something connected her mother and father. Now, standing with their arms angrily crossed over their chests, torsos leaning in opposite directions, they were like two negative ends of a magnet repelling each other, according to some irrefutable law of nature.

Miranda leaned her forehead against the scratched plastic window of the plane and looked down. Beneath her, a snow-covered mountain rose improbably out of a rosy nimbus of clouds. She checked her watch. They'd been in the air less than two hours. She turned to the pale young man next to her who had been reading a dog-eared copy of *The Brothers Karamazov* the entire flight. Whenever a passage seemed to strike him, he'd uncork a pen with his teeth and underline the words with a check in the margin. Normally, she would never talk to a stranger, especially one like him, but the newness of her adventure made her uncharacteristically bold.

"Do you know what mountain range this is?" she asked.

The young man craned his head over her body, first glancing at her chest. "Mount Hood," he answered, letting his eyes rest on her breasts, as if they were old friends.

"Mmmm," she answered, buttoning up the chartreuse cashmere cardigan she was wearing, one of Helen's best. She hadn't wanted to take it but her mother had insisted. "No reason to leave it for the moths." Miranda had pretended not to see the tears in her mother's eyes.

"First time to Alaska?" he asked, folding a corner of a page to mark his place and putting his book away.

"Yes," she said, and nodded, alarmed by the disappearing book. "I didn't mean to interrupt your reading."

"Dostoyevsky." He shook his head. "He's like chocolate. Delicious. But you can't eat too much."

Miranda tried to hide her wince behind a smile. She'd spent her childhood among young men similarly enamored with their own love of literature. When Miranda was finally old enough to read the works her father's graduate students talked about so lovingly, she'd felt like a frigid lover, unable to respond for fear of sounding like one of those pompous young men. It was one of the reasons she loved Jason. He liked to read. *Andrew Marvell. He's a poet. I know*. But for him it was something pleasurable. Not an existential road map for the rest of her life. And certainly not a way to make a living. Miranda loved her father but she did sometimes feel there was something unseemingly soft about teaching literature for a living.

"Martin Lane." The young man stuck out his hand and launched into his history without further prompting. He had work lined up on a Japanese fishing boat. Or he did, if the pollock were running. If the work was there, he could make enough money in three months to live the rest of the year in Los Angeles. If not, he could easily find construction work, though it paid less and was harder to do. "See all these blue-hairs?" He dropped his voice and looked around the cabin of the plane.

"Mmmm." Miranda hoped nobody had heard him use the term.

"They're all here to look at real estate."

"Really?" Miranda asked, unconvinced. "I thought old people liked to retire to warm places."

"Where else can you get oceanfront property for less than a hundred K?" Martin shrugged. "And pay no income tax. They come for the summer and leave for the winter. It can get up to ninety degrees in Ketchikan. The houses are for shit, though. After a couple of winters, most of them need to be torn down. That's what happens when you leave five feet of snow on the roof all winter. What about you?" he asked, glancing at her breasts again.

"I'm going to live with my boyfriend."

Martin looked disappointed. "Importing talent."

"Sorry?"

"There are, like, no women in Alaska. And the good ones get taken fast. I tried to get my girlfriend to come one summer, but after two weeks, she was, like, 'Yeah, Alaska, where the odds are good but the goods are odd.' So most guys import their talent. Is he a fisherman?"

"Who?" Miranda was trying to decide if being called "talent" was an insult.

"Your boyfriend."

"No." She shook her head. "He's a . . ." She hesitated. "A lumberjack."

"Whoa." Lane reared back and made a cross with his fingers. "Sleeping with the enemy."

"What do you mean?" she said testily.

"I'm not an enviro-freak, but you see the way they whack those trees"—Martin made a karate-type gesture and a sound like a B–9 bomber—"it's like a battlefield."

"I see. It's okay to fish the waters to the point of extinction but thinning the forest so they can make the books you read is a crime?"

Lane showed her the palms of his hands. "Don't shoot the messenger. I'm just saying your honey ain't too popular among certain types."

"Whatever." Miranda lowered the shade, put on her headphones, and buttoned the cardigan all the way to her neck. Let him look at someone else's tits.

23

Sophia could tell from the fresh lemon smell in Helen's room that Darius had been there recently. After reading a paper by a Swedish doctor theorizing that patients in comas could benefit from the sensory stimulation of strong tastes and loud noises, Darius had been squeezing fresh lemon on Helen's tongue, playing the theme from the *Magnificent Seven* for her on a pair of expensive German headphones every day, and alternating a feather with sandpaper on her cheek. She supposed it didn't do any harm, but she had seen a nurse rolling her eyes behind his back and had felt ashamed. Were they the crazy parents who couldn't accept the obvious? Every day, the hospital asked if they had decided where to move Helen.

"Ayyy, eeee, aye, ohhhh, yewwww."

Sophia cringed. As if to prod them to action, the hospital had recently moved another patient into the room. Only a thin polka-dot curtain hung from a built-in track on the ceiling separated Helen from a forty-two-year-old woman who had lapsed into a coma after a stroke caused by an overdose of diet pills. In the middle of a divorce, with no children, no parents, the woman had apparently eaten the pills until she passed out. If her ex-husband hadn't found her when he showed up to borrow a ladder, she almost certainly would have died. As it was, she didn't respond to any stimulus but, for reasons nobody could explain, she said the vowels over and over, like a record on an endless skip. *A, E, I, O, U.* The second Sophia heard them, her jaw began to clench with irritation.

She put a finger on Helen's cheek. "Hello, sweetheart," she whispered. After her initial awkwardness speaking to her, Sophia had settled on the childish endearments she had once lavished on the girls when they were little. By the time they'd become preteens, they'd begun to writhe in embarrassment whenever Sophia expressed any affection, but who could stop her now? She took Helen's hand and held the back of it against her cheek. It never ceased to surprise her how Helen's body continued to live, growing hair and fingernails, generating heat, pumping blood, all without any regard for the things that were generally believed to separate humans from animals—thought, language, memory.

"Your husband left half an hour ago." Sophia jumped. Peggy had switched to a day shift to keep her nights free for a new boyfriend.

"Is Miss Irritable Vowel Syndrome still at it?" The nurse drew the curtain back.

Peggy had been so proud of her pun when she thought of it. Sophia had tried to play along but she couldn't help seeing it as part of the general, free-floating contempt the nurses felt toward the bodies in their care. When she was around, they were gentle with Helen, carefully lifting her limbs, telling her what they were doing when they did it, just as the childcare books said to do with a baby. But Sophia saw how they treated patients who didn't have family around. Like sacks of flour on a warehouse floor. She had no illusions that they treated Helen any differently when she was not there, nor was she unaware that her own squeamishness was a direct contradiction to her arguments with Darius. If Helen was brain dead, what did it matter if her skin was washed with laundry detergent or the expensive French lavender bars Sophia bought and insisted the nurses use for her sponge baths? Or if the catheter leaked or the sun was too bright or the ammonia smell of the mop was too strong?

After an hour, the vowels drove her out, to the grocery store, then home. Since Miranda had left, a week earlier, Darius had seemed even more distant than usual, but when she saw him sitting at the table in their kitchen, she felt a momentary flicker of relief. As long as he was home, they could work on their relationship. She began unloading groceries, waiting for him to say something. But the longer he stayed quiet, the more agitated she became. What right did he have to project his disappointment onto her? She shoved the grocery bags under the sink, noting regretfully that the time between coming home and wanting a drink was getting shorter and shorter. She went to the refrigerator.

"Why is there never any cold wine in this house?" she asked, hating the words as soon as they were out of her mouth. They made her sound pathetic, like somebody who needed a drink, which she did, but why advertise it? She poured a glass of vodka from a bottle in the freezer, a leftover from one of Darius's graduate student parties. It poured viscous, like oil.

She sat down across from him. "What's wrong?" she asked, more brusquely than she intended, aware that the liquor had begun to release the impatience that was now her constant companion.

"You drink too much," he said.

Sophia looked at her drink. As the alcohol interacted with the ice, the water and vodka swirled together, creating a paisley pattern of clear on clear. "It's true. I do. Sometimes, I even smoke. Last week, I parked in the handicap zone at the hospital. Are there any other faults of mine you feel like discussing?"

"You've given up hope on our daughter and I can't forgive you for it."

Something cold ran through Sophia. She thought of what her mother used to say about those shivers.

Somebody just walked on your grave.

I don't have a grave.

Your future *grave.*

It had been inconceivable to the little girl that she would ever die. Not when a summer afternoon seemed to stretch on forever. Now death felt just around the corner.

"At least I didn't drive our only living daughter away by being a total asshole," Sophia answered. Darius's face turned red. She had been thinking it ever since Miranda announced her plans but she had tried her best to keep the thought bottled up inside her. Darius, she knew, would not forgive her for saying it.

"I did not drive her away," he answered coolly. "She made the decision to go on her own."

"Because you were so cold to her when she didn't want to set up camp twenty-four hours a day next to Helen's deathbed."

"Stop saying she's dead."

Sophia turned her head away from her husband's raised voice. That was when she noticed the set of black nylon luggage she had given him a few years before piled in the hallway. She could still remember what she had written on the card. *For all the trips we've yet to take.*

"What is that?" she asked, her heart beating fast with a sudden rush of fear.

"I'm sorry," he said, laying his hands flat on the table in front of him. "I can't do this anymore. Not now at least. Maybe it made sense when Miranda was here, but now we're hurting each other more than we're helping."

"You're leaving?" Her brain and mouth were moving at the same speed. Thoughts needed saying right away.

"Steve Chen said I could stay with him until I find something."

Steve was one of his graduate students, a brilliant first-generation Chinese immigrant who had broken his parents' hearts by choosing literature.

"Are you sure?" Sophia asked, stalling for time.

"He has a pull-out couch, it will be fine."

She supposed she should be grateful—she had a colleague who came home from work one day to find her husband had left, taking most of the furniture, the silver, and the cats with him. "It was the cats that killed me," the woman liked to say, because it made people laugh, but Sophia suspected otherwise.

"If this is what you want." She tried to affect an indifference she did not feel.

"We both know it's more complicated than that."

"'Complicated'?" She raised an eyebrow. Darius blushed. When the girls first learned to ask why of everything—Why is the sky blue? Why can't I stay up late? Why can't I have ice cream for breakfast?—they would answer, "It's complicated." Now it was just another bit of history blocking the driveway.

"I am going to move Helen in with me," he said. "As soon as I get my own place."

Sophia felt like one of those people who have been shot but couldn't feel it. "You can't do that," she said.

"I've talked to some lawyers. I am a legal guardian."

"I mean, you can't do it by yourself."

"You haven't really left me a choice." She heard bitterness in his voice. That was new.

"How will it work?" Her mind began to rush through the practicalities. Was she supposed to live in their big house alone? Could she afford to do that? Were they getting a divorce? What about Miranda? She felt an absurd desire to giggle. Her husband was leaving her for another woman. Her daughter.

Darius stood. "Kelly said there's room in the step-down facility at the hospital for at least a week."

Step-down facility? At first, Darius had resisted the hospital's jargon. Now he sounded like one of them. She watched as he bent over to pick up the luggage but did not offer to help. Monty, the dog, stood next to him, his tail working back and forth, like a metronome gone wild.

"What about Monty?" she asked.

"Steve's apartment doesn't take pets."

"You're joking."

"I'm sorry, Sophia, I can't take the dog."

"He loves you. You can't abandon him." She was pleased to see him blush.

"I'll come get him when I can."

"You're going to break his heart."

His upper body swayed like a tall tree in the wind. For a second, she thought he was going to lean over and kiss the top of her head, but then, suddenly, he was gone. Was that how a nineteen-year marriage ended? With the pneumatic *phhht* of the storm door closing? Monty lay next to the door whimpering. She finished the vodka, poured herself another, locked the doors, and went upstairs to lie down. In the sudden quiet of the house she noticed the same sounds she'd heard so acutely the night of the accident: The furnace rumbling on. The soft flutter of the clock as the numbers turned. The drone of insects in the yard. In the past, she had looked forward to the rare moments of being alone in the house. The delicious, snow-day feel of the empty house filled her with glee, and she had some-times fantasized about a sudden, painless death for Darius so that she might live forever in that state. This was different. This was alone without end. This did not feel so good. The vodka, which usually eased her into a happy state of worrilessness, did not seem to be working. Instead of making things blur, it made her feel more awake, more alive than she had in years. Her foot jiggled nervously and her jaw clenched and unclenched. It reminded her of the one time she and Darius had tried cocaine in the early 1990s, after a graduate student had given Darius as a birthday present a small envelope filled with the white powder. She'd been shocked by the drug, which made her feel massively, uncharacteristically, competent, as if she were suddenly capable of cleaning the house, finishing her thesis and having sex with her husband on the living room couch all in one day. She only actually managed to do the latter and then couldn't reach an orgasm but she'd seen enough of the drug to understand how easily it could exacerbate her feelings of unfulfilled potential. "Never again," she said to Darius the next morning. "Agreed," he'd answered.

The doorbell rang. Sophia looked at the clock. An hour or ten hours might have passed since Darius left. Only seven o'clock in the evening. Still. Who dropped by uninvited at that time of day?

Through the window next to the front door, she saw Harry Harlow's dumbly handsome face studying the lintel.

"Go away," she said.

"Please."

"No." She shook her head. Was he spying on the house? Did he know that Darius had left?

"I need to talk to you," Harry said.

Sophia saw a silver BMW parked in front of the house and opened the door. "Is that the car?" she used her chin to point to it.

"No." Harry shook his head. "I traded it in. There wasn't any damage but I didn't want to drive it anymore."

She looked into Harry's eyes. The flecks of gray and orange were like the granite countertops all her friends used when they renovated their kitchens. Why would he do such a thing? He could so easily be lying and she would never know. "This is not a good night," she said.

Harry hung his head and pressed his hand against his forehead, as if he were trying to shade his eyes from the sun. On the rare occasion a script had called for tears Harry had never been able to cry on demand, but now, standing on the McMartins' front porch, he was unable to stifle the sulfurous sobs that rolled powerfully through his lungs, up the larynx, and out his throat. Sophia was both moved and appalled by the extravagance of his grief.

"Oh, for God's sake"—she opened the door to let Harry in—"*I'm* the mother." Harry stepped inside. Determined to gather himself, he pushed his palms against his eyes, inhaled deeply and drew himself to his full height, as if to salute a general. The tears passed so quickly, even he wondered if they had been an unconscious ploy to get inside the house. Monty, who usually kept his distance from strangers, nudged his nose into Harry's crotch. "Monty!" Sophia chastised the dog, secretly pleased at its impertinence.

Sophia turned and headed toward the kitchen. Harry followed meekly behind. "I need a drink," she said. "Do you want one?"

Harry shook his head. "No, thanks."

Sophia scowled. Teetotalers depressed her.

"Maybe a beer." He changed his mind.

"We don't have beer."

"Wine?"

Sophia chose a bottle of her cheapest red.

Watching her execute the quick half twist of the corkscrew followed by the *thwock* of the cork leaving the bottle, Harry understood that Sophia McMartin knew her way around a wine bottle.

"Why are you here?" Sophia handed him a glass.

"They fired me from the show and my wife left me."

Sophia thought it might be a good time to point out how little a marriage and job compared to a daughter but settled for an unsympathetic "Mmmm."

"Actually, it's okay. I hated that show and my wife. . . ." Harry shrugged.

Sophia took a sip of the wine and winced. It was barely fit for a pot of coq au vin. "I'm so glad we could be of service," she said. When the girls became teenagers, she used to lecture them on the awfulness of sarcasm, but, what the hell, she was having a bad day.

"You hate me," Harry said sadly.

"I don't hate you. I hate what happened when you were driving your car." If Harry were a different person she might have hated him, but five minutes in his presence was enough for Sophia to see that he was just another lost soul. His looks only barely covered it up. Something about his misery made her open up. "My husband left me, too."

Harry's eyes widened in surprise.

Sophia took another sip of wine. Once it aired, it wasn't nearly so bad. Or maybe her expectations had merely fallen in line. "He wants to bring Helen home and I don't. She's not conscious and won't ever be. After the accident, the doctors said her chances would be good if she awoke in twenty-four hours. Then it was a week. Then two weeks. Now they don't look us in the eye anymore. Instead, they say, 'She's very sick.' Like I didn't know that." The alcohol made it easy for her to talk. Once, on a plane trip back from Ireland, she'd sat next to a chemical engineer returning to Ottawa from his father's funeral in Killarney. After three glasses of

Aer Lingus's complimentary Cabernet, she had confided her darkest thoughts about her marriage. *I think I married too young. I'm not sure my husband has talent. I should have finished my dissertation. You can always have children.* The engineer, a bland-looking man with wire-frame glasses, thin lips, a wife, and four children, shocked her by putting his hand on her thigh. "Tempting," she'd lied. "But I don't think so."

"For what it's worth," Harry said, "I think you're right."

"I know I'm right," Sophia answered.

"Is there anything I can do to help?"

"Such as?" Sophia asked.

"I don't know." Harry tried to think of what he could possibly offer. "Money?"

Sophia wondered if she should be offended. People always were when it came to money but she was more practical than that. The insurance from Darius's job was supposedly covering the hospital stay, but already bills with shockingly high balances had begun to arrive daily at the house. At first, Sophia had opened them and made a few halfhearted efforts to sort through the arcane codes by calling the 800 number at the top of the page, but now, when they arrived, she threw them into a Nordstrom shopping bag in the broom closet and forgot about them.

"Can you drive me somewhere?"

"Anytime," Harry answered.

"Now?"

Sophia saw Harry glance at the wineglass in her hand. "I'm not drunk," she said defiantly. Harry wasn't going to argue. He'd watched his mother enough to know exactly where Sophia was located on the drunkenness spectrum—seemingly lucid but prone to recklessness. And convictable if stopped by the police. Better him driving than her. "Where do you want to go?" he asked warily.

"None of your business," she answered.

"Okay," Harry answered. "Let's go."

Sophia hesitated. She hadn't quite expected him to say yes.

By the time they arrived at Bobby Goralnick's house, via an irrational set of directions printed off an Internet map site, the sky had turned the smudgy gray of an exurb night. "Drive slowly," Sophia said, looking closely at the houses, half of which had been torn down, replaced by cedar-shingled McMansions too big for their lots. Bobby had lived behind a run-down split-level ranch mostly obscured by a clump of funereal evergreens. Beyond the shrubs, she could see the outlines of a roof. She tried to imagine the house through Helen's eyes. To Sophia, it looked sad and neglected but Helen might have thought it romantic or, at the very least, exotic compared to the McMartins' tidy Colonial and well-kept front yard. Sophia got out of the car. Harry followed.

"Who lives here?" he asked.

"Lived. Bobby Goralnick."

"The kid?" She didn't bother to correct him. Already, she was beginning to question the wisdom of the outing. What was she hoping to find? Bobby Goralnick's dirty socks? A bong? *The Collected Works of Immanuel Kant?* She hadn't had a drink after the bad wine back at her house and the thirst was terrible. Harry followed an unenthusiastic three feet behind her, but she was glad of the company. She never would have had the guts to do it without him. Sophia turned the handle on the door to Bobby's house. It was locked.

"Oh, well," Harry sighed with relief. "We tried."

Sophia opened her purse, took out the key that Louis Carone had brought her, and put it in the lock.

"What are you doing?" Harry asked.

The door opened. Sophia stepped inside the dark house.

"I don't think this is a good idea," Harry said from the doorway.

Sophia found a light switch on the wall and flipped it back and forth a few times. Nothing. "Do you have a flashlight in the car?" she asked.

"Yes," Harry answered without thinking. "I mean, no. I really think we should go."

"The eyes adjust."

"This is breaking and entering."

"This is entering. I have a key."

The outline of a couch and a television became visible. Beyond that was a door. To the bedroom? Sophia inhaled deeply through her nose. The air smelled of unwashed clothes and incompetent plumbing, but underneath something smelled familiar.

"Do you smell that?" she asked.

"I don't smell anything," Harry said miserably.

She closed her eyes and inhaled again. "Murphy Oil Soap. Someone has been cleaning."

Sophia felt her way through the dark into the tiny kitchen. She didn't tell Harry what else she knew, that the person who had done the cleaning was a woman and probably not the maid. She doubted Bobby had a house cleaner. Light from the street revealed an oil lamp and a box of matches on the kitchen counter. She lit the oil-soaked wick. A flame threw her shadow dramatically against the wall, illuminating a garbage bag distended by pizza boxes in the corner. Sophia opened a cabinet door. A dozen cans of white clam sauce were lined up next to a five-pound bag of sugar. She held the light closer to the bag. Sophia wasn't a baker. When the girls were small, she'd made the occasional cake in the shape of a butterfly and, once, the number five, but the sadly lopsided results had always filled her with resentment—all that work for such mediocrity? The top of the bag had been clumsily opened so that a smattering of small white granules collected in the folds. A column of small brown ants marched up one side and down the other. Sophia frowned and closed the cabinet door.

In the living room, Harry was sitting awkwardly on the arm of the couch. He stood up when he saw her. "Can we go?"

"Soon," she answered, passing him on her way to the bedroom.

The room smelled of mold. She raised a venetian blind and looked out the window at a chain-link fence and the back of someone's garage. A sleeping bag lay crumpled on top of the mattress. Sophia put the lamp on the bedside table, stretched the sleeping bag the length of the bed, lay down, crossed her arms like an Egyptian mummy, and stared at the ceiling. A brown water stain surrounded a few small stalactites of plaster that had begun to peel and flake. If only the ceiling had collapsed on Bobby Goralnick in his sleep. Or the boiler had blown up or the mud slides had thundered down the Santa Monica mountains, engulfing the block, the house, the room, the bed. She could spend hours thinking of better ways for Bobby, né Virgil, to have died.

The elongated shadow of Harry appeared in the doorway. His face looked even more alien in that light. "Are you okay?" he asked.

"No," she answered. Something about Harry's comic gloom kept her honest.

Harry sat on the edge of the bed. "When I first moved to L.A., I lived in places like this."

"Before your ship came in," Sophia answered. She worried that he might lie next to her.

"Before my ship came in," he repeated. "Is this making you feel better?" He twisted his spine to look at her.

"Not really. You?"

Harry shrugged. "I don't matter."

"Who does?" Sophia sat up. Lying next to him felt too intimate.

"Your daughter. She mattered." Harry winced. He'd meant to say "matters." Present tense.

Sophia startled Harry by standing suddenly and moving quickly toward the kitchen.

"What is it?" he asked, following her.

Without answering, she opened and closed drawers until she found a wad of cheap plastic grocery bags, the kind she used to automatically throw out until she was responsible for picking up a dog's crap. Harry watched as she carefully placed the sugar in the bags. "Let's go," she said turning to him.

"Happily."

Neither Harry nor Sophia noticed the red Mercury Sable parked across the street from Bobby Goralnick's house on their way out. In the driver's seat, Misty Moon held her breath as they passed.

Harry turned the key to the ignition, or what used to be called a key but was now a small black thing the size of a matchbox with some kind of infrared doohickey that unlocked the doors and adjusted the rearview mirror, lumbar support, radio, and air-conditioner to levels preset by the driver. The engine came to life with a muted roar and Harry's eyelids drooped momentarily with pleasure. What was it with men and the internal-combustion engine? Even Darius got that same moony look when a Ferrari passed them on the highway. It must be the promise of an easy escape. As if such a thing existed.

"Where to?" Harry asked. Sophia searched her wallet. After the policeman Louis Carone had left the house, she'd been so angry she had thrown his business card in the garbage, then fished it out five minutes later. Coffee grounds had stained a corner brown, but otherwise it was readable.

"Can I borrow your phone?"

Louis Carone answered on the first ring.

"Detective," Sophia hesitated, suddenly unsure of herself. "It's Sophia McMartin. Helen's mother."

"Yes?" he answered. Impossible to read.

"I, um, think I have some evidence for you."

"What is it?"

"I'd rather bring it to you in person."

"I'll be in the office tomorrow."

"What about tonight?"

"It's almost nine." His mood was suddenly clear—irritation with a dash of indignation. In the movies, she wanted to say, detectives worked all night. Instead, she looked out the window at the heavy traffic on the 405, her mind helplessly drawn to the unanswerable questions of city life: Where was everyone going? How many hours of their lives had been spent sitting in traffic? Hundreds? Thousands? What might they have accomplished in that time? Why was she having these thoughts at this moment? She wanted to say something that would reveal the significance of what was lying between her feet at that moment but she sensed the policeman might be underwhelmed by the brick of sugar. Even Darius had shown remarkably little interest in finding out who put the sugar in Bobby's gas tank when she finally told him about it. "Will it bring Helen back?" he'd asked. "Will obsessing on cutting-edge medically inappropriate treatments bring her back?" she'd wanted to answer, but had not.

"My caller ID says Harry Harlow," the policeman interrupted her silence.

"I'm in his car." Sophia glanced at Harry hunched over the steering wheel, driving like an old lady. Only after saying it aloud, did she understand how that must sound. Her irony detector, usually so well attuned to the perverse couplings of fate, had somehow slept through that one. It must have been the Merlot.

"Hold on," Carone said, his voice suddenly alert.

In the background, Sophia heard voices talking excitedly.

"My kid loves that show." Carone came back on the line. "Could you meet us at Marie Callender's in twenty minutes?"

Twenty years in Los Angeles and she'd never been in the restaurant, but it was exactly as she might have imagined: laminated menus, gelatinous cherry pie on a slow carousel, crayons for the kids, a pendant light fixture for every booth, silverware tightly wrapped in white paper napkins, the faint smell of french fries and ammonia, and a weary waitress of Cycladic proportions. Through the outside window, she had seen Carone sitting in a booth across from a kid eating a piece of coconut cream pie. The child looked to be twelve, maybe thirteen, past the age of sugar-induced ecstasy, but incapable, for the time being, of carrying out his more destructive impulses. Seeing love and fury mixed so inextricably in the detective's face, Sophia felt a wave of sympathy wash over her—why was it so hard to love purely?

When the child saw Harry and Sophia walking toward him, his eyes widened. Carone turned, rose, and held out his hand to Harry. "Mr. Harlow," he said, "how are you?"

Mr. Harlow? Sophia could easily picture Carone leaning against the counter in her kitchen, glass of water in hand—*May I call you Sophia?*

"And who is this?" Harry squatted to say hello to the kid. Sophia winced. That might have worked for a six- or seven-year-old, but teenagers, especially the young ones, want to be treated like equals.

"Uh . . ." The kid looked down at the floor.

"Zachary. Zach for short," Carone said. "He's a real fan."

"Is he?" Harry asked.

"When are you going to come back?" Zach asked. "That new guy really sucks."

"Right now I'm kind of enjoying my break."

"Is it true the rats ate a woman alive?"

"Where did you hear that?" Harry asked.

"On the Internet. They also said that you had, like, gone crazy."

"Maybe," the policeman said, "you could talk to Zach about work in the television industry?"

"*Dad.*"

"I don't mean on camera but, you know, behind the scenes as a cameraman or, what do you call it? A grip."

A waitress appeared, pressing a menu against her ample chest. "Oh my God," she said, staring at Harry, "are you who I think you are?"

"No." Harry shook his head. "I'm not Brad Pitt."

Everyone but Sophia laughed. How awful fame was, she thought, watching Harry drown in their sweaty stares. Sophia touched Carone on his arm. "Could we?" She gestured toward the grocery bag in her hand.

"Go," Harry said, and nodded. "Zach and I will talk."

Carone settled in a few booths away, his eyes still on Harry. "I didn't know you and Mr. Harlow were friends."

"We're not. He's just trying to expiate his guilt by pretending to give a shit about me."

Carone forced his eyes back to Sophia and nodded slowly in the "Okay, I'm dealing with a crazy woman" way.

"Did you ever search Bobby Goralnick's apartment?" she asked.

"I would need a warrant to do that. To get a warrant you need a crime."

"Attempted murder is not a crime?"

"If the perpetrator is dead, that doesn't leave much incentive to prosecute."

"Not Bobby," she answered impatiently. "The person who put the sugar in the tank."

"Oh." Carone leaned back in the booth. "I shouldn't have told you about that."

"But you did."

"I told you, it probably had nothing to do with the accident. The sugar falls to the bottom of the tank and makes sludge. The fuel filter takes care of the rest."

"What if it didn't?" Sophia pressed.

Carone was looking at Harry again. "I almost didn't recognize him. The hair looks so different. And he's shorter in person. But I guess everybody says that."

"We went to Bobby's house." She placed the sugar on the table. "I found this in the kitchen."

Carone looked in the bag. "Sugar," he observed.

"It doesn't make sense that someone like Bobby Goralnick would have a five-pound bag of sugar in his kitchen. He wasn't the type to bake cookies. You said it was probably a woman. If you dust this for prints, I think we'll know who did it."

"Any prints would have been completely erased by the abrasion of this plastic bag."

Sophia stared at him in disbelief.

The waitress arrived with the decaffeinated coffee Carone had ordered. "Here you go." She smiled at Sophia. Having arrived at the restaurant with a celebrity, some fairy dust seemed to have landed on her own shoulders. "Anything else?" the waitress asked.

"No, thanks." Sophia couldn't imagine anyone mistaking the ghastly expression on her face for a smile, but the waitress seemed satisfied and left them alone.

The detective shook his head. "It's TV. Everybody thinks they're a detective." He took his spoon and held it over the bag. "May I?" he asked.

"Is that supposed to be a joke?" Sophia moved the bag from the table to her lap, where its weight pressed reassuringly against her thighs.

Carone shrugged and took a packet of sugar from a container on the table. "Even if we found prints, it wouldn't prove anything. It's not against the law to use sugar. Not yet. And if the person who did it hasn't committed a prior felony, they won't be in the system anyway. And as I told you, the kind of person who does this is generally not a hard-core criminal."

"I'd feel better knowing."

"Maybe you would. Maybe you wouldn't." Carone emptied two full packets of sugar into his coffee. "My first job was patrolling South Central in a black-and-white. At the end of the month, when welfare checks arrived, there'd be a dozen muggings in one day. We'd have to drive every victim around the neighborhood, slowing down whenever we saw someone who matched the mugger's description—which didn't win us fans among the young men in the neighborhood. Then we'd take the victims back to the precinct house, where they'd spend an hour going through mug shots. In all that time, we never made a single collar based on the information we got. One day I asked my captain why we were wasting our time. Know what he said?"

Sophia didn't answer.

"He said, 'You have something better to do than make a citizen feel like you give a shit about her misfortune?'"

Carone took a sip of his coffee. Sophia turned her head to watch Harry and Zach, who seemed to be doing most of the talking. Harry merely bobbed his head in agreement.

"You're divorced?" she asked.

"Separated. How did you know?" Carone twisted the gold wedding ring on his finger.

"Just a feeling."

Carone looked at Zach, then back at Sophia. "Let this thing with the sugar go," he said. "Whatever Bobby was thinking that day, he took it with him."

Sophia moved her hand to the bag in her lap. She guessed it weighed just under five pounds. When Helen was born, she had weighed 4.9 pounds. The doctors were worried enough to consider an incubator, but Sophia had refused. She knew she needed to keep her close, naked against her chest, where she could coax her into feeding and whisper the truth that only she knew. *You're going to be fine*, she'd told Helen. *A mother knows.*

24

*a*nton was eating dinner—black beans, rice, and contempt from the taco stand around the corner ("You don't want no chicken?")—when the doorbell rang. Of course he wanted chicken but it cost an extra four dollars he didn't have, so he lied and said he'd become a vegetarian, which made the boy behind the counter, who had made many a chicken taco for him over the last year, snicker. Which made Anton furious enough to consider forgoing his order altogether. But there was his empty stomach to consider.

"Who is it?" he asked through the door. If it was Scudder, he wasn't opening it. Scudder was working on a big-budget disaster movie at Universal and couldn't stop going on and on about the star's tits, the amazing pyrotechnics, the free craft-service lunch, the checks for overtime. Blah blah blah.

"Anton McDonald?" a female voice came through the door. "It's Emily."

Anton hesitated. He didn't know anyone named Emily.

"Misty. Misty Moon. From this morning."

Anton opened the door. "You're here," he said because he could think of nothing else.

"Yes." She half smiled, then burst into tears.

Anton stood awkwardly in the doorway. Should he hug her? Pat her arm or something? The tears had caused her mascara to run and her face was unevenly blotched pink, red, and white, like a half-healed bruise. Even her kind of magnificent body seemed stooped and sad, like an osteoporotic old woman. "What happened?" he asked.

"Can I come in?"

Anton moved out of her way.

Misty looked around the small living room: the brown plaid couch he'd bought from the Salvation Army; the black-and-gold torchiere lamp in the corner; the oversized television, which took up more room than it should; the steamer trunk used as a coffee table; and the vintage movie posters tacked to the wall. "Very bohemian," she said, and sniffled.

He knew her so little, he wasn't sure if she was being serious or sarcastic. "Thanks, I guess."

Misty sat in the middle of the couch, lowered her head as if in prayer, and began to sob once again. Anton went to the kitchen to get her a glass of water. Not that he really believed water would be of any solace, but he didn't know what else to do.

Back in the living room, her sobs had subsided into something resembling a mewling cat. Anton put the water in front of her. "Thanks." She took the glass, held it up to the light and frowned. "Do you have anything sparkling?"

Anton shook his head, relieved. How upset could she be if she could bust his chops over sparkling water?

"Okay," she said, putting it back on the table.

"What happened?" he asked, sitting across from her in the remarkably uncomfortable vinyl club chair left by a previous tenant.

Misty pushed her lips out, like a blowfish, then brought them back in. "Have you ever had a day where everything that happened seemed designed to push you over the edge?"

"You didn't get cast?" he asked hopefully.

"Oh, no." Misty rolled her eyes. "Today was my big break." She shuddered, picked up the water, and drank.

Anton wanted to hear the details but he also didn't. "I guess it's good you got it out of your system."

"You got that right." Misty leaned back on his couch and crossed her arms over her chest. Her tears seemed to be replaced by a simmery anger. "You know they all take Viagra?"

Anton didn't know that.

"It's like, long after a normal man would have, you know, finished, they just keep on going and going and going. And you've got to act like you're happy about it. 'Try not to look like you're in pain,' they kept saying to me but, I mean, hello? People say porno actresses can't act, but I think they all deserve a fucking Oscar." She paused. "A Fucking Oscar, that's a good idea."

"I think they have those, actually."

"Well, they should."

"I'm really sorry. It sounds terrible."

Misty snorted. "I wasn't crying because of the shoot."

Anton didn't say anything.

"Do you want to know why I was crying?"

"Only if you want to tell me."

Misty crossed her arms and leaned forward as if she were suddenly cold. "I haven't told anyone."

"You don't have to tell me."

"You promise not to tell anybody?"

"Maybe you shouldn't tell me."

"I think I killed someone." She covered her face with her hands after she said it and made a low, moaning sound.

Anton was pretty certain Misty Moon, née Emily whatever, had not killed anybody. That seemed like the kind of thing you would know if it happened. "What do you mean?" he asked.

"I mean, he's definitely dead. I just don't know if it's my fault."

"Go on."

"It was my ex-boyfriend. I was mad at him for dumping me, so I put some sugar in the tank of his motorcycle, because he loved that motorcycle. A few days later, he had an accident on the highway and died."

"Shit," Anton said.

"I know." Misty nodded solemnly. "And there was a girl with him. She's in the hospital."

Anton kind of wished that she hadn't told him. Was he now morally obliged to turn her in or something?

"You know how I told you I've been sleeping in my car? I only did that once. Lately, I've been staying at his house. It's going to be torn down soon, so the owners didn't bother to rent it out. But tonight, when I got there, some people were inside. After they left, I went in and the sugar was gone." She shook her head. "I think it may have been the police looking for me. I'm scared." She started to cry again.

Anton sat next to her on the couch and awkwardly put his arm around her shoulder. She leaned gratefully into his body. "I don't want to go to prison," she said, sobbing.

"Maybe if you turn yourself in, they'll go easier on you."

"That's what I was thinking, too." She pulled away from him. "But I don't have money for a lawyer or anything."

"If you're poor, they give you one free."

"Do you think that I'd be, like, on television or something?"

"What do you mean?"

"I don't know, I mean maybe it could be, like, the O.J. trial or something. I could write a book or play myself in the movie. Or something."

Anton could tell by the "or something" that even she didn't believe that was going to happen. "I think you have to be famous first," he said as gently as he could. "Otherwise, you just end up on some cheese-ball true-crime show."

"Yeah, I know. I got the order all wrong. The whole thing was so stupid. I didn't even like him that much. He was a real boozer. As I was pouring the sugar, it was like watching my feelings disappear. If I could have gotten it out somehow, I would have. And I never thought it would cause an accident. I swear." She stared glumly at the floor. "What's that smell?"

"What do you mean?" Anton glanced nervously at his bare feet. Did they smell bad?

"It smells like food." Misty put her hand on her stomach and started rubbing.

"Are you hungry?" he asked.

"Ravenous. I haven't eaten all day. I didn't want, you know, my stomach sticking out. But I don't know why I bothered, you should have seen the cellulite on some of those cows."

Anton brought his rice and beans from the kitchen.

"Thanks!" She used the fork like a shovel. "No chicken?"

"I was thinking of becoming a vegetarian."

Misty chased the last grains of rice with the white plastic fork, then licked it. "I'm still hungry. You want to get something to eat?"

Anton shook his head. "No, thanks."

"My treat. They paid me something today, though not nearly what they should have for putting up with those pigs." She reached down to pick up her white bag, took out her wallet, and began counting out neat piles of twenties.

Anton watched with admiration how unsentimentally she handled money.

"I was a bank teller one summer," she said, as if reading his mind. "It doesn't take you long to realize it's only paper." She put a thick wad of twenties in the zippered lining of her purse. "I'm going home. If the police want me, they can come get me in Amarillo."

"That's wise."

Misty held up three twenty-dollar bills. "My last night in Los Angeles. Where can we get a good meal and music for sixty bucks on a Friday night?"

Anton chewed on his pinky fingernail. He and Maddie always ate at the falafel stand close to school. Whenever he replayed the course of the relationship in his mind, that was one of his regrets. He should have taken her out someplace decent. "How about the airport Hyatt?" he asked. "I know someone who plays the piano there."

"You have a friend who plays piano at the Hyatt?" She said it like it was the funniest thing she'd ever heard.

"Well," Anton said hesitatantly, thinking of Cyrus Dumond's big hands and tolerance for human frailty. "I wouldn't call him a *friend*."

"You know that's where the whores work, right?"

"Really?" How did she know that?

"My car or yours?" She was already standing.

Anton hesitated.

"You're out of gas?" she asked.

Anton's face reddened. "Temporarily."

"God." Misty rolled her eyes. "No wonder you don't have a girlfriend. C'mon, I'll drive."

"I *had* one," Anton protested.

"That's your friend?" Misty whispered into Anton's ear.

Cyrus Dumond was hunched over a grand piano singing "Something," eyes squeezed shut, his massive upper body swaying back and forth with pleasure. His voice was smooth, regular. Nothing to be ashamed of, Anton noticed with relief.

A waitress came to take their order. Margarita, salt, on the rocks for Misty. For Anton, a Budweiser.

"He looks like a cop," Misty said.

"How so?" Anton asked.

"Every time I've ever been pulled over by policeman, he has been big and black."

"Isn't that, like, racist to, you know, make an assumption based on a few random experiences?"

Misty rolled her eyes. "How can it be racist if it's true? Don't take this personally? But we would be a terrible couple."

Anton turned toward the bar. He'd been hoping to see some genuine whores, but the only people drinking were a group of European tourists sharing a bottle of Blue Nun and an older couple nursing brown drinks with red cherries and orange slices.

The waitress arrived with their drinks. "Is this a double?" Misty asked.

"No," the waitress answered.

"Didn't I say I wanted a double?"

"No," the waitress repeated.

"Oh." Misty frowned and took a sip. "Could you make the next one a double? And how much are they?"

"Eight dollars."

"Okay." Misty nodded. "Do you have any, like, chips and dip or anything?"

"I'll bring you a menu."

"Cow," Misty said after the waitress left. "In Amarillo, there's this bar where they give you free chips and cheese dip all night if you're drinking. Plus, if they get your order wrong, they give it to you free." She stuck a straw in her margarita and took a long sip. "Will you drive if I get really drunk?"

"If?"

"It's my last night in town, I deserve to celebrate."

The waitress returned with a menu and Misty's second drink. Cyrus finished his song and surveyed the sparse crowd. "I got time for one request before I go on a break."

Misty raised her hand. "'Piano Man'!" she shouted.

Anton sank low in his seat.

Cyrus twisted his spine to get a better look at Misty. "'Piano Man'?" he asked. "'Piano Man'? I hate 'Piano Man.'" As he spoke, his fingers began picking out the opening chords of the song on the keyboard. "Every day, before I come to work, I say, 'Please, God, no "Piano Man" tonight.' It's not right to bother the Lord with such a small request, so to punish me, what is the first request tonight?" He began to sing: "*It's nine o'clock on a Saturday. . . .*"

"This is so cool," Misty said happily.

Anton smiled. Even the old couple at the bar seemed to have perked up.

Afterward, Cyrus came and sat at their table.

"You sang that great!" Misty, halfway into her second, stronger drink, leered at him.

Cyrus smiled and twisted a large gold ring on his finger. "Are we on a date?" He looked from Anton to Misty.

"No," they answered in unison.

Cyrus laughed.

"We met at work," Misty said.

Cyrus looked at Anton sternly. "You know what the law says. If you have a job, you need to let us know."

"N-no," Anton stammered. "I don't."

Cyrus laughed. "Oh, shit. I'm pulling your leg. You think I care?"

"How do you two know each other?" Misty asked, looking from one to the other.

"It's a long story," Anton answered.

"Why do people always say that when they don't want to tell you something?" Misty wondered out loud.

"He's my unemployment counselor," Anton answered. Why should he feel ashamed? Better men than him had been fired from better jobs than his.

"Really?" Misty looked with renewed interest at the pianist. "Can I get that?"

"Have you worked steadily for the last six months?"

"No."

"Did your last employer pay unemployment insurance for you?"

"No."

"Were you fired from your last job?"

"No."

"Well, then, that's your answer."

Misty frowned. "I never get anything for free."

The waitress returned with an iced tea for Cyrus.

"Thank you, Berenice."

"Could we get some bread and butter?" Misty asked.

"Do you know what you want?" Berenice frowned.

"Yes." Misty nodded. "Bread and butter."

Berenice opened her mouth to say something.

"It's okay," Cyrus said.

Berenice made a horsey noise at the back of her throat, took the menus, and left.

"Can I ask you something else?" Misty asked.

Cyrus opened his large hands. "I'm an open book."

"Me, too." Misty nodded her head vigorously. "What's the point in hiding anything? Everything eventually comes out. So . . . were you ever a cop?"

"Why would you ask me something like that?"

"You have cop eyes."

"I like her," Cyrus said to Anton. "She's sharp."

Anton shrugged. "We haven't known each other long."

"As a matter of fact, I was a policeman in my younger days."

Misty pumped her hands in the air, like a champion crossing the finish line. "I knew it!"

Anton rolled his eyes.

"The minute my pension kicked in, I left to pursue my dream." Cyrus looked around the room. "The piano man."

"Don't you think this is a sign?" Misty looked at Anton.

"For?" Anton asked.

"You know," Misty said, "that friend of ours with that problem."

Anton had no idea what she was talking about.

"I know someone." Misty fixed Cyrus with a look of such studied sincerity Anton understood exactly why she had never been cast in any of the 423 auditions she had gone on during the time she was in Los Angeles. She never looked phonier than when she was genuine. "This person may or may not have contributed to an accident through something this person did to some-one's motorcycle, though that was not ever this person's intention."

Cyrus knit his eyebrows together. "You poured sugar in your boy-friend's gas tank?"

Misty's eyes widened. "Holy fuck."

"At least you didn't start a fire with a flaming bag of dog poop." Cyrus laughed. "I saw that happen once. Destroyed a whole block."

"Did you tell him?" Misty looked accusingly at Anton.

"Yes," Anton said. "I used a secret set of hand signals while you were drinking your margarita to telegraph the entire story."

Cyrus chuckled, a sound like a lawn mower trying to start.

"It's just too weird." Misty's eyes filled with tears.

"Don't worry." Cyrus patted her hand. "The sugar dissolves. Tell your friend to have the gas tank drained. It costs about eighty bucks."

She blew her nose on a cocktail napkin. "Thank you. Thank you. Thank you. I think you just saved my life."

25

S ophia woke to the sound of Monty's tail thumping under the bed. She knew something had changed but it took a few seconds to remember what it was. Right, Darius was gone. Lying back on her pillow, she examined the fact in the light of day. She had seen enough friends divorce to understand how differently it affected people. Some women were hastened into old age by the surprise of loneliness after so many years of crowded rooms, while others—no other way to put it—blossomed like flowers. Without even realizing it, they'd been slowly bored to death by their angry husbands and solipsistic children. They made new friends, began working out, changed their wardrobes, took vitamins, traveled the world. Some went back to work or quit bad jobs for better ones. Every one of them said they had never been so happy. Darius had been a good husband, but it only took Sophia a second to choose the kind of ex-wife she wanted to be.

She began to feel a stirring of optimism, the way she had felt when she was eighteen and leaving home for the first time. Back then, she'd been convinced that one day she'd be famous and successful. She hadn't even picked a field—maybe art, maybe politics. The world, she felt, would point her in the proper direction after she'd done some real living. The young, she now understood, always feel that way. She could see the same certainty in her daughters and their friends. It never occurred to them that things might not go well for them. Even Miranda, whose cynicism was supposed to protect

her from disappointment, felt special. Sophia supposed all that idiot
optimism was a good thing. If somebody had told her when she was eighteen that she'd be doing what she was doing now, she'd have laughed. No
way. And she wasn't even doing so badly. She knew women who had it
much worse. Women whose lumps weren't the result of too much coffee.
Career-obsessed women who'd woken up at forty-five, bored by their jobs
and suddenly desperate to be a mother. Women whose husbands had cleaned
out the joint checking account and left no forwarding address.

She went downstairs and made herself a pot of coffee, something
Darius, the early riser, usually did. By the time she came down, it was
always slightly burned. She could have thrown it out and made a fresh pot,
but that would have been wasteful. For years, she had simply put up with
bitter coffee until it became what she knew and expected. She savored the
taste of a fresh cup and looked out the window. The neighbor's automatic
sprinkler system turned on. She and Darius looked down on the wasteful-
ness of watering the desert. "If they want to live in Connecticut, they
should move there," he always said. But, as a gardener, she knew her lawn
benefited from the runoff—the side that bordered them was much greener
than any other part. Now that Darius was gone, maybe she'd put in her
own sprinkler system? No, she made an effort to clear her mind of those
kinds of thoughts. They were too small. Too minor. What was required of
her now was something large. Something radical. Darius needed the house
for Helen. She needed to leave. It was that simple.

She took a piece of paper and a pen out of the kitchen drawer and sat
down at the kitchen table. The phone rang. For a second, she let herself
believe it was Darius calling to say he had made a mistake and wanted to
come home. But of course it wouldn't be. He wasn't the type. She let the
answering machine pick up. A few seconds later, Harry's voice filled the
room. "Hi! It's Harry. Harlow. I just wanted to call and see how you are doing. Last night was . . ." He paused and laughed nervously. "I mean, I hope
I helped. If you need something. *Anything*. Please. Call me. I mean that."

Sophia started writing.

1. Paris
2. Istanbul
3. An island. Washington State??
4. New York
5. London

Paris was out of the question. Her French was not very good, the exchange rate was terrible, and she didn't even like the city. When she was nineteen and the currency had been in her favor, she and the rest of America had gone for a visit. Everywhere she went, Moroccan men with bad teeth followed her, certain that she was eager to have sex after only five minutes of conversation concerning the new Michael Jackson album. Now she might be tempted to take them up on their offer—no-strings-attached sex with beautiful young men actually sounded pretty good, bad teeth or not—but now they wouldn't be interested in her. Too old. Perverse world. She'd only put Istanbul down to make herself seem more interesting than she was. She had no interest in a city of Muslims. An island was tempting. She had it in her to withdraw completely from the world. Once, she and Darius had rented a cabin for two weeks in the boundary waters of Minnesota. She had loved the perfect stillness of the place, but Darius had gotten lonely for the girls and suggested they leave four days before their lease was up. It was too soon for that. Also, she feared she might drink too much if left on her own.

That left New York and London. Several years before, Darius had exchanged jobs for a semester with a professor from the University of London. They had gone to live in the man's house in Camden Town while the man had moved with his wife and family into their Los Angeles home. Everybody in the family hated it. Except her.

"When are we going home?" the girls would ask after each friendless London school day.

"Soon," Sophia would reassure them, momentarily vexed by the intractable cool of the Brits. It was one thing to be snooty to her—she liked being left alone—but to children? The entire time they lived there, the girls were never asked on a single playdate. The few times she brought up the subject with other mothers, she'd been met with reactions ranging from bafflement to what seemed like outright hostility. Finally, an American mother with older boys (and therefore useless) told her that playdates were unheard of in London. "The family knows you or they don't. Plus, I don't think the English really want to encourage 'playing.'" It was even worse for Darius. He liked to joke that an Irishman from the United States teaching Shakespeare in England was like walking around with a Kick Me sign taped to your back. Even his students would say things like, "Well, I guess in the New World . . ."

"Can you believe they still think of America as the New World?" he'd fume when he arrived home.

But Sophia had loved it. After dropping the girls at school, she'd get a newspaper, sit and read in a café near the tube station, and spend each day exploring a new part of the city. She began with the obvious places—Hyde Park, Holland Park, Hampstead Heath, Cheyne Walk—but even the less touristy neighborhoods she wandered into—the tail end of King's Row, the nondescript row houses behind Victoria Station, the Indian hotels near Hyde Park Gate, the Arab embassies near Sloane Square—all stirred memories of the novels she had read as a girl. The Bennetts coming to London for the season; Isabel Archer buying, buying, buying; the dissolute party girls of Evelyn Waugh; the clerks of Shaw; the Schlegels of *Howards End;* the urchins of Dickens. Those characters had been her companions in a lonely childhood. Their lives and histories were vividly alive to her even now. The fact that London had changed, become a world capital struggling with waves of immigrants from places like India and Pakistan, made it even more interesting. When the nine months were up, she made tentative noises about making it permanent, but her family had been adamant. They wanted to go home. London without them was unthinkable. She'd read too many contemporary British novels about lonely middle-aged women to have any illusions about what her life would be like. In nine months of ordering meat from her local butcher, the man never once smiled at her.

So, New York. Sophia looked out her window at the bright white California sun. She'd been so entranced with the weather when they had first moved there. How could anyone live anywhere else, she'd ask Darius as each day bloomed more gloriously than the next. But now the sun had come to oppress her. She knew how ultraviolet rays could unscramble your DNA, sending silent, deadly messengers deep into the epidermis. She was ready for seasons. Rain and snow. A place where things died but then came back to life. A place where you could believe in new beginnings.

"Mrs. McMartin?"

The sound of a voice made her jump. Maria, the cleaning lady, came every Wednesday but Sophia was usually at work or, more recently, the hospital. It must have been a year since they'd actually seen each other.

"Maria! You scared me. How are you?"

"I am fine. I heard about your *hija*. I am so sorry."

"Oh." Sophia looked down at the table. "Thank you." She stood up. She hated sitting while others worked. "I'll be upstairs."

Maria nodded and turned toward the sink. Sophia noticed the bag of sugar where she'd left it the previous night.

"Maria," she said, "can you throw the sugar out?" She couldn't bring herself to do it.

Maria looked at the bag. "Okay," she said, and nodded. "Bugs?"

Sophia hesitated, then agreed. "Yes. Bugs."

26
♈

*M*iranda looked out the window. Snow. Everywhere. And coming down still. Growing up in Southern California, snow was an
abstraction. Something sprayed from an aerosol can onto the Nativity
scene at the Beverly Center. The few times the family had gone East to
visit her grandparents for Christmas, the massive white piles veined with
dirt and grime had been a bother. Watching it drift dreamily onto the
landscape, like confectioner's sugar on a cake, she suddenly understood
its magical allure. Below, she could hear Jason tending the fire in the
wood-burning stove.

"It's snowing," she said out loud. The house had no doors except the
one to the bathroom.

The clatter below paused, then continued.

Was it her imagination or was Jason different in Alaska? When she'd
gotten off the plane, he'd held her in a tight, reassuring hug as the old
people streamed around them, beaming at the young lovers, but by bag-
gage claim she noticed something stiff in the way he held himself, as if he
were embarrassed to be seen with her. Then again, how well did she really
know him? In California, he had been the gobsmacked tourist, the one
exclaiming in banal amazement over the dry hills dropping into the vast
blue of the Pacific Ocean, the orderly ant farm of traffic on the thruways,
the crush of Chinatown. Now she was the one gaping at the stuffed polar
bear in the airport lobby.

She took a deep breath, threw off the down comforter, and climbed out of bed. Goose bumps rose on her skin.

"It's blood rushing away from the surface of your skin, going to the organs that really matter," Jason had explained the night before, his hand creeping down to one of those organs. She had tried not to tense but something about the sex had felt false, as if they were feigning passion to justify the upheaval of the last six weeks.

Miranda climbed down the ladder from the sleeping loft, trying not to shiver.

Jason handed her a cup of steaming coffee.

She cradled the cup for warmth. "Is there milk?"

He shook his head. "Nondairy creamer," he answered.

"Fine," she said, as cheerfully as she could. She hated the stuff.

"I don't know what you usually have for breakfast . . ."

"Fruit," she said with a shrug. "Granola."

"How about Cheerios?"

"How do you eat them without milk?"

"You just. Eat them."

When they arrived the night before, the outside had been lit by a full moon reflecting off the white of the snow, but inside, the house had been pitch black. In the morning light—a weak, gray wash of color that more closely resembled five a.m. in California—she looked more closely at her new home, an unfinished A-frame built by a husband-wife team of accountants from San Antonio. In his e-mails, Jason had called it "luxurious," with indoor plumbing, a generator, and a snowmobile they could use sparingly. But looking around, Miranda was surprised by the exposed studs and baffles of pink insulation resembling cotton candy.

"Doesn't that, like, cause cancer?" she asked, pointing to one of the walls.

"Fiberglass?"

"Forget it," she answered, realizing too late that she had been thinking of asbestos.

"A lot of people out here don't even bother with Sheetrock. With all the contracting and expanding of wood, nails can pop right out of the wall. The natives had the right idea. They built their houses underground."

Miranda thought that sounded awful. Who wanted to live like a mole? Somebody—a woman, she guessed—had made a few poignant stabs at livening the place up. Panels of stained glass hung from the windows. Red-and-white gingham curtains covered the bathroom windows. (So the bears couldn't see in?) Embroidered poem fragments hung from bare nails. *We are all in the gutter but some of us are looking at the stars. God grant me the serenity to blah blah blah.*

"Can we take anything down?" Miranda asked.

Jason shook his head. "They're trying to sell the place. The deal is, we get it free, but we have to keep it in shape. People could come at any time to look."

Miranda guffawed. It had taken an hour by snowmobile to get there—a loud, uncomfortable ride that made her bottom sting—on what Jason claimed was an old mining road but contained only trees covered with snow. She saw him look away, an expression on his face somewhere between a scowl and pain. "I just mean," she said, "it's not likely someone is going to drop in."

"I told you it was remote."

Miranda felt a sudden desire to cry. Everything she said seemed to annoy him. Had coming here been a mistake? How long did she have to stay before she could admit her error and leave without feeling like a total fool?

"So," she tried to change the subject, "what do you think happened?"

"What do you mean?"

"To the accountants. Why are they getting divorced?"

Jason scratched the underside of his jaw. She could tell from the red rash and whiteness of the skin around his mouth that he hadn't been shaving regularly. "It takes a certain kind of person to survive solitude," he said finally.

"What kind of person?" She sat on an uncomfortable wood chair and took a sip of coffee. Maybe she could learn to drink it black. Her

Greek grandmother always said people who needed milk were weak of character.

"People with very high expectations. Or very low. Either way, they've been disappointed. They come here thinking the land will heal them."

"Does it?"

He shook his head. "Everything is just harder. But it does seem to make people appreciate what they had. I guess that's something."

"What about you?"

"I was born here. It's different." He checked his watch. "I need to get going."

"Where?" Miranda sat up, surprised. She thought they'd have a leisurely day together, getting reacquainted with each other.

"Check the trap lines," he said, pulling a fleece over the wool sweater he was already wearing. Until spring, when he and his father could start logging, the only money to be made in the woods was in trapping. Demand, he'd explained in his e-mails, had been depressed when rich ladies in New York were being spattered with red paint, but in the past few years, prices had bounced back, even higher than before. *It's the Russians and Chinese,* he had written. *They've got money to burn and the woods are full. Marten, lynx, fox, even wolf.*

"Yesterday," he said, "I heard about a dealer in New York who'll pay four hundred and fifty dollars for an intact wolf skin."

"They're not endangered?" Miranda asked.

Jason snorted. "Are you kidding? F and G will pay you to shoot them." He must have seen Miranda's perplexed expression. "Fish and Game. Wolves eat the caribou. And anything else. I've been in this house three weeks and they've already tried to eat the dogs twice. I tried to shoot them but they're too smart. A buddy of mine lost an ear last year trying to trap one. He would have lost more than that if his friend hadn't shot the wolf in the head, which was too bad, because it's hard to skin a wolf with a shot-off head."

It was the most Jason had spoken since Miranda arrived, but everything he said had made her feel queasy. "You have a gun here?"

Jason smiled. "We don't shoot people in Alaska, Miranda. Except for that guy in McCarthy."

"Who?"

"Some guy went completely crazy in the middle of the winter and shot half the town. When the mail plane came, he went running out to meet it shouting 'There's a crazy person shooting people!' The pilot told him to jump in. He almost got away with it, but as the plane was taking off, the rest of the town came out of hiding and started chasing the plane. I always thought that would make a good scene in a movie."

He finished his coffee. "You want to help feed the dogs?"

On the ride in, she'd heard the dogs before she'd seen them.

"What's that?" she'd yelled into Jason's ears.

"Dogs," he'd answered.

She'd wanted to hit him.

When they got to the house, the dogs hurled themselves the length of the chain staked to the ground, then whimpered when the collars jerked them back. Miranda, who was used to the domesticated dogs of Los Angeles, was shocked by their feral aggressiveness.

"They're just saying hello," Jason had said, patting one on the head.

A lazy orange light was beginning to bleed into the gray dawn like a watercolor painted in slow motion. The dogs leaped to their feet and began a low-pitched whine when they saw Jason. "These aren't my dogs," he said over his shoulder. "Half belong to my dad and the other half belong to a buddy of his. They're not used to working together, so it's been a little rough on the trail. When I have better control, I'll bring you with me."

Miranda found the dogs' ice blue eyes haughty and uncannily knowing, as if they had taken a measure of her worth and found her severely lacking, a position she would be hard put to argue against. But still. She didn't want to see that in a dog's eyes.

"I'm surprised wolves want to eat them," she said. "They look like close cousins."

Jason filled a bowl with chum salmon and handed it to her.

"Fancy for a dog," Miranda said, looking down at the bright orange fish.

"Would you eat six-month-old fish?"

She edged toward a large gray-and-white female who seemed slightly more calm than the others. The dog's eyes were fixed on the bowl. Saliva was dripping from her mouth.

"That's Mathilda," Jason said. "She's the lead."

Mathilda's black nose twitched as she lowered her head toward the bowl. Miranda put a hand on the white fur of her head while she ate. It was coarse, like the bristle of a brush. The animal glanced blankly at Miranda and went back to eating.

"Take me with you," Miranda said.

Jason slipped a blue harness over Mathilda's head. "It's cold out there."

"I don't mind."

"You're shaking like a leaf."

"I could get dressed in five minutes."

Jason didn't answer.

"What am I going to do here?" she asked.

"You could finish chopping the wood. You could boil those conibears on the table in the shed and get them waxed for tomorrow. You could make bread."

Miranda's eyes widened.

"I'm kidding," Jason said, and laughed. "It's your first day. Relax. Read a book."

Miranda nodded. She'd brought a lot of those. Novels. Biographies. A history of Alaska. Standing in the snow, watching the vaporized breath of the huskies in the cold air, she knew the books would be useless. Ever since Helen's accident, the minute she tried to read anything, even the newspaper, her thoughts would wander to her sister. It was as if her mind refused to accept any new information for fear of displacing some important memory of her sister. Already, the Helen most readily in her head was not the Helen who argued with her the morning of the accident, a Helen filled with the vibrant promise of life. The Helen she saw when she closed her eyes was sick Helen. Helen in the hospital. Helen in a coma. Pale, bloated, vacant. Nothing like her sister. Jason had been like a tonic to the problem. When she was with him, she didn't think about her sister at all. Maybe that was the reason she'd come to Alaska. And now he was going to leave her alone.

One dog refused to stay still for the harness over his neck. Jason pressed his full weight against the animal. At first, the dog struggled to get free, but when it realized Jason wasn't giving in, it went limp. Jason tightened the straps around its chest.

"Do the traps kill the animals?" she asked.

"Not always." Jason stood. The dog looked up at him with an expression resembling love.

"You shoot it," Miranda said flatly. The thought of Jason pointing a gun at a defenseless animal was appalling.

"No, Miranda, that's called hunting. I'm trapping. Look, you'll be fine here alone. The wolves don't come to the door dressed up as granny."

Miranda looked up at the house. The exaggerated, upside-down V of the roof did look like something out of a Grimm's fairy tale. "What's with the A-frame?"

"It makes the snow fall off the roof."

"I'm afraid," she blurted out. Always, before, when Miranda alluded, however vaguely, to Helen and the accident, Jason had been sympathetic. This time, she saw a flicker of irritation in his face. It made her step away from him and throw her shoulders back. He was right. She was being weak. Bad things happened to people all the time. Look at Jason and his mother. He survived. That was what one did.

"Being alone is part of life," Jason said, more softly.

"Oh, I know." She looked up into the sky. It was eleven in the morning. Would the sun ever appear? "I'll be fine."

Jason looked uncertainly at the dogs, all connected to one another by two straps running up the middle of the formation. "I guess I could skip another day."

"No," she said firmly.

He looked relieved. "If I catch a rabbit"—he kissed her on the forehead—"we'll have stew for dinner." He stepped onto the sled, yelled, "Hike!" and took off into the white woods, a swirl of snow in his wake. She shivered and realized she had no idea when he would be back. Two hours? Ten? In California, she could have picked up the cell phone and asked. Here, she would just have to wait and see.

27

Sophia stood at her bedroom window, trying to commit to memory all that she had taken for granted for so long. In one hour, a cab was arriving to take her to the airport, where she was going to catch a plane for New York City. Tomorrow, Darius was bringing Helen home. Almost six months to the day since the accident. She studied the splay of the pin oak branch, the orange tile of the neighbor's roof, the hedge of euonymus marking the end of the yard. How often had she felt stifled by the predictability of her life, but now, preparing to leave it, she felt suffused with unanticipated sorrow for the past. Nothing but nostalgia, she scolded herself. Suddenly, her eye was drawn to movement at the bottom of the driveway. A woman, neither young nor old, and a young man filled with the jaunty spirit of life were walking toward the house. For a second, she wondered if she had somehow conjured their presence by her concentration, but as they drew closer she realized it was Maria, her cleaning lady. Observing the young man's long saturnine jaw, close-shaved head, goatee, white T-shirt and wide blue jeans hanging loosely off his body, Sophia thought of a phrase her mother used about young men who intimidated her. *Rough trade*. Then again, raising teenagers in the first decade of the twenty-first century had taught Sophia that looks mean nothing. A kid could dress like him and be a choirboy. A girl could dress like the biggest whore on Hollywood Boulevard and be a virgin. Everything was topsy-turvy. She went down the front staircase to greet them.

"Maria?" Sophia smiled. Damn it. All those years and she couldn't remember her last name. The checks were always made out to cash.

"Mrs. McMartin." Maria bowed her head shyly and introduced the boy. "José, *mi hijo*. My son."

José held out his hand. His grip was firm and his smile was open, friendly, filled with healthy white teeth.

"Come in," Sophia said. She had called Maria two days earlier to tell her that she was leaving and that Mr. McMartin would be moving back into the house with Helen. She thought Darius might need an extra day of help. Maria had seemed nervous but amenable. Had she changed her mind since then? Or had Sophia bounced her last check in the confusion of closing old bank accounts and opening new ones? "Let's go to the living room."

"No, no, the kitchen is *mejor*," Maria said.

Once they were seated, Sophia noticed that Maria was nervously bobbing her head up and down, like a Torah scholar davening. "Is everything all right?" she asked.

Maria raised a trembling finger and pointed to José, who had put a small leather satchel on the middle of the table and was now staring at it.

"Yes, ma'am." José moved around in his seat as if he were trying to get comfortable. "We're here because . . . well, you remember a month ago, when you told my *mami* to throw out a bag of sugar?"

Sophia nodded.

"Well, she doesn't like to throw anything away." José smiled affectionately at his mother. "So she took it home with her instead."

"I'm sorry, Mrs. McMartin. I should have asked," Maria interrupted.

"Don't be silly," Sophia answered. "Better it not go to waste." A hard round ball of anxiety was beginning to form and grow in her belly. It was the size of a giant gumball, the kind the girls used to buy from vending machines for twenty-five cents, and seemed to be ricocheting throughout her upper intestines, like a pinball in a kid's game.

"That's what I said," José nodded. "Anyhow, a few days later she was making some cookies for a bake sale at the church, and found what she thought was candy in the bag." He snickered at this, as if it were a joke.

Sophia realized that Maria was watching her closely, as if to gauge her reaction. "I'm sorry?" Sophia asked, puzzled.

"Little pink-and-green pills with the Nike swoop on them? Rollis, Mitsubishis, whatever you want to call them."

"José." Maria looked relieved. "I told you she don't know."

"No," Sophia said, shaking her head. "I have no idea."

José leaned forward, unzipped the satchel, and took out a handful of small pink, green, and orange pills and put them on the table. Each one was enclosed in a tiny plastic Ziploc bag, a doll's version of the bags she used for the girls' sandwiches at school.

She leaned forward and picked one up. It was stamped with a flower, a zinnia if she'd had to guess. "Drugs?" she asked.

"X, Ecstasy, or MDMA, if you want to get technical." José nodded.

"Wow." Sophia shook her head. Drugs in the sugar. Not bad, Bobby, né Virgil, whoever you were. Even with it staring him in the face, Detective Louis Carone hadn't been able to figure that one out. But then, he wasn't the brightest light on the Christmas tree. Had Helen known? Sophia didn't think so. Through no particular efforts by her or Darius, the girls seemed to think drugs were uncool. Even Sophia had been surprised by Helen's lack of sympathy when Roy Beaudell's father got busted for pot. "What a loser," she'd said, and rolled her eyes at dinner one night.

"Two thousand hits," José said. "That's big. I don't know where you got it, but the quality is good, too. No caffeine or aspirin or all that other shit—excuse me." He glanced apologetically toward his mother.

"How do you know?" Sophia asked.

"There's a website. You send a sample with a hundred and fifteen dollars, and they post the results. When people want to buy, they can check the quality first."

Sophia nodded, impressed by the confluence of the free market, the Internet, and illegal drugs.

"My *mami* thinks X is bad because it's a drug, but it's not like other drugs. Nobody gets addicted. People just take it to relax, have fun. It's like a once-in-a-while thing. Right?"

Sophia shrugged. "I really wouldn't know." She tried to remember what she knew about the drug from hearing the girls talk, but drew a blank.

José leaned forward, suddenly businesslike. "Do you know the street value of this?"

"No," Sophia answered.

"Fifty thousand dollars."

"Well," Sophia replied, just slightly embarrassed by how prim she sounded.

The largeness of the number hung for a moment in the air.

"Do you know how long it would take my mother to make that?" José asked.

"*Hijo*," Maria said sharply.

Sophia had always congratulated herself for paying more than double the minimum wage but said nothing. She could see José leading her somewhere. She waited to see what it was.

"I mean, is somebody going to come looking for this?" he asked.

"I already took it to the police. They weren't interested."

José looked relieved. "Because if that is true, I know somebody who would be willing to buy the whole thing. Cash only. No paper, no nothing to link us to anything. I figure we split it fifty-fifty."

Sophia shook her head. "No."

José looked disappointed. "Okay." He twisted his lips. "Sixty-forty, but, remember, we didn't have to come back here. We could have sold it on our own."

"No." Sophia shook her head. "I mean, I can't sell drugs. I'm a . . ." She hesitated, what was she? "I'm an arts administrator." She laughed—risible but true.

"Well"—José spread his hands—"I'm a college student but I could use some paper to help on my tuition. And my mom is a cleaning lady but she could use a car that didn't break down every three months. And my cousins in Chihuahua could use some help getting to America and my sister, Reina, could use some diapers."

A few years earlier, Sophia had been at one of the endless faculty dinner parties she was required to attend as a professor's wife, when a visiting scholar from Tel Aviv had suddenly turned and looked at her. "When you come to a red light in the middle of night," he asked, "what do you do?"

"What do you mean?" she'd asked, nonplussed by his dark, distrustful eyes.

"I mean, no one is around. Do you stop?"

"Of course." She looked down at his hand to avoid his eyes. His knuckles were covered with wiry black hairs.

He seemed both pleased and disgusted by her answer. "Only in America. I ask this question all over the world. Israel. Lebanon. El Salvador. Everyone says, 'I go. Of course.' Not in America. You are a country of sheep."

She'd kept her eyes on his knuckles, trying to ignore the insult.

"You know why?" He leaned in. "You haven't seen war in almost two hundred years. You believe laws can contain man's evil."

"Well"—she'd taken a sip of white wine—"maybe if people stopped at the light, there wouldn't be war."

"*Baa,*" he'd answered.

Sophia took another sip of wine and looked away. Asshole.

"I guess this means you're not going to sleep with me," he'd said. "Too bad. I asked Ken to seat me next to a live prospect."

Sophia had stayed offended for weeks. Was she a sheep? Was she, a married woman, really considered a "prospect"? The worst part of it was, for months afterward, the image that kept coming to her mind during sex with Darius, the image, in fact, that could always push her over the edge to an orgasm was not Darius's face looming over her or his naked ass in the bedroom mirror, it was that man's hairy knuckles on her own treacherous flesh.

It wasn't just the idea of breaking the law that kept Sophia from agreeing to José's plan. Profiting from anything to do with Bobby Goralnick was unthinkable. Nor could she permit José, who seemed like a fine young man, to put himself at that kind of risk.

"José," Sophia tried to explain, "if you got caught and ended up in jail, I would never forgive myself."

"I won't get caught," he said.

"How can you know that?"

"I know." He half laughed.

"What about you, Maria?" Sophia asked. "What do you think?"

Maria looked surprised to be asked. After twenty years of cleaning other people's homes, Maria Rodriguez was used to never being asked anything. It had taken her a few years, but eventually she had come to understand that the American dream the politicians talked about so freely on the TV around election time would never happen for her, despite the green card that had arrived in an official envelope marked Special Delivery from the U.S. government five years before. Even the nice clients, the ones like Sophia McMartin, who picked up their dirty underwear before she came and paid her a big tip at Christmas, had no interest in seeing her as anything but the person who scrubbed their sink. No matter how many night classes in English she took or the citizenship test she passed. *What is the capital of Massachusetts? Name three signers of the Constitution.* She would begin her working life in America cleaning floors and she would end it cleaning floors. But for her son, it would be different. If the children of the rich people wanted to take drugs and ruin their minds, what was it to her?

"I think what José says is okay," she answered.

Sophia sighed. Her flight to New York was leaving in three hours. She thought about the policeman Carone and his lack of curiosity. José was right. The police would never catch him. If it was a onetime thing and it changed their lives so dramatically, where was the harm? More important, how could she stop him? He had the drugs. "Do what you want," she said to José. "But I can't take any money."

"For real?" José abruptly stood up, as if he were afraid she might change her mind.

Sophia nodded. For real.

28

Yo, Helen, whassup? Roy here. But I guess you know my voice.

—Man, it is so harsh what happened to you. I'm really, really sorry.

Magda told me she was, like, making these tapes for you and so, I thought, shit, I could make you, like, a CD, you know? So you wouldn't be falling too far behind on what was happening in the music scene. So there are, like, five songs on this CD. One for every year we were friends, which I guess is kind of corny, but someday, when you're better, we can listen together, and I'll tell you why I picked them.

—After your accident, I gotta tell you, I felt really low. Like it was my fault. I mean, if I hadn't left, you never would have ended up with that old guy. What was up with that? He sounded like a real loser. I guess I shouldn't say that. He was probably cool—'cause, I mean, you wouldn't go out with someone who wasn't cool—but I asked around a little in the L.A. music scene. Well, okay, I asked my dad. He asked his friend Larry and, like, nobody had heard of him. I mean, that's cool. Everybody has to start somewhere. It's just, you know, he wasn't that young or anything. It's just, what we had was so special. I don't know if that comes around ever again. My dad says the first time is always like that, but I don't think so. I think what we had was special. We could have even gotten married some-day. Maybe.

—I'm not blaming you for hooking up. I mean, shit, I hooked up with some chicks here in New Jersey. Because, I mean, you said that was okay.

But those girls were just, like, I don't know. Cold. You know what I mean? Cold-blooded bitches. Like everything was, what are you going to do for me? I guess that is the way of the world. But I never saw you that way.

—It looks like I might be coming back to L.A. Greg and I are thinking about getting a band together. He didn't get into any colleges he applied to so he's, like, let's hang. And I'm like, cool, because I didn't even apply to college. Education is so bogus, if you ask me. It's just, like, teaching everybody to think the same, act the same, dress the same. It's, like, University of Abercrombie, you now? Old Navy U. The College of Starbucks. Where's the originality? My mom is totally cool with that. As she pointed out, she didn't exactly have an extra fifty thou sitting around anyway. And my dad isn't exactly in a position. So, shit, whatever. I can always DJ bar mitzvahs until we're discovered.

—I don't think having me around was, like, really part of my mom's life plan. Some of her boyfriends are only, like, five years older than me. Isn't that so fucking weird? I mean, my dad always went for younger chicks, too, but that was different. I don't know. I mean, to each his own. But whatever. Sometimes I'd, like, play video games with one of her boyfriends and he'd be, like, this is cool, and my mom would be there, like, drinking her white wine, smiling in the background.

—Anyway, my dad's lawyer is filing a lawsuit to get me a share of the house. Did I tell you it sold? Yeah, we're not neighbors anymore. No more late-night visits, no more, "Arise, sweet Juliet" or whatever your dad used to say. I never understood half of what he said, but he was a cool guy. And your mom. She was a little scary, but I guess if I had kids, I'd feel the same way about someone like me. But shit. By the time you wake up out of that coma, I think I'll really have made it. You'll see.

—Okay, peace. Stay cool. Stay beautiful. I love you.

—P.S. I don't have the rights to these songs or anything, so don't, like, play this for any policemen or anything.

29

*h*arry paid for the too-expensive hotel Sophia stayed in while she looked for a place in Manhattan. Initially, she protested but he insisted, claiming he could write it off as a business expense for Swimming with Fishes, his new company, which was turning out to be a surprising success. Just the week before, he had posed in a swimming pool for the cover of *L. A. Magazine* holding a bottle-nosed pleckie between his thumb and forefinger. "It's a million times better than acting," he told Sophia. There were a few problems with the business. The fish still bit, but since so few of his clients actually swam in their pools, it was less of a problem than he had anticipated. Also, it was necessary to change the pool water every three months, which, given the fact that Southern California was a desert, did somewhat defeat the environmental benefit of the undertaking, but it was a point no one seemed to have noticed.

The expensive hotel was a pleasure. At first. Previously, when she and Darius had visited the city, they'd stayed at a Holiday Inn in Chinatown, ostentatiously congratulating themselves for having found the best deal in the city. "And so clean," they'd remark to their friends in California. But the particle board nightstand and polyester blend sheets of the place had always depressed her. It was the way of the city, she consoled herself—people went out as much as they did because their apartments were so crappy. At the expensive hotel, the satin sheen of the sheets gave her a small thrill when she went to bed, and though she was used to regular sightings of celebrities in L.A., in the hotel, you could practically see the pores on their noses. One night, she rode up in the elevator with an inebriated rock star who kept grabbing the breast of a girl less than half his age. The girl moved the hand away and smiled in a "*Men!*" way at Sophia, who could remember being nineteen and dancing to the man's voice. Another night, an aged movie star famous for her gravelly voice cast an imperious eye on the black sneakers Sophia liked to wear on her long city walks. But mostly, the people in the elevator were businessmen who ignored her. Once one of them arched his eyebrow at her in a way that seemed like an invitation. She was so grateful to be noticed, she could have kissed him. But she declined whatever he was offering with a half smile, demurely keeping her eyes on the floor. I am not fit for human contact, she said to herself.

By the end of her first week, the fawning doormen (did she tip them *every* time they got her a cab?) and the eight-dollar cups of coffee from room service began to oppress her. She needed a place of her own, but the furnished sublets she'd seen through real-estate agents had all depressed her. Each had the same pale beige walls, pull-out couch, banal seascapes, and packets of nondairy creamer in the maple-veneer cabinets.

"Don't you have anything with more personality?" she asked her real-estate agent, an unpleasant young woman who seemed to have constant problems with her shoes.

"Honey," the woman said, dangling a stiletto heel from her toe, "these apartments are designed *not* to have personality." Sophia sighed. Why was a woman fifteen years her junior calling her "honey"? And why did she have to pay her a month's rent for a six-month sublet? To finance her "sabbatical," Sophia had cashed in a mutual fund she'd started back when Helen was born. The money had grown considerably over the years, but at this rate, she'd be broke in six months.

It would be easier and cheaper to look for an empty apartment but she didn't want to be weighed down with objects. One of the worst parts of leaving Los Angeles had been the pain of leaving the house: Who would weed her perennial beds or chase the squirrels from her bulbs? Who would know where she had bought that pair of sheets with the cherry blossom pattern? That set of royal blue towels? Who would remember the thousands of meals served on that set of blue faience dishes? Sometimes, she felt the record of her entire adult life could be found only in those everyday objects, the tools she had used to serve her family's endless needs. And, in the end, for what? So they could leave when it suited them.

It was Miranda who suggested she check out one of the populist bulletin boards that had sprung up on the Internet. Mostly, people seemed to be looking for roommates who liked cats, did not smoke, play loud music, do drugs, or have overnight guests. Apartments that sounded like possibilities were in neighborhoods she had ruled out during her long walks. The Upper East Side felt too suburban, Midtown too chaotic, Chelsea too young, the Village unpleasantly overrun with tourists on the weekend, the Lower East Side too dirty. She liked the wide-open space of Tribeca and the cones of silvery light reflected off the river, but there were no listings for furnished apartments down there. Finally, on the Upper West Side, she found something that looked promising.

SUBLET AVAILABLE IMMEDIATELY—French professor (Columbia U.) seeks professional, mature adult to sublet charming book-, light-filled apartment on Upper West Side. NO pets. No shares. References.

The price was half what she'd been looking at and did not include a finder's fee. Sophia considered how best to reply.

Hi. My name is Sophia McMartin. I am visiting New York
from California . . .

She stopped typing. Why was she in New York? Could she write the truth, that a part of her had always felt that she hadn't really lived until she lived in New York? That one of her regrets in marrying Darius was missing the chance to measure herself against that city, to throw herself headlong into its hurly-burly and see how she fared? Now that she was there, wandering its busy streets, going to museums alone, ordering room service because she felt too self-conscious alone in a restaurant, she feared she had waited too long. The city seemed like a shop where every item on the shelf was spoken for. Walking the streets, going to movies, riding the subway, she felt envy for everyone—the Wall Streeters checking their watches and tapping their feet, ever mindful that time is money, money is time, the NYU kids with their arty self-absorption, even the weary West Indian nannies on their way home to Queens. They all had a purpose in life. A reason to get out of bed and propel themselves into the maw of life. No, that would be entirely too much information. It would make her seem too emotional, too unstable. She should be terse, to the point and, like a New Yorker, identify herself by what she did.

. . . on leave from my job at the Bollanger Museum. Please ring me for a convenient time to look at the apartment.

She hit Send. There were, according to the search engine on the site, twenty-one more entries that met her criteria. She knew she should keep looking, experience had told her that for every ten things you try in life, you can only reasonably expect one to work out. But she had a good feeling about this apartment. If she sent out queries on any other apartment, she feared she would compromise the pureness of the feeling. She took a walk, idly browsing the ludicrously expensive boutiques on Madison Avenue. When she arrived back at the hotel, pleasantly tired from her walk, the bar was buzzing with the after-work-drinks crowd. The first time she'd heard that roar, it had made her so wistful, she'd gone upstairs and fixed herself a martini from the minibar. After a few sips, she knew it had been a mistake. What was there left to do at six-thirty in the evening but get more drunk? At least if she had an apartment, she could busy herself with buying food, making dinner, cleaning up. Hotels took too much of the work out of life.

As she unlocked the door to her room, the phone began to ring.

"Hello?" she answered, breathless.

"Sophia?" the woman's voice was softly accented. "I am Micheline. You sent an e-mail about the apartment."

"Yes," Sophia answered, trying not to sound excited. People didn't like to give you things if you wanted them too much. "Is it still available?"

"It is. Could you come see it tonight?"

"Tonight?" Sophia started to say no, it was too spur-of-the-moment. She needed time. But time for what? That was the old Sophia talking, the one who had obligations that could not be dropped at a moment's notice. The new Sophia had nothing to do.

The apartment was on the third floor of a five-story limestone building, a few blocks south of Columbia University. The block felt prosperous and abandoned—perfect for muggers. She rang a buzzer and went back outside, as Micheline had instructed. Somewhere above, a window opened and a woman's head appeared.

"Hello!" the head yelled, followed by a falling sock weighted down with two keys. Sophia picked up the sock and used the key to open the door. She could tell from the marble floor and crystal chandelier in the lobby that the building had once been grand, but over the years it had been reconfigured and rented as apartments, reflecting the changing fortune of the neighborhood.

Micheline Theroux lived in a one-bedroom apartment that overlooked the street in the front and an airshaft in the back. There were details a real-estate agent would call charming—a nonworking marble fireplace, intricate moldings, and a parquet wood floor—but the kitchen was cramped and unrenovated, with linoleum that needed replacing and a bathroom faucet that leaked.

"It's perfect," Sophia announced, forgetting her vow to play it cool.

Micheline smiled. She was slim, around Sophia's age, with hair cut in a severe pageboy style and smudgy black lines under her eyes that made her look vaguely racoonish. Sophia wondered if she had been crying.

"I was so glad to get your e-mail because I am leaving tomorrow," she said, folding a shiny aqua raincoat, a color Sophia would never dare. "My father has had a heart attack and is in the hospital."

"I'm sorry," Sophia said.

Micheline shrugged her shoulders in the dismissive way of the French. "Your whole life, you know your parents are going to die before you. But when it happens, you're surprised."

Sophia nodded. She had a lot to say on that particular subject but kept her mouth shut. She was so out of the habit of talking, she couldn't be sure what would happen if she were to open her mouth. The last thing she wanted to do was let loose the unstable avalanche of loneliness that had been building inside ever since she had called Darius to say she was leaving for New York. Some part of her had been gratified by the stunned silence on the other end of the line. How dare he think himself unsurprisable when it came to her. Another part of her felt as if the membrane that kept the sane part of the brain from the insane part had been stretched too thin by the move. The other day at the Met she'd stood a full fifteen minutes in front of a Goya depicting madness as a winged monster hovering over a distraught man. According to the museum's commentary, the tortured man was the artist himself. *That's just how it feels*, she'd thought, wondering if the winged monkeys from *The Wizard of Oz* were based on the painting.

"Anyway," Micheline continued, "I need to do some work at the university in Paris, so it all works out. A friend has agreed to take my classes for the rest of the semester. If you take the apartment, everything will be perfect."

Sophia was startled by how quickly the woman made up her mind. If it had been Sophia, she would have agonized for days over a prospective tenant in her home.

"You'll want references of course," Sophia said.

"Tell me about yourself."

The question she dreaded. "I needed a change." She shrugged.

"Are you married?"

"Yes, but my husband stayed in California. He doesn't like the cold."
Sophia wasn't sure why she added that last lie.

"And what are you doing here?"

"I walk. I go to the theater."

"That's all?"

The bluntness of the French. She had forgotten.

"I am going to start art classes soon."

"Ah, where will you study?"

Sophia hesitated. It was true, she had thought about taking art lessons more than once but she had done nothing to make it happen. "I am still trying to decide."

Micheline reached into her purse to extract an electronic organizer she turned on with a roll of her thumb. "I have a friend who is teaching at the LeBraun School, you must call him."

Sophia recognized Micheline's type. She was the sort of woman who was forever fixing other people's lives, pushing phone numbers on them, making connections, insisting you follow her suggestions. At any other moment in her life, Sophia would have brushed her off as a know-it-all nuisance.

"His name is Coleman Kramer."

"It sounds familiar."

"Doubtful. He got one glowing review in the *Times* twenty years ago, but pretend you've heard of him, it will make his day." Micheline raised a plucked eyebrow as she handed Sophia the number. "A charming man, but not to be taken seriously." Sophia understood that to mean Micheline had slept with him.

"Does he know that?"

"He'll be the first to tell you."

"I'm actually separated from my husband," Sophia volunteered for a reason she didn't entirely understand.

"Yes, me too." The two women smiled at each other. Sophia left soon after with a set of keys, a handwritten receipt for three months' rent, and Coleman Kramer's phone number.

Later that night, while informing the clerk at the front desk of the hotel that she would be checking out the next day, she glimpsed the profile of a man at a desk through an open door. Something about him looked familiar. Going up in the elevator, she tried to place the man's face. Was he famous? Had she met him in California? Did Darius know him? In her room, she undressed, turned on the faucets of her bathtub, and lowered herself into the water. With her eyes closed, she let the excitement of the day settle into her. She had an apartment. A home. A place she could settle into, albeit temporarily. And it had all happened so quickly, as if it were somehow meant to be.

Suddenly, she remembered where she had seen the man at the desk. He was the one who had noticed her in the elevator. Her face went hot with humiliation. He wasn't flirting, he was paid to smile at her. How mortifying. She thought of the time a few years before, when she and Darius had agreed to meet in the bar of the most expensive hotel in Athens after a day of separate sightseeing. She had arrived half an hour late to find her husband in a state of aggravated self-pity. Apparently, a knockout Nordic— big tits, corn-silk hair, milky blue eyes—had sat next to him and struck up a conversation. He could hardly believe his luck. After a few minutes, she asked, in a very friendly, matter-of-fact way if he would be interested in a "date." Darius had blushed, thanked her profusely, told her he was immensely flattered but was, in fact, married and would have to decline her offer. She had smiled at his answer. "That's okay," she said, putting a hand on his thigh, "most of my clients are."

Sophia had laughed at the story. "You don't understand," he'd said, "there I was, all puffed up, thinking that the old man still had something left if a woman that good-looking would talk to me, and it turns out she was a bloody hooker." He was right. She hadn't understood. Now she did. She leaned over to pick up the phone in the bathroom. They hadn't spoken since she'd left Los Angeles two weeks ago. Maybe this would be a good opportunity to reconnect. She dialed the number of their house. It rang and rang. When the answering machine clicked on, she hung up. In Miranda's last e-mail, she had hinted that Darius might be seeing someone. Sophia had not asked for details. She tried to think of someone else to call, but knew that most of her friends would listen to the story, laugh a little, and then wonder if Sophia was losing it in New York. The only person who would receive the story the way she wanted was Harry Harlow, whose guilt was so deep and wide, he would laugh, take her side, be glad to hear from her—do anything she asked—but she willed herself not to call. Harry was a habit that needed breaking. Maybe that was the real problem with being so alone in the world, she thought, turning on the hot-water tap with one of her toes. If there's nobody to share the small stories, the series of unconnected moments that, taken together, constitute a life, how do you know you exist?

The next morning, Sophia packed her bags and took a cab across the park to Micheline's apartment. The Frenchwoman had left only that morning, but already the house seemed guiltily abandoned, as if its owner had been compelled to leave town hurriedly for unsavory reasons. A wire coat hanger lay on the floor, the waste basket overflowed with dry cleaners' plastic, a half-drunk cup of coffee sat on the counter. Sophia opened the refrigerator. Micheline had said she could help herself to whatever was in the kitchen, but eating another woman's cheese reminded her too much of the nights her mother brought leftovers home from the restaurant. She threw the perishables away, pushed perennials like Dijon mustard to the back of the refrigerator, and put the nonperishables in a plastic crate she stored at the back of the closet. She had wanted to do the same thing with Helen's bedroom. Seeing her deodorant on top of her bureau had felt too painfully immediate—as if she might walk in any minute. But Darius wouldn't hear of it. He hadn't even wanted Maria vacuuming in there. *You know how much dust is made of human skin cells?*

Do you hear yourself? You're crazy.

She shook her head like a wet dog to dislodge the memory.

In Micheline's bedroom, she labeled the framed photos with yellow Post-Its, stowed them under the bed, stripped the sheets, gathered the towels, and squeezed into the elevator for the basement. For so many years, she had resented the endless, Sisyphean drudgery of housework, but now she relished having a chore. Sliding quarters into the washing machine slot, she felt young again, like when she was in college. She thought of her mother and how every birthday she would say, bewildered, "But I don't *feel* fifty," or sixty, or most recently seventy. Sophia had always felt sorry for her. How could one get to be her age and be so clueless? But now that she herself was closing in on those ages, she knew exactly what her mother meant. Sophia did not feel forty-five, a neither-here-nor-there age. She felt twenty-six. Young, sexy, still ready for adventure.

Back in the apartment, she tried to restrain herself from going through Micheline's closet, but her resolve lasted only an hour. "Nosey, nosey," Darius would have said. "Healthy curiosity," she'd have answered. You've got to stop these imaginary conversations with your potentially ex-husband, she chided herself. The clothes were surprisingly high quality, but odd colors for the designers—fuchsia or citron, instead of their characteristic browns and blacks. Sophia thought of the aqua raincoat she'd seen Micheline pack the night they met. Were they the colors she preferred or the only ones left at the end of the season, when everything went on sale?

The phone rang. All morning, Sophia had listened as Micheline's voice instructed people to call her on her cell phone in Paris. When the ringing stopped, Sophia experienced a pang of loneliness so intense, her eyes watered as if from physical pain. She opened her address book to find the scrap of paper with Coleman Kramer's name and phone number. He answered on the first ring.

"Hello?" Only it sounded a lot like "Yellow?"

"Coleman Kramer?"

"You got 'im, unless you're trying to sell me something."

"I got your number from Micheline Theroux."

"Micheline!" She could hear the memory of sex in his voice. "How is the great lady?"

"Not so good, actually. Her father had a heart attack." Why had she relished throwing water on the man's lust like that?

"Oh, Christ, I'm sorry to hear it. I thought those frogs never got heart attacks."

Sophia suppressed a guffaw. She'd had the same thought about Franco smugness regarding the cardio-protective qualities of red wine, but never would have said it out loud.

"So what can I do for you, friend of Micheline?"

"She said you teach art." Was he always in such a good mood or was he flirting with her?

Coleman Kramer sighed. "In a manner of speaking."

"I'm looking to take a class."

"Well, you are out of luck for Advanced Painting and Drawing at the LeBraun School. We only have three weeks left in the semester and then I'm on sabbatical."

"Oh, I'm sorry to hear it."

"Are you any good?"

"I was once told I had an eye, but that was a long time ago."

"'Just an eye, but what an eye.'"

"Cézanne," Sophia answered.

"Oh, shit. An artist who knows her art history," Coleman answered, "no wonder you can't paint." Sophia laughed.

"What the hell. Come for the next few classes."

"Are you sure?"

"What's the fun of working if you can't fuck with your bosses?"

30

*M*iranda had always assumed she was a city person. But life in the middle of nowhere surprised her. After two months of living with Jason, she woke up, turned to mold the length of her body—neck, shoulders, stomach, legs—into his, and suddenly realized she was happy.

"What's wrong?" Jason asked.

She must have stopped breathing. "Nothing," she answered. "I'm happy."

"You sound surprised."

"I am. What kind of a freak is happy in the middle of an Alaska winter?"

Jason stretched. "Actually, this is the end of an Alaskan winter."

The first few days had been the hardest. After Jason left in the morning, she'd go back to the cabin and throw herself into cleaning. But even without a dishwasher or vacuum cleaner, two adults can generate only so much dirt. On the second day, she discovered *Frontier Skills* sandwiched on the bookshelf between a dozen romance and espionage novels. Written in cheerfully ungrammatic prose by Barbara Olatz, a Norwegian woman whose husband, "Fred," trapped the region north of Fairbanks for thirty years, Miranda was captured by the first sentence: *When Fred and I arrived, I was as green as the willows on the banks of the Tanana River.* She read the book in one sitting. And then again the next day. And the next. Until she had read the book five times. From Barbara, she learned (in theory) how to cure meat; properly split a log; tan animal skins with their own brains; preserve blueberries, cranberries, and rosehips; brew homemade beer; tell moose scat from bear scat; keep toddlers amused at thirty below—water thrown in the air will land as frozen marbles—and the best time of year for getting your moose—first week in October, after they'd been eating the whole summer. Winter moose was nothing but bone and gristle. "The dogs will hardly touch it," Barbara sniffed.

Truthfully, most of the skills Barbara wrote about presupposed a basic knowledge beyond anything Miranda possessed. *Harvest your barley early.* What barley? In the McMartin household, Sophia had done all the cooking and gardening. Miranda thought of her domestic ignorance as something temporary, even charming, like one of those city sophisticates too busy to bother, but now she felt a kind of retroactive shame for her ignorance. How did she think all those meals got prepared year after year? Now, with so much time on her hands and Barbara Olatz at her side, she was determined to learn something useful. Mixing mortar out of peat moss or chopping up dead mice for bait were out of the question, but after two days of trial and error, she did figure out how to make biscuits in the wood-burning stove. The trick was a steady temperature. For this, Barbara suggested a wet log. *The water slows the fire. Plus, the moisture will help in cooking. That's how the French get their bagetts* [sic] *crusty on the outside, and airey* [sic] *on the inside.* The book also included twenty-two ways to cook moose, a good thing, as their main source of protein was the cache of moose Jason's father had sent over the week before she arrived. Miranda found the meat stringy, like cheap stew, but if you cooked it for long enough, it wasn't half bad.

In the afternoons, Miranda wrote letters. Mostly, she wrote to her father because she knew he read them aloud to Helen. She had brought her laptop with her, but after the battery died, Jason refused to let her recharge it using the generator, which ran on diesel (four dollars a gallon).

"Longhand was good enough for Thomas Carlyle," he'd exclaimed.

Miranda had been so nonplussed by the Carlyle reference, she'd been momentarily struck dumb.

"If you can't, you can't." Jason softened his tone. "Just try."

Miranda sharpened her pencil and began to write. The words came so slowly, it gave her plenty of time to think about what she was saying. Somewhere between the emotion and the transcribing, she could see that most of what she thought she wanted to say was ill conceived. When she'd left California, she thought her mother had been on her side and her father had been against her. Now, she couldn't tell whom to be mad at—her father, for leaving her mother so quickly after Miranda. Her mother, for leaving her father alone with Helen. Helen, for getting on the motorcycle in the first place. True, Miranda had been the first to leave, but that was within the natural order of things. Children leave. Parents are supposed to stay.

She threw out the early drafts, berating them, and decided to keep her letters focused on things. She wrote about the dogs and their personalities, all of whom she fed while Jason skinned animals in the garage. *Mathilda is such a princess. Archibald is not to be trusted. Gus makes me laugh.* She wrote about the gaseous green fog of the aurora borealis at night, the heady abundance of stars, the strangers who came to look at the cabin for buying, and the men and women who lived in the surrounding area. She worked hard at finding original turns of phrase to describe the cold and snow but often failed. Even Barbara had been challenged in that department. *I kept thinking God was playing a joke with all that cold my first year. But the next year, it was the same. If I was going to make it, I could see I'd have to accept it. The next week, I traded four martens with an Inuit woman who taught me how to sew an anorak from a wolf Fred had trapped near Deadman's Gulch.*

Once a week, Jason took her by snowmobile to Judy and Pete Volker's double-wide trailer, fifteen miles away. The Volkers ran a generator 24/7, and if the weather was good, they could get an Internet connection from the satellite on top of their trailer. Miranda gave them the password to her account. If an e-mail arrived for her, they'd print it out and have it waiting for her. They refused to take any money, so each time Miranda went she gave them a bar of the expensive chocolate she had brought with her. She was sorry to see the chocolate go and was pretty certain they read the e-mails based on the motherly way Judy Volker sometimes engulfed her in her wide, soft arms, but those were small prices to pay for regular updates from the outside world.

She sat at the dining room table determined to reply to her father's last e-mail. But everything about it troubled her more than most.

Hello Sweetheart:

Thank you for your last e-mail. You wouldn't believe how much it means to me to hear from you. As you know, I was opposed to your leaving, but hearing how wonderfully stimulating Alaska has been for you, I see that I was being selfish. (That was what your mother always said.) I wanted you around, so I assumed staying was the best thing for you. What I am trying to say is, I am happy you are happy. (I am always telling my students to get to the point—I guess I should take some of my own advice.)

We are well around here. Helen is all moved back into her old room. She's got a very fancy motorized bed that will actually do exercises for her. I should get one for myself! To make room for it, I gave her old bed to the people who moved into the Beaudells' house. I met them one night when I was walking Monty. They are a young couple with two small children. It made me remember how excited your mother and I used to get whenever a new couple moved to the neighborhood with children either your age or of babysitting age. Apparently, the father invented the Internet, or something like that—when they said the name of the website, they looked at me like I should be impressed, but honestly I had no idea. When they mentioned the house was much bigger than their old one and that they had no furniture, I said I had a bed I was throwing away and would be grateful if they'd take it. The next day, two men showed up and moved the bed from the hallway.

You asked in your last e-mail how I spend my days. Honestly, not that different from before. Your uncle Fergal and his wife, Siobhan, came to visit. I tried to tell them it wasn't a good time, but they wore me down. It was surprisingly good to see them. You should see how their son, Danny, has grown. I am back to teaching a class this semester. Jack thought it would be good for me, and, truthfully, I am grateful for the distraction.

When I am away from the house, Wendy, a Jamaican lady who used to be a nurse, watches Helen. I've never seen anyone so reluctant to move. I've already fired two workers, however, so I am striving to be less judgmental. The first one lasted only a day. When I came home and checked on Helen, her catheter had come undone and the bed was soaked in urine. I asked the woman how long it had been since she checked on her, and she said, "Five minutes." When I observed that the sheets were already cold, she acted like I was the one at fault. It definitely gets on your nerves, the way they sit there all day watching soap operas. Then if you ask them to do something, like run a vacuum, they say, "Oh, no. That's not my job." Thank God for Maria. BTW, will you ask your mother why Maria doesn't cash my checks? It's been six weeks. Every time I ask, she blushes and backs away from me.

Did you ever meet Molly, the poetry professor from Montana? Thin, dark, curly hair, looks a little like Joyce Carol Oates, but not quite so intense? Well, she has become a good friend. No, not that way. I guess she had to take care of her sick father for several years, so when she heard what I was doing, she has come over a few evenings to play Scrabble and help keep me company. She's not quite up to snuff in the Scrabble department, but who is, compared to you?

What do you hear from your mother? I want you to know how sorry I am for how everything has turned out between us all. I do miss her. But don't tell her that. I think it would just make her feel bad, and she deserves a break from all this.

At night, I read your letters to Helen in her room. I am sure she loves hearing everything.

Sometimes I think your mother was right. It probably would have been fine to keep Helen in a place where they are trained to take care of people in her condition. Maybe soon I will need to take her back. If something happened to her here, I don't think those ladies would have half a clue about what to do. Assuming you could tear them away from the television. I have thought of disconnecting cable service, but the thought of them sitting blankly, staring at the wall, is even worse.

Your mother always said I didn't see half of what she did around the house. It's true. Her roses have gone all black and spotty. I went to Home Depot to ask for advice, but the girl in the gardening department was as ignorant as I was. She just read the label out loud to me. That's corporate globalization for you.

Well, that's all for now. You mustn't worry about Jason's father. I am sure he likes you fine. As a parent, it can be hard to believe anyone is good enough for your precious darling but in the end, what you want most is for your child to be happy.

Lots of love,
Daddy

P.S. If you speak to your mother, please don't tell her about the roses. Or Molly. You know how she worries.

Miranda remembered Molly well. At one of her parents' semi-regular Christmas parties, Molly had gotten tipsy and told Helen how lucky she was to have such a "top-drawer" father. Molly had studied poetry at Cambridge and thought she could say things like "top-drawer" without anyone noticing. But the phrase had become a joke between the sisters. Thereafter, anyone they considered even remotely pretentious was labeled "top-drawer." The fact that Molly was circling Darius, using the excuse of a dead father, made Miranda's stomach fall. He was as defenseless as a mackerel on a beach when it came to women.

More troubling were his hints about Helen and her condition. The women who cared for her sounded awful. In the beginning, Darius had used a service that hired nurses to watch Helen, but the cost had been prohibitive. The social worker at the hospital had hooked him up with an informal network of caregivers who took their salaries as cash at the end of the day. Rationally, Miranda had always agreed with her mother—Darius was deluding himself about Helen's condition—but on some level, she had been glad of those delusions. It gave her license to feel the same way at times, despite what the doctors were saying. Hearing him suddenly fatalistic about Helen made Miranda feel terrible.

Dear Dad,

    Thank you for your last e-mail. I am very sorry to hear that Helen is not well. What do the doctors say?

She stopped writing and began chewing on her fingernail. There was no point in asking. The doctors had stopped treating Helen months ago. She crossed out the last two sentences.

Dear Dad,

    Of course I remember Molly the poetry professor. Nervous woman with dark ringlets and pale skinny legs. She's had her eye on you for years. Yes, I am going to tell mom, who will probably hop on the next plane to California with a No Trespassing sign tucked under her arm.

She stopped again. Nothing sounded right. One was too grim. The other too breezy. She stood up and walked to the window. In the last few days, she had noticed that the afternoon light, normally a silvery steel-gray, had given way to a brighter, whiter light. A true afternoon. When she mentioned it to Jason, he had nodded. "First sign of spring," he said. She checked her watch. It was early for her afternoon walk, but the outdoor air would clear her mind, let her start over again.

Gus, the dog who usually stayed behind, jumped to his feet when he saw her.

"Hey there, Gus." She patted his head. She would have liked his company on her walks but Jason forbade it. It was too easy for a dog off-leash to get a leg caught in a trap. She set out on the trail, breathing deeply, imagining the cold air scouring the inside of her lungs clean, purging them of years of California's soiled air. Somewhere to the right of her, a spruce dropped its load of snow with a quiet *whoosh*. The first day Miranda went out on her own, she'd walked about a hundred yards and then run back to the house, suddenly spooked by the sense of a looming abyss in front of her. It was how she often felt treading water in the deep part of the ocean. What lay beneath was too vast to contemplate.

As she grew more familiar with the land, the way it rose and fell, how the trees leaned a certain way on the other side of the ridge, she got the confidence to push forward on her walks. If something were to happen to her, a sudden freak attack by a wolf, or a bear roused early from hibernation, Jason would come looking for her. He would find a patch of blood, a sign of struggle, the ripped interior of her down vest, and tell the small circle of people who cared. Maybe the police would even come investigate. To make sure he hadn't hacked her up himself with an ax. In the end, that was all one could ask for. To have one's death noted.

When she came to the top of an unfamiliar ridge, she stopped. About a hundred yards from where she stood, something dark was moving in the snow. It was a fox with a large steel trap attached to its leg.

"Shit," she said out loud, making her way to the animal.

The fox stopped. He kept his face pointed away from her, but Miranda could see his yellow eyes watching her with hatred, as if he understood that she was responsible for the disaster that had befallen him. When she got closer, Miranda saw bits of crushed white bone visible between the hard steel teeth of the trap. The fox was breathing hard, his chest rapidly falling up and down. Now that she was off-trail, the snow was at least three feet deep. She hadn't bothered to wear the gaiters Jason wore on the trail, and her boots were filling with snow.

The fox turned to face her. His whole body was trembling now—whether from pain or fear, Miranda couldn't tell.

"I'm sorry," she said out loud to the animal. He only growled and tried once again to hobble away. But Miranda's presence had seemed to deprive him of what energy he had left. He sank into the snow, his leg twisted at an awkward angle, and stared angrily at her, as if to say, What now?

Miranda knew what to do. Barbara Olatz had dealt with the exact same situation her first year in the Tanana valley. *I did feel pretty awful for the little fellow. But better a quick death than a slow one. When it's time for me to go, I hope someone will do the same for me.* Miranda lifted her shoulders and dropped them. "I can't do that," she said out loud. She turned back to the trail, eager to get away from the animal's obvious suffering. Just a few minutes before, the afternoon had seemed so wonderfully alive. Now she felt cold, weak, and slightly nauseous. A coward forced to look at herself in the mirror. Twenty paces down the trail, she stopped and turned. The fox was still lying in the snow. Miranda broke a branch the thickness of a baby's arm off a pine tree and started back toward the animal. The stick bobbed nervously in her hand. Her socks were wet from the snow in her boots.

Miranda stopped a foot from the animal and watched him close his eyes, as if he knew what was coming. She raised the stick overhead with both hands and brought it down as hard as she could across the length of his nose. Just as Barbara had predicted, the fox's body stiffened, then went limp. Miranda kneeled in the snow, took off a glove, and put her hand on the widest part of his chest, near the heart. Up close, she could see that the fox wasn't red at all. He was more rust-colored, with black, white, and gray markings around his face and eyes. Underneath her cold fingers, she could feel the slow thumping of his heart. She'd half hoped the blow alone would have been enough to kill him. *Stand on his heart and that will stop it dead, but more than once I have lost my balance doing that, so it helps to have a partner steady you.* Miranda brought the fox into her lap. She stroked the fur on the fox's forehead, then put her hands on both sides of its head. *A quick jerk to the left while he's out will do it.* She moved its head slightly. Barbara made it sound so easy but Miranda didn't think she had the proper torque. She closed her eyes, took a deep breath, and twisted the neck as hard as she could. She heard a bone snap. A last ripple of life shuddered through the animal's body, and a bright red rivulet of blood ran from his nose onto the stark whiteness of the snow.

Miranda shivered with disgust and pushed the body away until it was half covered with a shroud of snow. The animal's eyes were covered in a milky sheen, as if a shade had been lowered from its lids. She stood up and looked down at the carcass, looking for the certainty that she had done the right thing, but all she felt was soiled and guilty. The fox had seemed so *human* in its struggle to survive. If her leg had been caught in a trap, she probably would have acted the exact same way. She wanted to go home, to forget what had happened, but when she imagined explaining herself to Jason—*I killed the fox with my bare hands but left it for the wolves*—she knew she could not leave it in the snow. A mature red fox could easily bring seventy-five dollars from Jason's dealer. She took off her gloves, unhooked the trap from its chain, and carried the fox home, using the U-shaped trap as a handle. Each time she glanced down at the body swinging by the side of her leg, she felt her horror fade a tiny bit. A body without life was an empty container. Nothing to be afraid of. Nothing to weep over.

When she got closer to the house, she could hear Gus barking and hurried her steps, fearful that a wolf might have showed up. Parked in front of the house was an unfamiliar red snowmobile. The door to the house opened, revealing Judy Volker's parka-covered body. Miranda hurried up the steps. Judy opened her arms and enfolded her in a stiff hug. "I've brought an e-mail from your father," she said. "I'm so sorry."

31

*S*ophia almost never properly matched a phone voice with a face. Men who sounded huge and avuncular turned up tiny and elfin. Women with soft, feminine squeaks were looming, big-bosomed Helgas. But she got Coleman Kramer, the art teacher, exactly right. He had thick, graying hair cut in a modified buzz; a generous belly, shrewdly concealed by an expensive black shirt that, she guessed, he had not paid for himself; a handsome Roman nose; a plush lower lip; amused black eyes; and about thirty-six hours' worth of gray and white stubble on his chin.

"You must be the Micheline manqué," he said, taking one of Sophia's hands and resting his other on top of it, as if he were wishing her good luck on a long voyage.

The classroom was large and airy, with a high ceiling, old-fashioned skylights that looked as if they never opened, and fluorescent light fixtures that bathed everything in a harsh glare. Most of the students sat on high stools in front of easels staggered around a simple wooden stage set with a stool in its middle. Coleman led Sophia to an empty easel with a piece of white paper attached to a board. On the ledge underneath were several pieces of black drawing charcoal. "You'll be taking the spot of Mrs. Edna Fernblatt, who has recently decamped from New York for a ranch in Phoenix, thanks to her husband's worsening asthma. I heard all about it last night on the phone. And no, sadly, by 'ranch' she did not mean a sprawling horse farm of the sort elderly Republican politicians retire to. She meant a ranch *house*."

Coleman turned out to be one of those teachers who won his students' affection by insulting them. "It occurred to me after our last class," he said, leaping onto the platform in the middle of the room and rubbing his hands together, "that everyone in this room is a talented phony."

Sophia looked around the class. There were a few students who looked to be in their early twenties, but overwhelmingly the class was older and female, the kind of cultured, prosperous women who could be seen at the symphony or the ballet. Earlier in life, they would have been the mothers organizing school bake sales to benefit the Biafran refugees or the homeless shelter across town. Relieved of child-rearing responsibilities and living off their husbands' retirement accounts, they finally had the time to "do something for themselves." Sophia could easily imagine the conversations that led to the class.

"Well, Mom, what do you want to do with your life?"

"Oh, I don't know."

"You must have some interests."

"Of course I have interests."

"What about painting? You've always liked art."

"I suppose . . ."

Now those women were smiling self-consciously at Coleman's insult. He had called them all phonies, and that wasn't good, but at the same time, he had said they were talented, and that was something.

"What do I mean by 'phony'?" Coleman turned slowly, affording each student an excellent view of his substantial but not badly shaped ass. "You are all drawing the way you think you should draw. You've had your art history courses and spent endless afternoons at the Met, you know what good drawing looks like, so when you sit down to draw, there's a little voice in your head saying, 'Draw like Rembrandt. He's a real artist.' Only none of us, and I include myself, can draw like Rembrandt. Even if we're better draftsmen, we can't do it, because we're no Rembrandt. He's dead. So we end up with something that is, by definition, phony."

Now the women were glancing at one another, tentative grins on their faces. Oh, that's our problem. We think we're Rembrandt.

"So tonight, let's forget about what we know. Stop trying to draw like someone else. Let your drawing be bad. Let it be misshapen. Let it look nothing like the model. If people want verisimilitude, they can take a photograph. But whatever you do, make it *you*."

On cue, a heavy girl with a weak chin, broad nose, and the deflated air of someone who didn't expect much out of life, climbed on the stage, sat on the stool, and let the silk kimono she was wearing slide off her back. Coleman climbed on the stage, smiled at the girl in a surprisingly paternal way, and arranged her body so that she was leaning forward, palms on top of her thighs, like a runner waiting for the signal to start. The encounter startled Sophia. In her college art classes, the models had all been clothed after the feminist union protested that paying a woman to take off her clothes, even if it was in the name of art, amounted to prostitution. The art teachers had offered to use only men, but the feminists, sensing a rare victory, had held fast. A principle is a principle.

Sophia took her time studying the broad planes of the girl's white back, the slight roll of flesh around the waist, the ridge of her spine under the skin, the sloppy chignon at her neck. Instead of wandering the classroom, as Sophia had feared Coleman would do, he sat at his own easel, stared at the girl, and made loud, slashing marks against the paper. After a few minutes, he would sigh loudly and start over on a fresh piece of paper.

Sophia picked up a piece of charcoal and tentatively began to draw the line of the girl's back, slowly reacquainting herself with the connection between the eye, the page, and the object. It felt good to be in a room filled with people all bent to the same task, but almost as soon as she began to work, it came back to her why she had given it up. Look at that line, she despaired, it's terrible—out of proportion, wobbly, lacking conviction. Shut up, she scolded the judging voice in her head, and forced herself to continue.

"Not bad." She jumped. Coleman Kramer was standing behind her.

Sophia looked at the drawing and made a face. "Trite."

"It's the subject. What is there to say about a naked woman that hasn't been said? Personally, I prefer eggplants."

As the class was breaking up, Coleman asked Sophia if she wanted to get a drink. A few feet away, one of the art ladies frowned.

"Sure," she said, smiling at him.

He chose a dark West Village bar where, she was relieved to see, most of the patrons were over thirty. Maybe there was a guidebook she could buy—*Manhattan for the Middle-Aged*? After the waiter brought their drinks—white wine for her, bourbon and a beer for him—Coleman asked what she thought of her first class.

"Uncomfortable." She wrinkled her nose. "Like taking a bath with strangers."

He had a good laugh, the kind that made you want to keep amusing its owner. Sophia had never been able to laugh out loud. As a child, she had considered her laughlessness a strength, the sign of a critical intelligence not easily shaken. It was only as an adult that she realized she might be missing something. Even now, when she heard something genuinely amusing, the best she could manage was a smile and a descriptive "Funny!" Mostly, people didn't notice. They were too busy enjoying their own mirth to care about anyone else's. Darius had been the first to spot the flaw about three weeks into their relationship, when they'd gone to a comedy club to watch a fellow literature student on amateur night. The woman had surprised everybody with her dry wit and perfect timing, and did eventually achieve some small measure of fame before she was diagnosed with a rare but fatal case of esophageal cancer at the age of twenty-eight. After a joke that had the room howling—something about cunnilingus, if Sophia remembered correctly—Darius had glanced at his date to see how she liked the show. Sophia, he later told her, had been watching the stage with a confused expression on her face. Later that night, he mentioned it to her.

"Yes," she had agreed, thrilled to have been so acutely observed by an-other person, "it's my tragic flaw."

Darius vowed then and there to find her funny bone. During the weeks that followed, Sophia was forced to endure an endless succession of unfunny "guy walks into a bar," "Arab and a Jew," "How many Polacks does it take?" jokes. She always laughed but Darius (rightly) accused her of faking it. She began to develop sympathy for women who faked orgasms. His heart was in the right place, but listening to joke after joke was turning into a torture. Finally, after a joke involving Richard Nixon and the movie *Deep Throat*, Sophia reached deep down into the bottom of her diaphragm, let out a few, tentative coughlike exhalations, and then—ha, ha, ha—she giggled, eyes closed, mouth stretched wide in an approximation of hilarity. Darius watched her suspiciously. He was as adept as the next man at sniffing out fakery, but in the end, he, too, had grown weary of all the forced jollity. If his girlfriend was never going to laugh out loud, why should it bother him?

"I've made you laugh," he said.

"Yes, yes," she agreed, a little too quickly, "you have!"

Sitting across from Coleman Kramer, a man for whom laughing was as natural as breathing, Sophia wondered if she ought to have married some-one more like him. Three bourbons (him) and two white wines (her) later, Coleman looked into Sophia's eyes and told her she was "a very attractive woman, all things considered."

"What things?" she asked.

"You know," he answered.

"No," she said, "I don't."

"Come on!" he roared with laughter. "It was a joke. You don't get out much, do you?"

"No," she said, signaling for the check.

"Now, now." He reached over and trailed a finger up her arm. "Don't be like that. I like you."

Sophia shivered. "I like you, too," she answered. "More or less."

"Come home with me."

"Do people do that?" she asked. The check sat on the table between them, untouched.

"Have sex? All the time."

"The first night they meet?"

"In my experience, thinking about it doesn't improve it."

"In my experience," she answered, putting her credit card on the black folder holding the bill, "anticipation is the greater part of pleasure."

"Okay. Don't sleep with me. But let me walk you home."

"I live on the Upper West Side."

"So do I."

"Are you lying?"

"Only a little. If I bomb with you, there's a woman on Ninety-ninth and Columbus who is always happy to see me."

Sophia couldn't help looking shocked.

"I'm kidding." He paused. "She lives on Eighty-third and Amsterdam."

After a cab dropped them on Sophia's corner (paid for, once again, by her), Coleman took her arm as they walked down the street arguing unseriously about the merits of an artist's retrospective currently hanging at the Museum of Modern Art. He thought it overrated, she thought it the work of a genius. Sophia recognized that his passion on the subject stemmed from envy, but said nothing. With Darius, her blood had boiled when he disagreed with her or offered an opinion she considered obtuse. Arguing with a virtual stranger, she felt stimulated by a fresh perspective. So what if he was wrong? It was no reflection on her. Anybody seeing us, she thought, would assume we were two middle-aged married people still very much in love. Or maybe they were giving off the carnal glow of anticipated sex. After all, there was nothing stopping her from inviting him up to the apartment. The fact that he had counted on her resolve wavering was a little irritating, but so what? Wasn't this exactly the kind of adventure she'd craved when she decided to move to New York? As they approached her building, Sophia noticed a dark, stooped figure sitting on the steps. Something about the curve of his back made her stomach flip.

"Darius?" she whispered.

He stood up slowly, as if his coat—inappropriately thin for the cold night—were weighted. His hair appeared grayer, thinner at the top, and the skin around his eyes looked delicate and creased, like crumpled tissue paper. He looked embarrassed at finding her with another man. "Hi," he said wearily.

Sophia hugged him. There was a strange new smell to him. Something unpleasant, like food gone off. Snow, predicted all week, began to fall. Coleman shivered and adjusted his leather gloves.

"Darius, this is Coleman Kramer," Sophia spoke, sensing Coleman's desire to leave.

Darius held out an ungloved hand. Coleman hesitated, then stuck his own gloved one into his. Watching the two men appraise each other, Sophia felt acutely aware of their differences.

"Do you mind?" she said to Coleman.

"Of course not." He kissed her cheek chastely. "I'll see you next week."

Sophia wondered if she would ever see him again.

"Seems like a nice fellow," Darius observed flatly.

Sophia smiled at the choice of words. "I only met him tonight," she answered, shivering slightly at the snow and the ready way she distanced herself from him. Darius looked relieved.

"Do you have a bag?" she asked.

He glanced at a small black vinyl bag on the ground but made no effort to pick it up. Sophia bent over and grabbed its handle. The weight surprised her.

"My God," she said, "what's in here?"

Darius looked stricken by the question. "Can we go upstairs?" he asked.

"Is Helen okay?" Sophia asked.

Darius lifted his eyes to the windows of the building, as if he were trying to guess which apartment belonged to her.

Sophia suddenly felt like she couldn't breathe. "Who is taking care of Helen?"

"She died two days ago."

Sophia had known the news was coming for the last seven months. She had tried hard to prepare herself. But the shock of the actual news was like a physical blow. She gasped, raised her hands as if to beat the air, dropped them, and burst into tears. How could she not have known? She had lived the last twenty-four hours as if it were a day like any other. Had drunk her morning coffee, read the newspaper, taken a yoga class, shopped for food, finished a biography on Benjamin Franklin, gone to a new art class, and had drinks with a man she seriously considered having sex with, and all the while her husband was flying across the country, holding this terrible news in his head. She leaned her body against his and cursed her blasphemous heart.

They might have stayed that way for hours, covered in a mantilla of white, lacy snowflakes, had a restaurant delivery man dressed in white pants, white cap, and a puffy down jacket not approached them.

"You order?" the man asked, looking from one to the other. In his hand he held a white plastic bag printed with I ♥ NY; inside was a paper bag folded once and stapled shut. Darius, who hadn't eaten for twelve hours, realized he was suddenly ravenous. "How much?" he asked, and then tipped the man twenty dollars to make up for stealing someone else's food. Sophia watched him bike away, his tracks a graceful arabesque on the white of the street.

"Your food will get cold." She opened her purse to look for keys. Darius leaned down to pick up his black bag and the bag of food.

Inside the apartment, he put the bags on the dining-room table and sat down. Sophia got him a plate and watched him eat. "I want to know everything," she said when he was done.

It was a heart attack. Darius had been home, grading papers downstairs, when the monitor went off. "The doctors said to watch for random electrical impulses that would cause the heart to beat funny. In the hospital I'd seen her EKG go wild and then calm down several times. It would drive me

crazy, because nobody would come to check on her after it happened—
they said it was normal but I always thought they were just waiting for her
to die. So when the alarm went off—"

"What time was that?" Sophia interrupted.

"Around four o'clock."

Seven o'clock New York time. She would have just met Micheline.

"I went in and counted to thirty, like they told me to. When the pulse
didn't come back, I used the defibrillator." He shook his head. "When the
medics came, they said her heart was too weak and couldn't take the shock."

"Why didn't you call me?" she asked.

"I tried, but I kept getting the machine. I sent Miranda an e-mail, but I
didn't want to leave a message for you."

"Where is she now?"

"I had her cremated."

"Why?" Sophia's eyes filled with tears. Nothing left of her golden child
but ashes?

"It's what she wanted. Remember? After my mother died? We weren't
sure what to do. Miranda said, 'I want to be buried.' Helen said, 'I want to
be cremated.' She said we should scatter her ashes off Point Dume in the
ocean, but I didn't want to do it without you." Sophia didn't remember the
conversation, but she believed him. It was the kind of thing Helen would
have said.

"I brought her," he gestured to the bag on the table.

"You're joking."

"I didn't want to leave her."

She couldn't decide whether to laugh or cry until she saw her husband's
guilt-stricken face. "You did the right thing."

"Thank you."

Neither of them said anything for a long time, or so it seemed to Sophia.
Then again, it could have been only a minute. Time was bending in odd,
hallucinogenic ways. Finally, Darius reached into his pocket and pulled
out a cassette tape.

"I thought you might want to hear it," he said.

Sophia glanced at the clock. It was two-thirty in the morning. She put the tape in the stereo, pressed Play, and sat next to him on the couch. He put his arm around her. She leaned her head against his shoulder.

—Hi, Helen. Us again.

—Your loser friends.

—Speak for yourself.

—Oh, believe me, I am.

—This is Magda, Siri, and Anya. Louisa would be here, but she says she's working on her college essay.

—Insert awkward pause here because the deadline was two weeks ago.

—Maybe she got an extension.

—*Right.*

—Every college has the same question. Write about an experience that had a profound impact on your life. I started to write about my parents' divorce, but when I read it over, it sounded so whiny. "And then my dad wasn't there when I woke up, and my mother was crying all the time." Boo-hoo. Like anyone cares. I hate to say it, but your accident is the most interesting thing that happened to me.

—Which is kind of pathetic, because it didn't even happen to you.

—Um. Okay. Maybe you shouldn't be calling me pathetic in front of Helen?

—I didn't say you were pathetic. I said the behavior was.

—Guys. Can we?

—Anyway. I brought my essay and thought I'd read it to you. Do you guys mind?

—Go ahead.

—No, I mean, do you mind leaving the room?

—This is ridiculous. Why are we here if it's just going to be the Magda show?

—That's not fair.

—Do me a favor? Lose my phone number. P.S. If Helen were around, I really do not think she would be friends with you anymore, either.

Sound of door slamming.

—God. I mean, *really*. I think she's just jealous. About me getting into Stanford early acceptance. The best she's hoping for is UC Santa Cruz, which is a perfectly fine school. I so don't look down on her for going there, but I also don't see why we can't be honest. Santa Cruz is not Stanford. It just isn't. And I don't see why it's a crime for me to be a little proud of my accomplishment.

—Magda.

—Siri, if you want to say something, you can.

—No, no, it's okay. I'm going to see if I can find Anya.

Sound of door closing.

—Why does Siri always have to be such a Goody Two-shoes? Conflict is normal. That's what my mom, the shrink, says. But not in this group. The first sign of trouble and, *bam*, everybody's out the door. I mean, if someone had asked me a year ago who my best friends are, I would have said you, Louisa, Anya, and Siri. I'm sorry, I really don't mean to cry. I know that you are the one who has suffered. It's just, I don't know, everything has fallen apart. I know Siri would say I am gossiping and focusing on the negative, but the truth is, Louisa has a drug problem. Every weekend she does X with those kids from Pacific Palisades and I've even heard rumors that she's selling it. I'm not judging her for that. I don't care that people do drugs but, I mean, her grades have gone to shit. She has a whole different set of friends. She barely even goes to school anymore, and if she gets caught selling, she could go to jail. Her mother actually called me and started crying on the phone because she didn't know what to do. And all that stuff about Anya being jealous of me? I don't really think that's true. What I think is, Anya is sick. Really sick. She looks like a Holocaust victim. She must weigh ninety pounds. When she first started losing the weight, everyone kept saying how great she looked, but then it got to a point where it was scary. Her arms are, like, pipe cleaners. The last time we met at Java Juice to plan the next tape, I went to the bathroom after her, and it totally smelled like vomit. When you look at her arms, it's like she's growing fur, which you usually can't tell, because she mostly wears long-sleeve shirts, but last week, I could see a little bit under the sleeve. That's what happens when a body gets too skinny—it starts growing extra hair to keep warm. If she keeps this up, she won't be going to college, because she's going to be dead.

And I know Siri is, like, an angel and everything, but all that God and Buddha shit is driving me crazy. I mean, if she was talking about Jesus, people would think she was a freak and they'd be worried, but because it's Buddha and she wears tie-dyed skirts, it's, like, oh, that's cool. But whenever you try to talk to her about a feeling, she's like, it's in God's hands. It's God's way. Ours is not to question. Like it was God's way for your accident to happen and, I'm sorry, I don't accept that. I don't believe in God, but if I did, I'd have to seriously question why He or She or whatever you want to call "It" would let something like that happen to someone like you, because I can see now what a cool person you were, Helen. I mean, I always knew it and I guess I was kind of jealous of you because you had the gift. Everybody liked you. I know I sound like I am sucking up, but what would be the point of sucking up to you now? Look at your own family. When I heard that your sister had moved to Alaska and your mother had moved to New York, I have to say, I was shocked. I mean, I knew your parents fought sometimes—whose don't?—but they seemed solid. Without you, I guess everything fell apart. You were, like, the sun. You kept things in orbit. Only we didn't know it. We thought we were our own galaxies, but it turned out there was a universe and you were at the center. Okay, now, I am crying too much and I think I should stop. Actually, Helen, I think this is going to be my last tape. The problem is, every time I start talking into the microphone, I just get really sad and I am always depressed for a few days afterwards. My shrink—Shit. Oh, well. I guess it's not that big of a deal. I'm seeing a shrink now. I know I swore I would never do it, but that was just adolescent rebellion by a shrink's daughter. She's the one who made me do it. She said she was really worried about me and she knows what depression looks like and she made me take some dumb test that was, like, Have you lost interest in the things that used to give you pleasure? Are you tired all the time? Do you think about killing yourself? Of course I answered yes to everything. I mean, I'm sad. My best friend is in a coma. It's normal I would be sad! It's not as bad as I thought it would be. Boyd, he lets me call him that instead of Dr. Davis, thinks that making these tapes is keeping the accident too alive in my mind. He thinks I need to move on. He says I can keep you in a room and go there to mourn, but I shouldn't live in that room. It's funny, because I always thought compartmentalization was unhealthy, but he says no, they've been rethinking that and it can actually be healthy. He's pretty cool. And did I mention he's hot? I know, how clichéd, falling for your shrink, but he's married with two little kids, so don't worry, no chance of anything happening there. Still, a girl can dream. Did I mention that Boyd is practically the one who got me into Stanford? When school started in the fall, I guess I slacked off a little. I know it was supposed to be my senior year and really great and all that but, I don't know, I just found it hard to get out of bed. I guess I didn't actually go to school that much because I didn't really pass any of my classes. Well, the nice teachers gave me incompletes, but basically I was toast. I mean, I couldn't even fill out my application, except for the essay I wrote about you, which everybody agreed was kind of brilliant. So Boyd wrote a letter to the school explaining the situation and asking if they could just consider my transcript up until the point of the accident. Luckily, I had taken an early version of the SATs just as a warm-up, and they were able to use that score. Mrs. Buttsucker, the college counselor, says she thinks Boyd's letter is what got me in. It made me "angular," she said. That's the new word. Angular. It's not enough to be a smart, all-around good person anymore. You've got to have an angle. So I guess I have you to thank for making me angular. I'm sorry I have blabbed on so much. It's amazing how much easier it is to talk when nobody is around. Before, I always felt kind of self-conscious around everyone. Today, everything just flowed. So, Helen, just because I am saying good-bye, it doesn't mean I don't love you and think of you all the time. I do. I don't know if you can hear me or if everything is just kind of hollow, and I don't know what would be better. But if you're in there and all you have is your past to think about, well, you're probably kind of lucky, because you were just awesome.

A NOTE ON TYPE

The text of this book is set in Fournier,
based on designs by
PIERRE SIMON FOURNIER
from around 1742 in his
Manuel Typographique.

This book was designed by
NICOLE LaRoche.

This book was printed and bound
by R. R. Donnelley
at Bloomsburg, Pennsylvania.